POOL OF DEATH

When finally I went to sleep, it must have been three o'clock. I must have practically passed out, for I felt as though someone had been shaking me for some time before I wakened.

To my astonishment it was Bill. He was in bathing-trunks and dripping wet, and his young face looked pale.

"For God's sake wake up, Lois," he said as I sat up. "Something horrible's happened. There's a woman's body in the pool."

I grabbed a sweater and ran down the stairs. When I got to the pool, I could only stand and stare in horror.

She was on the near side at the shallow end of the pool, where the little brook flows in. There were three cement steps there, and she was on them—still half in the water, with her back toward us. Her black dress and blond hair eddied in the stream in a horrible parody of life and movement.

I took a step forward. With a sense of utter shock, I saw who it was . . .

MARY ROBERTS RINEHART
THE SWIMMING POOL

ZEBRA BOOKS
KENSINGTON PUBLISHING CORP.

ZEBRA BOOKS

are published by

Kensington Publishing Corp.
475 Park Avenue South
New York, NY 10016

First printing: October 1985

Printed in the United States of America

Chapter 1

One day last fall I ordered the swimming pool destroyed. For we were leaving The Birches, our family summer home for many years, and our asylum after the panic of '29. For various reasons neither my brother Phil nor I myself cared to stay there any longer, and the fear of the atom bomb had at last enabled us to sell it. The family that bought it had small children, so they did not want the pool.

But standing there watching a man at work, it seemed incredible that only the spring before, having sold a short story for more than my usual price and received another unexpected check, I had had it put into condition after years of neglect. Had repaired the old diving-platform and the bench along the side, and even restored the picnic table under its falling roof.

I must have been very small when it was built, but I could remember my father watching the work and not looking particularly happy. He had liked the small creek that was to feed it, and which had been temporarily detoured. But he had saved the valley above it, below the stables, and had kept it in its wild state, with trilliums and May apples and other humble little plants, even an occasional jack-in-the-pulpit on the bank. None of the gardeners was allowed to touch it.

So the pool was built over his protests, because Mother insisted on it. A swimming pool was a sort of cachet in those days, as later it was in Hollywood. But I think it worried him for other reasons, too. The water, he said, would be cold, and there was always the danger that I, at five or thereabouts, might fall in. I remember him looking down at me as it began to fill. He was a tall man, usually reserved except with me, and I have wondered since just how he came to marry Mother, or whether he was ever really happy with her. They were so different.

Anyhow, that day at the pool he was definitely worried.

"You'll have to learn to swim, baby," he said. "We can't have you falling in the thing, unless you know how to get out."

I was always "baby" to him.

As a result it was he who gave me my first swimming lessons that summer, his hand under my skinny tummy and his own lips blue with cold. After that I taught myself, usually with a frightened nurse or governess screaming at me. And the day I jumped in from the diving-platform, feet first and holding my nose, the mademoiselle of the moment actually fainted.

Yes, the pool had plenty of memories for me, some good but at least one tragic. I was glad to see it destroyed.

It is hard now to remember the extravagance of those days. True, the stables were no longer used, although the coach house still held a high trap and Mother's old surrey, and a case on the wall of the tack room showed the ribbons Father had won at horse shows and so on. I think in his mild way he resented the motor age, although he never said so.

But he loved the Birches, so called because of a grove of them on the hill near the house. He was always happy when, each early June, the family hegira from the city house began. The gardeners had been working all spring, the flower borders were beginning to show their colors, and while we were too late for the forsythia and the dogwoods, we still had the peonies and roses. Father always hurried to his wild garden, to which he had added lilies-of-the-valley, and the first time I was allowed to visit his grave I carried a drooping bunch of them and laid

6

them there.

That was later, of course. It was years before I was told how and why he died.

As I watched the man working that day, I was thinking of those mornings of the late 1920's. Perhaps children remember more than we realize, and the expedition from town house to country place was certainly impressive: the six or seven servants, including a butler, we four children with nurses and governesses, Mother and her personal maid, and usually a dog or two, excited at the prospect of freedom and strange new scents. Inside the big house everything would be in order. Mother would look it over with complacency: the enormous drawing-room with the conservatory opening off it—both closed now for years—her morning room, the library, and Father's den. She would glance in at the service wing, where Helga and the kitchenmaid were already fussing with the huge coal stove, but she never stayed in the kitchen. That was Helga's realm.

After that she would go up the stairs to her big bedroom over the front veranda—the one where years later my sister Judith was to nail the windows shut—and watch her maid unpacking the trunks. She was a large woman, Mother, dominant and, I realize now, very proud of her wealth and social position.

She would stand by while her handsome clothes came out of the trunks to be hung on perfumed hangers, and her jewels went into the wall safe beside the big old walnut bed. If I was lucky she would not notice me, so I could stay. Sometimes, however, she ordered me out.

I think now I understand why she never really cared for me. She looked after me, of course. No one could say any of the Maynard children was neglected. But it must have shocked her profoundly when, ten years after Judith, she found I was on the way. My sister Anne was fourteen then, Phil was thirteen, and Judith was ten. That was after the first great war, when the world was pretending to be at peace, and we were carrying on as

7

though there was no such thing as taxes, or an approaching end to our sort of living, or even another and more devastating conflict.

I arrived, however, a black-haired squealing baby who remained skinny for years, and a living, breathing embarrassment to Mother up to the day of her death.

Outside of that, in summer the Maynard family carried on much as usual for several years. In the mornings the chauffeur and the high Pierce-Arrow carried Father five miles to the railroad, where he commuted to New York and his brokerage house, and met him in the evenings. In the afternoons Mother either drove about the countryside making calls at the other summer places, or sat at home in state to receive them. I can still remember her, sitting beside her tea table with its glittering expanse of silver and china, and the butler of the moment carrying in trays of thin bread and butter, hot buttered biscuits or scones, and cakes of all sorts.

Perhaps all this background is not necessary to my story, but in a way it is. So much happened at The Birches years later, and so much of it was the outgrowth of those early days. Young as I was—I was only six or so—I remember clearly when Anne was married there in the summer of 1928.

It was a huge wedding, with a marquee on the lawn, a band there for dancing, and an orchestra in the house. And of all things I was a flower girl, in white tulle and a white lace cap! Phil said I looked like a charlotte russe, which I do not doubt. But Anne had married rather poorly, according to Mother. Martin Harrison was an unsuccessful architect, and nothing much to look at, but I daresay Anne loved him. At least she stuck to him, which is more than Judith did.

I realize now that Father hated ostentation. When I missed him I often found him down by the creek, and we would stay there for hours. But it was rare for him to make any protest. As I have said, he was a quiet man, soft-spoken and gentle, and I adored him. I would slip out of my nursery in order to waylay and hug him on his way out to the incessant dinner parties that were a part of the summer season. But I always disappeared before Mother came rustling out.

I could see her, however, by peeping around a corner. She was handsome, as Anne was later, but never the beauty Judith became. And she always wore the pearls in which Laszlo had painted her, and diamond bracelets on her left arm almost to the elbow.

I know now it was Judith who wanted the pool, Judith to whom Mother could refuse nothing. According to Anne, Father objected. Not because of the cost. Apparently there was plenty of money, but already in her teens boys gathered around Judith like flies. They broke down his shrubbery and trampled his little wild-flower garden.

"Why turn the place into a picnic ground?" he said. "It's bad enough already, with every young punk in the neighborhood cluttering the house."

Mother got her way, of course. Or rather Judith did. Judith was a curious mixture of beauty and determination. Years later Anne said she was a psychopathic troublemaker and liar from the time she was born. I don't know about that. Perhaps Anne was jealous. However, I do know that either she got what she wanted or would sulk for days until she did.

But how lovely she was! I liked to watch her brush her long beautiful hair, and put on the extravagant dresses Mother bought for her. Phil has said since that she was Mother's ace in the hole, to offset Anne's unfortunate marriage. I imagine he is right. Judith was to marry money and position, as eventually she did.

No one had any plans for me. I was still the ugly duckling in those days. My straight black hair and ordinary gray eyes, as well as the fact that I was always missing a tooth or two, were probably the reason Mother found me a real disappointment. As a result I was allowed more or less to run wild, to climb trees and wade the creek, and—after the pool was finished—to watch the boys swim and to swim myself.

I could dive, too. I would climb to the high top of the

9

platform with Judith's crowd below, and yell at them.

"Watch me!" I would shriek in my little girl's voice. "Watch me dive!"

I don't think they ever did. All they saw was Judith, sitting on the cement rim of the pool or on the bench beside it. Even the girls would be watching her, and she was something to see. She had cut her hair sometime or other. I don't remember when, but I do remember Mother bursting into tears when she saw her.

"Oh, Judith, your lovely braids!"

It suited her, however. It grew out into small blond curls all over her head, and she hated wetting it. Then, too, she swam badly. She could ride well. She could play the piano magnificently, but she hated the water. She was always afraid of the water. Perhaps that excuses her for what happened years later.

I can still see her in her bed at the hospital, with a policeman on guard outside the door, and most of her beauty gone.

"I was afraid, Lois," she said. "I tried, but it wasn't enough."

I was thinking of all this that day last fall as I stood by the pool. The bench had already gone, the bench where the unknown woman had lost her cameo pin, and the dizzy platform from which Anne's boy Bill looked down and saw something in the water. The long picnic table was gone, too, where an old snapshot I found one night showed Dawson, our sardonic butler at the time, carving a ham.

Curiously enough, I did not remember seeing Ridgely Chandler there, the man Judith married twenty years ago. For one thing, he was older. The youths around the pool were mostly college boys, while he was well on in his thirties. He must have been there, especially during the summer of 1929. He must have watched Judith, as the others did. But knowing him later I doubt if he joined the rest in the noise or in the surreptitious drinking of those Prohibition days.

Apparently no Chandler ever broke the law.

They drank a lot, Judith's crowd, and I suppose Judith herself did, too, although she was careful on account of Father. But on Sunday mornings, running through the shrubbery to the pool, I would find bottles and flasks, empty and discarded, and once I cut my foot rather badly on one of them.

I speak of 1929 because that was our last happy year at The Birches. When we went back after the crash, as we were compelled to do, it was to make it our permanent home. All around us the big country places were empty and on the market, with no buyers. The Adrian place, nearest to ours, was closed and on the market for years.

No one had any idea of that, of course, when we moved back to the town house in late September of that year. It was always a blow to me, going back to the city, to school, to dancing-class, to all the things I hated. The city house in the East Seventies was a tall one, elegant but dreary, the halls dark, the windows heavily curtained. The nursery—I still rated a nursery, to my disgust—as well as my nurse's room, was on the fifth floor, and instead of the grounds at The Birches I had only Central Park.

It was all behind me, of course, that fall day when I stood by the pool. We had sold the furniture, and a junkman had bought the surrey and cart and some of the old stuff from the attic where I found Judith on her knees one night years later. But in clearing out my desk I had found a scrap of paper which brought back to me a sleepless night when, confused and frightened, I had sat up in bed, and picking up the pad from the stand beside me, had absently found myself drawing the outline of a cat.

I am no artist, but a cat is easy to draw: two circles, just one small and one larger, then add the ears, dot in the eyes, and wrap a tail around it.

Only this cat was a solid black, and the window curtains around it were hanging in rags.

11

Chapter 2

It must have been in February of last year when Anne drove out to The Birches. It was a wet day, with rain melting the snow, and Anne was in a rotten humor. She stalked into the living-room, which had once been Mother's particular habitat, as Phil called it, and looked around her with distaste.

"How you and Phil can stand this shabby old ruin!" she said. "Why at least don't you paint it?"

"What with?" I inquired, less than grammatically. "Can you see Phil on a ladder, with a brief in one hand and a brush in the other?"

Phil was a lawyer, and not a successful one. He had very little help at his office, so he often brought his work home at night. Anne only snorted.

"Do you run to a cup of tea?" she asked. "I suppose there's no use asking for a whisky and soda."

"We're not as bad as all that," I said. "I'll mix you one, if you'll sit down and relax."

She drank her highball, but she did not noticeably relax. I gave her a cigarette and lit one myself, eying her as I did so. Anne at forty-two was still handsome, but stout and matronly, as well she might be, with two children to raise and educate and not too much money.

"Bill and Martha all right?" I asked.

"So far as I know. They're both away, Bill at college and Martha at school." She put down her glass and faced me. "See here, Lois," she said, "what's wrong with Judith?"

"Probably nothing that a rest cure wouldn't help," I said indifferently. "Judging by the columnists she's still the most photogenic as well as one of the ten best-dressed women in America. Also she's the leader of what they call café society, whatever that may be. What more can you ask? Or she?"

Anne frowned.

"I know. That awful treasure hunt, with a flower from Woodlawn Cemetery and a hair of the mayor's mustache! How she's kept her looks so long I don't know." She put out her cigarette and dropped it into an ash tray. "But I think she's breaking. She's been going to a psychiatrist for a month or two. Ridge told me. And she's changed. My God, Lois, how she's changed!"

"What do you mean, changed?"

"She's thinner, for one thing, and she doesn't run about the way she did. I saw her at the Stork Club one night. She looked like a death's-head."

"What about the psychiatrist? Maybe he's slowed her down."

"I wouldn't know. He's a man named Townsend, on Park Avenue. Of course, it's smart to be analyzed these days, but I understand he's good."

"Maybe she's fallen for him," I said lightly. "That's part of it, isn't it? They call it transference or something. Anyhow Judith's almost forty. It's time she settled down."

"Women of forty are not precisely senile," she said stiffly. "Anyhow I'm not thinking of Jude. I'm thinking of Ridge Chandler. She's led him up the garden path for a long time. He's had no sort of life with her. That wild crowd of hers, drinking and staying out all night, and God knows what! He quit it years ago."

I'm afraid I grinned. "He's pretty much of a stuffed shirt. The Chandlers can do no wrong."

"Don't be ridiculous. He has a proper sense of his own dignity and position. He inherited a good name and a lot of money, and Judith's throwing them both away. I might as well tell you. She's going to divorce him."

I was shocked. Although I seldom saw her, for years I had envied Judith. Not only her beauty, I still had the little sister's admiration for that. But I had envied her her marriage: the big apartment, luxurious and with plenty of servants, her cars, her clothes, her jewels. To throw all that over was incomprehensible to me.

"Why?" I said. "What on earth is the reason? She's got everything. I don't think Ridge is any ball of fire, but the Chandlers don't divorce. Or do they?"

Anne lit another cigarette, a sure sign she was upset.

"Of course, she never loved him," she said. "Mother made the match. I found her crying the morning she married him. Her wedding dress was on the floor, and she was tramping on it. I had to press it before she could wear it."

"She didn't have to marry him. Mother couldn't have forced her to a thing like that. She adored her."

"I suppose he meant safety," Anne said thoughtfully. "You know how things were after Father's death. Selling the town house and moving out here. And Ridge meant security. He was old enough, too, to know what he wanted. All I can say is he got it, and more."

We were silent for a while. I had tried for years to forget Father's death, and only to remember his gentleness and kindness. And as I have said, the stark fact of his suicide had not registered until years later. The crash had ruined him. He had paid as much as he could of the debts he owed, but in January of 1930 he had gone back to his office at night and put a bullet through his head. We had not even known he had a gun.

Anne was remembering, too.

"Funny," she said. "Mother never would realize what had happened to the country. She gave a big dinner the night

14

Father—died." She glanced up at the Laszlo portrait over the mantel. "Martin and I were living there, you know. We were pretty hard up, so I cut the train off my wedding dress and wore it. She had terrapin, I remember."

"Do you mean to say he had to sit through all that before he—" I didn't go on. I could not.

"He was quiet, I remember that. But he was always a great gentleman, Lois. He just got up and went out after the coffee. Nobody missed him."

She saw it was a dangerous topic. She went back to Judith.

"Ridge says she's asked him for a divorce," she said. "She doesn't give him any reason. Just says she wants to live abroad, or in South America. Of all the idiotic things!"

"That doesn't sound like the psychiatrist, does it?"

"Well, you know Judith. She's liable to do anything. She was a brat as a child. She'd lie at the drop of a hat, and she'd either sulk or raise a stink if she didn't get her own way. If Ridge had only turned her over his knee and spanked her, it might have helped. But he was too damned well-bred. He just gave her her head, and now she's lost it. I've always blamed Mother. She practically sold Jude."

Neither of us said anything for a while. I suppose Anne was thinking of Mother. I know I was. Phil had once said bitterly that she took Father's death as a grievance rather than a grief. It was a cruel thing to say, but I could remember when the town house was sold soon after, and her refusal to part with much of the furniture, as well as the tapestries and her Aubusson carpet, all of which she insisted had to go to The Birches. Along with her portrait, of course.

We had had to sell them later, over her bitter resentment. After all, we had to eat. But neither Phil nor I had the heart to sell the Laszlo. It was still over the mantel in the old library, now our living-room, and Anne got up and stood looking at it.

"Why do you think she forced Judith to marry Ridge?" she asked. "I've often wondered about it. Do you think he helped her out in some way? Money, perhaps?"

"I suppose it's possible. He must have been crazy about Jude to—well, to buy her."

"He was, of course. He was mad about her." She looked at her wrist watch and picked up her bag.

"I have to get home," she said. "As usual the maid walked out on me yesterday, so I have to cook Martin's dinner. I thought I'd better warn you about Jude. You certainly don't want her here. And if you pick Phil up at the station, be careful. The roads are hellish."

I saw her into her old sedan and watched her down the drive. Then, with a couple of hours to spare, I went back to my typewriter and what I hoped would be a novel someday. I had moved into Mother's room after her death, because the light was better and it was easier to heat. But I did no more work that day. The talk about Judith had made me uneasy. Also Anne had said something on the big front porch as she left which set me to thinking. She stopped and looked at me there in the gray winter light.

"Are you always going on like this, Lois?" she said. "You're a very pretty girl, you know. And nobody would guess you're twenty-eight years old. Isn't it time you stopped looking after Phil and began looking after yourself?"

"I'm doing all right. I even earn my keep, in a small way."

"What about men? Do you ever see any?"

"I've had a few passes made at me," I said, and I'm afraid I giggled. "Nobody I wanted."

She left then and went back into the house. Her news had really startled me. I went into the living-room and looked up at Mother's picture. Anne had said Judith had never cared for Ridge, that Mother had forced the marriage. And perhaps she had. I remembered her before she died. She had hated her new poverty, the skimping and saving of the years after Father's death. But somehow she had managed to give Judith a big wedding. Like Anne's, and less than a year after Father's death.

I never knew where she got the money, but I was too young in those days to worry about it. I remember that Phil gave

Judith away, in our small local church, and that she wore sweeping white satin and carried white orchids. But Anne said she had had to press the dress that morning, because Judith had thrown it on the floor and tramped on it.

I knew something else, too. Until she died five years later Mother had had a small income from some unknown source. She never spoke of it, and Phil said it was probably Father's pension from the Spanish-American War. But now I wondered if Ridgely Chandler had paid it. Certainly, wherever it came from, it ended with her death.

Yet, I don't think Mother was ever satisfied about the marriage. Not that Ridge Chandler was not a good husband. He was pretty nearly a perfect one so far as we knew. But a month or two before Mother died she asked me to look after Judith, if anything happened to her. I was only thirteen at the time, and I remember staring at her.

"What in the world can happen to her, Mother?"

She gave me a long, rather odd look.

"She's not like the rest of you," she said. "She's the kind to get into trouble. And beauty can be a curse, Lois. I'd feel better if you would promise to look after her."

"Of course I will, Mother."

"I spoiled her badly, I'm afraid," she said feebly, "and the sins of the fathers *are* visited on the children. I know that now."

"Everybody has always spoiled Judith, Mother."

She nodded her poor head. It was queer, but as she failed and depended more and more on me, I found myself giving her the affection I had never felt as a child. We could not afford a nurse, so Helga and I looked after her, with Phil giving us a hand when he could. And I was alone with her that day.

"I've made a good many mistakes," she said. "Some I felt were for the best, but I knew she wasn't in love with Ridgely when she married him. But you were a child then. You don't know how things were. I thought Judith needed someone to look after her. She was too attractive to men. And Ridge was

17

older. All those boys—"

Just before she died, a few weeks later, I think she tried to tell me something more. But Helga came in just then, and she never finished it. I have wondered since if she meant to tell me the whole story, and if it would have helped me if she had.

So there I was, after Anne's visit that day, bound by that old promise to look after a Judith whom I scarcely ever saw—a Judith in some sort of trouble after twenty years of marriage. A Judith, too, who, although she was thirty-eight when she went to Reno, could pass for thirty any time. And also—as though she knew of the promise to Mother—was to change her plans and decide to come to The Birches. For safety.

We did not want her. Both Phil and I knew from the beginning that trouble was her middle name, but there was nothing we could do. A part of the place was legally hers, and there was plenty of room. There should be a law against families who, in the luxurious years before two world wars, built vast country places and then left them to their descendants. Here we were, with a hundred acres and the big house in Westchester County, and with two maids we could barely afford. As Helga, now an old woman, never put a foot beyond the kitchen, we had to have a general housework girl as well. Her name was Jennie.

I don't want to sound bitter, in view of Judith's tragedy, but she had been the spoiled beauty of the family far too long, and after the way she had lived for twenty years it must have been hard for her to adapt herself. Not that she really tried. It was no help to my work that she chose the times when I was at my typewriter to play the fine old Bechstein piano Mother had salvaged from the wreckage of the town house. And I noticed after she came that Phil increasingly took refuge in the library, under pretense of work.

But I have not told how she came to The Birches, or why I went to Reno with her. Nor that at first when we got home she refused even to mention Bernard Townsend, her psychiatrist. We pretended not to know about him, but she was in such

18

nervous shape and sleeping so badly that Phil finally suggested someone of the sort.

Her first reaction was one of sheer fury and, I thought, of suspicion.

"Don't be a fool," she said. "If you think I'm going to spill my guts to one of those Peeping Toms you can think again. 'What do you dream about?' 'What is the earliest thing you remember?' It's childish. It's sickening."

She slammed out of the room, and Phil grinned.

"I guess Anne was wrong," he said. "She hasn't fallen for the guy, nor he for her. I don't know why he hasn't. After all she's a damned attractive woman, and I don't suppose her idiosyncrasies would bother a chap like that. He must see a lot of crackpots."

Because by that time we had decided that something was definitely wrong with Judith. I suppose every now and then some family has somebody like her; someone who has gone slightly off the rails psychopathically—if that's the word. Phil thought she had a persecution complex, for certainly she was terrified of something, or somebody. I knew that on the train coming back from Reno, when she fainted in the vestibule of our car.

But that faint was definitely not psychopathic. She *was* terrified, although it was only after long months of what I can only call travail that we learned the reason for it.

Chapter 3

In a way I have already jumped the gun in this record. To make things clear I must go back to a day or so after Anne's visit, when, looking up from my typewriter, I saw Ridgely's car coming up the drive.

It was Jennie's day out, so I went down and let him in. It was still slushy, and the snowplows had not got around to clearing the roads. He stamped the melting snow off his feet, apologized for the mess, and then remembered to shake hands with me.

Looking at him as he took off his overcoat, I thought he looked half sick. I had never cared for him, and so far had our paths diverged that it was a couple of years since I had even seen him. For one thing, he was thinner, but as always he was immaculately dressed. He was a smallish dapper man in his late fifties, with an arrogant manner and an already balding head.

Some of the arrogance was gone that day, however, as I took him into the library and put a match to the fire there. He looked, I thought, rather desperate.

"Sorry to bother you, in case you were writing," he said. "I see you still have the Laszlo. It's a nice piece of painting." And he added, "She was a strong woman, your mother, and a dominant one. It's very like her."

"Yes," I said. "Nobody has ever taken her for Whistler's mother. Would you like a drink? It must have been a nasty drive."

20

"Not now. Perhaps later."

He waited until I sat down, and then seated himself. I had an idea that never in his life had he sat while a woman stood. He did not speak at once. He seemed to be wondering how to begin. When he did, his voice was dry and hard.

"I'm not going to beat about the bush, Lois," he said. "I suppose you know why I'm here. Or do you?"

I nodded. "Anne told me. It's Judith, isn't it?"

"Yes. It's Judith," he said. "She's not herself. She hasn't been for the past month or so. I'm worried about her."

I hedged a bit. "What do you mean? Isn't she well?"

"Oh, she's well enough, or at least she has been until lately. Good God, she must be as strong as an ox, the way she's been getting around. I'm not feeble myself, but I couldn't take it. Haven't for years. Lois, do you think it's possible she's fallen in love with somebody?"

I wanted to say she was in love with herself and always had been. I couldn't, of course.

"She's always had men around her," I told him. "Like any woman with her looks. But I think it's unlikely, Ridge. She's—well, she really doesn't care for men. Not the way you mean, anyhow."

"I realize that," he said dryly. "She only cares for herself. I had some hope when she married me, but it didn't work out. I suppose I was a fool. I wasn't married a week before I knew she didn't really give a damn for me."

"You've stuck it out a long time," I said.

He gave me a chilly smile.

"What was I to do? I come of an old conservative family. We have stood for something in the city. Even in the country itself. Much like your own people. I—well, I put up with a lot for that reason. As for divorce—"

I found myself feeling sorry for him. He had been twenty years older than Judith when she married him. Now I wondered if it had been twenty years of martyrdom for a proud man.

"I must confess I don't understand it," he went on. "I've

never given her any grounds for it." He smiled faintly. "You might say the shoe should be on the other foot! I have stood for a great deal for a good many years. Not that I think she'd commit adultery, but she hasn't been a wife to me for a long time. Years, in fact. She—has she talked to you about it?"

"No. I hardly ever see her, Ridge."

He seemed rather at a loss. He took a cigarette from a gold case and lit it before he spoke.

"She sprung it on me at breakfast a day or two ago. She didn't often get up so early, but that day she did. I was surprised, because she'd been out late the night before. She simply sat down at the table and threw it at me."

"She always did unexpected things," I said. "Her life's full of exclamation points. You hadn't done anything to annoy her, had you?"

"Practically everything I do annoys her." He looked rather grim. "Outside of that, no. There isn't another woman, either, although the way things have been between us for years she probably wouldn't have minded that much. No, Lois. I'm well past the stage of extramarital affairs."

He hesitated.

"Perhaps I'd better tell you about the night before that breakfast when the divorce came up," he said. "I'm not proud of it, but maybe you can make some sense out of it."

What developed was that they had occupied separate rooms for years, and that he seldom even heard her come in. That night, however, he did, and did not go to sleep again. After a while he realized that she was not following her usual bedtime routine of bath, face cream, and so on. Instead she was walking the floor.

"It puzzled me," he said. "It wasn't like her."

I looked at him impatiently. I have no use for men who let their women trample all over them.

"Why on earth didn't you go in and find out?" I said.

He shrugged his padded shoulders.

"I told you. We haven't been on terms like that for a long

22

time. I suppose it was my fault. I work hard and I need my sleep. I couldn't take her routine, and if I looked at the clock when she came in she thought I was checking up on her."

"Well, for heaven's sake, why wouldn't you check up on her?" I said indignantly.

He let that go. He was gazing up at Mother's portrait again.

"I don't know exactly why I'm telling you all this," he said. "It's damned unpleasant. After all, she's my wife. But I have to know why she's leaving me, or what has happened to her the past few weeks, and especially the past few days."

Some of what had happened, when he finally got down to it, was queer enough. It seems he lay in his bed, expecting to hear her usual ritual before going to bed. But as it turned out she was not going to bed. So far as he could make out she was walking about the room, her high heels clicking on the hard wood between the rugs. Then she must have decided something, for he heard her working at the safe where she kept her jewels. As she never bothered to put away what she had worn until the next morning, this surprised him.

He must have picked up his courage at that point. Anyhow, he got up and went to her door. Her back was to him, and she did not hear him. She had got out everything she owned: the diamond bracelets, the pearls, the emerald earrings and necklace, a dozen or so clips and brooches, and she added to them the huge ten-carat solitaire which was her engagement ring. She was examining them piece by piece.

"As if she was appraising them, by the Lord Harry," he said. "And some of them had been my mother's."

I stared at him incredulously. He had left her there like that, he said. He had returned to his room and finally gone to sleep. But, idiot that I considered him, he was not entirely weak minded. It had looked like blackmail to him. What else could he think of?

"Only apparently it isn't," he said. "When she said she wanted a divorce, I asked her if she was in any sort of trouble, and if she was I was willing to help. She could have any money she needed. Do you know what she said to that?"

"What?"

"That all she wanted was to get out of the country! She intended to live somewhere abroad."

"And no reason?"

"No reason whatever. By God, I began to wonder if she'd killed somebody!"

"You don't think so now?"

"No. She's not a passionate woman. She has a temper, of course, but she's pretty well controlled. She would never risk a thing like that. She's played around. She likes admiration, but she'd never get into trouble about a man. Even if she did, why would she want a divorce? You'd think she'd want to stick to me, at least for safety's sake. And she's no child, Lois. She's kept her looks, but she's facing middle age. And there's nothing she can do about it."

I was puzzled. Whatever Judith felt about Ridgely, she had cared passionately for the life he enabled her to live. He had plenty of money, and she liked money. He had position, too, and, like Mother, that meant a lot to her. To throw everything overboard like this sounded crazy to me.

"Maybe she didn't mean it," I said. "You know Judith. She has erratic spells, when she does crazy, silly things. She's always had them, but they're never serious, and she gets over them in time."

"She's not getting over this," he said, his voice grim. "She's going to Reno as soon as I can get space on a train. Yes, she's let me do that. And she's in a hurry. She wants to get out of town. I left her packing her clothes. I think I'll have that drink after all, Lois. I guess I need it."

I got a bottle of Scotch from the liquor closet and cracked some ice from the refrigerator. We had no ice cubes at The Birches. The big gloomy kitchen was empty but warm, and I went over to the coal range and stood there for a minute, thinking. That Judith was in a jam of some sort was obvious, but what sort of jam? I agreed with Ridge that it was not like an

24

affair of any kind. A more generous woman might let herself go in that fashion, but not Judith, unless she had something to gain by it.

Then what? Or who? Some millionaire who had fallen for her looks and was offering her a yacht or a house at Palm Beach? But the sea made her sick, and she could go to Palm Beach any time. Then, again, why get out of the country?

I put the question bluntly to Ridge when I gave him his drink, but he only shook his head.

"You tell me," he said heavily. "Tell me why she hasn't been herself for the past few weeks, and why she locks her door at night. She's not afraid I'll bother her. What's she afraid of, Lois?"

"It's not like her to be afraid of anything, Ridge."

"It's possible, of course, that she's afraid of me. But why? We had established a pretty fair modus vivendi. I couldn't live her sort of life. She liked gaiety; she wanted crowds around her. Sometimes I felt as though I was running a night club. Or she'd be out late and I'd be afraid she had had an accident with her car. You know how she drives. Of course, the very fact that I worried got on her nerves. She wouldn't take the chauffeur unless she couldn't help it."

I knew all that. Judith at the wheel of one of her smart cars— she had a new one every year or so—was enough to set one's teeth on edge. How many times she had been arrested for speeding I didn't know, but Ridge probably did. He must have had to bail her out fairly often.

"You don't think it's a hit-and-run case?" I asked. "If she ever hurt anyone—or killed them—she would lose her head, probably. Just go and keep on going."

"Why would that make her divorce me?"

I looked at him. Even when he married Jude he could not have been a romantic figure. Now, in Father's old leather chair and clutching his highball glass, he looked what he was, an elderly gentleman of what we used to call the old school who was, to use more modern jargon, in one hell of a mess.

25

"Of course, it must be blackmail," I said. "Nothing else would explain the jewels, would it?"

"I'm not blackmailing her, and it's me she's leaving," he said sharply.

I thought of the old woman who left her husband because she had just lost her taste for him, but I said nothing.

"Anyhow, blackmail for what?" he went on. "I know she's seen Anne. Has she told her anything?"

"Anne's as much puzzled as you are, Ridge. She doesn't know what it's all about."

Curiously enough, he seemed to relax at that. He finished his highball and leaned back in his chair.

"Good whisky," he said.

Apparently we were through with Judith for the time, but I still thought him rather a pathetic figure. After all, he had stood by Jude for a good many years, submitted to her crowds, her hectic life, and her vagaries, which had ranged from parties for dogs and other pets—in the apartment!—to taking over the piano in a night club and transposing the music so that the soprano burst into tears and left the platform. The treasure hunt was only one of a series, and Ridge showed the wear and tear of those years, although she had been less often in the papers recently.

"Living with her has certainly been an experience," he said with his cool smile. "But in spite of the fact that we've lived separate lives for so long, I still don't believe there is anybody else. She likes admiration. She likes being one of the best-dressed women in America. She likes crowds around her. But she prefers notoriety to scandal, if you know what I mean."

He looked rather better after he had finished his drink. The divorce was settled, he said. He had even arranged what alimony he was to pay her, which, oddly enough, was all she asked. Also he had already had his lawyer wire another one out there in Reno to do the dirty work, and I wondered if there wasn't a bit of relief behind all these plans. He was certainly shocked and bewildered, but he was tired and not too young. I wondered, too, whether he rather looked forward to peace and quiet after what he had endured for so long.

It was, however, what came next that got me up, so to speak, all standing.

"What brought me here," he said, "is that she is frightened about something. It's real. She's not dramatizing herself. Personally I don't believe she's in any sort of danger, but you know her. I've always looked after her as much as I could, and before we were married your mother did the same thing. I suppose we've spoiled her, but there it is. She's reckless and unstable, and I don't want her to get into trouble out there. I thought, if you went with her, you could—well, keep an eye out for anything which might turn up."

I think my very soul revolted, but at least I managed to keep from shrieking.

"She would hate it, Ridge," I said. "She's never been fond of me. And I'd be useless in any sort of crisis."

"I don't expect a crisis, as you put it," he said grimly. "But I do expect her to behave herself. Also I have a right to know what, if anything, she's afraid of or why she wants to leave this country. And I think she means to take her jewels, and she's careless about them."

"In other words," I said, "what you want is a Saint Bernard dog with a keg of brandy around its neck. No, thank you, Ridge, you can do your own spying."

He was annoyed. He put down his glass and stood up.

"Look, Lois," he said. "Think back and you'll realize you owe me something. The money that took you through college was not from some old stocks you had forgotten. It was mine. And as long as your mother lived I paid her a small annuity. Now I want a little help, and you refuse it."

Well, there it was, take it or leave it.

I thought of the crime book I was writing. The story was just beginning to jell, and we needed the money for the old house. I have always said that when I died the words "guttering and spouting" would be found written across my heart, like Bloody

27

Mary and Calais. I suppose he saw my face, for he hurried on.

"I'd be prepared to pay for your time, if you'll go with her," he said rather apologetically. "Say a thousand dollars and all expenses. You may be able to work out there, too. She won't stay in town. She'll be on a ranch. Horseback riding if you like it, that sort of thing."

The horseback riding didn't interest me. By the time I was old enough to ride anything but my pony the horses were gone from the stables at The Birches. The thousand dollars did, however. In a burst of optimism the previous spring—as in the case of the swimming pool—I had repaired and furnished the lodge at the gates, in the hope of renting it to someone for the summer. But no one had taken it, and Phil called it Maynard's Folly and said it depressed him every time he passed it on the way to the train.

"When is she going?" I said feebly.

"In a day or so. She wanted to go today, but it's not easy to get a drawing-room just now. She's afraid to fly."

In a day or so! There must be something badly wrong, I thought, to cause such haste. It could not be Ridgely himself. You don't live all those years with a man and insist on leaving him in hours.

"She won't tell me anything, you know, Ridge. We've never been close. And what will I do if she won't have me?"

"She'll have you," he said, still rather grim. "It's one of the conditions I made, and she didn't object. She hasn't many women friends. Only that crowd of hangers-on and parasites who trail around with her." He put a brotherly hand on my shoulder. "You'll do it, won't you? I'll feel a lot better with you around. She's in a queer mood, Lois. Badly as she's behaving I don't want her taking an overdose of sleeping-pills, or something of that sort."

I think that was the first time I really felt the situation was serious. For I realized that Ridge was not only the deserted husband. He was frightened himself. Something was wrong. Under all his urbanity he was suspicious and alarmed. All through our talk he had been tense with strain.

"I suppose I'll have to do it," I agreed finally. "Only I wish I had some idea what to look out for. If you know it you should tell me."

"My dear girl," he said paternally, "if I knew I wouldn't be asking you to go to Reno. Whatever it is it must have happened suddenly. She hadn't been well for a couple of months, but when she went out to dinner the night I speak of she was entirely herself. She was wearing a new evening wrap, ermine and sable, and it suited her. I was at my desk in the library when she passed the door, and I'll swear she was normal as you are. She even waved good-by to me."

So she had waved good-by to him! It seemed as little as any woman could do for a new ermine and sable wrap, and when I thought of my own shabby muskrat I wondered why he had not strangled her.

But I was trapped and I knew it. I knew something else, too. As he drove away that day he looked not only relieved. He was a little smug, as though by making me his stool pigeon he had achieved something important to him. For all his air of ignorance I wondered if he knew more than he admitted about Judith's terror.

I went upstairs feeling that I had sold my birthright for a college education, a small annuity to Mother while she lived, and a thousand dollars in cash. And the mood continued while I put away my manuscript and slammed the cover on the typewriter. That annuity to Mother worried me, too. I sat there in what had been her room and thought about her. Why had she forced Judith to marry Ridge? If she did. And why on earth had Judith agreed? She could be as stubborn as a mule when anything displeased her. Yet she had gone through with the thing, with Mother still in black for Father pulling out her white satin train and then marching stiffly up the church aisle on an usher's arm. For all the world like a woman who had accomplished something and could now sit back comfortably and let Providence take care of the rest of it.

The roads were horrible as I drove in to town to meet Phil's train, and he looked so tired that I waited until he had put on his old smoking-jacket and mixed his evening cocktail before I told him.

"I'm going to Reno in a day or two," I said.

He almost dropped the shaker.

"For God's sake don't tell me you've been married all this time!" he said.

"Don't be an idiot. I'm going with Judith. She's divorcing Ridge."

He stared at me incredulously. "Don't tell me she's letting go of ten million dollars," he said. "I don't believe it. Not our Judy. That's fantastic."

"Ridge was here this afternoon. It's true all right."

He sat down, his jaw dropped, and his long thin body looking collapsed.

"I don't get it," he said. "What's sending her off the rails this time? Got something better in sight?"

"Ridge doesn't think so."

He drank his cocktail thoughtfully.

"Well, it's a break for him," he said. "I don't think our dear sister has been much of a wife. But if you ask me she's not leaving the soft nest she's got unless she has a plush-lined one waiting for her somewhere else."

He couldn't have been more wrong, of course. But when he learned I was serious about going with her—and within a day or so at that—he blew up.

"Don't be a fool," he said. "You never got along with her. Who could? And what's the idea, anyhow? A woman thirty-eight years old! If she can't take care of herself by this time she never will. As a matter of fact, she's always taken damned good care of herself. And why all the hurry? What's she running away from? Ridge?"

"He doesn't think so. He believes something has happened to her," I told him. "That she may be in trouble of some sort. She talks about living abroad."

"I'd be for that," he said callously. "What's she been doing? Stealing some woman's husband?"

"Not so far as he can find out."

"And why you? Can't she hop a train by herself?"

"I'm being paid. A thousand dollars. To act as Ridge's stoolie."

Phil's reading does not consist of crime fiction, as mine does. He only looked confused.

"I'm to watch Jude and report to him," I explained. "It's a dirty job, but I'd fall still lower for a thousand dollars. Think of the coal it will buy!"

He grunted and looked depressed. The furnace was his job. Then Jennie announced the evening meal in her inimitable manner. It consisted of opening the library door, yelling "Dinner" loudly, and disappearing. Phil looked still more down in the mouth.

"I seem to remember a time," he said sadly, "when some impeccable individual of the male persuasion politely opened that door and mentioned the fact that food was ready to be served. If Judith ever wants to come here—which God forbid—one week of Jennie would send her flying."

"That's silly. Why in the world would she come here?"

"Just out of general cussedness," he said, "and our usual bad luck."

Which again might have been funny if it had not been so horrible.

We had to drop the discussion during dinner, with Jennie in and out of the room, and when she slammed down the dessert, which was bread pudding, Phil stared at it with distaste.

"When I think of the poor little hungry birds outside in all this snow," he said sadly, "I wonder why I have to eat all the stale crusts. Jennie, can't you convey to Helga that it's too late for them to make my hair come in curly?"

But Jennie only giggled and banged out of the room as usual. Phil ignored his dessert and lit a cigarette.

"If I were Ridgely Chandler," he said, "I'd be cutting capers

31

all over the place tonight. Only, of course, the Chandlers don't do things like that. As it is, all I am grateful for is that Judith's going abroad after it's over. The very thought of having her here makes me shiver."

I left him there with his coffee and went upstairs to look over my clothes. They were a skimpy lot compared with the old days when Mother's handsome silks and brocades hung there. But as it turned out they did not matter. Nobody in Reno noticed me when Judith was in the vicinity.

There were times when I felt like her shadow, and when I had to gaze in a mirror to convince myself of my own reality. I did not really feel like myself until we were on our way east, and Judith fainted in the vestibule of our compartment car.

Chapter 4

The trip was uneventful, but when I met Judith at the railroad station in New York I realized that something had happened to her. Her face looked thinner, and she seemed to be watching the crowd feverishly. Her "Hello, Lois," was rather less than sisterly, but as I had not seen much of her for years I had not expected anything else.

She was traveling without a maid, to my surprise, and—also to my surprise—she looked almost shabby. She was wearing her hair differently, too, as though she had made a feeble effort at disguise.

"What!" I said. "No mink coat?"

"I won't need it out there."

"I thought it was cold in Reno."

She did not answer that. Her eyes continued to stare at the people around us, and not until we were inside the train did she seem to relax. Even then she showed that she did not intend to bother with me, or even that I was particularly welcome. "What's the idea anyhow?" she said peevishly. "If you're spying for Ridge, just forget it. There's nothing wrong. He simply can't understand how anybody can divorce a Chandler."

"Personally," I said, "I don't give a tinker's dam about Reno or your business there, Jude. I'm simply going along for the ride and a substantial check. I need the money."

She looked startled. Then she laughed.

"So Ridge is keeping an eye on me!" she said. "Well, he won't learn much, or you, either. You have the compartment next to my drawing-room, and I won't need anything. I am going to rest and read. Just amuse yourself."

I took the hint, and she spent almost the entire trip shut in her room and in her berth. I know she ate, for stewards brought trays and took them away, and once or twice the porter brought her ice, which I daresay meant a cocktail. After Chicago, however, the tension lessened. She even had the door opened between our rooms, and once we went to the diner together.

She had abandoned the semidisguise of the railroad station. Also she looked better, and as we went to our table I saw people looking at her, as they always did. It is hard to describe Judith. She is a blonde—an editor once told me that I must hate blondes, as I always made them obnoxious characters in my fiction—and her eyes have a little uptilt at the outer corners, which is unusual and attractive. But beauty is too hard to define. After all, the human individual universally has two eyes, a nose, a mouth, and a chin. It is the assemblage of those features that counts, and believe me Jude's counted.

It was in the diner that day when she asked me about The Birches.

"I haven't seen it for years," she said. "How is it? Lonely as ever?"

"Pretty much. The village is slowly dying, since so few of the big houses are open. I'm fixing the old pool this spring. We need it in hot weather."

"Do you still have Helga?"

"Yes, by the grace of heaven. But she's getting pretty old. She has arthritis."

I had no idea what she had in her mind that day: that The Birches might be a haven sometime, or even a hiding-place. I prattled on in my innocence, while my bad angel patted me on the shoulder for being a good little fool, and Judith ate fresh

34

mountain trout and listened.

We were better friends after that. Not intimate. Certainly not sisterly. But I began to realize that her early coldness had nothing to do with me. She was simply absorbed in herself and her problem, whatever it was. Because there was a problem. She would sit for hours staring out the car window but seeing nothing. And once or twice I saw her shiver, although the train was warm.

"We used to say that meant somebody walking over our graves," I offered once when she had been shaking for some time.

"Oh, for heaven's sake!" she snapped at me. "Why don't you read or pick up some man in the club car? Or does Ridge insist you watch me all the time?"

But she had lost all her color, and for a moment I thought she was going to faint.

Reno was not too bad. We were on a ranch outside of town, and I learned to ride a horse and like it. Judith rode, too, but also she spent a lot of time in town, she said at the movies, but I had an idea she was gambling. It wasn't my affair, of course. I saw very little of her. When I did, she was usually surrounded by cowboys or the men who were guests at the ranch.

I have the carbon of a letter to Ridge which I wrote on my portable after we had been in Reno a couple of weeks.

Dear Ridge: We are comfortably settled and getting along nicely. Judith is fine, sleeping well and looking much her old self again. Apparently it was New York which did not agree with her, as she improved steadily all the way west. I do not see much of her, however, and it looks as though I am here under false pretenses. She seems to feel entirely safe, as I am sure she is.

Personally I wonder whether she was merely tired to the point of exhaustion before we came here, and so got some sort of delusion of persecution. You might ask her psychiatrist that. As things are I am rather like a third leg here so far as she is concerned.

35

Better burn this letter, and it's not necessary to reply. She knows you sent me and why, and I think it amuses her, which shows, I think, how normal she is. Yours, Lois.

I gathered that the divorce was being arranged, but she never mentioned it, nor did I. And whatever purpose the shabby disguise had served, it was not resumed after we left Chicago. She broke out in gay little dresses and evening gowns, hired a car and drove it recklessly, and on the proper day and surrounded by assorted males threw her lovely platinum wedding ring into the Truckee River and proceeded to pack for the East.

It was a few days before we left that she came into my room to say she had decided to stay at The Birches until she made up her mind what to do.

"The Birches!" I said with a sinking heart. "Why on earth The Birches? You never liked it there, and you'd go crazy, after what you're accustomed to."

"If you remember, a part of it is mine," she said coldly. "I've never asked any rent from you and Phil, nor has Anne. But I certainly have the right to live there if I want to."

"I thought you were going abroad," I said in a sort of desperation.

"I need to be quiet for a while," she said. "I can make other plans later. I'm better now. Thank God I don't have to live up to the Chandler virtues any more."

I stared at her, but she apparently meant it, so I let it go.

"How's the Bechstein?" she inquired. "I need to catch up with my music."

"It hasn't been tuned for years," I said. "Now look, Judith," I added desperately, "we simply can't have you at The Birches. Most of it is closed. We only use part of it. And I write. I have to earn money, and I need quiet to do it."

"Aren't you forgetting Ridge's little contribution?" she said nastily. "That ought to help."

36

But I still didn't believe her. Not until she told me she had wired Phil to have the Bechstein put in order. The immediate result was a telegram to me from Phil.

Don't understand but strenuously object. Paying small boys in neighborhood to plant a few skunks, etc. Insist this must not happen.

A day or two later there was an air-mail letter from Anne along the same lines:

What in the world is this idea of Judith coming to The Birches? She was always a troublemaker, and this divorce certainly shows she is still unstable. I am sure Ridge would let her have the apartment if she wanted it, and I simply cannot see her in the country. You may have servant trouble, too. Helga never liked her, and you don't want to lose her.

I have not talked to Ridge since, but as I told you there is something queer behind this divorce. Do you think she is in trouble? And if so, why Reno? I have asked around among the gang she played with, but they say no other man.

I have been worried about you, too, Lois. How can you write with her around all the time? If she wants the old Bechstein, let her have it. Give her anything else she wants. But for heaven's sake don't have her at The Birches. She will drive you crazy.

Anne was the practical member of the family, as well as the oldest, and I read her letter carefully. A solidly built woman and entirely domestic, she was only four years older than Judith, and consequently knew her better than I did. But the divorce came up about that time, and I saw very little of Judith until we started east.

37

So far as I know, however, she had been perfectly well. As usual she had two or three men see her to the train, and she looked beautiful and barely thirty that day. I remember we had two boxes of flowers, three of candy, and a bottle of Chanel No. 5 to help us survive the trip, as well as innumerable magazines and books. I stood on the platform in an effulgence of reflected glory as the train pulled out, the men waving, Judith smiling, and myself trying to hold the accumulated tribute.

Then, when it was all over, I turned to follow Judith into the car, and saw she was unable to move.

She was standing there, holding to a rail, and no amount of make-up would hide the fact that she was practically fainting. I tried to hold her, but she kept sliding out of my grasp. Then a tall man standing behind us realized the situation and together we got her to her drawing-room. She really fainted then, passing out in her seat like a light, and the tall man stood in the doorway, looking uneasy.

"Think I'd better get a doctor?" he asked.

"No. She'll be all right. She's done it before. But thank you, anyhow."

He disappeared then, and a moment later Judith opened her eyes. I had a glass of water in my hand by that time, but I had been startled enough to be irritable.

"For heaven's sake, what happened to you?" I asked. "One minute you're all smiles, waving to that posse out there, and the next you're going to pieces on me. What was it?"

She sat up then and ran her hands through her hair.

"I just got dizzy," she said shortly. "And take that water away. I'm all right. Stop staring at me with your mouth open. You look like an idiot."

I shall always believe that what Phil called Judith's agoraphobia—which he explains as fear of the market place, or her *idée fixe*, to use his own words—began that day. I only know that she behaved very strangely. For one thing, the moment she recovered from her faint she insisted on having the door locked, only permitting me to open it to let the porter bring in fresh linen for her berth, and so far as I know she never left her bed until we were drawing into New York.

Even I was shut out, and I could only get in by rapping twice and then once, and after that first day she never let the porter in at all. The dining-car waiter didn't matter—she ate almost nothing, and I took in her tray. But the porter did. His job devolved on me. He would give me the fresh sheets, with a queer look on his face, and I would have the backbreaking job of making up the berth.

"Lady have a bad scare about something?" he said once.

"She's a nervous case," I explained lamely.

He showed beautiful white teeth in a smile. "Sometimes Reno do that to them," he said. "Other times they act like they very happy. Never can tell."

I was puzzled, but also I was sorry for her. The flowers faded. The candy and magazines were not even opened. She simply lay there, looking like death and refusing to explain anything.

"Why don't you tell me, Judith?" I would say. "You're afraid of something, aren't you?"

She scowled at me. "Can't I be sick without you bothering me?"

"I don't think you *are* sick. You're scared. All this locking yourself in is silly. What on earth can happen to you on a train?"

"People have been murdered on trains," she said, and shivered.

That was as much as I got out of her on the trip. I sat in my compartment next door and tried to puzzle the thing out. Whatever had happened had been as the train was ready to move out. There had been the group of waving, grinning men, piling her arms with tribute, a red-capped porter or two, and the train conductor. A taxi or two had driven up at the last minute, but their passengers were two laughing women and an elderly one who walked with a cane.

To save my life I could see nothing menacing in that departure of ours. I wondered if the trouble was some passenger on the train, and the second day I began to look it over. It was a long train, and if there was anything sinister about any of the passengers I could not discover it. All I saw were tired and bored people, the women reading or trying to doze, and none of the men with what my detective-story reading told me should be the bulge at the left shoulder that indicated a holster and a gun.

Whatever Judith thought, I could not see Nemesis in wrinkled suits, crying babies, and tired-looking women who had left Reno and their former lives for the unknown future that lay ahead.

I daresay any train east from that Nevada city carries its own load of drama, but I had no idea it was carrying ours.

Chapter 5

It was not until the second day that I saw again the man who had helped me with Judith. My legs were tired from my search of the train, and so, when I reached the club car, I sat down for a cigarette and a drink.

He was across a table from me, and when I searched for a match he leaned over and offered me a light.

"How is the lady?" he inquired.

"She's better, thanks," I said. And that was all for the moment. He was a big man, broad shouldered and powerful, wearing dark glasses with shell rims, and with heavy hair going gray over his ears. There is something disarming to me about gray hair. It shouts respectability, for one thing, although he was not old; in his early forties, perhaps. And beyond asking about Judith he let me alone until I had had my highball. Then he turned and said something about the scenery. As I had had a bellyful of scenery I merely nodded, but he seemed to be lonely, for he kept on.

"In Reno for the usual reasons?" he inquired.

"I'm not married," I said coldly.

He was not easily snubbed, however.

"I've seen you going through the train," he said. "Not looking for someone, are you?"

"I've been looking for Nemesis," I said shortly, and he laughed.

"And why," he said, "should a pretty young woman like yourself be expecting Nemesis?"

It was the first time I realized he was Irish. Probably only Irish descent, but it was there, in the turn of phrase, in the quick uptake and the laughter. But I had an idea he was watching me through those dark glasses, and for just a moment I wondered if it was he who had terrified Judith. It was impossible, of course. He had been behind her, and she was staring out when it happened.

"I don't know," I said vaguely. "Something made my sister faint yesterday. I thought perhaps she saw something. Or somebody. She's really quite strong. It bothers me."

He nodded. "I have an idea I've seen her somewhere," he said. "Either her or her picture."

"Probably her picture," I said, with some bitterness. "The New York columnists use it a lot."

"They would," he agreed. "She's very good-looking. I think I remember now. She's Mrs. Ridgely Chandler, isn't she?"

"Judith Chandler. Yes. You were very kind. I meant to thank you."

He ignored that. He seemed to be thinking.

"What do you think frightened her?" he said. "Or are you imagining something? After all, the strain of getting a divorce must be something."

I didn't tell him that you could have put Judith's strain about her divorce in an eye and not even blinked. It had gone through her like a dose of castor oil. But I did intimate it.

"In this case it was practically painless," I told him. "No, it wasn't that."

"Sure of it, are you?"

"Positive."

He looked thoughtful.

"Then why not let me look over the train for you?" he said. "It's more in my line than yours, anyhow. And if you don't object to meeting me in the diner tonight about seven o'clock I'll tell you what I find, if anything."

He did not explain his line, and I did not ask him. But I found myself liking him. Also I was lonely and feeling rather forlorn, so I agreed at once. He took me back to Judith's drawing-room, and stood by while I gave the customary raps. He smiled down at me.

"Like something out of a book, isn't it?" he said.

I was annoyed.

"I wouldn't put anything so silly in a book of mine."

He looked startled. "You mean you write books?"

"I've done one or two," I said modestly. But he only stared at me.

"Good God!" he muttered, and left abruptly.

I was in two minds after that about having dinner with him. To say I was annoyed would be a considerable understatement. On the other hand, I couldn't very well go into the diner and show my resentment by sitting by myself, and I ended by putting on fresh make-up and what I hoped was a highly literary expression.

It did not seem to impress him. He was waiting for me at a table for two, with a couple of cocktails ready and a beaming smile. He seated me with considerable manner.

"I hope you like Martinis," he said. "It seems like a good idea to drink to a train as innocent as this one."

"You found nobody?"

"A couple of con boys. I wouldn't worry about them."

In a way it was a relief, but I found myself eyeing him curiously. He did not look like a policeman. I was sure he was not flatfooted, he was well dressed, and his hands were well cared for. His diction, too, was good. In a rather rugged way he was good-looking, but his face was strong rather than handsome.

"You seem to know a lot about that sort of thing," I said tentatively.

"I should. I'm a cop myself. Or I was," he added. "I've been

43

in the army. Got knocked about a bit. All right now, however."

Perhaps it was the cocktail. Or perhaps there is something about a train trip which is rather like being on an ocean liner. You make contacts, but because you know they are brief, or perhaps you are bored, you talk rather more than you should. So within an hour or so I knew that my big friend's name was Terrence O'Brien. "With two r's, my mother insisted. God rest her soul." That he was usually called "Irish," that he had been a lieutenant of Homicide in the New York Police Department, had left it for the South Pacific during the war, and having inherited "a little something" was now at a loose end.

"Thinking of getting a small place out of town," he said. "Maybe raise a few chickens. That sort of thing."

I wondered just what he meant by being knocked about a bit. If ever a man looked in the pink of condition, he did.

"You'll miss your work, won't you?" I asked.

"Maybe. Maybe not. I have a lot of reading to do. I got thrown out of college." He grinned. "In a moment of exhilaration it seemed like a good thing to take the pants off the campus policeman," he said. "Which is funny, because I went on the force myself later on. I'd always wanted to be a cop," he added. "I suppose most kids do."

But he reverted to Judith almost immediately.

"You can tell her for me there's nobody dangerous on this train," he said. "Or, on second thought, just leave me out of it. It won't hurt her to shut herself away for a while. And by the way, I don't know your name. Maybe I should, if you write."

"You don't like writing women, do you?"

"Never knew any," he said promptly.

But he didn't laugh. He looked appalled when I told him my name and that I wrote crime stories.

"Don't tell me," he said. "I know. The guy is a private eye. He keeps a fifth of Scotch in a drawer of his desk, he's blackjacked and then gets up and goes about his business instead of being taken to a hospital where he belongs, and he solves the crime when the regular cops are running in circles."

44

In spite of myself I had to laugh.

"Not quite," I said. "My detective is a woman."

He looked really disgusted then, but as dinner arrived at that moment we let the subject drop. Nevertheless, I felt during the meal that he was quietly observing me. I had no idea why.

I didn't tell Judith about him when I carried in the tea and toast that night. Policemen to Judith are men who give you tickets when you park a car or hale you up in traffic court for one thing or another. But I felt a little safer having him, so to speak, on call. He looked so reliable.

I saw him only once again during the trip. That was the same night. After I had rubbed Judith's back, given her two sleeping-pills, and heard her lock herself in, I wandered back to the club car again. He was where I had seen him first, only he had abandoned the spectacles, which made him look younger. He got up when he saw me.

"I was hoping you'd come," he said. "I've kept this chair for you. Sister any better tonight?"

"She's just about the same," I said. "She's still locked away, if that's what you mean."

"Still no idea why?"

"No idea why."

He dropped the subject, got out a rather handsome cigarette case, and after giving me one took one himself.

"I've been thinking about you," he said abruptly. "Read a book of yours out on the islands. *The Red* something or other, wasn't it?"

"*The Red Urn*," I said, probably with a lilt in my voice.

"You slipped up in it, you know," he said. "Why don't you crime writers learn something about police work? And that heroine of yours was a dilly. No character. Nothing but looks. As for that woman detective of yours— Why for God's sake a woman? Know what I think?"

"I haven't an idea," I said coldly, and with the lilt certainly gone.

"This sister of yours," he said. "She's a beauty, and so

probably you were brought up to believe she was God's gift to the world. It doesn't work out like that. Look at the ugly women some men marry! Not that you're that, God knows," he added magnanimously.

That made me laugh, and before long I was telling him of my childhood, of The Birches and our reasons for living there, to Phil and Helga and Jennie, and even to the rehabilitated swimming pool and the gatekeeper's cottage I had done over and could not rent.

He said it all sounded very pleasant to a tired New Yorker. He was pretty much at a loose end himself. He'd thought of a farm, but he realized that a farm without a woman might be pretty lonely, and he had never married. "Been too busy," he added.

Months later I was to think back over that talk of ours, and to wonder that I had not realized its undercurrents. Except for his helping me when Judith fainted in the train at Reno none of it was accidental. If I had not gone to the club car he would have managed to meet me somehow. Before I told him he knew perfectly well who Judith was, and almost certainly my own identity. And what is more, he knew what she was afraid of.

He had done, I thought resentfully, rather a professional bit of acting!

I had no suspicion of him then. When I finally said good night and went back to my compartment, the connecting door into Judith's drawing-room was closed and locked on her side, so I hoped she was settled. At one o'clock in the morning, however, she shook me awake.

"I'm not going to New York at all," she said. "We can take a train from the station as soon as we get there, can't we? I'm going directly to The Birches."

"Well, you can't do it in the state of Illinois, or wherever we are now," I said peevishly. "For goodness' sake go back to bed and let me sleep."

But I didn't sleep much after that. Lying in my berth I could see Phil's face when we arrived, and Helga's. I thought of the quiet days at my desk in Mother's room, and the Bechstein underneath. I thought of the salad or sandwich that was my customary lunch, and Judith's ideas on food. And I wondered how in heaven's name we could lock up a great rambling place like that if Judith persisted in behaving as she was doing then.

It was daylight before I slept.

I did not see my policeman again. Apparently he had left the train somewhere, perhaps in Chicago. I missed him, for I could have used a little help. It was Judith, of course. She would not leave the car at Grand Central until the entire train was empty, and even then only the warning that it was going out to the yards finally evicted her. By that time there was not a redcap in sight, and had it not been for a benevolent conductor I might still have been there, surrounded by luggage.

Luckily there was a local ready, and as I had wired Phil, he met us at the station with our rattling old car. I expected Judith to make some comment on it, but she did not. She ducked in as though all the fiends of hell were after her, and kept looking behind all the way as though she expected to be followed.

Even Phil, resentful as I knew he was, finally noticed it.

"What the devil's the matter with you, Jude?" he said. "Expecting your ex-husband to follow you?"

"Of course not," she said sharply. "I thought I heard a state trooper behind us."

"They know this heap," Phil said dryly. "When they stop me it's for obstructing traffic." He turned around and eyed her as she sat in the back set, surrounded by her handsome luggage. "Why don't you relax, Jude? You'll find The Birches a fine cure for the jitters. All we ever get there is an occasional scream in the night. Got any plans for the future?"

"Plans?" she said. "I'll stay at The Birches for a while, anyhow. The house is as much mine as yours, isn't it?"

"Such as it is," he said. "The food, including Jello and bread pudding, both of which I detest, is paid for by Lois and me. So are the taxes, the light, the heat, the telephone, and the man who wanders in a few times a year to cut the grass. We count

47

that and upkeep as rent. You'll have to ask Lois if she wants to take a boarder."

There was very nearly a row right then in the car. It ended, however, with her agreeing to pay a part of the expenses while she was there, but by her demanding Mother's old room in return. I was furious.

"Sorry, Judith," I said stiffly. "That's mine now. Has been for years. I certainly don't intend to move out."

"If I'm to be a boarder I have a right to it. It's the biggest. Anyhow I have my own reasons for wanting it."

"What reasons?"

She declined to say, so it was a stalemate until we reached the house.

In spite of everything I was glad to be home. As I have said, spring at The Birches is wonderful, with the grass brilliantly green, the forsythia golden yellow, and the trees showing their new young leaves with pride. Like mothers with young babies, Father always said. As we drove in I saw the pool was finished and was slowly filling, and Judith looked at it with an odd expression.

"I thought you'd let it go," she said.

"We did. It's just been restored."

I thought she shivered.

"I always hated it," she said, and closed her eyes.

Then the house was sprawling before us. The white elephant, as Phil called it, was no longer white. Even the big pillars of the porch were now scaling and gray. It was still impressive, however: the center three stories high, with the top floor the large attic; and the two wings, one the service one with the pantry, kitchen, storeroom, and laundry in it and eight or ten servants' rooms above; the other containing what had been the morning room and was now our living-room. In the ell on that side was the library, what had been Father's gun room but was now empty, and beyond the drawing-room the unused conservatory, much of the glass gone and looking rather as though it had been bombed.

Judith had not been there for years, and she looked shocked when she saw it.

"What do you mean by upkeep?" she said indignantly. "The place is a ruin!"

"Guttering and spouting," I told her. "New tiles on the roof so we don't sleep under umbrellas. Toilets and bathtubs that work. What did you expect? Buckingham Palace?"

She said very little when she was inside, although her face was a study. The long hall that ran from the front to the rest of the house was carpetless, except for a rug or two, and some impulse on Jennie's part had opened the door to the drawing-room, although it had been closed for years.

It stood there, naked and enormous, with what little furniture remained covered with sheets, including the piano, and the glass chandeliers and the mirrors similarly protected. She stood gazing in at it.

"Welcome home," I said. "You can't say I didn't warn you, Jude."

"But it's dreadful. Where's Mother's Aubusson carpet? And all the rest of her lovely stuff?"

"Sold," I told her. "Sold long ago when Phil was getting a start. It went for food and doctor bills, and when Mother died it buried her."

I think she hesitated, then. She looked as though she meant to turn and leave, but some second thought, some secret reason, decided her to stay. At that moment Helga and Jennie appeared, and I saw by Helga's expression that there was going to be trouble.

"You'll have to take us as we are, Miss Jude," she said. "We live pretty plain. Not the way you're used to."

But Judith had pulled herself together by that time.

"I only want to rest," she said plaintively. "I don't expect a great deal, Helga. Just peace and quiet."

"That's all we've got," Helga said, her face grim, and decided to offer a gnarled old hand for Jude to shake. "This is Jennie. She's not what you're used to, either, but she can get about,

49

which is more than I can."

All in all it must have been an unpleasant home-coming—if you can call it that—but Judith had apparently made her decision. She may have had some qualms, however. She stood at the front door, gazing down the drive while Phil carried in her luggage.

"I don't remember it like this," she said. "It used to be so gay. And it's frightfully lonely. Aren't there any neighbors?"

Phil put down some bags and mopped his face.

"Quite a lot has happened to the world since your day," he said. "Or perhaps that crowd of yours in town didn't know it. No, there are no neighbors, Judith. Take it or leave it. And my own suggestion is to leave it."

She only shrugged her shoulders, and I left her there to go back to the kitchen and Helga. She was standing by the stove stirring something and her old shoulders looked bent and depressed.

"I'm having lamb stew for dinner," she said, her voice stubborn. "She can eat it or let it alone. I don't want her here, Lois, and that's flat. I've seen you and Mr. Phil struggling for years while she lived on the fat of the land, and not so much as a visit from her. Now when she's in trouble she's here."

She sat down on the edge of the big kitchen table.

"What do you mean, trouble, Helga?" I said. "I wouldn't call her divorce that."

Helga eyed me dourly. "Maybe you haven't really looked at her," she said. "She's in some sort of jam, and I don't like it. She looks haunted-like. She's thin, too. What's she done? Killed somebody?"

"Don't be an old fool," I said, and put an arm around her. "She won't stay long. We'll have to make the best of it. That's all."

I found Judith already ensconced in Mother's room, with an entranced Jennie opening bags and taking out the lace-trimmed underwear and nightgowns they contained. A country girl from the village, she had certainly never seen things like that

50

before. Nor anyone like Judith, anxiously examining her face in the mirror of my toilet table. Already my typewriter and table had been moved into the hall, and I was almost speechless with fury.

"You always get your own way, don't you, Jude?" I said, my voice shaking. "If you ask me, this is a pretty dirty trick. There are plenty of other rooms."

"I won't be here long. I've told you that."

"Then why throw me out?"

"I have all my jewels with me. I need the safe, Lois. It's still here, I see."

I was appalled.

"Do you mean to say you took all that stuff to Reno?"

"Why not? I always carry it with me."

"Is that why you locked yourself away in the train?"

She looked at me in the mirror.

"Of course. What do you think?"

I didn't believe her for a moment. She was lying, and I knew it. She had had it on the way west, and never bothered about it. But she followed it up cleverly.

"That's why I want Phil to nail those windows shut over the porch," she said. "The other two will do for ventilation."

I stood staring at her.

"That's ridiculous," I said. "No one knows you have anything valuable with you. Anyhow you have the safe. And we never have burglars. They know we have nothing worth stealing except Mother's Georgian tea set, and that's been on the sideboard in the dining-room for twenty years."

She looked stubborn.

"Anyone could climb those porch pillars," she said. "I'm taking no chances."

Jennie had gone out for something by that time, and I confronted Judith with what I daresay was not a particularly sisterly face.

"What are you afraid of?" I demanded. "Don't pretend to me, Jude. You're scared to death. You've done something,

51

haven't you? Something wrong. Maybe something terrible. What is it?"

She did not like it. I thought for a moment she was going to slap me. Then she thought better of it.

"Don't be absurd, Lois," she said. "What could I have done? And if I had, do you think I could get away with it, as well-known as I am? That's simply silly. I'm taking normal precautions, like any sensible person. You're building up something that actually doesn't exist."

It was her round. I'll grant you that. She had won Mother's room and even Phil's reluctant support. For the last thing I heard that night was the sound of a hammer as he nailed her two windows shut.

I was back in my old nursery by that time, still seething, but in spite of myself I had to smile, remembering dinner that night. Judith had come down to dinner in an exquisite negligee, had waited for the soup course, which did not arrive, and winced when Jennie slammed her plate of stew in front of her. Phil watched her without appearing to until the dessert appeared.

"I'm sorry, Judith," he said, "but we've had to let the butler go. Got into the wine cellar and turned up plastered. But I can recommend this lemon gelatin. Not fattening but full of energy."

Whereupon he ate the stuff, which I knew he detested.

Chapter 6

Ridgely called me up the next morning. He sounded irritable.

"I didn't expect to have to learn from the papers that you were back," he said. "When did you get in?"

"Late yesterday. She's here at The Birches, Ridge. I don't know why."

"I suppose she has her reasons," he said coldly. "I'll mail you a check today."

He hung up without so much as a good-by, and as I put down the receiver I wondered again why he had wanted me to go to Reno. It seemed singularly pointless. He was not even interested in why she was where she was.

I had my first chance to talk to Phil when I drove him to the station that morning. I told him the whole story, the fainting at Reno, and the way she had locked herself away on the train. But I did not mention O'Brien. It seemed unnecessary.

Phil was thoughtful, especially after I told him of Ridgely's call.

"Suppose she's afraid of him?" he asked.

"He wasn't in Nevada," I said. "Or on that train. And she's not afraid of him. She never has been."

It was true, of course, and Phil nodded.

"I suppose he's out," he said. "Certainly he's behaved damned decently, but then as a Chandler he would. Think she got mixed up with some man out there?"

"Not seriously. No, Phil, it's not Ridge, and it's nobody else I can think of."

He grunted.

"Well, I wish to God she'd take her troubles somewhere else," he said heavily. "Just as we're beginning to see daylight—"

I did some marketing in town after I left him at the station. Town is what we call the bustling small city where the station is situated. The village, a mile or so beyond our gate, is merely a huddle of houses. Thus I buy our food in town, shop for clothes in the city, and get our grass cut—so to speak—by the village. So I bought the groceries in town that morning, and then drove slowly home.

The Birches sits on a low hill, with higher ones behind it, and the drive slopes gradually from the cottage to the house, some five hundred feet or so. The Adrians' neglected entrance was not far beyond ours, and as none of us had money to do any pruning, we were practically drowned in shrubbery. I had managed to clear a bit around the pool, which lay halfway to the house on the Adrian side.

I looked at the cottage as I turned in. It was still closed, and I decided to open and clean it soon. I had put it in the hands of an agent again. And I stopped the car by the pool and got out. It must have rained recently, for the water was slightly muddy. It looked cold, too, and I wondered if after all it would ever justify its cost. Maybe, when the weather got really warm—

I was startled to hear someone behind me, and turned to see a young man with a camera in the drive.

"Any chance of my getting a shot of Mrs. Chandler?" he asked cheerfully. "Famous beauty in bucolic surroundings. Resting after Reno. You know the sort of thing."

"I haven't an idea," I told him. "She's never objected before, so far as I know. You can try, anyhow."

He went toward the house, and I walked up to what I called Father's garden. The banks of the little stream—it was only a

54

foot or two across—were still pretty bare, but here and there small green things were pushing their way up after their winter's sleep. I could still see him there, holding my hand and calling me baby. And I could still remember the wilted lilies-of-the-valley from those very banks which I had carried to his grave, long after his death.

What would he think of us now? I wondered. Or of the bleak old house? Or of Judith and the mystery that apparently surrounded her? He would be patient, I thought. Patient and understanding. He was always understanding. It was he who had established the small cemetery under the birches where we buried our pets, the dead baby robin I had found and wept over, the kitten one of his hunting dogs had killed. In later years Phil and I still carried it on, and the green mounds were always neat.

As I walked to it I thought drearily how much of the family history was there: the early pets, my turtle, the little alligator Phil bought somewhere and kept in his bathtub, even the cats kept in the stable to catch the mice there. Then the long interval after Father's death, with Mother at The Birches refusing, as she said, to turn the place into a zoo, without even a dog allowed. And after she was gone Phil's terriers and my own series of Pekes with their small tragedies, usually traffic ones. After Chang died I had had enough heartbreak. I had no other dog but, as I say, we still kept the place in order, although the little wooden crosses had long lost the inscriptions on them.

I was pulling some weeds from one of the mounds when I heard footsteps again, and saw the photographer coming toward me.

"Look," he said. "Do you live here?"

"I do. Why?"

"Well, I want you to take a good look at me. Would you say, just casually, that I am a thug or a gangster? Or that I've got horns and a tail?"

"Not casually," I told him. "I don't know what investigation

55

might disclose."

He managed a grin.

"Thanks," he said. "It's like this. Mrs. Chandler was in the hall when the maid opened the door. She just took a look at me, yelped, and ran up the stairs." He took off his hat and mopped his face and head with a handkerchief. "Darnedest thing you ever saw, or heard."

So Judith was really in hiding. It was the first time I had actually believed it. It was silly, of course. It had already been in the press, as witness Ridgely's call. But as she never looked at a newspaper, perhaps she did not know it.

My cameraman left after that, and I wandered slowly up the stream toward the old stables. The birch grove was on my way, and I stopped to stroke the smooth silver-white boles. They were big trees now, and I was a big girl. Too adult at least to be as uneasy as I was beginning to feel. And the grove quieted me. It had always done that. There is something soothing about a tree. It is so permanent, and in a way so patient.

I was feeling better when I went back to get the car, although Helga was indignant when I carried the groceries into the kitchen.

"You're late," she said snappishly, "and what's all this about some man attacking Judith? Jennie says she's locked in her room and won't come out."

"Nobody attacked her. A newspaperman wanted a candid-camera shot of her. That's all."

"And when did she ever run from a camera?" Helga asked shrewdly. "The attic's full of snapshots of her down at the pool in the old days."

None of it made any sense to me. How on earth did she expect to hide? She had always been the columnists' delight, and while we were out at Reno Anne had sent me an envelope of clippings. To quote one is to quote them all:

The beautiful Judith Chandler is in Reno, ending an apparently

56

happy marriage of twenty years. She and Ridgely had been drifting apart for a long time, Judith preferring the white lights while he stayed at home and read a good book. What Judith plans for the future is unknown, but if there is a romance involved no one seems to know.

I never showed any of them to her, but I think it was the cameraman's visit that put her virtually in a state of siege. For days after it she did not go beyond the front porch in the daytime, although at night she would put on a dark cape and walk up and down the drive. She always left the front door open, however, and if she could induce either Phil or me to go with her she seemed happier.

I made the best of an uncomfortable period. My old nursery was in the wing over the living-room and, I hoped, remote enough to enable me to work. It was not too comfortable, of course. Shelves which had been adequate for a little girl's books did not begin to hold mine. Also I had forgotten the piano, and it seemed to me at that time that I never went to my typewriter but Judith simultaneously sat down at the Bechstein.

She did not do it deliberately. I want to be fair. It was simply something for her to do when I was not available. For the curious thing was that she had apparently cut herself off entirely from her old life. She telephoned nobody, and such bits of mail as came for her outside of her alimony checks seemed to be largely advertisements or travel circulars.

Even Phil noticed it.

"What's happened to her old gang?" he asked inelegantly. "Don't they call her up or anything?"

"Out of the papers out of mind," I suggested.

"Well, I suppose there's a difference between alimony and ten million dollars," he said philosophically. "See here, Lois, I haven't said this before, but has it occurred to you that Judith has some sort of persecution complex?"

"Who on earth is persecuting her?"

"How do I know? But I've watched her. I begin to think she's a schizophrenic, although God knows what that means. Can't you sic her back on Townsend—or whatever is the psychiatrist fellow's name?"

But Judith was no schizophrenic, although ultimately she did go back to Doctor Townsend. I must admit, however, that even I was puzzled when she had been back a few weeks—it was early in May then—when one day a locksmith came out from town and asked for her. I was in the hall, and I stared at him.

"A locksmith," I said incredulously. "What are you to do? Or did Mrs. Chandler say?"

"I've got it here." He put down his bag and got out a card. "It says new locks and bolts on main bedroom and bathroom. All right with you?"

I had no chance to answer. Judith appeared on the stairs then and took him up with her. She never explained, nor did I ask, but the next time I heard her at the piano I investigated. In the early days, I suppose Mother's bathroom had served several of the family, for in addition to opening into the bedroom it also opened into the hall. Later on, of course, other baths were installed. Even my nursery had one. So did Phil's, and several of the guest rooms. Now, however, there were heavy new locks on both Judith's bedroom and bath, and a chain on each of them.

I stood staring at them for some time, and that night I told Phil. He did not seem surprised.

"I told you," he said. "Now maybe you'll listen to me. If she won't go back to Townsend, get her to go to someone else. Suppose she sets fire to herself with a cigarette? We'd never get her out."

I hesitated. We were getting along rather better, Judith and I. She was never sisterly to me, but at least she no longer seemed to regard me as one of the help. The only open warfare in the house was between Helga and herself. It puzzled me. I even wondered sometimes if Helga knew something about her, but if she did she kept it to herself.

Then, too, something happened a day or so later which took my mind off Judith as having nothing to do with her. Or did it? I was not even sure of that.

The spring was well advanced by that time. One day our itinerant gardener appeared and cut the lawn, and I was reminded of the cottage which I hoped to rent.

It was a pleasant little place, a one-story bungalow-type house, with a shed behind it where in the early days the men at work on the grounds had stored their tools.

I walked down that afternoon armed with the keys and a broom and dustcloth, and wearing an old pair of slacks. As usual I stopped at the pool, which was clear by that time, and I saw a car in the drive next to ours. As the Adrian house had been closed for years, this rather surprised me. I saw nobody around, however, and promptly forgot it.

The cottage stood close to the main road, with a path from our drive leading to it, and it smelled musty and damp when I went in. The door led directly into the sitting-room, and beyond it were two small bedrooms, a bath, and the kitchen. As all were shuttered, the place seemed dark and uninviting.

I stopped as soon as I went into the kitchen. Someone had been smoking there. The ashes apparently from a pipe had been dumped into the sink, I thought rather recently, and the reek of smoke was over everything. I was annoyed rather than startled. After all, the agent had another set of keys, but if he had sent someone to see the place I should have been notified.

Rather indignantly I opened a window and the shutters, and I had just stepped back when I heard a car on the road. As it is not a main artery, there is not much traffic on it. What with most of the summer places closed what usually passes us are delivery trucks to the village a mile or so beyond, an occasional pair of lovers seeking privacy, or a family out for a Sunday jaunt. So I glanced out the window, to see the car I had noticed leaving the Adrian drive and going rapidly toward town.

It was a yellow taxicab from the city. Our local ones are

59

cream colored with blue fenders. But I had no time to see who was in it. As I looked around the cottage, however, it became more and more clear that someone had been inside it, perhaps for some time. There was a glass on the living-room table where the intruder had taken a drink of water, and further investigation showed a defective shutter and a window not entirely closed. Whoever it was had not been sent by any agent.

I did no cleaning that day, although I was angry rather than frightened. And as that was the night Phil chose to suggest a psychiatrist to Judith, I promptly forgot it.

Chapter 7

Judith had been more relaxed since the extra locks had been placed on her doors, but she still looked drawn and tired. She must have realized it, too, for at the dinner table she said she really needed a shampoo and a facial. Phil pushed away the tapioca pudding he loathed and looked interested.

"Do you good," he said. "Go to a beauty parlor and get fixed up. Can't neglect yourself at your age, Jude. How about the old nerves? Sleeping better?"

"My nerves are all right," she said sharply.

"Then you certainly don't show it. They can sure play the devil with a woman's looks." He had touched on a raw spot, and he knew it. "You've been ready to jump out of your skin ever since you came back from Reno. Why don't you see somebody about it when you're in town? A good psychiatrist might help you."

Which was when, as I have already written, she told him not to be a fool; that she had no intention of spilling her guts to any Peeping Tom. She was suspicious, too. We were not supposed to have known of the Townsend visits.

"I suppose you have someone already picked out for me!" she said. "If you have, forget it."

"Not me," Phil told her. "Pick your own, or consult the old girl Lois writes about. Of course, if you want to lose your looks that's your business. When I go to bed I go to sleep. That's how I keep my beauty."

But if Judith repudiated the idea of a psychiatrist, I did not. There was something badly wrong with her, and in common humanity I felt we should know about it. I resolved that night to see Doctor Townsend, and making the excuse of having to see my publisher, I called at his office the next morning.

I had no appointment, so it was some time before I saw him. Anne had been right. He was a handsome man, and he looked relieved when I said I was not a patient, but I had called about one. He glanced at the clock on his desk.

"I can give you ten minutes or so," he said. "Who is this patient, Miss—Miss Maynard?"

"My sister, Judith Chandler, Doctor."

He gave me a quick glance.

"Mrs. Chandler left me some months ago. You know that probably."

"Yes. Of course, she had been in Reno. Now she is living with us in the country. Do you mind saying why she came to see you, Doctor? I'm not merely curious. It may be important."

"What do you mean by important?"

"She's not well. She's—well, she's in a curious state of mind. My brother thinks she has delusions of persecution. I don't agree with him."

"So?" He looked thoughtful. "Well, Miss Maynard, so far as I know she came to me because she was not sleeping. I suppose that's understandable. If she was contemplating divorce—"

"I don't think she was really," I said flatly. "I think something scared her. I don't know what, but she's still scared into panic, and I believe she needs help."

"Yes," he said. "Quite definitely she needed help when I saw her. Only—suppose you tell me what you know."

I did. No halfway measures were any good, and I knew it. Also I felt I could trust him. There was something quieting about him, too, as though no depths of the human mind would

62

shock him. I began with the night Ridgely had found her with her jewels, and went on from there to her sudden determination to go to Reno, and what happened at the station there and on the train. He listened absorbedly, as though he was trying to reconcile it with what he knew of Judith.

"Of course," he said, "if this terror is real, it is a matter for the police. On the other hand, your brother may be right. I have no idea why she wanted a divorce. Quite frankly she never mentioned it to me. But you have to remember that divorce in itself is often a sort of psychic shock."

He went on. He had to deal with such people quite often. They had reached the end of one road, and unless another opened up they felt lost and confused.

"Especially with divorced women," he said. "Up to that time they've been sheltered. At least there was someone around they could depend on, in case of burglars, for instance!" He smiled at me. "Someone to keep house for, order food for, even to dress for. If they marry again, all right. At least they are back in a familiar groove. If they do not, what have they? They haunt the movies and the beauty shops, they gamble frantically, and some of them end up in this office, out of sheer loneliness and despair."

"I suppose she does miss her old life," I agreed, "but she's not only lonely. She's sick with fright. If someone like you could find out what it is—"

He shrugged.

"She was difficult," he said. "I often wondered why she came at all. She only talked about unimportant things. Of course, it's normal for the human mind to protect its privacy, and we don't use medication, Miss Maynard. In this job of mine all we have is words. I get sick of hearing my own voice sometimes," he added. "Your sister did, I know, but she never really came clean. Actually I never knew what she was thinking. And it was deliberate. She didn't want me to know."

"Would you try again, if she came back?"

He hesitated.

"If she came of her own free will," he said. "Otherwise it would be the same story all over again."

"Perhaps if you called her up and talked to her—as a friend," I went on hastily, seeing his face. "You see, it's not only Judith who needs help. We all do. Life isn't really bearable just now. This locked-door business is only a part of it. She hasn't left the house, except at night when no one can see her. She doesn't go far even then, only up and down the drive a short distance. And while she talks of going abroad I don't believe she really will. She seems to have no initiative."

He nodded.

"That's understandable," he said. "Someone else—her husband, I suppose—always arranged things for her before. But you must realize I can't very well ask her to come back. However—wait a minute." He rang a bell and the nurse appeared. "Miss Robey," he said, "did anyone ever claim that gold compact?"

"Not yet, Doctor."

"I see. Thank you." He turned to me as she went out. "I might call her about that," he said. "Ask if it's hers. I rather think it is. She left me pretty abruptly the last day she was here."

He looked at his watch, and I got up.

"Don't expect too much, Miss Maynard," he warned. "We may get her over her agoraphobia. The fear of open spaces, if that's what it is. But if she is in real danger I suggest the police."

I was depressed when I left him, but to my astonishment his call that night worked like a charm. Not immediately. At first, as I have said, she was not only suspicious but resentful. But two days later she came down to breakfast, hitherto unknown, and announced she was going with Phil to New York. She was dressed in a thin spring suit, and with careful make-up she looked more like her old self. But she did not mention Bernard Townsend. She was, she said, going to have a shampoo and a facial. But she wore a heavy nose veil and a scarf she could pull up over her chin.

It looked for all the world like an attempt at disguise. I did not mention it, however. And in spite of my growing sympathy for her it was a relief to me to get her out of the house. I did the first real day's work I had managed since she came. Phil reported later that the excursion had taken on all the attributes of high adventure.

"She wouldn't get out of the car at the station until the last minute," he said. "She sat there, eyeing everybody in sight, until I felt damned conspicuous. Same in the city. Look, Lois, why is she afraid of taxis? She wouldn't take one. Wouldn't go near one, in fact."

"Even in the city?"

"Certainly in the city. She shies off like a frightened horse when she sees one."

I was tempted to tell him about the one in the Adrians' drive, but it seemed rather pointless. After all, there might be a dozen reasons for its being there, or someone breaking into the cottage. Curiosity perhaps, or someone thirsty and needing a drink. As for her phobia about cabs, I had no idea what caused it. Certainly she never explained it, although from that time on she went regularly to New York. It existed. I knew that. When I could not take her, or Phil's train was too early for her, she used Ed Brown's rattling one, which he kept in the village. She was looking better, however. A shampoo and a rinse had brightened her hair, and she was using a new make-up.

I suspected she was seeing Doctor Townsend again, but she never admitted it.

Perhaps I am spending too much time on that interval, before our real mystery began to develop. My only excuse is the change Judith made in our living, with the old peace gone, with Phil growing increasingly irritable and my own work suffering. The servants, too, were hard to manage. Jennie even threatened to leave, after Jude sent her breakfast down because she maintained the coffee was cold. I found her crying in the pantry.

65

"How do I know when she's going to ring?" she said. "And that coffee was boiling when I poured it. Only two of us in a house this size, and her acting like she was a duchess or something."

I spoke to Helga that day. It was raining and her arthritis was bothering her. But I knew and she knew that after forty years with us and at her age she could not get work elsewhere. Also she had known Judith since she was born, and apparently nothing she did surprised her.

"She's what she is, Lois," she said. "She was a spoiled child from the day she could walk, and looking like a little angel all the time. She was sly, too. Your mother never knew half the things she did. But she's not so young now. She isn't cute any more, or anybody's angel, either."

However, she promised to talk to Jennie, and in the end Jennie stayed on.

But I was still uneasy. Judith not only locked herself in her room at night, but sometimes in the daytime. She was losing weight. As Phil said, if she was fooling herself she was making a good job of it. Then one day I had a brainstorm. I decided to talk to Ridgely.

It was early June by that time, and quite warm. The little wild garden Father had planted by the creek was flourishing, and when Phil came home in the evenings he would take a dip in the pool. I used it, too, although the water was still cold. And I was sitting on the bench beside it one day after a swim when I thought of him.

I had gone back mentally to the old days, when Judith would be there surrounded by boys of all ages, and I would climb to the top of the platform, an often toothless straight-haired seven-year-old, and yell to them to watch me dive. Just to prove I could still do it, I climbed the ladder, and suddenly I remembered the one time I had seen Ridgely there.

He had been standing by the pool watching me, and he said, "That's too high for you. What's the idea? Showing off?"

Funny! I had forgotten that entirely until then. To my

childish eyes Ridgely had appeared out of the blue, walking down the church aisle with his bride on his arm!

Judith was in town that day, so I called him on the telephone and asked him to have lunch with me as soon as possible.

His voice sounded apologetic.

"I've been meaning to call you," he said. "If you don't mind the Yale Club, meet me there at one tomorrow. How is everything?"

"I'll tell you when I see you," I said, and hung up.

He was not particularly cordial when I met him. He said he hadn't much time, and to get on with it. He was as dapper as ever, but I didn't think he looked well. I suppose a divorce is as hard on a man as on a woman, although I was sure he had long since ceased to care for Judith. He ordered cocktails and then sat back and surveyed me.

"You look a trifle desperate, Lois," he said. "You're thinner, too."

"That makes a pair of us," I said. "Judith is losing weight, too. Ridgely, when she left you, you thought she was in some sort of trouble. Did you ever find out what it was?"

"I thought she might be being blackmailed. Why?"

"Because I don't think it's that. She's afraid. Physically afraid. Blackmailers don't kill, do they?"

"Not as a rule," he said dryly. "Who's she afraid of, Lois? Not me surely."

"Not you, of course. I think it's somebody she saw in Reno."

"Reno? For God's sake, why Reno?"

But, of course, I had no idea. I told him the story, the locks on her doors, her windows over the porch nailed shut, and her attack on the train from Reno and her odd behavior after it. He seemed puzzled rather than uneasy.

"Sure she's not merely dramatizing all this?" he asked. "She was rather good at that sort of thing."

"She's making a real job of it if she is. I wondered—Is she really afraid her jewels will be stolen, Ridge? That's the excuse she gives."

He shrugged his well-tailored shoulders.

"She was always fairly casual with them. I can't imagine such extreme measures."

"Well, I'll ask you another," I said. "Was she always afraid of taxicabs?"

"Taxicabs?" He looked astonished. "Not that I know of. Of course, she didn't use them often. She had her own cars. What's all this about taxis? It doesn't sound sane."

"Maybe *I'm* crazy," I said. "Only it looks odd to me. Even Phil has noticed it. So have I. I think she's gone back to Doctor Townsend, too. But she walks everywhere here in the city, rain or shine. She won't use a cab. Did she ever have any trouble about one? Run into it or something?"

He shook his head. If she had, he said, he had never heard of it, and he almost certainly would if it had been serious.

"I can think of a lot of things," he said grimly. "If the trouble is real—and you know Judith, she imagines a good bit—it may be blackmail. Only the hell of it is I can't learn anything about it. As a matter of fact, I put a private inquiry agent on it after she left me. I felt responsible in a way. He worked for six weeks. He went back a dozen years and turned up a lot of dirt about some of the people she played around with, but nothing about Judith. Absolutely nothing, Lois. She always—to use his own phrase—landed in her own bed, and no mistake about it."

So that was that. No blackmail. No lovers. Probably even no anxiety about her jewels. Then what?

I felt vaguely dissatisfied when I left him. He was too cold, too detached. After all, she had been his wife for a long time. I wondered that day if her life with him had been any bed of roses. He was a gentleman and a Chandler, but he must have known something, or why had he paid me to go to Reno? And why of all things a private detective?

As it happened, it was that same evening that Jennie added her mite, if you can call it that, to our general bewilderment, which led Phil, sweating and exhausted, to drop into a chair and light a cigarette with shaking hands.

"If I've ever made any cracks about having Judith committed," he said, "just forget it. I'm the one who needs it. A cell and a nice strait jacket sound like heaven to me."

Yet the incident itself was not hair-raising. It was simply bewildering.

We were in the living-room, and I had been telling him about Ridge. He was listening comfortably, his highball nightcap in his hand, and looking up now and then at Mother's portrait over the mantel.

"So what?" he said when I finished. "He doesn't give a good goddam. After all, since Judith never cared for him, why should he bother?"

Then we heard Jennie. She was running screaming toward the house, and the next moment she was in the room, still shrieking. Phil dropped his glass and catching hold of her shook her.

"Stop that noise!" he shouted. "What the devil's the matter? Stop it, I say."

She began to cry then, and little by little we got it out of her.

She has what she calls a boy friend in the village and, as Helga strongly forbids "followers," their usual meeting-place is the bench by the pool. What Jennie said, after she became intelligible, was that she had been waiting there for him when a man came through the shrubbery from the unused Adrian place, and pointed a gun at her from across the pool.

"A gun?" Phil said. "It was dark, wasn't it? How could you see a gun?"

She didn't insist on the gun after that, but she did insist that he spoke to her.

"He spoke to you! What did he say?" Phil asked.

"He said I was to stay there until he could talk to me," she said surprisingly. "And that I knew damned well what it was about."

"And that's all?"

"That was plenty, if you ask me, Mr. Phil. I just yelled and ran."

Luckily Judith had gone to bed, or we might have had trouble. As it was, the two of us, Jennie not voting, made a careful search of the grounds that night. We found nobody, but there were some broken branches among the rhododendrons across the pool, and above it someone had crushed a few of the lilies-of-the-valley Father had planted there.

But it seemed incredible that Judith had heard nothing, and later I was to wonder whether she did. Whether she had not lain shivering in her bed that night, listening to those shrieks of Jennie's and realizing that The Birches was no longer a haven.

I think she did, for the next day she began to make inquiries over the telephone about ship sailings. She was too late, as it turned out, for that was the summer of the great hegira to Europe. But those inquiries of hers eventually led to her tragic undoing.

Chapter 8

Later in the month to my amazement I happened on the O'Brien man again. I had almost forgotten him, but there he was, big and smiling and holding out his hand. I had been to the butcher's in town that morning, and I was clutching a leg of lamb when he confronted me.

"Well, look who's here!" he said. "I thought you lived somewhere in this neck of the woods, Miss Maynard, but I certainly never expected to see you."

He had been smoking a pipe. He emptied it and dropped it in his pocket, and we shook hands like old friends. After which he insisted on taking me into a drugstore and buying me a Coke. Over his glass he inspected me with some care.

"You're thinner," he said. "Anything wrong? Or is your lady detective working you too hard?"

His eyes were keen and very blue. Also he was not wearing his spectacles, although he got them out later and put them on. But I realized he had the trained eyes of a policeman. What he looked at he really saw. They could be cold, too. Oh, God, how cold they could be!

"I'm all right," I said. "I'm not working well, but I have those spells. All writers do, I think, especially if their heroines have only looks, no character."

He ignored that. "And your sister? How is she?"

"She's staying with my brother and myself at The Birches, five miles out of town."

"Five miles!" he said. "That's a short ride but the devil of a long walk. I like your neck of the woods," he went on. "I've been looking it over. But I'm not sure I'm cut out to be a farmer. I have no natural affection for cows or even pigs. Chickens are about my limit."

I laughed and his eyes twinkled.

"What I really need is a small place somewhere," he said. "I'd like to sow some seeds and see what comes up, if anything. Maybe keep a few chickens, and get an egg or so at the source, so to speak. What about that little place of yours? Rented it yet?"

It was too casual, too easy, somehow. And there was that pipe of his in his pocket.

"No," I said. "Didn't you like what you saw of it the other day?"

"What's that supposed to mean?"

"You were out there, weren't you? In a taxi? I saw the cab, and I knew someone had been inside the house."

He actually looked startled.

"I've never been near the place," he said. "What's this all about? Been having trouble?"

I told him about Jennie's intruder, and he listened carefully.

"No idea who he was?"

"None whatever."

He was thoughtful, but I still was not trusting him entirely in spite of his disarming manner, and just then he put his hand in his pocket and rather sheepishly threw a bunch of keys onto the drugstore counter.

"I'll be honest," he said. "I've never even seen your place, Miss Maynard, but I've been in to see your agent just now, and he gave me those keys. Want them back? Or shall we go out and look it over?"

I hesitated.

"What about your job?" I said. "Does a lieutenant or

72

whatever you were in Homicide simply walk out and raise chickens?"

He looked impatient.

"I've told you all that," he said. "I had some trouble in the Pacific. Not mental. I didn't have to take sitz baths and weave rugs! But enough so I've got what you might call a protracted leave of absence. Got shot in a lung and am supposed to have a good rest and breathe some good country air. Your agent says that's what you have."

Of course, his being a wounded veteran made a difference, I told myself, but I thought, too, that it might be a good idea to have a policeman on the place. What with Jennie's experience and someone breaking into the cottage itself, some of my former confidence in the peace and security of The Birches was rapidly vanishing.

"We have the air," I conceded. "I'm not so sure you'll have a rest." Which, as he told me later, was not only prophetic, but an understatement of considerable magnitude.

The clerk behind the counter had disappeared, so sitting there I told him my story: Judith's terror and the extra locks, Jennie's man with or without a gun, even the yellow taxi in the Adrian drive, and the intruder in the cottage. When I finished he was looking grim.

"I don't know what it all adds up to," I said. "It's a sort of Chinese puzzle, isn't it?"

"What it all adds up to," he said soberly, "is that I'm taking the cottage, whether you want me or not. No reflection on brother Phil, but if there's dirty work at the crossroads I don't think it's precisely a lawyer's job. But," he added, "I'd better tie a string to this. I'm not going there as a cop. For one thing, I don't believe your sister would care to have an ex-policeman at her heels. She hasn't been very co-operative about her trouble, has she?"

"She seems deadly afraid we'll learn what it is."

"Good enough. I'm a veteran, with a hole in my chest and maybe a bit of business to take me into town now and then.

73

How about it? And how about another Coke?"

"Thanks, but it so happens I loathe the stuff."

He reached out solemnly and shook my hand.

"So do I," he said, and we both laughed.

It is hard to remember how cheerful I was that day! Because I liked him, and I thought he liked me. Because there was something dependable about his big strong body and steady eyes. And perhaps because, shut away in the country as I had been, I had been lonely for a long time, and here at last was a good companion and what I suspected would prove a loyal friend.

We made a small procession that day on our way to The Birches, I ahead in our old sedan while he followed in an equally shabby coupé. The place looked beautiful in the sunlight, and he got out and stood looking about him with a pleased smile on his face.

"Wonderful," he said. "And don't tell me that's a swimming pool over there! I can't believe it."

I told him it was and that he could use it whenever he wanted, although the water was still cold. Upon which I had some difficulty getting him into the cottage at all. Once inside, however, with the shutters opened and the windows raised, he stood in the sitting-room with his hands in his pockets, gazing about him complacently, although his size dwarfed the small room.

"It's swell," he said. "And that shed back there would be fine for chickens. I'm right handy with tools. And if you don't mind chicken wire, I could make a place for them to run. How about it?"

"Do anything you like," I told him recklessly. "I'll go so far as to buy your eggs, too."

"Well, maybe now and then I'll make a present to your cook. There will be no money passing between the lady of The Birches and Terry O'Brien. I can tell you that."

It was a little time before he settled down. Then I found him in the kitchen, inspecting the ashes in the sink.

"Fellow was a pipe smoker like myself," he said thoughtfully. "Where's the glass he drank out of?"

It was still on the sitting-room table, and I was about to pick it up when he yelled at me.

"Haven't you ever heard of fingerprints?" he demanded. "Find me some paper, can you? If there's real trouble afoot, this is as good a start as any."

I found him some newspaper in the wood box by the fireplace, and he wrapped the glass carefully and put it in his car. He was thoughtful when he came back.

"Any chance your sister will remember me?" he asked. "That might be awkward."

I didn't think she would, and told him so. After all, she had not seen him when he picked her up, and she had really fainted after that. But he thought it best to try before he settled in so I took him up to the house for lunch.

He need not have worried. Jennie was having her day off, and a disgruntled Helga limped around the table, eyeing him as she did so. But when Judith wandered in, beautiful in a blue-silk house gown, she merely gave him a long stare as I introduced him.

"Mr. O'Brien has taken the cottage for the summer, Judith," I explained. "This is my sister, Mrs. Chandler."

She nodded and sat down.

"I always thought it was a dreary little place," she said, without interest. "Maybe Lois has fixed it up." Then she gave him a double take and scared me almost out of my wits. "Haven't I seen you before, some place?"

He smiled. "It's possible, Mrs. Chandler. But if I had seen you anywhere, be sure I would never forget it."

That is all I remember of the lunch, Helga's smoldering eyes on him and Judith's failure to show any interest whatever, especially in the chickens he insisted on discussing. I know she left the table as soon as the meal was over, and he looked thoughtfully after her.

"She gave me a bad minute or two," he said. "She's seen me,

all right. Hit-and-run case, where the woman died. We never proved anything on her, and she denied it, of course. It was years ago."

"Would that be the trouble now?" I asked. "Some relative, or something like that?"

But he shook his head.

"The old girl had no family. The city had to bury her. I have an idea Mr. Chandler suspected his wife at the time, but I don't know."

I remember showing him the lower floor of the house after that, and finding him totally unimpressed, except with Mother's portrait. He stood in front of it for some time.

"Looks like a woman who knew her own mind," was his comment. Then suddenly: "What happened to the pearls?"

"I suppose they were sold long ago, like everything else."

"Pity," he said. "They'd look nice on you." He turned and looked at me. "I'm beginning to think you've had the hell of a life, and that it's not getting any better fast. You might just remember that I'll be around in case of trouble. Or in any case," he added.

We walked down to the cottage, and at the pool he stopped and pulled out a small black book. As I had always had the police in my fiction carry just such books, I was entranced to see him writing in it.

"You've got some sort of clue already, haven't you?" I asked breathlessly.

"Clue?" he said. "Oh, the book. No, I'll need some bathing-trunks. That's all."

After which anticlimax I simply sat down on the running board of his car and laughed until I cried.

He arrived to stay a week later. Jennie and I worked hard over the cottage, and I must say it looked wonderful. The living-room-dining-room had shelves for books, and I carried down some of my father's and a few recent novels. There were bright rag rugs on the floors, a big center table in the living-room, and one easy chair with a lamp beside it which I thought

76

he would like. At least it was large enough for him!

I had not seen him since the day he took the place, although a huge roll of chicken wire had come, and some lumber I supposed was to turn the shed into an adequate chicken house. I had finished my work and was locking the door when he arrived, and my first impulse was to laugh. His car was loaded to the roof with what I gathered were his lares and penates, as well as with cases of provisions; and on top of everything else was a crate with six bedraggled hens in it.

He grinned as he got out.

"Got to get the girls out of there," he said. "They've raised hell all the way."

Then and thereafter those hens were "the girls" to him, and in time I found myself calling them that. He took the crate out and set it tenderly on the ground.

"Now behave yourselves," he admonished them. "Tomorrow you can run all you like. Only remember you have a job to do."

He wanted no help unloading the rest of the car, but he did allow me to arrange his provisions in the kitchen. He seemed to be delighted with the place. Also it was evident he did not mean to starve.

"Someday," he said, "when the girls get going, you must have breakfast with me. I learned to make griddle cakes at Childs' when I was working myself into and out of college, and I like fried ham and cream gravy. I hope you do."

I did, and said so. But when the car was about empty and he was picking up a few last things, I saw him take a gun out of the glove compartment and drop it in his pocket. He didn't think I saw him, but it gave me an uneasy feeling. After all, what did I know of the man? I had not asked him for any references. I was not even certain that he had been hunting a country place. So far as I knew he might have been the man Jennie saw at the pool, and for a panicky moment I wondered if he was a part of Judith's terror.

On the other hand, she had not really recognized him. As a

77

matter of fact, she had practically ignored him. But Helga had been suspicious, and I wondered why.

The gun was out of sight when I went back into the house, and O'Brien himself was busily laying out a half-dozen bottles. When he saw me he held one up.

"I was thinking of a drink to celebrate," he said. "Does the lady of the manor drink with her tenants? This is all new to me, Miss Maynard. How about it?"

I suppose it was his smile again. Somehow I could not associate it with anything evil. So I sat down in the midst of all the confusion and let him put a drink in my hand. Possibly it was the highball, or possibly it was because I felt I had misjudged him, for before long I was telling him about the early days at The Birches, and about Father. He liked the idea of the wild-flower garden.

"You'll have to show it to me someday," he said. "He must have been quite a man."

Perhaps it was the glass in my hand. Perhaps I could not talk any more about Father. But I remembered then the glass he had taken to the city with him, and asked about it. At first he affected not to know what I referred to, then he remembered.

"Oh, that!" he said. "Prints all right, but none on record."

I did not think he lied easily, but I was sure he was lying then. He changed the subject too quickly.

"I've been learning a little about your sister," he said. "I hope you don't mind, but with things the way they are—Of course, you know she's been pretty well-known around the night spots for years. Nothing against her," he added rather quickly, "but she was meat and drink to the society editors. Isn't it possible she's tied up with someone in her old crowd?"

"Her husband says not."

"Oh! So you've talked to Chandler about it?"

"He gave me a thousand dollars to go to Reno with her. That's partly how I paid for the pool. That, and a check for a story I sold."

He looked surprised. Then he grunted.

"Thank God for Ridgely Chandler," he said. "And in case you're interested, I bought the trunks. To a guy who learned to swim in the East River that pool is pure temptation."

I was rather thoughtful as I went back to the house. I had installed a policeman at The Birches and told no one I was doing so. Now I was a little frightened. Perhaps the sight of the gun had done it. Certainly I felt guilty, and when I saw Judith's door open, I went in. She might feel safer if she knew about him, or again—

She was sitting at my toilet table, the one I had substituted for Mother's big walnut bureau. It was littered now with elaborate bottles of perfumes, with her gold-backed brushes and mirrors, and the innumerable jars of creams and cosmetics she used. At the moment she was painting her fingernails, and she looked up at me unsmilingly.

"So your chicken man has come!" she said. "I tell you here and now, if he has a rooster to wake me in the mornings, I'll kill the creature."

"No roosters," I said. "Half a dozen hens is all."

"Who on earth is he, Lois?" she asked. "I hope he has references."

"The agent in town attended to that. He's a veteran. He was wounded in the South Pacific. That's good enough for me."

"The war's been over out there for five years. He's had plenty of time to get well."

Luckily for me she dropped the subject. She sat waving her hands in the air to dry her nails, and wondered if it was true that Paris was wearing shorter skirts. If Jennie could sew, she could turn up some hems for her. It was useless to tell her that Jennie had plenty to do without that, or even that her own chances of getting to Paris that summer were negligible.

One thing, however, was clear. She was no longer the terrorized woman she had been not long before, and that day, working on her face after her nails had dried, she told me she was seeing Doctor Townsend again.

"I'm glad, Judith," I said. "Do you think he's helping you?"

She gave me an odd little half-smile.

"I don't need his kind of help," she said. "But he's a darned good-looking man."

"So what? He's married, isn't he?"

She laughed. "What's that got to do with it? Don't be naïve, Lois. Anyhow there is such a thing as divorce."

"You ought to know!" I said, and left her.

Phil stopped in to see our new tenant that evening on his way home. He had used Ed Brown's taxi, as he did occasionally, and when he came to the house he was grinning broadly.

"Nice fellow, your new tenant," he said. "But have you seen his girls?"

"Only in the crate. Why?"

"He's got six different breeds of chickens, including a White Leghorn that won't stay out of the house. He calls her Henrietta, for God's sake! I've asked him up for a cocktail. Get the stuff out, will you, while I wash?"

I knew I should have told him who O'Brien really was. After all, Phil was the understanding sort. But the dove of a new peace had apparently settled down on us just then, and who was to know that it was really a vulture?

Chapter 9

The alfresco cocktail party was a success, and after it for a few days everything was quiet. As it turned out, O'Brien played bridge, and once or twice in that time he made a fourth and easily won from all of us.

Otherwise he seemed to have settled down comfortably, although the occasional sound of a hammer showed that he was being active. I imagine he used the pool, too, although I never met him there. He had no visitors, except that one day looking up from my typewriter, I saw a woman knocking at his door. She wore a black hat with what looked like a wreath of bright flowers on it. After a time she gave up, and I thought she was dispirited when she left. She stood for a time on the road, evidently hoping to thumb a ride, and someone must eventually have picked her up, for she disappeared.

It was not until after O'Brien had been installed for some time that he asked us all down to supper at the cottage, and gave us a thick steak done to a turn, French fried potatoes, and peas, and peaches with what he called a Russian sauce of whipped cream, eggs, and brandy.

The cottage was immaculate. Even the bed where we left our wraps had the corners squared, I suppose military fashion. But to our amusement the little white hen refused to go to roost with the other chickens. She trailed him around the kitchen with alert bright eyes, and he scolded her for getting under his feet.

"You're a nuisance, Henrietta," he would say. "Get out of here. Go where you belong."

In the end he had to pick her up squawking and take her out to the roost with the others. He came back looking apologetic.

"Must have been some kid's pet," he said. "Darned if I know what to do with her."

But I had an idea that he had a good many lonely hours there in the cottage, and that Henrietta at least allowed him to hear his own voice. By tacit agreement I had made no effort to see him, and for that brief period there seemed no reason to do so. There were no more intruders. Judith still locked herself away at night, but she was much less restless, and down at the cottage I gathered that O'Brien had finished his chicken house and now had a dozen girls and boasted of the eggs they produced. He must have been catching up with his reading, too, for at night from my old nursery in the wing of the house I could see his light on until all hours.

My book, too, was moving, slowly but surely, and I had settled down to work and what proved to be a factitious peace, broken only by an occasional swim in the pool. Then one day toward the end of the month Anne called up. She was in a state bordering on tears.

"I'm in a jam," she said. "Martha has been visiting in Boston since school ended, and now she has appendicitis. I'm going there tonight to be near her in the hospital. They're operating in the morning. And Bill's home from college and at a loose end. Can you possibly take care of him for a few days? I have no maid, as usual, and while Martin can go to the club, I can't leave Bill here alone."

Of course, I was glad to do it. I liked Bill, who had steadfastly refused to believe I was his aunt and had called me Lois since he could talk. He was a tall rangy boy of nineteen, too thin for his height and still given to pimples, but with a cheerful grin and an enormous appetite.

I went back to the kitchen and told Helga, who smiled and looked cheerful for the first time since Judith's arrival.

"We'd better lay in a good stock of food," she said. "That boy's hollow all the way down. And maybe I'll make some gingerbread. Keep him from raiding the ice-box at night."

He arrived late that evening during a heavy summer storm, and in a thing on wheels he called the Ark, because he said it pitched within and without. I heard it rattling up the drive, and the next moment he was in the hall.

"Hello!" he shouted. "Bill's here! Come arunning, one and all."

I ran down to meet him, and he grabbed me and lifted me up in the air.

"Getting skinny, aren't you, kid?" he said. "Or maybe I just don't know my own strength. Anything around to eat? I missed my supper."

I took him to the kitchen and watched with sheer amazement while he finished a cold roast of lamb, cold potatoes, some cold string beans, and a whole square of gingerbread. Then, replete for the time, he leaned back and surveyed me.

"Who's the gent at the gatehouse?" he inquired.

"That's our tenant. He's taken the place for the summer, and he's nice, Bill. We all like him very much. Do be nice to him."

"Like that, is it?" he said. "Maybe you can contemplate him with equanimity. I can't. Gray hair and spectacles! I'll bet he's forty if he's a day! You ought to do better, even at your age."

As I was only nine years older than Bill, I treated this with the scorn it deserved, but I was curious to know when he had seen O'Brien. He snorted.

"Seen him!" he said. "I damned near ran over him. As I turned into the drive he shot out his door as if the fiends of hell were after him. He had a flashlight, and he turned it on me before he'd budge out of the way. Then he said, 'Sorry, old man,' and beat it back to his house. I think he had a gun, too. It looks crazy to me."

But Bill's statement kept me awake for some time that night after I settled him in the guest room, with another shot of gingerbread in case he got hungry in the night. It looked as though O'Brien was indeed watching us, or watching over us. And I wondered if he still felt he had to protect us.

I was positive he knew something about Judith which he had not told me. He had certainly lied about the fingerprints on the glass, and the night we dined with him I had seen him watching her, as though she puzzled him. He had seen me observing him, and when she and Phil had started home, he tried to explain it as he picked up my light summer coat.

"Amazingly beautiful woman, your sister," he said.

I was annoyed, for no particular reason.

"Yes," I said. "She got all the looks in the family."

He looked astonished.

"I don't agree with you, Miss Maynard," he said. "Not for a moment."

Which, I was to learn, was as near to a sentimental speech as he usually came.

There in bed that night I lit a cigarette and lay thinking. What sort of danger threatened Judith, if any? And how did he come into the picture? That he had fully meant to take the cottage, I already knew, and I had a brief thought he might be the man Ridgely Chandler had employed to check on her. I abandoned that, however. Ridge had said that was over, and he thought she was only dramatizing herself anyhow by her locks and bolts.

It was unseasonably hot that night. There was a breeze of sorts, but it was from the south and only made things worse. At one time I thought I heard someone on the stairs, but the old house always creaks and groans in a wind. And still later I heard Ed Brown's ancient village taxi go by the road and a minute or two later pass again on the way to town.

I wondered drowsily if the Adrians had at last decided to open their place to escape the heat of the city. Not, of course, that they would have escaped much, but there is a pleasant theory that the country is always cooler than New York. When finally I went to sleep, it must have been three o'clock. I must have practically passed out, for I felt as though someone had been shaking me for some time before I wakened.

To my astonishment it was Bill. He was in bathing-trunks and dripping wet, and his young face looked pale.

"For God's sake wake up, Lois," he said as I sat up. "Something horrible's happened. There's a woman's body in the pool."

"A body!" I said, shocked. "Whose body, Bill? You don't mean— It couldn't be Judith, could it?"

"It's not Judith. I never saw her before. And Judith's locked away. I tried her door first. It was nearer. Get up, will you? I have to wake Phil."

I got into a pair of slacks and a sweater as being the quickest things I could find, and ran down the stairs. Bill had left the front door open, and it must have been half past six by that time, for the birds were singing and the sun well up. But as nothing rouses either Helga or Jennie until seven, there was no sign of life from the service wing.

It took me a couple of minutes' hard running to get to the pool, and Bill caught up with me as I reached it. I could only stand and stare, for there *was* a woman there, or a woman's body, anyhow. Bill grabbed me by the arm.

"Don't you go and faint on me," he said hollowly. "I dived in on top of her. She was at the deep end. I dragged her where she is before I knew she was gone."

Where she was was on the near side at the shallow end of the pool, where the little brook flows in. There were three cement steps there, and the woman was on them. She was still half in the water, with her back toward us. She had no hat, and her black dress and blond hair eddied in the stream in a horrible parody of life and movement.

I never heard O'Brien until he was there. He was in his bare feet, and he had only a bathrobe over his pajamas. But he looked shocked, if that is the word. Incredulous is better.

"Good God!" he said. "Who is it?" He did not wait for an answer. He was down beside her in a few seconds. Then he was raising her head, and I can only say there was pure relief in his face.

He straightened and looked across at us.

"Anybody know who she is?" he called.

"I haven't seen her face yet," I said feebly.

"Don't try just now," he said. "Go back to the house and get some coffee. She can wait. She's not in a hurry."

"But you can't leave her like that," I protested. "Half of her is in the water! It's beastly."

He came back then, moving more deliberately.

"Look, my dear," he said. "She can't be moved yet. Either she fell in, and that's police business, or she was thrown in, and that's the same thing." He looked at Bill. "Suppose you use my phone. It's nearest. And call the chief of police in town. This is county stuff, but the sheriff's on a vacation. The chief's name is Fowler. He's in the local book. Just tell him what happened. Don't trim it any. I'll stay here."

Bill looked injured, but he did as he was told, and O'Brien turned to me.

"I suppose you'd better have a look at her," he said dubiously. "You may recognize her. After that go up to the house. If I know Fowler, he'll be here soon, with some of his outfit. And the state police will be sure to horn in. There will be a photographer, too. You don't need your picture in this."

I could only nod, and I held my breath while he turned the dead face for me to see. But I did not know her. The face was singularly peaceful, as though indeed she had gone to sleep where she was. She was not very old, I thought. Perhaps in her forties, rather small and slight, and with her hair bleached a golden yellow.

"Where's her hat?" I said, vaguely feeling she was the sort to wear one.

"It may be in the pool. Her bag, too. Look here, Miss Maynard, are you sure you don't know her? She must have had

86

some reason to be here."

"Maybe she meant to kill herself, and the pool was handy. You thought it was someone else, didn't you?"

"I thought it was your sister," he said soberly.

He didn't explain, and Judith chose that minute to arrive, with Phil holding her arm to steady her. It was typical that routed from her bed, with her hair flying, without make-up, and clad only in a dressing-gown, Judith should look as lovely as ever. Somehow it irritated me, with that dead woman lying there. Partly, of course, it was relief, for I, too, had thought at first it was she in the pool.

"Who is it?" Phil said. "I always claimed that pool was a deathtrap at night."

Unluckily he had released Judith's arm, and she took only one look at the body and crumpled up. It was a real faint. Her nose looked white and pinched, and her lips had no color whatever. All my resentment faded. She looked pitiful and forlorn lying there, and I sat down on the ground and put her head in my lap. Phil was all for throwing water on her, but I stopped him.

"Just let her alone," I said. "She used to do this, years ago, when she was excited. She'll come out of it all right."

She did, of course. She moaned a little and opened her eyes. Then she tried to sit up.

"Get me up to the house," she said. "I don't want to see that—that thing. It's dreadful."

Well, it wasn't nice, of course, so when she could walk, young Bill and I took her home. She still looked pretty awful, but we poured coffee laced with brandy into her until she could climb the stairs. We got her into her room and I tried to put her to bed. But she wouldn't have it. She waited until we went out and then locked the door behind us. Young Bill stared at me.

"What goes?" he said. "What the hell does that mean?"

"I don't know. She always does it," I told him. "She's afraid of something or somebody. I don't know who."

"Not old Ridge, by any chance?"

"I think she'd like us to think so. I don't believe it."

Breakfast was late that morning. Both Helga and Jennie were on the fringes of the crowd that had gathered down by the pool. O'Brien had been right. The state troopers were there as well as the chief of police and a half-dozen men, uniformed police and detectives. And as I stood on the porch I saw them giving way to Doctor Christy, the medical examiner for the county.

The public was being kept out, but the main road was lined with the cars of passers-by who had stopped to see what the excitement was about, and not until an ambulance had carried the body away did the crowd disperse and our household staff return.

They were in a state of wild excitement, having been asked if they could identify the body.

"We told them no," Helga said, "but it might be someone from the summer places around. One or two are opened this year. Maybe she just walked across and never seen the pool. Looks like it. No hat. No bag."

Chief Fowler came up while Bill and I were eating a belated breakfast. Phil had already gone to his train, so I gave the chief ham and eggs and coffee. He seemed grateful, but rather uneasy.

"Hate to ask you, Miss Maynard," he said, "but I've got to drain that pool of yours. Way it rained a couple of days ago we can't see into it, and there may be something of hers there."

"Of course. Go ahead," I told him. "Only what could be there?"

"Nothing probably, if she came from around here. Point is, nobody seems to know her. So if she came from a distance it stands to reason she'd have a bag. A hat, too, at her age. She must be forty or so. But we've looked around the place. No signs of them."

"We would have to get a man from town to open the gate at the lower end," I said. "It's old and pretty rusty. As the pool is fed all the time, we don't have to clean it. We only empty it for the winter."

He nodded and looked at Bill, young and fresh faced in a bathrobe over his trunks.

"Tell me again about it, son," he said. "You didn't see her before you went in?"

"Well, I did and I didn't," Bill said. "Not from the side of the pool, no. But when I climbed the rickety old diving-platform I saw something dark. I didn't think it was—well, what it was. It might have been mud from the creek. When I got down, though, I knew."

"And then?"

"I was kind of scared." Bill grinned. "I came up for air and to see if there was anybody around to help. There wasn't, so I went down again and got hold of her. I dropped her once. I guess I was pretty nervous. But I got her to the steps and left her there."

Fowler nodded and prepared to go.

"Thanks for the breakfast," he said. "I needed it. And I'm sorry about your sister. Kind of a shock, of course. But soon as she's better I want her to look at the body. We need an identification, and she may have seen her somewhere. You're sure you haven't?"

I said I was sure, but there was something in my mind which kept escaping it. Then, just as he was leaving, I remembered.

"There's one thing," I said. "I'm pretty sure I heard Ed Brown's taxi on the main road last night. It seemed to go as far as the Adrian drive next to ours, then turn around and go back."

"Ed's taxi! What time was it?"

"I haven't an idea. It was hot and I was restless. It sounded like Ed's the way it rattled. That's all I know."

"Sure the Adrian family hasn't decided to move out from town?"

"The maids here say they haven't. You can't see the house from here. It's not near, and there's all that shrubbery. But the gardener's been working there now and then, as he does for us. He may know the woman, if she works for them."

"Doesn't seem as though she worked very hard for anyone," he said. "Hands don't look like it. Of course, the way folks work today that don't mean much." •

I watched him down the drive in his car. There was a state trooper by the pool, and after he stopped and spoke to him, the trooper took off through the woods to where the distant sound of a mower showed the gardener at work. The chief himself turned toward town, and without apparent purpose Bill sauntered down the drive.

I knew what he meant to do, but he was just too late. The moment the trooper disappeared, O'Brien in a pair of bathing-trunks made for the pool and dove in. I was curious. It was only too obvious that he had been waiting for the chance, and for some reason I could not understand. I only knew that when at last he reappeared on the surface he was clutching something, and that he looked completely disgusted when he saw Bill there, and me not far behind him.

He forced a grin, however, as he crawled out.

"Got her bag," he said. "Now if you pair of ghouls can keep your mouths shut maybe we'll learn something."

Bill, whose jaw had dropped, managed to close it.

"You're being damned nosy about all this, aren't you?" he said. "The police will want that."

"The police will have it. Don't worry, son. You'll give it to the chief and tell him you found it. I think her hat's in there, too. Better try and find it."

There was a moment when I thought Bill would revolt, but there was something authoritative about O'Brien's voice and his big muscular body. He turned to the pool.

"Keep an eye on that guy, Lois," he said, and dived in.

O'Brien opened the bag and shook its contents out on the grass. It was made of some sort of fabric, and the contents were soaked. There was nothing exciting that I could see: the usual compact and lipstick, a small money purse with five or six dollars in it, a handkerchief, and a scrap of yellow paper. Then he examined the bag itself. There was a zipper pocket which he opened, only to pull out a water-soaked newspaper clipping, yellow either from the pool or with age, and now a sodden mass. Even I could see that it was barely decipherable, and I was surprised when he tucked it into the belt of his trunks.

"That trooper's coming," he said. "Put the stuff back in the bag, will you? I'll have to dry this scrap."

I suppose I was distracted at the moment, for Bill appeared with the soaked remains of what had been a woman's hat. It was of black straw, with a wreath of bright but now woebegone flowers around the crown, and it looked forlorn and pitiable. But it looked more than that. It looked vaguely familiar.

Bill scrambled out with it, to hear the trooper bellowing at him.

"What are you doing there?" he yelled. "You know goddam well you were told to keep away from here."

"Oh, drop dead!" Bill said. "I got her hat, didn't I? That's more than you did, fancy britches! And this is my family's pool. Try to keep me out of it!"

The trooper leaped the narrow stream at the head of the pool and made for Bill with at least mayhem in his face. Then he saw me, and I gave him as sweet a smile as I could muster at the moment.

"Bill has been fine, Lieutenant," I said. "He got her bag, too. The chief said he wanted them found."

Either the smile or the rank I gave him mollified him, or the mention of the chief did. At least he laid no hands on Bill.

"Sergeant," he said. "I suppose you've looked through that bag," he added disagreeably.

"Certainly not," I said virtuously, and prepared to empty it on the ground again. He yelped in anguish.

"Don't *do* that," he said. "There may be fingerprints, all sorts of things." He looked completely discouraged. "See here," he said. "Thanks for finding the stuff. Now I'd be obliged if you'd both just go back to the house and let well enough alone. Go back and take a nice rest. I'll manage by myself for a while, and I'll do all right. Don't worry."

We did not go at once, however. I stood staring at the hat, and fighting the feeling I had seen it before. After all, there were probably one million black hats with wreaths in circulation in and around New York. And O'Brien had not reappeared. I could not ask him about it.

We were still there when a loud thumping and rattling announced the arrival of Ed Brown's taxi, and it was followed by the chief's car. Both of them passed our gate and went on a short distance. Then we heard them coming back, and they turned in at our drive.

The chief got out, but Ed remained in his car. He has always claimed arthritis in his legs, which prevents him from carrying suitcases or even golf clubs, or helping women under any circumstances. Just now he looked surly.

"How do I know she came here?" he said. "I let her out at the other drive. She paid me for it. That's all I know. As for getting a man out of his bed at this hour, I ain't standing for it, police or no police."

The chief eyed him coldly.

"Didn't she say anything? Weren't you to come back and pick her up again?"

"No. Looks like she meant to stay. She said to take her to the first drive beyond the Maynards'. That's what I did."

"Kind of late for you to be out, wasn't it?"

"I seen some folks off on a train to the city. They'd been out to dinner. So she comes up at the station and says am I a taxi, and I says yes."

"Did she get off the train going toward town?"

"I wouldn't know. She just came up like I said."

"Did she have a suitcase, or anything of the sort? Like she was staying somewhere?"

"I didn't see any. I got this trouble in my legs. Folks handle their own bags."

The first car with a couple of reporters and cameraman arrived just then, and Bill and I beat it. O'Brien had still not shown himself, and I had an idea he wouldn't, with the press around. But Bill was grinning to himself.

"Maynard Mansion Scene of Mystery Death," he said. "Picture of swimming pool, center of many gaieties, where body was found. *Social Register* family bewildered. Say, O'Brien ain't so old, is he?"

"I haven't an idea," I said coldly.

He looked at me.

"He was watching for somebody last night when he shot out at my car. Think it was that woman?"

"If you think he murdered her, I'd think again, Bill."

"So you like him, eh? All I can say is that one good push from those arms of his and she's gone. And what's the idea, his getting the bag? He was damned anxious about it, if you ask me."

Chapter 10

Anne was on the phone from Boston when we got back to the house. She said the operation was over and Martha seemed all right. She'd like to stay a few days, however, if we could keep Bill.

"Try and get me away!" Bill said. "Home's nothing like this. Let me talk to her, Lois."

The last I heard as I went upstairs to dress he was telling Anne we were finding bodies all over the place, that he was under suspicion of murder, and that he'd call her from the jail, if and when. I let it ride. If Anne didn't know her own son by that time she never would.

To my shocked surprise, as I reached the upper hall, I saw a suitcase standing outside Judith's door, and heard her moving rapidly around inside the room. As I had left her in a virtual state of collapse, I was bewildered. I lifted the bag, and it was evidently packed. It looked as though she was leaving, and leaving in a hurry.

As usual her door was locked, and when I knocked all sounds ceased. But when she spoke it was from close by.

"Who is it?" she asked.

"It's Lois. What's all this nonsense out here?"

"Are you alone? Is anyone near you?"

"I'm alone," I said with such patience as I could summon.

"Don't be a fool. Open the door and let me in."

Her room was a mess, clothes all over it, on the bed and the chairs. Even the floor. And Judith herself wasn't much better, her hair in all directions and her face without makeup. She was almost as white as she had been at the pool, and her eyes looked almost demented.

"I'm getting out," she said. "I thought I'd be safe here, but I'm not."

"Safe from what, for heaven's sake?"

"Never mind that, I'm leaving. That's all."

"Look, Judith," I said. "Let's get at this thing sensibly. Did you know that woman who came here last night?"

"No, of course not. How should I?"

There was a ring of truth in that. Judith could lie, and do it well, when she wanted to, but I was sure she was telling the truth now.

"You fainted when you saw her," I said. "If you didn't know her why pass out like that? It looks darned funny to me."

She sat down then, as though the strength of desperation had suddenly abandoned her.

"Why wouldn't I faint?" she said. "She was horrible, dreadful. I don't write crime books. I'm not used to dead bodies, or murdered ones."

I eyed her.

"So you think she was murdered? You don't know who she is. You never saw her before, and even the police don't say it was murder. You'd better get a better story than that, Judith, before they begin to question you."

She did not answer at once. She tried to light a cigarette with shaking hands, and when she finally succeeded she took a long puff before she spoke.

"You saw her," she said. "Her hair is like mine, and she's almost my build. I think she was killed because she was mistaken for me."

"Don't be ridiculous! Who on earth wants to kill you? If you think it's Ridgely you're crazy."

"It's not Ridge. I can't talk about it. Let me alone, can't you? I'm not staying here, that's all."

"Now listen, Judith," I said impatiently. "If you're in real trouble you need police protection. I'll get the chief up here and you can tell him all about it. Or tell me, if you'd rather. Maybe you're wrong. Maybe you're just scaring yourself. In any case let's find out."

She gave me a quite dreadful look.

"If you bring the police into this I'll kill myself," she said. "I mean it. I'll do just that."

I eyed her. Erratic as she was she did mean it, and I knew it.

"But there has to be a reason for all this," I argued. "What have you done? Have you killed someone? What else am I to think except that you've committed some sort of crime and now it's catching up with you? That's what it looks like. And don't blame me for thinking so, Judith. It's all you allow me to think. And I'm calling Phil on the phone. He'd better come out and talk some sense into you."

"Phil won't change me, unless you both want me murdered."

She got up determinedly, and I had started for the door when a belated thought stopped me.

"Anyhow," I said, "you can't leave yet. The police have a body. Whether they think she was murdered or not, we'll all be interrogated. There will be an inquest, and we'll have to be there. You can't just get on a plane or a ship, and you know it. And what are you going to tell them? That she was killed in mistake for you? They'll want to know why."

Nothing, however, was more obvious than that she had no intention of telling anybody anything. I made one more attempt, though.

"What about Doctor Townsend?" I said. "Can't you tell him what's wrong? That's his business, isn't it? Or does he know already?"

"It has nothing to do with him," she said, her face tight. "I don't want him involved."

I left her after that, feeling pretty hopeless. It was lunchtime, and Bill and I ate hash and his favorite popovers. But he was rather quiet, for him. When Jennie had slammed the pantry door for the last time, he looked up from his coffee.

"Think all this has anything to do with Aunt Judith?" he asked.

I tried to look merely interested.

"Judith?" I said. "Where on earth did you get that idea?"

"Oh, Jennie talks," he said. "And all this locking herself in looks queer as hell. If she's in a mess why not tell somebody, get help, get the police?"

"I've tried that, Bill. She won't talk about it."

"Not Chandler, is it?"

"Your guess is as good as mine. He had twenty years to kill her, if that's your idea. Why wait until now?"

"I'll bet he pays her a cracking good alimony."

"I never heard of alimony as a reason for murder."

"Well, if he could get away with it," he said, and lapsed into thoughtful silence, as though the idea of Ridgely Chandler threatening Judith because of alimony was not unpleasant.

I suppose the local police were pretty busy at that time of year, and the town was understaffed, anyhow. Anyway, it was two state troopers who came back that afternoon. They stayed around the pool, and they seemed to be looking for something on the ground. At least they went over it inch by inch. Whether they found what they were looking for I did not know, and except for a couple of reporters, who had learned Judith was staying with us and hung around hoping to get a picture of her, the afternoon was quiet.

O'Brien's car, which he left out in all weathers, was missing, so I gathered he was off on some business of his own. I learned later that the chief and the state police were not only canvassing the village and surrounding countryside, but were getting in touch by telephone with the crew of the train from which, according to Ed Brown, she might possibly have come.

As it developed, the conductor of the train was pretty sure

97

he had seen her. He remembered her hat. But as it was a local train from up the river, he had no idea where she had taken it. A walking party from the city had pretty well filled it. Also his wife was about to have a baby, and I suppose his mind was not exactly on his job.

Phil had a case in court that day, so I could not get in touch with him. But by six o'clock the police were about where they had started. Even the bleached hair was no help. Our local beauty people said it was probably a professional job, and done not too long before. Perhaps a month ago, or less.

I was relieved to see that Judith had taken her suitcase back into her room. Evidently she had decided to stay, for a time at least, and when I met Phil that evening—Bill had rattled off to see a girl, named Janey, having learned her family had arrived for the summer—I told him of my talk with her.

"So she thinks it was murder," he said thoughtfully. "Anybody said that to you? When I left they'd about decided it was accidental. If she knows anything she should tell it."

But when I told him of her threat to kill herself if she had to see the police, he was annoyed.

"She's still dramatizing herself!" he said. "Don't let her scare you, Lois. She's too fond of herself for that." Then he saw my face. "All right, all right. Maybe she is in trouble, but what? She played around with a pretty wild crowd, but according to the papers they're all still healthy enough. Although God knows why, the drinks they drink and the hours they keep."

"Judith never drank a lot," I protested.

"There are other vices than liquor, my innocent. Drugs and adultery, for example. Have you any idea if she takes drugs, Lois? It might account for a lot of things."

But somehow I did not think so. There was a curious sort of rationality about what appeared to be her vagaries. She was afraid of somebody or something, and she took what steps she could to protect herself. Grant that, and much of it fell into line. As to the adultery Phil mentioned, Ridge himself had apparently cleared her of that.

We had our after-dinner coffee on the big front porch that night. Hot as it was nobody thought of using the pool, but Phil looked tired and I was sorry for him.

"Everything passes, Phil," I said. "This will go, too. Judith's going abroad as soon as she can get a ship. As to this dead woman, none of us know her, not even Jude. It can't mean real trouble with the police."

He only shrugged, but I had apparently reminded him of something.

"Speaking of police," he said, "I saw your tenant in town today. He was going into police headquarters at Centre Street. What is he, anyhow? Or do you know? He's a pretty close-mouthed customer about himself."

I suppose I colored, for he laughed.

"Him and his girls," he jeered. "If ever I saw a cop, our Irish friend is one. It stands out all over him. Maybe he did go to college. Maybe he's spent four years in the army. Maybe he's off the force now. But I wouldn't be too damned sure even of that."

"He's not on police business here," I said hotly. "He's been in the army and he's tired. You know all that. And if he wants to see his old friends certainly that's *his* business."

"Once a cop always a cop," Phil retorted. "And if he thinks those specs fool me he's gone in the head. Only what's he doing here? Up to now we've been a pretty law-abiding crowd. Think he's keeping an eye on Judith?"

"Why should he?" I said. Nevertheless, I was more than a little troubled. He had had a purpose in getting the dead woman's bag out of the pool, and he had taken something from it before he handed it to me; something he did not want the local authorities to know about, and which I did not doubt he had taken to police headquarters in the city that day.

Perhaps Judith was right and it was murder, after all. There were other things, too. What had the state police been searching for on the grass by the pool that day? Whatever it was, did he have it, as well as that wadded-up and soaking wet roll of newsprint? And did he know who the woman was? Had she been the one I had seen at his door only a few days before?

It was almost dark when I heard his car come in. The girls had apparently gone supperless to roost, and he did not disturb them. By that time I was practically ready to go down and denounce him, for being in Reno not by chance but by design, for picking me up on the train and inducing me to talk, and for concealing information from the local men.

I did not, of course. Judith came downstairs, saying her room was too hot to stay in, and she was barely settled with us on the porch when Chief Fowler arrived. He mounted the steps and took off his cap.

"Evening, folks," he said. "Warm night, isn't it?"

Phil asked him to sit down and offered him a whisky and soda. He refused, however.

"It's still working-hours for me," he said. "Looks as though we've got real trouble on our hands. The boy's not here, is he?"

"Bill? No, he's out somewhere," I said. "Why? Do you want him?"

"Only because he found the body. You see, this woman—the deceased—has a bad cut on the back of her head. No fracture but, well, maybe she was knocked out and then dropped in the water. In that case it's murder."

"Sorry to hear it," Phil said, "but since none of us knew her—"

The chief coughed.

"Well, as a matter of fact, that's why I'm here," he said. "I know none of you recognized her this morning. But she looks better now. I'd like you all to see her. Nothing to worry anybody. Just peaceful and quiet." Which last I thought was at least supererogatory. "Ten o'clock too early? Inquest's at eleven."

"I suppose not," I said. "Who is she, Chief? Somebody from around here?"

"Not if Ed Brown's story's true. Only it beats me why a

100

woman would drive five miles in a taxi, get out and send it away, and then fall or get pushed into that pool of yours. It doesn't make sense. What about this fellow you rent the cottage to? Know anything about him?"

Nobody had any decided opinions about O'Brien, except that he seemed like a nice person, and at last, after saying that both Bill and myself would be wanted to attend the inquest the next morning, he went away. Not far, however; I heard his car stop at the cottage, and it was some time before it drove away.

I stayed on the porch when the others had gone. The fact that I was wanted at the inquest seemed definitely sinister to me. After all, I had not found the body, but I had had the bag. It worried me considerably, and after the chief had left the cottage I walked down toward it. I did not like passing the pool. The memory of the dead woman in it was too recent. But the window of O'Brien's sitting room was open, and it gave me courage to go on.

I stopped at the window and glanced inside. O'Brien was sitting in the big chair by the lamp, but he was not catching up with any reading. He was not wearing his spectacles, either. He had two long strips of stiff transparent cellophane in his hands, and he was busy binding them together with what looked like Scotch tape. What seemed like a press clipping was between them, and in the lamplight his face was so grim and intent that when I spoke he practically leaped to his feet.

"Oh, it's you!" he said. "What do you mean, scaring a guy out of his wits! The door's not locked. How about using it?"

I heard him open a drawer of the table and slam it shut, and when he let me in whatever he had been working on was out of sight.

"I wasn't spying on you," I said. "But if that's the clipping you took out of that woman's bag, I imagine Fowler would be interested in it."

"It wouldn't have meant a thing to him. And I wish to God, Lois, that you'd keep your pretty nose out of what doesn't concern you."

It was the first time he had called me that, but he was too irritated to notice it.

"I have to be interested," I said. "I have to testify at the inquest tomorrow. What am I to say about the bag? That you took something out of it?"

He flushed. I think for a minute he wanted to throttle me. Then with a jerk he opened the table drawer and pulled out the clipping in its cellophane covers.

"All right," he said. "So I think a clipping twenty years old is worth preserving. And that it wouldn't mean a damn thing to Fowler or the medical examiner, either. It does happen to be my affair."

"I see," I said. "So Phil's right, after all."

"Right about what?"

"He says once a cop always a cop. And he believes you're here on police business. That you came here to watch us, or maybe Judith. That's true, isn't it?"

"I haven't made any particular secret about that part of it, have I? Only let's play it differently. Let's say I think your sister may need protection. In fact, I'm damned sure she does."

But I was still indignant.

"It was all neatly arranged, wasn't it?" I said. "The pick-up on the train, the renting of this place, the whole bag of tricks. Even that woman in the pool! You recognized her, didn't you? I think she was here the other day to see you, but you were out."

"Say that again!"

He was so astonished that I knew he was not acting.

"She was here?"

"I think it was her," I said, ungrammatically. "At least the hat looks the same, and she's about the same size."

"So that's it," he said, and seemed to be thinking over something. Clearly it bothered him. Then abruptly he flung the cellophane arrangement on the table.

"Maybe you'd better read that," he said. "You'll understand

a few things. If that woman is who I think she is, I've been hunting her for twenty years."

I picked the thing up. It was neatly done, an ancient yellow strip of newsprint, carefully placed between two sheets of transparent material. I glanced at the date. It was December 10, 1929, and it had to do with the murder of a girl named Mollie Preston in the old slums down by the East River. According to the paper, she had been strangled to death after a quarrel with a youth who had been seen with her a number of times, and he was being held for the murder.

I was completely bewildered as I put it down.

"This hasn't anything to do with us," I said. "I don't understand."

"No," he said. "How old were you then? Seven or so, weren't you? It's ancient history, but the woman today was a witness in that case. And she'd kept this clipping in her bag. Why? What did it mean to her? And why did she bring it here with her? If I knew that, I would know why she was killed."

"Killed! You think she was murdered?"

"I do," he said grimly. "Knocked out and then pushed into the pool. This man your maid Jennie saw—has she any description of him?"

"None at all. She was paralyzed with fright."

He sat down and picking up his pipe proceeded to fill and light it.

"If you have time I'd like to tell you a few things, Lois. But I'm going to ask you something first. Why do you think your sister fainted this morning, at the pool?"

"It wasn't a pretty sight."

"You don't think she recognized her?"

"I don't know," I said uncertainly. "Of course, it's possible. I don't think it's likely."

"All right. Maybe she did. Maybe she didn't. But let's think back to that year of 1929. For most of it the country was riding high, wide, and handsome. Everybody was getting rich. This property of yours was still a showplace. So were a lot of big

103

estates. This dead woman may have been employed around here, or even at The Birches itself. But I doubt it."

"I wouldn't remember her if she was," I said. "What happened about the Preston murder?"

"The boy was found guilty," he said. "Better forget it. Just a dirty miserable slice of life in a tenement. Girl probably a prostitute, boy maybe a little better, but not much. What would it have to do with you, the spoiled darling of a wealthy family?"

That was when I laughed, remembering the ugly brat I had been, remembering the gay crowds around the pool in the summer who never saw me, remembering—but this only faintly—Anne's wedding at The Birches, the marquee with its wooden floor for dancing, and Judith one of the bridesmaids. Remembering Mother in pale taffeta with a big hat and plumes and Father fussing about his morning coat. And still nobody noticing me. But he was right in one way. Riding high we certainly had been, when I was too young even for bands on my teeth.

"You're away before my time," I told him. "I was only seven in 1929 and Judith hadn't even come out. She always had a lot of boys and girls around, but they were the boarding-school-prep-school sort, with a great deal of excitement when a college man showed up."

"Just the same," he persisted, "that woman—her name was Kate Henry when I knew her—had a reason for being here. She didn't come near this cottage last night. I know that. Then who else? Could it have been your sister?"

I felt a small shiver up and down my spine, remembering as I did the creaking of the stairs the night before. He saw my face and nodded.

"All right," he said. "Let's forget it. Somewhere I think Conan Doyle says it's important in any case to reason backward. Have you talked to Mrs. Chandler?"

"Yes. She says she never saw the woman before, and I think she's telling the truth. But she was really terrified today. She wanted to get out of the country. She was packed this afternoon, but I talked her out of it."

"Where was she going?"

"Anywhere a ship would take her, I imagine."

He was thoughtful.

"It wouldn't be such a bad idea, at that," he said. "But if she makes a move to leave I want to know it, Lois."

He took me up the drive that night. It was still hot, but it had started to rain, a thin summer drizzle which was utterly depressing. He said very little on the way, and I felt that he knew more than he had told me, but less than he liked. Only at the foot of the porch steps he stopped, and with any other man I might have thought he meant to kiss me. After all, I had had more experience than I had intimated to Anne. But not O'Brien. He had to stand there and make what amounted to a speech.

"Every now and then," he said, "even a smart cop can be wrong. I'm beginning to think I've laid an egg here, and it's not one of the girls'. I'm going to ask you a favor," he added. "When you're called at the inquest tomorrow keep me out of it, will you? It may not come up at all, but if it does it's all right to say I found the bag, but don't say I opened it. It may be damned important."

Which, one way and another, was a poor preparation for a good night's sleep.

Chapter 11

I cannot honestly say that the dead woman worried me greatly that night. After all, I did not know her. Whether she was murdered or merely fell into the pool and drowned seemed to have no relation to any of us. But I was worried about Judith. Her reaction to the situation seemed ridiculously exaggerated, if she had not known Kate Henry, which O'Brien said was her name. Also the mere idea that she had slipped out of the house and gone to the pool in the middle of the night was sufficiently out of character to amount to absurdity.

At eleven o'clock the telephone rang in the lower hall, and I slipped on an old bathrobe and went down to answer it. It was Ridge, and he sounded annoyed.

"You seem to have the faculty out there of getting into the papers," he said. "What's all this about a woman drowning in the pool?"

"Well, she did. That's about all I know."

"Who was she? Any identification yet?"

I thought quickly.

"I don't believe so, Ridge. She had no cards or automobile driver's permit on her. I suppose it's only a matter of time."

"How's Judith taking it?"

"She was shocked, as we all were. The police think it may have been murder, that someone hit her on the head and then threw her in the pool. I don't suppose that's in the papers yet. It may come out at the inquest tomorrow."

"More likely she stumbled and fell in. I always said that place was a deathtrap."

I went back to bed and tried to think back to the fall of 1929. The crash had come, although Mother refused to recognize it. Phil once said she maintained she had lived through at least three of them, and nothing serious had ever happened. I had a vague recollection of the last dinner party she gave the night Father killed himself; of sitting on the stairs in my night clothes, watching the men give their arms to the women, the chattering, beautifully dressed procession moving toward the dining-room, and—although I did not see him—Father slipping out to his downtown office when the men were closeted with cigars and liquors, and using the gun no one knew he had.

I felt a deep wave of pity for him. He had been gentle and kind, a quiet undramatic man who loved his children and his home. Why had he done it? Not because he had lost his money. I did not believe money had ever been important to him, and other men had weathered the storm.

One thing I did remember. Mother had not stayed to see the city house dismantled. She had taken Judith and fled to Arizona not long after the funeral. She made the excuse of Judith's cough, but I felt now that she could not bear the loss of the lares and penates that were so important to her. She had protested over the sale, and I had trailed her around as, red eyed and shaken, she had pasted labels on the things that were to go to The Birches.

Someone—the auctioneer probably—followed her, protesting.

"But, madam, those chairs are a part of the assets of the estate. I have no right to let you keep them."

"They are mine, not my husband's. I bought them myself."

And willy-nilly a van had come and taken them away.

After that she went to Arizona. Phil returned to college, the

107

servants with the exception of Helga disappeared, and one day Anne appeared and drove Helga and me out to The Birches. It was still cold. The damp mustiness of the place was disheartening, and the furniture from the town house had been merely stacked in the hall and left. I think Anne got help from the village eventually, but that first night Helga and I had curled up together in Mother's big walnut bed, and I had cried myself to sleep.

It was late spring when Mother and Judith returned, Mother in deep black and looking harassed, and Judith blooming and beautiful. There were no more picnics around the pool, but Ridgely Chandler was there a great deal. One day I saw the huge square-cut solitaire on Judith's finger, and was told she was engaged to him.

They were married in the fall in the small local church. There were no attendants, and as I may have said, Anne found Judith crying bitterly before she put on her white satin dress. I overheard her, but when I went to Helga about it she told me to hush up.

"All brides cry," she said. "Just be glad she's getting a man. Maybe now she'll settle down."

Only she never had. I suppose Doctor Townsend would say the extravagance of her life after the marriage was pure escapism. And of course, behind her locked doors, she was still escaping.

I wondered if in those more prosperous days before the crash the drowned woman had been employed at The Birches. In that case she should have known the pool, however, and Judith might have remembered her. She had not, I was sure of that. Nor had Helga, who seldom forgot a face.

Only three of us went to the inquest the next day, Phil, Bill, and myself. For Judith was sick. She had worked herself into a fever, I suppose because she always hated the idea of death. And O'Brien's cottage was closed and his car gone.

Before the inquest they asked Bill and me to identify the body as the one we had found in the pool, and I stood for a minute or so, looking down at the woman. It seemed utterly sad to me that she could lie there among strangers. For someone she must have worn that flower-trimmed hat and bleached her hair. And at one time she must have been a pretty girl. Even now she was not wholly unattractive. They say drowning is an easy death. I don't know. I don't want to know, but her face was peaceful.

But, as we waited for the inquest to begin, I wondered about her. Why had she carried that clipping in her bag? What connection could she have had with the murder more than twenty years ago of a prostitute in the New York slums? She must have been young then herself. She was not much over forty now. If she was Kate Henry, she had evidently known this Mollie Preston. There must have been some reason for her keeping the account of that murder all this time, and having it with her when she died.

And why had she disappeared for all those years? What did she know? Or why again had O'Brien been trying to find her?

At the inquest later it was evident that considerable local interest had been aroused. The room was crowded, and Phil leaned over and told me the district attorney for the county was present.

"They're not sure," he said. "Maybe a murder, but they've got to prove it."

It took a little time to get organized, and to call the proceedings to order. But I was still calm, merely interested, until my own turn came. Doctor Christy was presiding, and there was some medical evidence by one of his assistants about the nature of the wound in the back of the woman's head. It had been inflicted with a sharpish instrument, but probably not a hatchet or anything of that sort.

"What do you mean by not a hatchet, Doctor?"

"I only used the word in a general sense. For instance, a hatchet makes a sharp clean cut. The edges of this injury are contused, broken down. The deceased had a thick skull, or there would probably have been a fracture. Considerable force was used."

"Could it have been self-inflicted? Or caused by a fall?"

"Absolutely not."

"You cannot state the weapon used?"

"Not of my own knowledge."

"Was it the blow that killed her, Doctor?"

"No. There was no fracture. She died in the pool, but she was almost certainly unconscious, or semi-conscious, when she hit the water. Actually she died by drowning."

"Can you give an estimate as to the time of the death?"

"I can only say some hours before the body was discovered."

"But approximately?"

"The water in the pool was pretty cool. I would guess five or six hours. It's purely a guess. Rigor was well established."

But it was Bill who was the star witness, and I think he rather enjoyed it. He identified photographs of the pool and the old diving-platform at the deep end from which he had seen the body.

"Not that I thought it was a body then," he said. "It was just something dark. But when I got down to it, I knew what it was."

"What did you do then, Mr. Harrison?" Doctor Christy inquired.

"I got up for air as fast as I could. Then I yelled for help. I thought she might still be alive. But there was nobody around. So I went in again and pulled her to the shallow end of the pool, so her head was out of the water. Then I ran up to the house and wakened my aunt, Lois Maynard."

"You still thought she might be alive?"

"Well, no," Bill admitted. "But I couldn't just leave her there and go swimming, could I?"

"It didn't occur to you to call the police?"

"I guess I was pretty excited. By the time we got back, the man who lives in the old gardener's cottage came running over.

His name's O'Brien. He sent me to telephone the chief of police."

Doctor Christy looked around the room.

"Is Mr. O'Brien present?" he asked.

Fowler, the Chief of Police, stood up.

"Mr. O'Brien was called away," he said. "I have his deposition here. The body was already found when he reached the pool. He dove in and recovered the deceased's bag, but that's all."

Ed Brown came next. He limped to the chair and sat down with the air of a martyr.

"All I did was take her out from town," he said, looking outraged. "That's my job. I never seen her before, and she didn't talk. Some folks rattle on as if I had nothing to do but listen to them. Only time she spoke was to ask if I was a taxi, and when she got out how much she owed me. I said did she want me to wait and she said no. When I turned around she was still standing there by the road to the Adrian place, like she sort of wanted me out of the way."

He didn't know whether she had got out of the train or not. It was his bedtime. He didn't like to work late. He had bad arthritis. But as soon as she knew he had a taxi she was inside the car.

"You mean she got in in a hurry?"

"I'll say she did."

"As though perhaps she did not want to be seen?"

"Maybe. Maybe not."

I had no idea I was going to be called until, after the usual preliminaries, I heard my name and saw that wretched bag on the table.

"You were present, I believe, Miss Maynard, when this bag was taken out of the pool."

"Yes. I watched Mr. O'Brien take it out."

"Did you by any chance happen to open it?"

"No," I said. "Why should I?"

111

He looked at me.

"It would be natural, wouldn't it?" he said. "After all, you might want to find out who she was, provided you didn't know her."

"But I didn't open it," I insisted. It was the truth, of course. O'Brien had done it. But the medical examiner leaned forward and, picking up the awful thing, opened it and dumped its contents on the table.

"This may be a case of accident or suicide, Miss Maynard. Or it may be one of murder. I want you to be careful what you say. This woman got off a local train here late at night. She is unknown in the town. She did not bring anything with her to indicate she meant to stay. Now what would that indicate?"

"I haven't an idea," I said truthfully enough.

"Isn't it possible she would have a return-trip ticket with her?"

The question was unexpected, and it left me practically paralyzed. What had happened to that yellow scrap I had seen on the grass? Did O'Brien have it, too? And if so was that why I was not to say he had opened the bag? I couldn't speak. I could only hear Doctor Christy's voice, cold and severe.

"As a matter of fact," he said, "the conductor of the train believes she did have a return-trip ticket. In that case it has disappeared. Perhaps I'd better rephrase the question. Did you at any time touch the contents of the bag? For example, the compact?"

"I—I may have," I said, feeling like an utter fool. "The thing fell open and the stuff spilled out on the grounds. I put it all back."

"Then that would account for your fingerprints on the compact?"

I wanted to sink through the floor, and a small titter showed the crowd was amused. I was not. But the doctor banged on the table with a gavel and went on inexorably.

"During this—er—accident," he said, "did you or did you not see the return-trip half of a railroad ticket?"

"There might have been one. I don't remember."

It must have sounded honest, or at least moronic, for at last they excused me. Not without reservations, I realize now, but the inquest was not over. There was a stir in the back of the room as a newcomer entered, and someone announced that a Mr. Kirk had arrived.

I had never seen him before. He was a tall sandy-haired man with spectacles, and Doctor Christy got up and shook hands with him. He apologized for being late and took the witness chair. The doctor turned to the jury.

"In view of certain developments in this case," he said, "I took the liberty of asking for assistance from the New York Police Laboratory, which is better equipped than the one in this county. Now, Mr. Kirk, will you state just what you received from us?"

"One item was an envelope, marked as containing scrapings from under the deceased's nails. The other was a small scrap of soft leather found, I believe, beside the pool where the body was discovered."

There was a stir through the room. This was what they had come for. Doctor Christy rapped for order.

"You examined these?" he inquired.

"Yes. Under the microscope. There was a filament of this same leather in the envelope containing the scrapings."

"Will you tell us what you then did?"

"I compared both with various types of the leather used for gloves, as they showed salt from human perspiration. In view of the nature of the wound I considered other possibilities."

"Such as?"

"The grip of a golf club was one. A golf club is an excellent weapon, and on investigation I found that the leather so used corresponded with the sample I had."

"Would you say that a golf club was used?"

113

"I cannot answer that. It is a possibility, of course."

Phil had the nerve to grin and punch me with his elbow, and I knew what he meant. His own clubs stood in their bag in the main hall of The Birches, and had done so for years.

"Good-by, Lois," he said. "Write me now and then, won't you? And a bottle of Scotch would come in handy."

"Oh, shut up," I said savagely.

To my surprise the inquest was adjourned almost immediately, but only after the district attorney had a low-voiced colloquy with Doctor Christy.

Phil looked serious as we left.

"I'm afraid it's murder, he said. "The police must want more time. What the hell made you say you didn't open that bag?"

"I didn't," I said indignantly. "O'Brien did. He dumped the stuff out on the grass. All I did was to put it back."

"Why on earth didn't you say so?"

"He asked me not to, but if I ever lay hands on him he'll be sorry. He made a fool out of me, and I fell for it."

"I told you he was a cop," Phil said smugly.

I was in a cold fury by that time, and Bill suggested a Coke at the drugstore near by.

"You look as though you need something," he observed. "So O'Brien's still a cop. Hot diggety dog! Ain't that something? And don't let that deposition stuff get you. They knew darned well where he was, and why. Only what about that clipping he snitched? Did he give it to Fowler?"

"Why don't you ask him?" I said bitterly. "I never want to see the man again. He got me into this mess, and he can damn well get me out of it."

"Such language! And I thought you'd fallen for the guy!"

Phil had not come in with us, so I sat there at a small table with a lot of school kids shouting and the usual drugstore smell of scented soaps, drugs, and soda fountain around me, and tried to think. Bill had wandered off to the juke box and, of course, had somehow picked up a pretty girl on the way. But I was worried as well as angry. Not about the dead woman. After

114

all, I could not see how she concerned me, except that I had made a fool of myself at the inquest. But about the clipping O'Brien had taken. What had a murder twenty years old to do with us? Phil had been away at college at that time, Anne was already married, and Judith not yet even eighteen.

Yet somehow it did concern us. Angry as I was at O'Brien he had been sure the presence of the dead woman had something to do with us. Actually, of course, with Judith. He had said she might be in danger, and there was no question her terror was real. She had been deadly afraid since Reno. Now she insisted the woman had been mistaken for her and deliberately drowned, and while I knew she was a good actress, there had been no acting when she packed her bags and tried to leave that day. She had been as near desperation as no matter.

Bill was still at the juke box when I went to the telephone booth and looked up Doctor Townsend's number in New York. His nurse answered. She said the doctor was out and who was speaking.

"It's Lois Maynard," I said. "Mrs. Chandler's sister. Could I see the doctor sometime tomorrow?"

"Mrs. Chandler has her regular appointment tomorrow."

"I don't think she'll be coming. She's not well."

"Just a moment. I'll look at the book."

She came back in a minute or two, said I could come at eleven-thirty, and seemed relieved when I said I didn't want Judith to know about it. She said she thought the doctor would be glad to see me, and hung up as though she had said too much.

I don't know how Phil felt when we got home that day, but I drew a long breath of relief when I saw his golf bag in the hall. The clubs were all there. I counted them.

Chapter 12

As usual I made my publisher the excuse for going into town the next morning, although I had practically abandoned work. As no one in the house ever considered me seriously as a writer this brought no comment from Phil. But Bill spoke up briskly.

"How about taking me along?" he asked. "I'll tell him you're a prime suspect in a murder case. That ought to be good publicity. 'Novelist Detained in Mysterious Death. Writer of Crime Fiction Involved in Murder Herself.' How's that?"

"I'm not involved, and it isn't funny. You're not coming."

He was persistent, however. He needed new bathing trunks. Did I want to see his derrière through the old ones? I retorted that as I had watched diapers put on him as a baby he was no treat to me. But his Janey, whoever she was, saved the day for me. She called him up and asked him to lunch, so I was able to draw a free breath again.

I saw Judith before I left. As usual she was locked in her room, but after some grumbling she admitted me. I saw at once something had happened. She looked worse than the day before, if possible, and her hands shook as she crawled back into bed and tried to light a cigarette.

"You'll burn yourself to death someday doing that," I told her. "How are you? Fever gone?"

She did not answer. She took a puff and then put down the cigarette.

116

"What's this Jennie tells me?" she said. "About a man at the pool with a gun?"

I could have strangled Jennie at that moment, but I was for it, and I knew it.

"Apparently some tramp wandered in, but he had no gun," I said as cheerfully as I could. "That's pure imagination on Jennie's part."

"How do you know it was imagination?"

"Well, look, Jude. It doesn't make sense. Jennie waiting for boy friend on bench. Man appears across pool, points gun, and disappears. Jennie screams and runs. The end."

"What do you mean, the end?" she asked peevishly. "She saw someone, didn't she? And Phil found the place all trampled. I wish you'd stop treating me like a child or a lunatic. I'm neither."

I did not argue with her. I had a train to catch, but it only struck me later that she had not asked about the inquest. However, for once she had a morning paper, so perhaps she had read about it.

On the way out I saw that O'Brien's cottage door was still closed and his car gone. Not only that, but his girls were raising a terrific racket, as though they needed feeding. I made a mental note to do so when I came back, but personally I never wanted to see him again. Whatever he had meant by vitally important, he had gone away and left me literally holding the bag, and I was fed to the teeth.

The train was crowded, but I got a seat, and sat there thinking about a number of things. The newspaper clipping, for example. It was dated 1929, and I tried to remember that period. I had learned some things about it as I grew up, that it was the time of the boyish form, of rolled stockings, and I think the Charleston. Of the short skirt, too. The photograph of Anne on a table in the living room showed her in her wedding dress, the skirt to her knees showing her rather sturdy legs, the waistline down around her hips, and the long satin train which only made the whole outfit grotesque.

117

From Anne to Judith was only a step. She said she was neither a child nor a lunatic, and in spite of Phil I began to believe her. Nevertheless, I was determined to see Doctor Townsend. Somewhere there was a key to what he termed the privacy of the human mind, and I hoped he had found one for Judith.

He had not, however, although he seemed pleased to see me. "I'm glad you came," he said. "I read the papers, and this death must be a real shock to your sister. How is she taking it?"

I told him: her fainting at the pool, her impulse to escape, her fever and inability to attend the inquest. He listened attentively. He had her file in front of him, as though he had been going through it, but he shook his head when I finished.

"All pretty bad for her," he said. "I don't know how long she can carry on. As you know, she's been coming back to me, but I've not really been able to help her. As I told you before, she doesn't co-operate. When you were here you told me of the jewel episode and of her leaving her husband. Also that she had fainted on the train platform at Reno and seemed to be terrified. Have you anything to add to that?"

"Only that she's still terrified. I'm quite sure she thinks someone intends to murder her."

He took that in his stride. I daresay it was nothing new to him. But he asked me to give him her early history, and I told him what I knew: how she had been spoiled as a child by Mother, had been taken to Arizona for several months, and been married the fall after her return. I said, too, that I did not think she had been in love with Ridge, but apparently they got along well enough. Only she liked to go out and he didn't, and in the end they were merely living in the same apartment.

He nodded, as though he already knew much of it. When I had finished he went back to what I had told him before, about the night she came home and Ridge found her with her jewels, as though she were appraising them.

"Rather a startling thing, of course," he said. "Has he ever said what he thought of it?"

"He wondered if she was being blackmailed. He went into that later after she left him. Apparently there was no reason for it. She still has the jewels, or so she says. And she had never had a lover, or anything of the sort."

"I see. Also he probably knows that as a rule blackmailers don't murder, or even make the attempt." And he added, rather dryly, "Why should they?"

He knew her side, of course, about the divorce and Reno. She had been willing to talk about it, but apparently she had told him she left because Ridgely had another woman. Trust Judith to say that, and perhaps even make herself believe it.

"I don't know whether Mr. Chandler had an extramarital arrangement or not," he said delicately, to spare my virginal sensitivity. "It's possible, of course. He and his wife had not lived together for a long time. You don't think this dead woman—"

"Was his mistress? I don't think so, Doctor. She wasn't young, or even beautiful. She looked and dressed like—well, like a housewife."

He abandoned Kate Henry then, if that is who she was, and took me back to Reno again. "You say you saw nothing to induce that fainting attack. But she must have seen something, Miss Maynard."

"I can't imagine what it was. I searched the train after it happened, and there wasn't a large crowd at the station. Just porters and a chauffeur or two and a few taxis. Taxis!" I said excitedly. "That's queer, Doctor. She won't use a taxicab. She walks or takes a bus. Does that mean anything?"

"Possibly. It seems carrying things rather far. It may be an *idée fixe*. We get a good many of those here. It is carried to extremes sometimes. I had a young man here yesterday, perfectly sane in other respects, who believes he is an adopted son. He is not, according to his mother. I have seen his birth certificate."

"Listen, Doctor," I said urgently. "I know all that. It happens, of course. Only you can't measure Judith by the usual yardstick. She sleeps in a locked room, with the windows over the porch nailed shut. She won't go into the grounds if she can avoid it. When she does it's at night, in a long black cape. She looks spooky. And I still don't know why she came to The Birches. She would be better off in a good hotel."

"Perhaps The Birches means sanctuary to her, Miss Maynard. She must have been happy there as a girl. She's not entirely normal, of course, but The Birches is easy to explain. It's like—" he decided to disregard my virgin status—"it's like going back to the mother womb."

"Well, the mother womb in this case is having a lot of birth pains," I said. "Judith fainted when she saw the body. That could happen to anybody. But the real reason it worries her is because she thinks this woman was mistaken for her."

"That's curious," he said. "Why would she think that?"

"They were the same build in a way, they were nearly of an age, and they both had blond hair. The other woman's was bleached, I understand, but on a dark night—well, it's possible, I suppose."

He sat thinking for a few minutes, his head on his chest. When he looked up his expression was grave.

"Of course, it's possible she's really in danger," he said. "We both know she is a psychiatric case, or we believe she is. But we must not let that close our eyes to other things." And when I nodded he went on. "I'd better talk to you rather frankly. I can say this. Usually after this lapse of time I can read a patient's mind pretty well. I'm only a listening-post, you know. They talk. I ask questions and listen to the answers. With Mrs. Chandler it's different. I can go so far. Then, as I told you before, there's a wall, and I can't either break it down or get over it. You can't remember anything in her past that would cause—well, let's say a shock, a psychic shock."

"No," I told him. "She's had an unusually easy life until now. She's had plenty of money, she's had the looks of the family, and for years she had a good husband. I can't think of anything."

120

He smiled.

"What do we mean by a good husband?" he inquired. "A good provider, who stays home and is at least technically faithful?"

"I wouldn't know. I've never had one."

"As to Mr. Chandler, I don't know him. There was certainly incompatibility, and he may be a hard man to live with. It's not unusual for me to have a woman here and after a time discover it is the husband who should be my patient. Do you think Mr. Chandler would talk to me?"

"Not on this couch of yours! He may come. He'll sit where I am, offer you a dollar cigar, and ask if you think Judith ought to be committed."

He grinned.

"I may try to see him," he said. "I like a good cigar. Now I'm afraid I'll have to let you go. I have rather a heavy day. But I suggest you think over what I have said. This danger may be real."

I was out on the hot street before I realized I hadn't asked him about Judith's idea of going abroad. But there was one thing he had said which I found thought-provoking. That was the idea that sometime, somewhere, she had had a psychic shock, and the inference that after years of normal living whatever it was had caught up to her.

Anne might know, I thought, so I found a telephone pay booth and called her up. Her voice was not too amiable. She had got in from Boston that morning, and the apartment was a mess. She wanted to know if I would keep Bill a little longer, and was he actually suspected of drowning the woman.

"No," I said, "but he's enjoying it. Of course he can stay. We're glad to have him. He has a sort of heavy date there with a girl called Janey. She doesn't seem to have any other name."

"They never do," Anne said resignedly. "Any more deaths? And how's Judith?"

"Not so well. Look, Anne, may I have a bite of lunch with you today? I'm in town."

"If you'll take potluck," she said. "Can't you wait until I've got my breath?"

"No," I told her firmly. "I want to talk to you, and it's important."

She agreed unwillingly, and I found her in the kitchen, savagely attacking a pile of dirty dishes. She had the harassed air I always associated with her. She had been a pretty girl, and in a way she was still a handsome woman. But Martin Harrison had been a disappointment. The crash had practically ruined him, and I could faintly remember those days when their house on Seventy-Ninth Street had been sold, and they had come to stay with us. There was a night, I believe, when Anne found him with a gun and had to take it from him by force.

Things gradually improved, of course, in the building line, but he was never an ambitious man, and for years she had had to struggle. It had left its mark on her, and I always suspected her of being jealous of Judith's prosperity.

That morning she eyed me grimly after she admitted me.

"Don't tell me I look like the wrath of God," she said. "I know it. You look like the devil yourself. Judith wearing you down?"

"We have had some trouble, such as a murder."

"A murder! I thought it was an accident."

"The police seem to have discovered something," I said vaguely. "I'd rather not talk about it. We don't even know who she is—or was."

She sat down heavily and kicked off her shoes.

"My feet are killing me," she said. "I suppose my poor Bill had the shock of his life when he found her."

"He's had the time of his life ever since! He was the star performer at the inquest yesterday, or don't you read the papers?"

"I've had a fat chance to see a newspaper this morning."

I asked about Martha, who was coming home before long, and in due time I suggested lunch. She shrugged.

"There's practically nothing in the place," she said. "I can fix some scrambled eggs, I suppose, and there is a hambone. It looks as though Martin's been living on ham. I saw it in the refrigerator. It doesn't look too moldy."

As a result I made a ham omelet, and over the kitchen table I had a better look at Anne. Washed and with her hair brushed she looked more like her old self. But as usual she was curious about Judith.

"How are the psychiatric treatments going?" she inquired. "Are they helping her any?"

"I don't think the doctor is satisfied. I saw him this morning. Anne, did Judith take Father's death very hard?"

"I don't think I noticed. Why?"

"The doctor thinks she's had a shock sometime or other."

"You have to remember how things were at that time." She poured herself another cup of coffee. "Martin and I were completely broke. He'd been in the market, too. I had to ask Mother for money even to take a bus! I think she resented it. After all, I had married and she had every reason to think I was off her hands. Then we landed back on her like a pair of parasites! It was sickening. No wonder she got out from under."

"Then it wasn't because of Judith's health they went to Arizona?"

"Listen to me," Anne said. "She's my own sister, and in some ways I'm fond of her. But Judith never had a sick day in her life."

"But it took money, Anne. Where did it come from?"

"I always thought Ridge Chandler financed them. I know he and Mother had some long conferences at that time. He'd gone completely overboard about Judith, poor devil. I meant to ask you something, Lois. What about Doctor Townsend? Has she fallen for him?"

"I don't know. She said something once that sounded like it."

She shrugged, and began picking up the dishes.

"They often get that idea, don't they?" she said vaguely. "I

123

gather that's part of the treatment. Don't worry about it, Lois. She'll get over it."

"You don't have to live with her," I retorted. "Look, Anne, you remember her as a kid, and I don't. Was she in any trouble?"

She laughed.

"She didn't have a baby when Mother took her west if that's what you mean. She was too busy taking care of her pretty little self. She's never had one since, either. I think Ridge has always resented that. The Chandler women always had them, to carry on the name."

"Then what or who is she afraid of? Because she's good and scared now," I said. "Phil thinks it's all in her mind, but she insists someone is threatening to kill her."

"I've felt like that myself sometimes."

"It isn't funny," I said indignantly. "I've wondered. That woman in the pool. Do you think she came to The Birches to see Judith? She fainted, you know, when she saw the body. And Phil's clubs were in the hall at The Birches."

"What about Phil's golf clubs?"

"They say a weapon of that sort was probably used. Not necessarily a club. Something like it."

Anne laughed.

"So you're suggesting that our dear sister took one of Phil's golf clubs and brained her! You know that's funny, if nothing else is. Judith, who wouldn't break a fingernail to raise a window, marching down to the pool in the dead of night, with a club over her shoulder and murder in her heart! Don't be fantastic, Lois."

I dried the dishes for her, and we let Judith alone for a while. Anne, however, was thoughtful.

"I saw Ridgely the other day," she said. "The poor old boy looks dreadful. He's aged ten years. Why did she leave him, Lois? Has she ever said anything?"

"It's not Ridge she's afraid of. I'm sure of that. She thinks the woman who was killed was mistaken for her. Anyhow why would he do such a thing?"

"It would save alimony," she said curtly. "But he's as puzzled as we are. He has an idea she was being blackmailed, and I suppose you know he put a private investigator on the case. But it was no soap. He says she always landed in her own bed."

"She would," I said. "I imagine it takes a generous sort of woman to get into that kind of mess."

She laughed at that, and we finished cleaning up before I left. Anne was still in the kitchen mopping the linoleum when I was ready to go, and I realized she had already practically forgotten Judith and even myself.

"Well, thanks for the lunch," I said. "I'd better be going. I have to catch the train and get home."

She looked as though she had just remembered I was still there.

"Glad to have you," she said absently. "And if Helga decides she can't take Judith, send her to me, will you?"

"Judith?"

"No, for heaven's sake! Helga."

I glanced around the apartment on my way out. It looked small to have raised two children in, and the furniture showed abuse. Phil and I sent her some of Mother's stuff after her death when we closed off part of The Birches. It had helped, but now it looked shabby and neglected. Seeing the place I could understand her resentment of Judith, who had had everything and apparently thrown it away.

Chapter 13

As I passed the cottage on my way home, I saw that O'Brien was back. His car was outside, looking dusty—usually he kept it very clean—and the girls were clucking contentedly. I did not stop. I merely stepped on the gas and sailed by, my head high with sheer fury.

It did not help my morale to see a town policeman and a state trooper near the pool. Each of them had a rake, and they were combing the grass and even crawling under the shrubbery. So the case was not closed, and this was verified when Jennie said Fowler had been there that afternoon.

"He took Mr. Phil's golf clubs when he left," she said. "He asked Mrs. Chandler if he could, so I guess it's all right. He said he'd bring them back tomorrow."

"Then he saw Mrs. Chandler?"

"Oh, yes. He was here a long time."

Phil was not yet home, and Jennie said Bill was meeting his train with the Ark. I felt practically dazed as I went upstairs. Judith's door was shut, so I did not speak to her. I went on to take a bath and change, but what I call my brain was past all reasonable thinking. The case was not closed. It had only moved from the swimming pool to the house itself.

Rather to my surprise Judith came down to dinner that

night. She looked better, and she even took a cocktail.

"I hope it was all right to give the police your golf clubs, Phil," she said. "But I can't imagine why they wanted them, Can you?"

"Very definitely," Phil said. "The idea is to give me free room and board for a time, and maybe a meal I can select before thay shave my head. Or do they shave heads? I can't seem to remember."

She fixed him with those curiously tilted eyes of hers and looked puzzled.

"Do you mean those clubs are important?"

"Important! Do you know what they cost? Oh, well, maybe we'll have an atom bomb in time. One can always hope!"

Bill choked over his drink, and I sat down because my legs were shaking.

"Fowler was really nice," she went on. "He asked a lot of questions, and one of them was funny, Phil. He seemed to think you'd know the woman in the pool. He didn't use the word 'mistress' but that's what he meant. I said I was sure you hadn't had one. Your morals—"

"Not morals. Money, my dear. Such ladies are expensive."

"But he was really very pleasant. He said I was not to worry about anything. Just leave it to him."

Phil looked at me and winked.

"It's not limited to birds," he said. "A little salt on anything male and it's all over."

Judith looked blank, but as just then Jennie opened the living-room door, yelled "Dinner," and slammed it shut again, the discussion ended.

I ate very little that night, as did Phil. Not only was he worried about the clubs. I found myself watching Judith and wondered what Doctor Townsend meant by a psychic shock. So far as I knew her life had been one grand sweet song until a few months ago. And if leaving Ridgely and going to Reno was a shock she had certainly recovered fast; playing roulette and

127

the slot machines and shooting craps, always with her entourage of men trailing her. She called them her boys, and they loved it.

It was possible, I thought, that the shock—whatever it was—had come, not in her earlier days, but on the train the day she fainted.

We had coffee as usual on the porch that night, but as the late summer evening turned to night I found myself there alone, Bill announcing that he had to see Janey and would probably propose to her.

"At your age, Bill!" I said. "Don't be absurd."

He grinned at me.

"It's just part of the game," he explained. "Keeps other fellows away, gives me the right to do a little necking, and lets me in to dinner now and then. They have a damned good cook." He saw my face and laughed. "Anyhow, I'd better get some influences behind me, such as her father. You see, I've been using Phil's clubs."

After he had rattled off, Phil took his brief case into the library, and with Judith gone to bed I found myself alone.

I couldn't decide what to do. O'Brien's lamp was lighted, and I had plenty to say to him. On the other hand, things seemed to be breaking too fast even for imagination. Sometime, too, during that interval I heard a car pass on the road and stop somewhere beyond. It must have been eleven o'clock by that time, the moon was rising over the trunks of the birch grove, and I was about to light the final cigarette of the day when I saw someone standing there.

It was a man, and at first I thought it was O'Brien. Then I realized he was not tall enough. Whoever it was he stood gazing up at the house, his hands apparently in his pockets. One hand was not, however. It was clutching something, and to my shocked surprise it seemed to be a rock.

It was a rock! After seemingly assuring himself that no one was around, he stepped out of the grove onto the drive that led to the stable, and with an easy pitch lobbed it up at one of Judith's open windows. I heard the distant crash as it hit the floor, and Judith's faint scream, both almost simultaneous.

He was gone before I realized it, fading among the trees, and before I could recover from my astonishment, I heard a car start up on the main road. As though that was not sufficient, I saw O'Brien running up from his cottage. As the car started, however, he slowed down to a walk, but he kept on coming. He was almost on the porch when he saw me.

"Who is it?" he said, peering up.

"It's Lois," I told him. "I'm afraid your friend's gone. After he heaved a rock through Judith's window, of course. That's not mayhem, is it? Mayhem is an attack on the person. But it seems a rather lethal form of amusement."

I doubt if he heard my last sentence or two. He was in the house and upstairs banging on Judith's door almost before I finished. I followed him up as fast as I could, to see him stop at Judith's door, and to hear him calling her name.

"Mrs. Chandler!" he said. "Are you all right?"

She did not answer him at once. When she did her voice was sharp.

"Of course I'm all right," she said. "What on earth is the matter?"

"The rock didn't hurt you?"

"What rock? I don't know what you're talking about, Mr. O'Brien."

"Didn't one come through your window just now?"

"I was taking a bath. I'll look around." There was a short silence, while she ostensibly made her search. O'Brien did not look at me. He put a sizable ear close to the door, and I saw he was wearing an army overcoat over his pajamas.

There was a short silence.

"There's no rock here," she said. "I can't imagine what all the excitement is about."

"Won't you let me in to look?"

Then she laughed, the light artificial laugh I knew so well.

"Really I can't do it," she said, her voice close to the door. "I'm just out of the tub. If Lois is around she would call it *in puris naturalibus*. College, you know. Good night, Mr. O'Brien, and thanks for looking after me."

O'Brien turned and looked at me.

"All right," I said in a whisper. "I'm a liar. There was no man and no rock, and everything's nice and friendly in this best of all possible worlds."

He grinned.

"She jumped that hurdle pretty fast," he said in a low cautious voice. "Had a lot of practice probably. Want to come down and talk about it?"

I did. I even wanted a drink to settle my nerves. I got two highballs and carried them to the porch. He evidently had his pipe with him—he had dozens all over the place—for when I went out he was smoking. He looked almost complacent. He sampled his drink, stated it was what the doctor ordered, and then told me to go ahead and—as he put it—add a bit.

Nevertheless, he was serious enough as I told him what had happened: the man's approach by way of the grove, the crash of the rock, Judith's scream, and then the car and the unknown's flight presumably in it. He did not speak until I had finished. Then he told me to stay where I was, and went down the steps and around the corner of the house.

When he came back he was holding a sizable stone in his hand.

"She threw it out the window after we got there," he said. "Notice anything about it?"

"It's just a piece of rock, isn't it?"

"It's rough, and it's squarish. You can tie things to a shape like this. I'm not psychic, but I can tell you what your sister is doing right now. She's either burning the note this carried, or she's flushing it down the toilet." He thrust a big hand into a pocket. "She's pretty thorough, you know, but she slipped up

130

in one thing. She threw the cord, too."

He produced it and handed it to me. It was an ordinary piece of white string, not too clean, and O'Brien took it back and put it in the pocket of his overcoat again.

"People get excited and slip up on some little thing," he said. "That's where the police step in. They're looking for the slip."

"I still don't understand," I said blankly. "Why not write her a letter?"

He smiled.

"Well, there's a bit of drama in this sort of delivery," he said indulgently. "Makes her read it, for one thing. No human being could resist a note tied to a rock and flung, so to speak, at one's feet."

He was not so complacent as he sounded, however. He had been taking a shower when the car drove past and he had not heard it. He had seen it later in the Adrians' drive, and started at once for the house, only to be too late.

"But what's it all about?" I wailed. "Who is he? It wasn't Ridge Chandler. He was bigger than Ridge. If he has to see her or communicate with her why not simply ring the doorbell?"

"Maybe he has his own reasons," he said evasively. "I told you once even a smart cop could lay an egg now and then. Maybe I'm not smart, for I think I may have laid one here. Only, damn it all, I can't get in touch with the fellow."

"You know who it is, don't you?"

"Look, sister," he said. "A lot of things have been going on around here. Some I understand, some I don't. The hell of a lot I don't. And I won't have you involved. Think that over, my dear."

He got up abruptly, stood undecided for a minute, and then stooped quickly and kissed me.

"Been wanting to do that for a long time," he said, and departed.

I was still sitting there in stunned amazement when Phil came out. O'Brien had taken the stone with him, so I could not show it, but he listened to my story with only a mild interest.

"She denied it, did she?" he asked when I had finished.

"Yes. Absolutely. She even laughed. Through the door, of course. She wouldn't open it."

"Well, don't let her get you, kid. She's doing all right. They say lunatics are always happy—in their own way, of course."

"Doctor Townsend says she's sane enough. He thinks she's had a psychic shock of some sort. And certainly she didn't stand on the drive and sling a stone at herself, Phil."

"Probably another lunatic," he said, and yawned. "Maybe they like company."

Perhaps I was on the verge of a good crying spell or perhaps he merely realized I was considerably unstrung. He lit a cigarette and leaned back in his chair.

"All right," he said, "I'm sorry. Only I don't like to see you losing weight and worrying. Let's look at this thing. If ever a woman was petted and coddled all her life it's Judith. She's what she's always been, spoiled and a trifle off center. Probably the shock was when someone took her rattle away when she was a baby!"

"That wouldn't make her terrified now. And she is. She's really afraid. That man tonight—"

He moved impatiently.

"I don't know anything about her private affairs. Maybe she has a lover. Who knows? Only remember this, Lois. You say she thinks someone wants to kill her. Well, maybe so, but look at the facts. She's been the beautiful Judith Chandler for twenty years, and she's still something to look at. Maybe when she left Ridge she meant to marry someone else, but he hasn't come through. Or maybe she changed her mind. She doesn't want him, after all. So she not only hides from him, she dramatizes the affair. Either she's his or nobody's. He may even be desperate enough to kill her. Second act curtain."

He yawned again and got up.

"That poor creature in the pool played right into her hands," he said. "Same color of hair and same build, so she

132

insists the fellow meant to kill her and got the wrong woman. Better get to bed, Lois, and stop fussing. She's having the time of her life."

I did not believe him. I was sure he did not believe himself. And when later events proved how wrong he had been I was too busy to remind him. I was, at different times of course, to be visiting both O'Brien and Judith, and of all places in the world, in the local hospital.

Chapter 14

Bill had not come in by midnight. As he seldom did, I was not uneasy. But I was not Phil, with his humor and his factual mind. I knew I would not sleep until O'Brien had explained just why he had run up the drive, or what warning he had had of trouble. He could not have heard Judith's scream, yet he had come pelting along as though all the fiends of hell were after him.

I wasn't a child, to be put off with a pat and a kiss, I thought indignantly. Or to be shown up as a liar at the inquest. He owed me something, and I intended to collect it.

His light was still on, and after an uneasy moment when I remembered the man with the rock, I decided to go down to the cottage. As an afterthought I took one of Father's old canes from the umbrella stand in the hall, and cautiously made my way down the drive.

I think the cane amused him.

"All armed for an attack, aren't you?" he said. "Well, come in. I'm not going to apologize for that impulsive act on the porch, if that's what you're after."

I took a leaf from Judith's bag of tricks.

"What impulsive act?" I said coolly.

He stared at me. Then he laughed.

"All right," he said. "Just the way no stone was fired

134

through your sister's window, isn't it? Only you might remember there was a stone, and I found it."

"I didn't come down for double talk. I want to know how that man got to the house tonight."

"Easy. His car was parked in the Adrian drive. I saw it there."

"Then you know who it was, don't you?"

"Let's say I have a theory about it. Remember Jennie's man, and a few other things. All I want is to lay hands on the fellow."

"You know that woman was murdered, don't you?"

He did not answer at once. He closed the two windows and drew my chintz curtains across them, picked up a pipe, and gave me a cigarette and lit it before he sat down.

"She was, yes," he said. "But I wasn't thinking only of her. Someone else may be in danger."

"You mean Judith?"

"Possibly. Certainly *she* believes it. I'm not sure."

"Doctor Townsend explains her state of mind as the result of a psychic shock, perhaps years ago. I can't think of anything of the sort. I can only remember how carefully she was raised. Until she made her debut she hardly moved without Mother or a nurse, or a governess. She went to a private school in town, but the car took her and called for her. Mother had a sort of fixation about her, and when she was dying, although I was only a youngster, she made me promise to look after her. Judith knows that. I think that's why she came here to The Birches."

"Any idea what your mother was afraid of?"

"She wasn't afraid exactly, but Judith was the family beauty. Then, too, she had been a difficult child. Mother might have been afraid she'd go off the rails somehow. As she has."

"The divorce, you mean?"

"That didn't bother Jude. She never really cared for Ridge Chandler. No. I think she was glad to be free. She was practically normal until we started east. She was going abroad as soon as she could book passage."

He thought that over for a moment or two, knocking out his pipe and refilling it. When he spoke again it was about the inquest.

"Sorry I let you in for that. Of course, I didn't know they had your prints. How did that happen?"

"I was an air-raid warden during the war. The police took all our fingerprints."

He nodded. It was very quiet. The only sounds were when once a sleepy hen gave a faint cluck in the chicken house or when now and then a car passed along the road. For there were a few cars now. Summer had come, and here and there a summer place had been opened. But O'Brien was not listening. He was still fiddling with his pipe, and his face looked unhappy.

"I've about reached the end of my rope," he said finally. "I need some help, and I think perhaps you can give it to me. Only I'll have to tell you a story, and go back a long way to do it."

He reached into the drawer and pulled out the clipping from the dead woman's bag, in its cellophane frame.

"It has to do with this," he said. "It doesn't sound important, does it? Yet it may be. It may mean not only this Madam X of ours was murdered. It may explain why. I've tried to trace her and failed. But I need help. In the first place, look at this."

He reached into the drawer again and pulled out a yellow scrap of paper. It was the return-trip half of a railroad ticket to a small town up the Hudson! I suppose I looked jolted, for he spoke quickly.

"Don't judge me yet, Lois," he said. "I had a reason, and a damned good one."

He gave me no chance to speak. He went right on.

"I've told you I'd always wanted to be a policeman," he said. "Maybe you think that's funny, but a lot of kids are like that. Anyhow I stuck. I flunked out of college to do it, and my family was furious, but in the end I got on the force.

"I guess I was a pretty obnoxious young punk at first. Because my people had some money I had the idea that God

136

had made me a little better than the other men. Then one day a Homicide man twice my age took me around the corner and knocked hell out of me. I was laying for him after that. I had a Lower East Side district, and I was prepared to shove him into the river whenever I got a chance. His name was Flaherty. Inspector Flaherty.

"He knew it, too, but he didn't let it bother him, and when there was an opening, he got me transferred to Centre Street in his department. He grinned when he sent for me.

"'I'll feel safer when I have you where I can see you,' he said. 'And you have the brains to make you a good cop, as well as the build of one. That's why you're here, O'Brien. I asked for you.'

"Well, you don't shove a man into the East River after a thing like that, and after the first few months I guess I would have let Flaherty tramp all over me. Most of what I know he taught me. He was hard as nails outside, but—oh, hell, I don't want to talk about him. He had only one ambition. He wanted to have a chicken farm when he retired. I guess that's the reason for the girls out there.

"I was still with him a year or so later when they found that girl in the clipping you've read. It wasn't my first murder, but it was bad enough. She'd been a pretty kid, and she had three or four younger sisters and brothers to support. She worked in a cheap store down there, and maybe she made some money on the side. You couldn't blame her. They had to eat.

"The district's changed since then. Not so many pushcarts on the street, for one thing. They sold everything from hot baked potatoes to men's pants and shoes. Now the traffic men have moved them back to the pavements or even into small stores. But it's still a messy place, washing and beddings hanging on fire escapes, and the kids staying out until all hours.

"The Preston kids—you've read that clipping: her name was Mollie Preston—were out until midnight that night. And when they came home she was dead on the floor, strangled. We had the hell of a time getting any story at all, what with the screams and all that. But a girl on the floor below said she saw a young fellow going up the stairs to the Preston flat that night, and that she heard a noisy quarrel. Her name was Kate Henry, and unless I'm crazy she's the woman your Bill found in the pool.

"It was Flaherty's case. I came into it because I'd learned shorthand. And Flaherty took it pretty hard. He'd known the girl since she was a baby.

"Well, it looked like an open-and-shut case. She'd been seeing a young law student from Columbia named Shannon— Johnny Shannon—and Kate Henry identified him in the line-up and before the grand jury. He admitted he'd been there that night, but only for a few minutes to call off a date. The girl was angry because he wouldn't stay, and she was pretty noisy about it. He said there was no quarrel and he claimed an alibi, but it didn't stand up, so he got a life sentence.

"It killed his mother. Only the funny thing is that Flaherty never believed he was guilty. Up to the time of the trial he kept working on the case. He found homes for the Preston children, but even after the trial he was convinced Kate Henry had lied.

"Kate had disappeared by that time. Then one day he told me he thought he had located her in a small town up the Hudson. He didn't tell me its name, except that it wasn't far from Poughkeepsie, and that he was going there the next day. Only he never got there. He was shot and killed on his way home that night."

He stopped, as though he did not want to go on.

"A good Joe," he said heavily. "The best ever. They don't make many like him. But the way it looks someone knew he was getting too close, so he was murdered."

He drew a long breath.

"Sorry. It's a long story, isn't it? But you had a right to understand. I don't want these local guys to gum things up. This is my case. In a way I've been on it ever since he died.

"I wanted to know who killed Flaherty. Maybe it's an obsession with me now. It was a long time ago," he added.

138

"You never knew him, or heard of him. But he was like a father to me, only more than most fathers. People knew he was fair, even the ones he sent up. He was shot because the next day he was going to that town up the Hudson, the town the dead woman came from.

"That's why I kept the ticket stub as well as the clipping," he said. "Flaherty is my case. So was Shannon, if he was innocent. I didn't want Fowler or any of the state cops going up there and spilling the beans. You'll notice nobody from there has claimed the body. That's suspicious in itself."

I sat gazing at the return-trip ticket in my hand. The town was probably thirty miles or more away, and I was bewildered. I was seeing him the day I had met him in town, when he had insisted on buying me a coke at the drugstore.

"Why did you come here?" I asked. "What have we to do with all this? None of us knew her, or Flaherty. Certainly not this Preston girl. I don't understand it."

"No," he said, "you wouldn't. You were pretty young at that time. Anyhow, what would you or your family know about a girl murdered in a tenement down on the East Side? Anyone could have killed the girl. She was that sort. All kinds of men visited her. As I said, Flaherty was out to prove the Shannon boy was innocent. Beyond that I think he didn't care."

"You still haven't said why you're here," I persisted.

He hesitated.

"It doesn't clear anything, Lois, but I'll tell you. I got an anonymous letter after I came back from Reno. It said Mrs. Chandler was in danger. She may have had one, too. It would account for a lot if she did. But the postmark was from Kate Henry's town, and I think she sent it."

"But why?" I asked. "Didn't it give any reason? Judith may have enemies. Lots of people don't like her. But to threaten her—"

"The letter wasn't a threat. It was a warning. Whoever sent it was trying to prevent trouble, not make it. You see, it's pretty well known I never gave up the Flaherty case. Let's say

139

Kate knew something about it. Maybe she was scared. Maybe she needed protection herself. I don't even know how she located me here, but it looks as though she had. She probably knew I had a car, too. She didn't ask Ed Brown to come back for her. But I never saw her that night. Personally I think she was followed here, attacked, and thrown into the pool."

I felt slightly dizzy and certainly confused.

"Who would have followed her? She came by train. That's pretty fast."

"She came on a local. Anybody in a car could beat her time. There's a damn good highway most of the distance, too."

"Then it has nothing to do with us," I said flatly. "Or at least with Judith. It doesn't explain her at all. Yet you think she may be in danger. You came here to watch her, didn't you? Why? Don't tell me she killed the Preston girl, or Flaherty. That's ridiculous. She was only seventeen."

"Kids that age do commit murder. But I don't think she ever killed anyone. No, this woman had some dangerous knowledge. Maybe her conscience troubled her, maybe she was afraid. That's as far as I go."

He got up and put the clipping into the drawer. Then he came over and put a hand on my shoulder.

"I'm wondering if a girl like you would be caring to help a bit," he said, lapsing into the brogue I had noticed on the train. "I'll tell you now it's beyond me. I've been to that town and all around it since I saw you last. No woman has disappeared, according to the police there. It's a dead end, in more ways than one."

"And I suppose," I said rather feebly, "that this town is where I come in?"

"That's where you come in, my girl. And only God knows how I need you."

Chapter 15

I suppose all those small towns up the Hudson River have a basic resemblance. There is a shabby and usually dirty railroad station, a warehouse or two and perhaps a factory by the tracks, and one business street with a movie house, a drugstore, a couple of groceries, and nearly always a beauty parlor, a doctor and a lawyer, and possibly a dentist, usually the offices upstairs over a shop.

This one was a little better. It had two such streets, including a woman's dress shop, a milliner, and a tobacconist, as well as a dozen or so small businesses, including a garage.

But it improved beyond the business section. There were houses neatly set in well-kept lawns, and I imagined that beyond them and up the hill there were some large estates. But I did not drive there. Whoever the woman was she almost certainly did not belong there.

I had our old car. I had left Phil at the station as usual, but I did not go home. It was Judith's day to see Doctor Townsend and I suppose she was raving, but I knew Bill and the Ark would look after her. Nevertheless, the whole excursion looked like a wild-goose chase to me. As I told O'Brien I had only one clue, the bleached hair, but he only laughed at me.

"For a girl who writes fiction you show a lamentable lack of imagination. What's the matter with her leaving her purse on the train and you finding it?"

"And keeping it all this time?"

"You were afraid to turn it in at the station. Somebody might take the money. So you watched the ads in the paper instead. You knew she came from here. There's the return ticket."

It sounded absurdly easy, put like that, but I was nervous nevertheless. Even the drive did not help much. I kept seeing that dreadful body at the end of the pool, the state police as well as Fowler and his men, and the crowd being held back along the road. I felt annoyed, too, at having let myself in for such an excursion. O'Brien's story about Flaherty had moved me the night before. He had been on the case for twenty years, which in itself was touching. But what had I to do with Flaherty, or for that matter the dead woman?

Perhaps it was suspicious that no one had claimed her, but how did I know it was? Maybe no one had missed her, or nobody cared. Or, again, she was supposed to be away on a visit. She could still have had the return ticket.

One thing was sure. If she lived in that neighborhood she had no car. I stopped at the garage for gas, and I went into my spiel at once. It was easy, for the pleasant young man who waited on me was curious about me.

"Don't live around here, do you?" he asked.

"No. I was just going through, but I meant to stop, anyhow."

"Know some folks?"

"Not exactly. You see, I found a woman's purse in the train the other day. No name in it and no papers, but it had a return ticket here."

"Lot of money in it?"

"Just a few dollars. She hasn't advertised it, so I kept it. I don't know her name, you see." I went on. "She was sitting across the aisle from me, a bleached blonde, maybe forty or so, in a black dress and a hat with a sort of wreath of flowers on it."

He had lost interest, however, either because of her age or

the amount.

"I wouldn't know," he said vaguely. "Half the women in this town could answer that description. Why don't you just forget it? If she wanted it she'd have advertised. Did you try the Lost and Found Department at Grand Central? She may have reported the loss there."

"Thanks, I hadn't thought of that."

He looked at me as though he thought my IQ was pretty low, and as he stood in the doorway watching me, I had to drive around for some time before I tried elsewhere. The conversation at both grocery stores followed practically the same lines, but I had kept my ace up my sleeve. That was the bleached hair and the beauty parlor. And there I struck pay dirt.

Gertrude—that was the name on the window, Gertrude's Beauty Shop—was busy when I went in. She was giving a permanent, but her young assistant was free. With inward qualms I asked her for a manicure, and seated at a small table received the usual disapproving query.

"Keep them pretty short, don't you?"

"I use a typewriter," I explained.

She glanced up at me quickly.

"Stenographer, eh?" she observed. "Well, the cuticle's pretty good, anyhow. I'll see what I can do."

And it was there, to the rasp of an emery board, that I got my first clue.

"Bleached hair?" she said. "Well, if she's from here, you can bet we did it. And that hat—Say, Gert," she called, "remember that bleach job you did last week. Old girl in the funny hat? Remember her name?"

"I should remember all the jobs like that I do. What's the idea?"

"Girl here says she left her purse on the train and she found it. Wants to give it back, only don't know who she is. Says the return ticket says she comes from here."

Gertrude, however, was convinced that the woman in question never left her purse anywhere. "Nor a half dollar, either," she added with some bitterness. But she was completely uninterested. "You might look in the appointment book, Edna," she said. "Not that I give a damn."

The manicure was better than I expected. I paid for it, added a tip, and suggested that Edna follow Gert's suggestion. She got a dog-eared small ledger from a desk drawer and with a long nail ran down lists of names for the past week. On a Monday she stopped.

"Listen, Gert," she said, "wasn't it Benjamin? Seems like that rings a bell. Didn't he run that tobacco shop before he died?"

Gert nodded indifferently.

"Guess that's right," Gert agreed. "Lives somewhere around here. Hair was a mess. She'd been doing it herself."

They had no address for her, however. I got it finally from one of the grocery stores I had visited previously. But the clerk observed that she was probably not at home.

"Didn't come in Saturday," he said. "Regular as clockwork, she was. Lost her husband a few months back. He left her plenty, but if that's her purse you found she's probably having a fit. She'd squeeze a quarter until the eagle screamed. Funny she didn't advertise."

He gave me her address. It was up the hill a half mile or so, a small white-framed house set back from the road, with a gate in a picket fence and a path to the front door. It sat alone, with the next houses some distance away, and screened by shrubbery, and as I got out of the car and opened the gate I saw a curtain moving at a window. I began to feel rather awkward. If someone lived there with her, my story was no good, and I would have to get out as best I could.

No one answered the bell, however, and as I stepped back and looked at the window I saw the reason. A huge black cat was on the sill, scratching at the glass and meowing wildly. And behind it the curtain was torn almost into shreds, as though by its claws. That the poor thing was desperate was obvious. Possibly it had been shut in when the Benjamin woman left, and it must have been starving, or dying of thirst.

Up to that time I had merely done what O'Brien wanted, managed to identify her and locate where she lived. The rest was up to him. The cat, however, changed things. I couldn't leave it there to die. It was scratching at the glass again, its big eyes fixed on me appealingly, and when I tried the front door, I could hear it in the hall, still yowling.

The door was locked, of course. I went around the house to the rear, where there was a small porch, but that door was locked, too, and I felt fairly discouraged, especially since the cat had followed through the house and was scratching frenziedly at the back door. I looked around, but there was no one in sight, so I tried a kitchen window. It was fastened but rather shaky, and I needed something with which to pry it open. There was nothing in sight but a garbage can, so at last I went back to the car, got a tire iron from the heterogeneous mass I call the tools and, praying I had not been seen, went back to the window.

The cat was there, on the sink. It seemed to know what I was doing, too, for now it was quiet and watchful. I had expected it to rush out once the window was open, but it did not. Instead it ran to an empty pan and equally empty water bowl on the floor by the stove, and waited for me to co-operate. I filled the bowl from the cold-water faucet, and it drank delicately, after the manner of all cats, but steadily and for a long time, giving me time to look around.

The Benjamin woman had been a good housekeeper. The kitchen was neat, the linoleum on the floor worn but clean, and a row of tea towels had been washed and hung up to dry. There was a door to a small dining-room, with a drooping fern on the table, four chairs, and a china closet rather sparsely furnished with dishes. I did not go to the front room at once. The cat was brushing against my feet, and I knew it was hungry, so I went back to the kitchen. I found a can of salmon in a cupboard and opened it. The cat was on the table before I could put it in the pan, so I emptied it onto the plate, and it was half gone before I could rinse out the can.

I was increasingly uneasy. Not only had I broken into the house, but my inquiries in the town might have aroused interest in the missing woman. And not only that. My car was sitting at the gate. I thought resentfully that O'Brien would never have left it there. He would have parked it elsewhere and walked unobtrusively to the house. Well, let him do it, then. I had attended to the cat. Now all I wanted was to get out and away from there.

But black cats are bad luck. When I looked out the front window a half-dozen school kids were standing around it and eying the house.

"She's back!" one of them yelled. "The cat's gone."

"How do you know it's her? She hasn't got a car."

"Well, somebody brought her. That's easy."

In time, however, they wandered on, and I stiffened my shaky knees and prepared to leave. It is due to what Bill calls my gluttonous curiosity that I did not. For, after all, the woman whose home this was was dead. I had been sure of that as soon as I saw the cat. She had left her house expecting to return either that night or the next morning.

Instead she had died in our pool.

The front room was a parlor. It had the unused look of such rooms in small houses, with a fan of paper in the empty fireplace, a suite of overstuffed furniture, a sofa and three or four chairs, and an old-fashioned marble-topped table. There was only one incongruity, a roll-topped desk, closed but not locked. I don't know why I opened it. I was tired and hungry. I had a long drive back, and no business whatever being where I was. But I walked to it and rolled up the front as though no black cat, fed and grateful, had been rubbing against my ankles.

It looked innocent enough at first. Certainly it was tidy. A block of unused billheads announcing *Walter Benjamin, Tobaccos* had been stuck in one of the pigeonholes, and there was a photograph of an elderly and bearded gentleman who was, I presumed, the said Walter beside them. Loosely in another compartment were a few receipted bills, one for a black dress from the village shop, several bankbooks, and two or three clippings. I glanced into the bankbooks. To my amazement they showed a balance of well over thirty thousand dollars in a New York savings bank, the deposits made almost twenty years ago, and with apparently no withdrawals since that time.

I stood staring at it. Sometime, somewhere, Mr. Walter Benjamin had had a windfall. In any event he had left his widow a considerable estate. If she owned the house and had sold the tobacco business, she was comfortably off. I thought O'Brien would be interested in the bankbooks as well as the unframed photograph, and I slid all of them into my purse.

The clippings seemed unimportant. They were largely local and New York notices of his death, the latter merely announcements in the obituary columns. I was standing with them in my hand when the doorbell rang, and it so jolted me that I dropped them also in my bag. I knew I was trapped. I had only time to close the desk before it rang again, and I had to open the front door.

There was a woman on the steps. She was in a house dress, a middle-aged stoutish person who eyed me with considerable suspicion.

"Oh!" she said. "I—has Mrs. Benjamin come home? My boy says she has."

"I'm afraid not," I said, recovering as best I could. "There's no one here but the cat and me. Why? Has she been away?"

"She's been gone for days. I got sort of worried. Not that we were ever friendly. If you know her you know she doesn't make friends easy. But the milkman said no one was taking in the bottles, so I stopped them. She may not like it, but it seemed such a waste."

"I'm sure it's all right," I told her, and once again went into the story about the purse and the return ticket.

"So I stopped in to get a manicure, and when I said I thought her hair was newly bleached they sent me here. They thought they remembered her."

She was still suspicious, however, until I told her about the cat and showed her the torn curtain.

"I declare," she said. "I forgot all about him. She thought the world of that Tom of hers. Maybe the children saw him, but you know what kids are. That curtain's ruined. She'll have a fit."

"You say she isn't very neighborly. Do you mean she is quarrelsome?"

"Not exactly, but she and that old husband of hers were no mixers. He did pretty well with his business—tobacco, it was—but he had all sorts of things on the side. Pipes and cigarette cases and lighters. Magazines, too. But he had a bad heart, and he was too stingy to buy a car. I always said this hill would kill him, and it did."

"She's a widow, then? I wouldn't have thought so. She wore a flowered hat."

"She doesn't believe in mourning. They were out in Indiana, visiting his sister, and he just fell over. I don't believe she's grieving much, wherever she is."

"Then you have no idea where she went when she left?"

"Didn't even know she was gone until the milkman told me."

I showed her the kitchen window and she said her husband would fix it. Also she would take the cat until Mrs. Benjamin came home, and at last I was free to get into the car and start home. I had eaten nothing since breakfast, but somehow I was not hungry. I was seeing Mrs. Benjamin at the end of our pool, her newly bleached hair about her face, and her thirty thousand-odd dollars in a New York savings bank.

They could not help her now. Nothing could help her. But why had she come to The Birches? What did she know that caused someone to kill her?

148

Chapter 16

It was, however, merely the beginning of what was to be an unpleasant day: my job of housebreaking, my near discovery by the woman next door, and the long tiresome trip home. For Judith was in a furious temper when I got there.

There had been no sign of O'Brien at his cottage, and as his car was gone, I drove straight to the house.

Helga and Jennie were having tea and toasted muffins at the kitchen table, and I sat down with them. I was still there, eating ravenously, when Judith stormed in.

"So here you are!" she said nastily. "Perhaps you'll tell me why you chose to go off and leave me this morning. You knew I was going to the city."

"You had Bill," I said. "And anyhow the car is Phil's and mine. I don't have to account to you for where I go."

"That rattletrap of Bill's! And he drives like a lunatic."

"Well, he got you there and got you back, apparently."

"No thanks to you. And I'll remind you I'm paying my way here, including the gasoline for the car. I have a right to expect decent treatment, and what do I get? Rotten food, everyone spying on me, pretending people throw rocks at me at night! I was a damn fool ever to come here."

"The food's as good as you'll get anywhere," Helga said indignantly.

"I notice you do all right by yourselves!"

Both of the women had risen when she came in, something they never did for me, but she ignored them completely. For the first time since my childhood I saw her in what Helga called one of her tantrums. She picked up the plate of muffins from the table and flung it, cakes and all, at the stove. Then she turned on me.

"What were you doing today? You were out with O'Brien, weren't you?"

"Certainly not. I haven't seen him."

Under her make-up she was white with anger.

"You're plotting something against me. Oh, I'm not blind. I've seen you slipping in and out of his cottage. You were there until all hours last night, and God knows how many others. An Irish cop! And don't tell me he isn't a cop. It's written all over him. A cop!" she repeated shrilly. "You sicked the police on me, and I won't have it."

She picked up another plate and was about to throw it at me when Helga went into action. She caught the plate with one hand, and with the other she slapped Judith in the face. It was a real slap, too. It almost knocked her down. Certainly it surprised her. She stared hard at Helga and then at me, and suddenly the wild look was gone.

"I'm sorry," she said, and dropping into a chair put her head down on the table and began to cry, deep choking sobs which shook her whole body.

Helga looked at me.

"I had to do it," she said. "I did it when she was a child, too." Then she moved over and put a calloused old hand on Judith's lovely hair. "It's all right, Judy. Don't cry, darling. Don't cry."

I belong to a different generation, I suppose. The old soothing methods do not occur to us. We don't like our bruises patted or kissed. And our usual answer to any emergency is a drink. At any rate I shot out of the kitchen, got Phil's decanter of brandy, and brought it in with a glass. Judith was still crying, but more quietly.

"Here's some brandy, Judy," Helga said. "Just take a sip of it. It'll help. You're worn out, darling, and scared, too. Just a little taste now, for old Helga's sake. And, Lois, if you'll fix her bed, Jennie and I will get her upstairs."

I knew it was a sign-off. Helga wanted to get rid of me, and I was glad to go. I went up to Judith's room and after turning down her bed I filled a hot-water bottle—a relic of my air-warden lessons—and put it between the sheets. Then I retreated to my nursery, and to my utter amazement burst into tears myself. I was still crying, face down on the bed, when Helga came in.

She came over and stood beside me.

"No use crying over spilled milk, Lois," she said. "She probably won't even remember what happened."

I managed to sit up. Helga got some tissues from my bed table and handed them to me.

"I'm not crying about what she said," I told her. "I'm crying because I'm so damned sorry for her."

"You'd be sorrier if you'd taken off her clothes," she retorted. "She's nothing but skin and bones. She's been padding her breasts and hips so she could wear her things and we'd not notice. I'll bet she don't weigh more than a hundred pounds."

"What is it, Helga? Haven't you any idea what's scaring her?"

"I can think of a lot of things," she said evasively. "From the day she was a baby. I wouldn't try to see her yet, Lois. I gave her one of her sleeping-pills, and she's best let alone."

She stood looking across the room, with the geese and frolicking lambs on the walls and my typewriter covered on its table.

"How's the book coming?"

"Book?" I said bitterly. "You don't write books in a lunatic asylum."

"She's not crazy, Lois."

"Then I'm about to be."

I doubt if she even heard me. She turned and went out, and I could hear her creaking down the stairs.

I lay back on my bed. It had been a long day and a wretched one: the long drive, the breaking into the Benjamin house and being caught there, and Judith's strange outburst. All, I thought resentfully, because of a newspaper clipping and a man named Flaherty.

What did Flaherty matter to me? Or the fact that O'Brien had loved him like a father? I had got myself out on a limb for no good reason whatever. Even O'Brien was not sure the Benjamin woman had anything to do with that dead-and-gone case. Yet she had been murdered. Murdered and then thrown helplessly into our pool.

Why had she come there? To see O'Brien after her previous failure? Why then have Ed Brown leave her at the Adrian's drive and have to break through dense shrubbery on a dark night?

I wondered what my woman detective, yclept Sara Winters, would have done under the same circumstances. Probably made fun of the regular police and at the end triumphantly produced the real criminal, someone like Phil, for instance, whom nobody had ever suspected.

For some reason that apocryphal case cheered me. I got up and dressed for dinner, putting on the new pale-blue silk I had paid for with part of Ridgely's check, and was rewarded when, over cocktails in the living-room, Bill burst in and gave a loud wolf call.

"Who's the family beauty now?" he inquired. "You're a knockout, Lois."

But he was full of Judith's excursion to the station in the Ark, and at the table he related it with gusto.

"She said it would probably fall to pieces on the way, and she made me dust the seat before she got in. As to speed, I could have kicked a barrel faster." He glanced at Phil, who was surveying with disgust the tapioca pudding in front of him.

"See here," he said after Jennie left the room, "who's she afraid of? Don't tell me she isn't. She watched one man for ten minutes before she'd get out of the car. Then he turned around, and I guess she saw it was all right. Anyhow she began to breathe again. So did I."

He wolfed down his dessert, lit a cigarette, and sat back.

"I don't get it," he said. "Locking herself in her room, sticking in the house this hot weather, and making someone go with her when she walks out at night. It doesn't make sense. What's the idea, if any?"

Phil had apparently forgotten the tapioca, for he grinned.

"You don't know your Aunt Judith very well," he said. "I imagine she's dramatizing something or other. A sort of play, with herself as the star. Maybe Ridgely Chandler is the villain. I wouldn't know. Man at the station look like Ridge?"

"No, Ridge is short. This fellow was tall."

"That wouldn't make any difference to her. She has to have a villain. That's all."

He glanced at me complacently, but Bill was not having any.

"Look here," he said, "do you mean she has a persecution complex? That's not so good, is it?"

"Whatever she has I imagine she's enjoying it," Phil said cheerfully. "Gives her the center of the stage again. She's used to it, you see. She's been the society editors' baby for years."

I can look back on that evening now with a certain amount of perspective: Judith locked in her room and shaken by terrors we did not understand, Phil's easy acceptance of her fears, and young Bill's bewilderment.

I got up and blew out the candles.

"Let's talk about something else," I said. "I'm fed to the teeth, if either one of you cares. Only don't let Phil fool you, Bill, Judith is scared, and plenty."

Phil was free that night, and Bill's Janey was otherwise occupied. To my annoyance I found myself with two men on my hands, and no chance to go to the cottage. The result was canasta, at which I lost three dollars before Bill began to yawn.

153

It was half past eleven by that time, but from the porch I saw that O'Brien's light was on, and by midnight when the house finally settled down I got my bag and started down the drive.

The night had turned cool, so I took Judith's black cape from the powder room where she kept it and wrapped it around me. It was very dark, no moon and no stars, but as I knew every foot of the way I was walking fast when I heard a movement among the rhododendrons by the pool. The next moment someone caught hold of me and held a hand over my mouth.

"Don't try to yell," he said roughly. "If you do I'll drop you in the pool. We're going to have this out if it's the last thing you ever do."

He jerked off my cape and to my utter amazement picked me up like a child, ducked into the shrubbery and toward the pool. I did not dare to scream. He was strong and muscular, and I realized he had meant what he said. At the bench, however, he paused.

"You she-devil!" he said. "I ought to drown you, but I need you first. And you're going to talk. Believe me, you're going to talk and talk fast. You know what I want. You got my note all right."

I had got my breath by that time.

"What note?" I gasped. "I don't know what you mean." He was certainly startled. His hold on me relaxed, although I was still in his arms.

"Good God," he said. "Who are you?"

"Lois Maynard," I said, "and if you don't put me down I'll scream my head off."

He seemed as stunned as I was, but he still held onto me. Then unexpectedly he laughed.

"All right, scream!" he said, and pitched me into the pool.

It was the deep end, and I went in with my mouth wide open. I swallowed a lot of water before I fought my way to the surface and could swim enough to get out. Even that was not easy. The skirt of my new dress wrapped itself around my legs, and I was still coughing and choking. I stood there, dripping and shocked

154

as well as outraged, until I heard a car starting and moving off, and I realized he was gone.

Somehow I staggered to O'Brien's cottage and knocked at the door. His face was a study as he saw me, and I must have almost fallen, for he caught me up and carried me to a chair. He gave me a drink and put a match to his fire before he let me speak. Then he said, "Don't tell me you fell into that pool. I don't believe it."

"I was pitched in."

"I see. Bill playing tricks, or what?"

"No. I suppose it was the man who threw the stone through Judith's window. He picked me up from the drive and carried me through the shrubbery to the bench by the pool. He said I had got his note all right, and I was to talk. To talk a lot. So I asked him what he meant. I guess my voice scared him. He asked who I was, and when I told him he pitched me into the pool."

"Rather drastic, wasn't it?" He was being calm, but he didn't fool me. His face was set as he filled his pipe. "I suppose he escaped again?"

"He had a car. I heard him start it."

And then he said something which almost brought me out of my chair.

"The crazy bastard!" he muttered. "The poor crazy bastard!"

I stared at him.

"You know who it was, don't you?"

"I have an idea. I could be wrong."

He had been standing on the hearth, with a dressing-gown over a pair of slacks, and for all the attention I got after that I might have been a stuffed codfish.

"How long ago was all this?"

"I don't know. I swallowed a lot of water, and I had to swim the length of the pool. Ten minutes maybe, or more."

He did not say anything. He went to the telephone and called a number in town. When he got it he lost no time.

155

"'Try road into town from here," he said, "and be quick about it. Put somebody by the reservoir, too. Better block the road— Oh, hell, put your own car across it, man! Just see that you get him.'"

Then for the first time he really looked at me. I was not a pretty sight, with my hair in dank strings, one of my white pumps missing, and my new dress a complete wreck.

"Of course, I had to wear the best thing I own," I said sourly. "I don't think the damned thing was meant to wash."

He roused at that. He pulled my chair closer to the fire and threw another log on it.

"You'll have to get out of it," he said. "Better strip off everything. No use your taking pneumonia. What else have you got on?"

In case he expected a maidenly blush from me he was disappointed.

"I'm wearing exactly one slip, one bra, and one pair of panties," I said. "I'll keep the slip and let the others go."

If he recognized the paraphrase he did not show it. Instead he simply pulled my dress off over my head and wrung it out over the hearth.

"Get out of the rest," he said. "I'll turn my back if you're too modest. Better hang them on the fire screen to dry."

We made quite a picture when I finished, I in my low-cut white slip, with my dress, panties, and bra draped on the screen. I'm afraid I giggled, thinking of Judith that afternoon. O'Brien saw nothing funny in the situation.

"I suppose you didn't get a good look at this fellow?"

"I never really saw him at all. He seemed pretty strong."

"You think he mistook you for your sister?"

"He mistook me for somebody. Not necessarily for Judith. Anyhow, what has Jude to do with all this? Don't tell me at the age of eighteen or so she shot and killed your Flaherty! I don't think she's ever owned a gun in her life, or fired one."

He smiled, for the first time.

"Still the loyal little sister!" he said. "Of course she hasn't.

156

In fact, I think it might be as well if she did have one. I don't like this thing tonight."

"Maybe you think I do!" I said.

He only nodded, which annoyed me.

"Why do you think he thought I was Judith?" I asked. "You do, don't you? Something's really threatening her, and that's why you're watching the grounds. It's this man, isn't it? Why don't you tell me who he is? What is the danger? I have a right to know. After all, she's my sister."

"Of course," he said. "Only I'm not certain. There are things I still don't understand. When I get those straightened out— The man tonight wasn't Chandler, was it?"

"No," I said. "Absolutely not."

"What about today?" he said, as if he had suddenly thought of it. "Did you learn anything?"

I nodded. Suddenly I remembered.

"My bag! It must be in the pool. I know I had it when he threw me in."

"Anything in it?"

"Everything," I said despairingly. "Bankbooks, her husband's picture, the works! And they're gone."

"Who was she?"

"She's a widow. Her name was Benjamin, Selina Benjamin. There was a cat in the window. That's how I found her."

"Of course. A cat. That explains everything," he said. "When you've stopped scaring me to death you might tell me about it. What did you find out from her house? And are you sure it's the woman from the pool? We can't afford to make a mistake there."

It had never occurred to me that I might have been mistaken; that a bleached-blond woman named Benjamin might have left her home and her cat and been killed by a taxicab in the city. Or had merely chosen to disappear, leaving thirty thousand dollars in the bank. And as I told my story I could see he agreed with me.

"We'll have to get an identification, of course," he said.

"The cat woman may be anybody. But what's this about all that money?"

"It was deposited a long time ago. That's all I know."

"And the name of the bank?"

"I didn't notice."

He looked rather disgusted.

"You'd better stay here and dry out," he said. "Take your stockings off. They're soaking. I'd better make a try for the bag, although there's only a remote chance I can find it in the dark. Where did you go in?"

I told him it was the deep end, and he grunted. But he disappeared into his bedroom and when he came back he wore only his bathing-trunks. Annoyed as I still was I had to admit he was the fine figure of a man, broad shouldered and narrow hipped. He was muscular, too. Not muscle-bound. Just strong. But he had a scar on his chest I had not noticed the morning at the pool. He almost dared me to mention it now.

"If the telephone rings, get the message," he said. "And lock the door behind me. I may be some time. Only for God's sake be sure who it is before you open it."

He put another log on the fire. Then he was gone and I was alone. I smoked one of his cigarettes and tried to think. Nothing was clear, however, except that he considered Judith's danger was real. But I had had a long day, and the fire was warm and comforting. I put my head back and was about to go comfortably asleep when a noise in the kitchen aroused me.

I had not dreamed it. As I jerked my head up, it was repeated, and for all the world it sounded like a chicken shaking its feathers.

It *was* a chicken shaking its feathers. Sitting on a nice small roost in a corner, with a newspaper spread beneath it as a sanitary measure, was Henrietta. I stood in the doorway and laughed, while Henrietta inspected me, first with one eye and then with the other. I had no idea then that the determined little lady was to play her own part in our mystery. As it was, she went back to sleep, and it was not long before I followed her example.

It was two o'clock in the morning before a rap on the door roused me. It was O'Brien, and big and strong as he was he looked exhausted as well as blue with cold. He did not say anything. He threw my other pump on the hearth to dry, flung my sodden bag on the table, poured himself a huge slug of Scotch and drank it straight, asked if the telephone had rung, and when I said no disappeared into his room. When he came back he was wearing his old dressing-gown over his pajamas, and he looked better.

"Sorry," he said, "but I'm no fish. I'd about given up when I found the thing. How about some coffee? You probably need it. I know I do. And leave the bag. I want to open it myself."

The coffee tasted wonderful, strong and black. It stimulated me as no whisky could have done, but as a result of waiting for it, it was half past two before at last he carefully opened the bag. As it was leather the contents were wet but not sodden. And to my surprise it contained not only the bankbooks and the photograph but a half dozen or so newspaper clippings. Then I remembered the woman pounding at the door, and having my hands full of things.

"They were in the desk," I said. "I must have picked them up, and when that woman rang the doorbell I dropped them in my bag. I haven't looked at them since. I just forgot I had them."

"Mrs. Benjamin evidently had the clipping habit," he said. "People do, you know. Like collecting stamps. Let's dry them out, and the bankbooks, too."

He did so carefully in front of the fire, and it was the bankbooks he inspected first. He made a note of the amount of the deposits, and their dates, but when he glanced at the clippings the first one he saw was about the woman herself, and there was no doubt of her identity. It was from a local newspaper. It showed her picture, and according to it she had won a prize at a charity card party. O'Brien showed it to me.

"Our woman all right," he said. "Good job, Lois. You'd

make a pretty good detective yourself."

"It was easy," I said modestly. "I just thought what Sara Winters would have done, and did it."

"Winters? Who the hell is Sara Winters?"

"She's the woman detective I write about."

He snorted and went back to the clippings.

Among the others there was the obituary notice of a Walter Benjamin, aged sixty-four. It was brief, and dated some months before. It did not give the place of death. And there was one which O'Brien held for a time and then reluctantly handed to me. It was one of the articles about Judith's divorce and her return to The Birches, and a picture of her, evidently taken previously, with a gay party at the Stork Club.

I sat staring at it.

"Rather interesting, isn't it?" he said. "Your sister says she didn't know her, never saw her. But this Benjamin woman cuts her picture out of the paper and keeps it. What do you make of it?"

I was trying to think.

"I think it's very unlikely Judith would know her," I said. "She's lived for years in that little town."

The telephone rang just then and he answered it. Someone was speaking at length.

"I see," he said finally. "Well, better luck next time."

As usual, he refused to explain further, and when I had put on my dress and my shrunken pumps and gathered up the rest, he took me back to the house. I was fairly confident that he had his gun in his pocket. He carried a flashlight, too, and when he reached the shrubbery he stopped and examined it. There were some broken branches and a few fresh leaves on the ground, which bore out my story but told nothing else. He seemed reluctant to leave me at the porch, however.

"Who locks this huge barn of a place at night?" he said.

"The last one to go to bed, although we don't bother much about the windows. We've never had any trouble."

"It might be a good idea to take a few elementary

precautions," he said rather dryly. "It's more than possible that your Mrs. Benjamin was pretty deliberately murdered. It's not a nice thought."

There was a moment then when he stood looking down at me, and there was a softer tone to his voice.

"You see," he said, "I don't want anything to happen to you, Lois. You're—well, you're a damned nice girl."

He waited until he heard me lock the front door before I heard him going down the drive. He walked lightly for so big a a man, but I felt certain that he was not going back to the cottage.

He did not. I was barely up the stairs when I heard his car start and drive furiously toward town. I forgot about him immediately, however, for Judith's door was open and her room empty.

Chapter 17

She had been in bed. It was mussed, the sheet thrown back, and the book she had been reading lay on the floor. I went panicky for a second or so. If that man was still in the grounds and he found her—

Judith, however, was not out in the grounds. As I stood there I heard faint sounds overhead, and realized where she was. The house has only two stories, but above them are the huge attics where ever since the place was built everything was stored: the usual old trunks, broken furniture, and even ancient toys. It was years since I had been there, since the time when I was getting out Phil's battered hobbyhorse for young Bill, and I doubted if Judith had ever been up there at all.

She was there now. There was a candle on top of a box, and she was kneeling on the floor before a small old-fashioned trunk. Its lid was up, and I shall never forget her face when she turned her head and saw me. I don't think she could speak at first. Then:

"What do you mean, following me around?" she demanded irritably.

"I heard you, and your room's empty. If you're looking for something, maybe I can help you."

She slammed the trunk lid and got up.

"It was hot and I couldn't sleep," she said, more quietly.

"Mother had a lot of my wedding pictures, so I thought I'd look for them."

I remembered what she had said about Doctor Townsend not so long before, and I wanted to say something about setting forth the funeral baked meats for the marriage feast, or whatever it is. I did not, of course. She was still pale, but whatever she was looking for it was not the huge expensive photographs of her wedding. The trunk in front of her I knew was filled with old snapshots taken hither and yon, but nothing else.

"I think there are a few in the library somewhere," I told her. "I'll look in the morning."

She got to her feet and picked up the candle. Without make-up and with a glaze of cold cream on her face and neck she looked her full age that night, and older. But I let her get back to her room and wash her hands, which were filthy with the dust of years, before I asked her what I felt I had to ask. She was rubbing some sort of lotion on her hands when I spoke.

"There was a man in the grounds tonight, Judith," I said. "I'm sure he thought I was you. He grabbed me and started to carry me off. When he found he'd made a mistake he pitched me into the pool. Do you know who he is?"

She stared at me. My hair and my wrinkled dress told her I was telling the truth, and at first I thought she was going to faint. She did not, however.

She simply sat down on the bench in front of her dressing-table. The bottle of lotion fell and spilled all over the place, but she paid no attention to it.

"Yes, I know who it was," she said, in a dead voice. "It's someone who intends to kill me."

"Why? Why should anyone want to kill you?" I insisted. "What did you do, Judith? It must have been something."

And then, sick as she looked, she gave me a queer ironic smile.

"What did I do?" she said. "Well, for one thing I married Ridgely Chandler."

"It wasn't Ridge, Judith," I said.

"Of course not," she snapped. "He wouldn't have the guts."

It made no sense. Even now it does not make a great deal. But I got nothing more from her that night, nor did I get much sleep when I finally went to bed. Again and again I went over what I knew. What O'Brien had said about her danger, and her own fears ever since Reno. But why would anyone intend to kill her? What had she done, petted and cared for all her life as she had been? And what had she meant about marrying Ridgely?

There had certainly been no murder in the man who had stopped me in the drive, although his voice had been hard, almost fierce. But if it was Judith he was after, he had not meant to kill her. They were to have something out. She was to talk, but about what? And why had he killed the Benjamin woman, if he did?

Sitting up in bed with a cigarette and getting more and more wakeful every minute, I could not see how she belonged, or even why she had come to the pool. To whom could she have been a menace, that middle-aged woman with her clean kitchen, her big black cat, and her small fortune in the bank?

I watched the sun come up that morning. My room faced the east, and finally I got up and drew the shade, to try and get a few hours' sleep. I could see the edge of the pool from the window, and after a moment or so I saw O'Brien there. He was sitting quiet on the bench, smoking his pipe, and I was pretty sure he had been there—or near there—all night.

I had my second talk with Doctor Townsend that afternoon. I had no appointment, and the Robey woman looked annoyed. However, he seemed to be free and, I thought, even glad to see me.

"I've been worried about your sister," he said. "She was rather strange yesterday. Has anything happened?"

"That depends on how you look at it, Doctor. She blew up when she got home. I wondered if anything here upset her."

"I don't know," he said thoughtfully. "Perhaps I probed a

bit too deep. You have to remember what my work is. Not to use too many technical terms, the theory is to bring any subconscious worries to the conscious mind; in other words, to make the patient dig up the buried anxiety and face it. Mrs. Chandler refuses to do it."

"But it's there—the worry, or whatever you call it?"

"It's there, yes."

"Would that account for her hysterical spell yesterday?"

He didn't answer immediately. He pushed a cigarette box at me, and over the desk lit one for me. When he sat back he smiled.

"I'm sorry it happened to you," he said. "You've been having a bad time for months, haven't you? As to yesterday, let's say a neurotic temperament under strain will occasionally blow up. It's a sort of mental explosion. Usually when it's over it's over."

"Our cook, Helga, has been with us for years. She thinks Judith doesn't remember much about them afterward."

"That's possible. It relates to something we call the censor, the thing that works while we sleep, and raises hell with our dreams. Has it ever occurred to you that she regrets her divorce?"

"Never," I said definitely. "She detests him. I don't know just why. He's behaved very well. And," I added, "you have to remember he's a Chandler. They always behave well, the Chandlers, summer and winter, cold or hot, up and down and sideways."

He laughed a little, but when I told him about my experience of the night before his expression changed.

"I see," he said. "Well, it's been apparent all along she is afraid of something or somebody. This man wanted her to talk. That's it, isn't it?"

"It's what he said. She'd talk or he'd kill her."

He sighed and put out his cigarette.

"We're not infallible, you know," he said. "A shock or long-continued strain is often mistaken for a neurosis, and I gather this man is a fact, not a delusion."

"He is, unless you think I went swimming in my best summer outfit."

"Then it changes things considerably, doesn't it? You see, it's easy to say people have delusions, or persecution or what have you. A paranoid psychosis, if you like. I was inclined to think that of your sister. But now she has produced what looks like a real neurosis and is actually a fact. You say she won't explain him. Who he is? Why he wants her to talk, and what about?"

"Only to say he means to kill her. Period."

He opened her file and examined it. Then he slapped it shut.

"Just how much do you remember about her marriage?" he asked. "You were—what? Seven or eight, weren't you? Children often have surprisingly good memories."

"I don't remember much, but my sister Anne says she found her that morning kicking her wedding dress on the floor. It doesn't sound particularly ecstatic, does it?"

"Yet she stayed married for twenty years."

"If you call it that. Personally I don't think she was really married after the first week."

"And you're still sure her husband has nothing to do with this terror of hers?"

"Not directly, although she said a curious thing last night, after I found her in the attic and she said someone meant to kill her. I asked her what she had done to be so afraid, and she smiled and said, 'For one thing, I married Ridgely Chandler.'"

"That's interesting," he said. "Did she intimate that he killed the woman in the pool?"

"Absolutely not. After all, why should he? Even if he thought she was Judith? He had had a good many years with her, plenty of time for a murder if he wanted it. So he waits until he's free of her and then knocks her out with a golf club!"

He was very thoughtful when I left. He seemed puzzled, and I wondered what his science did for him against a problem like this. I daresay he went home and ate a hearty dinner with a wife he was fond of, saw his children, if any, and played bridge or went to the movies later. But I carried a heavy load back with me.

It was on the train I considered Father's suicide, and wondered if it could have been the psychic shock he had mentioned. It seemed impossible. Judith was only seventeen or so at the time, and not a particularly devoted daughter; and I at seven had been shut in the nursery of the city house and knew nothing about it. I had missed him, of course.

My nurse would not talk about it, so I would slip down to Helga in the kitchen.

"Where's Daddy, Helga?"

"He's gone away, darling. Don't you worry about him."

"But I want him. He didn't say good-by to me."

"He doesn't like saying good-bys. You know that. Here's some cookies. You'd better eat them here, so you don't get scolded."

There had been a butler at that time. I remembered him only as a rather dark sardonic person. He and Helga did not get along, and my only real picture of him was when Mother was going to Arizona, and he was carrying her bags and Judith's to a taxicab. I did not remember him after that. I suppose he left with the rest when the house was closed.

O'Brien's car was gone when I drove in past the cottage, so was Bill's jalopy, and Phil and I ate dinner alone. With Judith still in seclusion, it was my first chance to talk to Phil in several days, and I asked him what he remembered about Father's death.

"Why bring that up?" he said. "It just happened, like plenty of others that year. The poor old boy was broke. That's all."

"Doctor Townsend spoke about some sort of psychic shock for Judith," I persisted. "I wondered if that was it."

"It was a shock for everybody. I think Judith fainted when they told her, but as I remember she was going through one of her queer spells at the time, anyhow; having a hysterical fit one minute and the next shut in her room and looking lost and forlorn. I think that's why Mother whisked her off to Arizona."

"She wasn't engaged to Ridgely then?"

"No. At least I don't think so. Not until they came back."

"Look, Phil, did she want to marry Ridge?"

"She married him, didn't she? Nobody pushed her to the altar—although Mother might have given her a shove. She was pretty keen about the match."

With some difficulty I got him back to Father's death. He seemed surprised how little I knew about it.

"Of course, you were only a kid, but I suppose you know when he did it?"

"After a dinner party, wasn't it?"

He nodded, gave a look at the canned peaches Jennie offered him, and waved her away.

"I was there," he said after she had disappeared. "I hadn't gone back to college. It was the Christmas holidays, you know. The party was over and I had started to undress when the butler of the moment—I forget his name—rapped at my door. He said there was a police officer downstairs, so I put on a dressing-gown and went down. It seems the night watchman had been making his rounds and heard the shot. Anne and Martin were living with us at the time. Martin had gone broke after the crash, and I seem to remember Anne was pregnant. Anyhow I got Martin, and we went down in the police car. There was nothing to do, of course."

"You're sure he killed himself?"

He stared at me.

"Certainly I'm sure. He left a note for Mother on his desk. That was queer, too," he said reminiscently. "I opened it, with the police all around, but it wasn't just what you'd expect. All he said was that he could not and would not do anything against his conscience, even to save her pride. I told Martin about it, and we tore it up. Mother was up against enough without that."

"It doesn't sound like him, Phil. He was never cruel. And

what did he mean? Why his conscience?"

"Well, he was broke. Maybe she had some not-too-honest idea for getting money, like robbing a bank! But you didn't live through those times," he added patronizingly. "Plenty of men were doing the same thing."

It was not until we were having coffee on the porch that I told him of my experience of the night before. It startled him out of his usual equanimity.

"For God's sake!" he said. "Why didn't you call the police?"

"He was gone by the time I got out of the pool. I heard his car start."

"What's this about his mistaking you for Judith?"

"She says so. She says he means to kill her."

He took a minute or so to think about that, placing his empty cup in its saucer, and then putting them both on the table.

"Then you don't think she's inventing it?" he asked.

"She didn't invent the man. He was real enough. And Doctor Townsend thinks her trouble is real, too. I've seen him."

"This is the hell of a place for her in that case," he said. "Anyone can break in. See here, Lois, I'm going to the police. We need protection, or she does. I'll get Fowler out here, or some of the state police. You might even get that good-looking big guy of yours in the cottage, too. Unless he's the fellow himself." He looked at me with sudden suspicion. "Maybe he is, at that!"

"No," I told him. "It wasn't O'Brien. And don't call him my guy. I wish he were."

I don't think he even heard me, for as if Phil's mention of him had summoned him we saw Fowler's car coming up the drive. He climbed the steps, wiping his face with a large white handkerchief, and greeting us politely.

"Glad you've had your dinner," he said, seeing our coffee cups. "Always hate to disturb people at their meals. But I have some news for you. We have identified the woman in your pool."

Phil asked him to sit down and offered him coffee, which he refused. He sat down, however, seeming, I thought, rather pleased with himself. He did not glance at me, which was fortunate. I must have looked shaken.

"Yes," he said. "Her name's Benjamin. Selina Benjamin. Any of you know her?"

Phil said no, and I chimed in thinly.

"She's a widow," Fowler went on. "Comes from a small town up the river. Well off, too, or at least comfortably fixed. Funny thing, her coming here. She didn't expect to be gone long. Left her cat in the house. No reason for suicide apparently. Anyhow if she wanted to drown herself she had the whole Hudson River almost within spitting distance."

Phil was smoking calmly, but my hands were shaking too much to light a cigarette. Curiously, too, Fowler was still not looking at me.

"I'm glad you identified her," Phil said. "But I'd like to know myself what she was doing here."

"That's the question," Fowler said, and settled himself in his chair. "You see, we've got a funny story about her. Seems she'd been missing for some days. Nobody noticed it. Apparently she lived pretty much to herself. But a neighbor of hers got suspicious when she didn't come home, and she called up the local police. That was only yesterday, but she tells a sort of queer tale."

He looked at me then for the first time.

"Seems like the house had been broken into. She thought it was all right at first. The girl—it was a girl—said she'd seen the woman's cat tearing the curtains of the front room, so she broke in a kitchen window to see what was wrong.

"This neighbor—her name's Hunnewell—said it seemed all right to her at first. Then she told her husband, and he didn't like it. Said the girl had no business breaking in. She ought to have talked to the neighbors first, or even called the police. Anyhow, he took her to the local authorities last night, and they went to the place.

"The woman was gone all right, and they knew what we had here in town. They brought the two of them down here today, and they identified the body at the mortuary. Full name was Katherine Selina Benjamin. She used the Selina. This afternoon they got some fingerprints in the house. Hers were all over the place, but there were some others, too. I guess, Miss Maynard, you know whose they are."

Phil's jaw had dropped. He stared at me incredulously.

"What's all this, Lois?" he said. "What's it got to do with you?"

I think if at that moment I had had O'Brien near by I would have strangled him with my bare hands. Him and his Flaherty, I thought bitterly. The case that was never closed? And here I was, on the verge of arrest.

"It's not very difficult to understand," I said, as calmly as I could. "I saw the cat in the window. It looked desperate, so I tried to save it. It was almost dying of thirst. I fed it some salmon too, if that's suspicious."

"You didn't feed it at the desk in the parlor, did you?"

"I don't know what you mean. Anyone who would leave a cat like that to die—"

"Look, Lois," Phil said. "Of course, you're not mixed up in any real trouble. That's preposterous. But what the hell were you doing there at all? That's the dickens of a way from here."

"Can't I take a drive?" I demanded. "I haven't been able to work for days. When I get a spell like that I often drive around. You know it, Phil."

Fowler was having none of that, however.

"You knew her," he said. "You knew where she lived. And she died in your pool. She didn't commit suicide. She was struck with something before she fell in, which makes it murder, Miss Maynard. Now her bankbooks are missing. Mrs. Hunnewell says she often saw them in the desk, but the Benjamin woman didn't have them with her the night she died. They weren't in her bag."

Phil got up. His usual bland cheerful face was set and hard.

"Are you trying to arrest my sister?" he said. "If you do, I warn you that I'll have you turned out of office if it's the last thing I do. It's absurd. She didn't even know the woman. None of us did."

"I haven't said I'm arresting her," Fowler said with dignity. "I am saying she was in the Benjamin house that day. And I'll go this far. The district attorney wants to see her tomorrow. Maybe he'll believe in black cats. I don't."

He went away, jamming his hat on his head as he went down the steps and slamming the door of his car as he gave me a last suspicious glance. Phil watched him out of sight. Then he turned to me.

"All right," he said. "Let's have it. Of all the lame-brain stories I ever heard yours was the worst."

"I'm sorry, Phil," I said feebly. "I just can't tell you. But I didn't kill her."

He gave me a long hard look.

"I'll accept that," he said. "You didn't kill her. I merely wondered why Chief Fowler came here and took away my golf clubs."

I regret to say I laughed.

"I'll write often, Phil," I said. "And if I send you a cake look out for a file in it."

Chapter 18

I don't know what he would have done, outside of throttling me, had Judith not chosen to come out at that moment. She looked really ill, and she had not bothered to use any make-up. She dropped into a chair, and when she took the cigarette Phil gave her, I saw her hands were trembling. Which made two of us.

"Wasn't that the chief's car?" she asked.

"It was," Phil said gruffly.

"What on earth did he want?"

"Don't ask me. Ask Lois. It seems she's been saving black cats, or something of the sort."

She looked relieved. What I did or did not do evidently did not interest her just then. She only looked somewhat blank.

"Did you tell him about the man in the grounds last night?" she asked.

"No. I clean forgot." Phil looked uncomfortable. "What's a man to do with a pair of lunatics gumming up the works? Suppose you come clean, Judith. What do you know about this man? First Lois tells me he dumped her into the pool. Then the chief of police comes and threatens to arrest her because a woman named Benjamin left a black cat when she died in our pool. Now it's a strange man in the grounds who wants to kill you, Judith. I must have missed part of this movie. It doesn't make sense."

Judith said nothing. She sat very still, as though she had not heard him, but she was still shaking. It seemed a good time to attack her.

"What Phil hasn't said," I told her, "is that I'm likely to be arrested for murder tomorrow."

"Murder!" She looked appalled. "What murder?"

"The woman in the pool. I'm supposed to have killed her with one of Phil's golf clubs."

"But you didn't do it. Why on earth would you?"

"That's the sixty-four-dollar question, Jude, and I have an idea you know the answer."

When she didn't speak I turned to Phil.

"I'm not in Judith's confidence," I said stiffly, "but if she won't talk I will. As I've told you before, she's been afraid of her life for months. I don't know when it started, but I believe it was before she left Ridgely. If she would tell us about it, we could protect her. As it is, one man is trying to do it for us. His name's O'Brien, and I think that's why he rented our cottage."

Judith stared at me.

"O'Brien?" she said. "What does he know? Or what has he told you, Lois?"

"So far the shoe's been on the other foot," I said curtly. "What I know is his. What he knows is his, too. But it may interest you both to know he didn't go to bed at all last night after Judith's friend attacked me and then ran. He stayed up and watched this house until daylight. I saw him."

"What the hell does he say it's about?" This was Phil, looking completely confused.

"He doesn't say. Perhaps he doesn't know. Only he does believe Judith's in danger."

"Why?" Phil said sharply. "Don't tell me you don't know, Judith. And don't sit there like a damned fool and let an ex-cop look after you. You have a family, even if you chose to forget it for a good many years. It's up to us to protect you and I wouldn't say The Birches is the place to do it in."

"It wouldn't matter where I went," Judith said dully. "I know that now. Unless I get out of the country."

I suppose it was idiotic to feel sorry for a woman who seemed bent on her own destruction. I did, however. I didn't think she was merely stubborn, either. She was concealing something because she felt she had to do so.

She got up before I could speak, said a brief good night, and went into the house, leaving Phil cursing under his breath and me in a state of pretty complete helplessness. It began to look as though I was going to be held for the murder of a woman I had probably never seen until she was dead. And also as though Judith would let me go to the chair before she revealed what she was hiding.

All in all, it wasn't the end of a perfect day, and I noticed that Phil locked up with extreme care before he went up to bed that night. When I told him Bill was still out, he merely grunted.

"He's got a car," he said. "He's got a home, too. It wouldn't hurt him to go there once in a while. I'll let him in. You look as though you could stand some sleep."

In spite of that I slept very badly. Quite obviously the police were not accepting my explanation of why I had been in the Benjamin house. And equally obviously Judith would die or be killed before she explained her own terror.

The strangeness of that attitude kept me turning restlessly in my bed. It was certainly abnormal. Or was it? Was she afraid to tell the truth, and if so why? She was a grown woman, not an adolescent pushed into a marriage she loathed. She knew the man she said meant to kill her. It was she he had expected at the pool. Hadn't he said she had the note he had thrown through the window? And she was to talk. Only talk.

It didn't sound like any prelude to murder to me. Or to Sara Winters, either.

I thought of Phil's story about Father, about the incredible note he had left for Mother. It was brutal, as only a man in a brutal situation could be. But what *was* the situation? Why had Mother made her frenzied escape to Arizona, taking a sulky

175

Judith with her? There had been no pregnancy, Anne said. There might have been something else, however. There was the time in the summer of 1929 when Father had a ruptured appendix and had to leave the three of us at The Birches.

Suppose Judith had slipped over the Connecticut border and married one of the boys who always surrounded her? There might have been a divorce or an annulment, or—knowing Mother—there might have been neither. She was quite capable of ignoring such a complication and marrying Judith to Ridgely Chandler without benefit of the law.

The fact that Judith might possibly have an unknown husband throwing notes attached to rocks through her window was intriguing, to say the least.

But I had my own problem to face that night. The next morning I was going to be interrogated by the district attorney, and I had no real answers. Mrs. Hunnewell would be there to identify me. Gertrude of the beauty shop could say I had asked where the Benjamin woman lived, and my story to her about a lost purse would blow up with a bang. Also—unless O'Brien told about the return-trip ticket—they would believe I had known all along what town she came from. He would have to talk now, I thought sourly; have to admit he had sent me to locate her, and why.

And he was going to do it, or else!

All evening his cottage had been dark, but now there was a light in it, and at last I put on a pair of slacks and a shirt and went carefully down the stairs. As I opened the front door, however, I had to choke back a scream. Someone was standing on the porch with a handkerchief to his face, and it was a moment or so before I realized it was Bill.

He staggered into the hall and dropped into a big Italian chair there which was a part of Mother's loot.

"Sorry, Lois," he gasped. "Suppose I could have a drink? I've had the hell of a time."

I got him some brandy from Phil's decanter in the dining-room, and while I have never considered brandy the miracle worker most writers do, he did begin to look a little better. Evidently he had been in a fight of some sort. His black dinner tie was somewhere under his collar and hanging loose, his coat was torn, there was a large welt over his right eye, and his lip was cut and bleeding. He managed to grin at me, however, as he handed back the glass.

"Chased a fellow and caught up with him," he said. "Only he was stronger than I was. He got me down and banged me with a flashlight. Or maybe it was a gun," he added. "I didn't have time to examine it."

I felt weak and shaky.

"Where was all this?" I asked sharply.

"Down the drive near the pool. I saw him skulking there, and I didn't like the idea. When I asked him what he was doing there, he tried to get away. Only like a damn fool I could run faster than he could. He—I guess he knocked me out. When I came to I was flat, anyhow, and he was gone."

He seemed apologetic rather than worried. He would have done better in the scrimmage, he said, only he was tired. His car had run out of gas a mile or two from The Birches, and he'd had to walk home.

"That's how I came to see him. My feet were sore, so I came up on the grass. He almost jumped out of his skin when he saw me."

"Did he drive off in a car?"

"He may have gone up in a balloon for all I know. I was having a nice little nap. I don't think he's still around, if that's what you mean. I imagine he wasn't feeling any too good himself."

"Did you get a good look at him, Bill?" I managed to ask. "Was he big or small?"

"Quite a hunk of man," he said. "All muscle, too. The minute I grabbed him I knew it was an error and the side was out."

So Mr. X was still around, or had been. Whoever he was he was certainly tenacious, and something had to be done.

"Look, Bill," I said, "can you walk?"

"Walk where?" he asked suspiciously. "If you mean up to bed I guess I can make it."

"Down to the cottage," I said. "It's important, Bill. I'm—I think I'm to be arrested in the morning, and I'm not going along that drive alone."

His young jaw dropped.

"Arrested? You?"

"They think I killed the woman in the pool. Don't ask me why. Just get me to the cottage. Then you can leave. O'Brien will bring me back."

"So that's the way it is!" he said, yawning. "Well, I can only try. If I drop I trust you to carry me back to ole Virginny."

He staggered to his feet, still rather glassy eyed and certainly no protection. But I was too weary to explain anything to him as we more or less weaved down the drive, and although he asked innumerable questions he was not in too good shape himself. Luckily O'Brien was still up and dressed. I suspected he was about to look around the grounds, for he had a gun in his hand when he opened the door. He slid it in a pocket when he recognized us, but I am sure Bill saw it.

"What's this?" he said. "A late call?"

Then he saw Bill's battered face and pulled him inside and into a chair.

"What happened?" he asked. "Been in a fight?"

"It turned into that." Bill grinned. "I chased a fellow, only I'm too good. I caught up with him."

"Where?"

"Here. On the other side of the pool."

O'Brien examined the bruise and the cut lip while Bill explained about his car. The injuries were not serious, O'Brien said, but Bill would look a trifle odd for a day or two. Then at last he looked at me.

"Was Fowler at the house tonight?" he asked.

"He was," I said. "It is now known that I murdered the Benjamin woman and stole her bankbooks. I've been identified, and my fingerprints are all over the house. I did it with one of Phil's golf clubs, and I'm to be interrogated tomorrow—this morning, rather. The district attorney expects to have quite a day."

He straightened. For the first time since I knew him he looked uncertain. Then apparently he made up his mind.

"Afraid you'll have to go back to the house and put yourself to bed," he told Bill. "I'll see Lois gets in all right. And"—he hesitated, then he pulled the gun out of his pocket—"if you see this fellow again take a shot or two at him. I won't cry if you get him."

Bill looked highly gratified. He took the gun and pushed down the safety catch, then shoved it in his pocket.

"One if by land and two if by sea," he said, and considering it a good exit line cheerfully took himself off.

O'Brien shut the door behind him and turned to me.

"Now," he said, "what's all this?"

He listened carefully while I told him what the police probably knew: Gert's beauty shop where I learned where the Benjamin woman lived, the fingerprints in the house, both Gert and Mrs. Hunnewell to identify me—the works, as Bill would say. When I finished he shook his head.

"They can't arrest you," he said. "Where's your motive? But this plays hell with my own plans. There's only one answer, of course. You found the return-trip ticket and kept it. So you thought you'd play detective and find out who she was."

"And kept my mouth shut after I did!" I said furiously. "You have a lot of nerve, Terry O'Brien. I do your dirty work and you go calmly about your business and let me go to jail. I have no intention of doing any such thing. You and your Flaherty, who's been dead for years!"

179

I saw him really angry then for the first time.

"I suppose you think I like what I'm doing," he said with cold fury. "I like watching these grounds of yours instead of getting a decent night's sleep. I like trying to save your sister's life when maybe it isn't worth saving. And I suppose I like hiding behind a girl's skirts, or pants, or whatever she's wearing! A few days in jail wouldn't hurt you. At least you'd be safe and I could stop worrying my fool head off about you."

"Nobody asked you to do any of those things," I said. "And don't bother to deny you came here under false pretenses. As if you really wanted to raise chickens! If you ask me you hate them."

Then unexpectedly he laughed.

"As a matter of fact," he said, "they grow on you. They're pretty good girls, you know. They've been contributing quite a bit to your breakfast."

"Are you still going to insist on that ticket thing?" I demanded.

"I'll change the story, if you like. There *was* a slip in the bag, but the wind blew it away. A day or two later you found it. How's that?"

He got it out of the desk and held it out to me. After its immersion in the pool it looked crumpled enough to have been out in the weather. I took it reluctantly.

"Just where does Judith come in in all of this?" I asked. "Don't tell me she killed Flaherty, or the Preston girl."

He closed the desk drawer with a snap.

"No," he said. "Someday before long I'll tell you her story. It goes back a long time, and it isn't pretty, Lois. But I don't want her killed. I want her kept alive and well. It's important. In fact it's vital."

"Don't tell me it has anything to do with Flaherty!"

"Not necessarily, no," he said.

He clammed up then, got his car and drove me to the house. Evidently he was taking no chances without his gun. The key was under the porch matting as he had ordered, and I got his

180

gun from the hall table and held it out to him.

He didn't take it. Not immediately, that is. He simply wrapped me in a pair of arms that could have squeezed a bear to death and kissed me hard. Then he released me.

"Sorry," he said. "Just an impulse. Don't think anything of it."

He was off the porch before I could slam the door.

Chapter 19

When I reached my room I was astonished to find it was only two o'clock. I had thought it was almost morning. I was not sleepy, naturally. Too much had happened, or was going to happen, including O'Brien himself.

Not the kiss. A girl these days who lays any emphasis on a thing like that must have been raised on a desert island. But what he had said about Judith puzzled as well as alarmed me. All those years of marriage, when the press always referred to her as the beautiful Mrs. Chandler. Her music. Her parties. Her big apartment, done by a good decorator as a setting for her. And all this time something hanging over her; perhaps something dangerous.

I found myself going back to the early days when Judith had been my big sister, to whom I looked up with a mixture of jealousy and admiration. Even then she had been popular. And now and then she had gone to subdeb parties, with Mother or my governess to chaperon her, much to her disgust.

I was allowed to stay up and see her off when that happened. She would stand in the lower hall, in white chiffon, or rose taffeta, and turn around for my benefit.

"Like it, Lois?"

"It's wonderful. You're wonderful, Judith."

And Mother standing by, her pride in her eyes, as though she could not believe she had given birth to so much beauty.

Compared with Judith I had been allowed to run wild in those early days, to ride my bicycle, to play even with the East Side kids whenever I got a chance, to roller-skate and ice-skate while nurse or governess talked scandal with others of her kind on the park benches. And at The Birches I learned to swim like an otter. I had an idea that Anne had had the same upbringing as mine. Judith was different, however. Looking back I think Mother was hardly normal about her. She watched her like a hawk, but Judith could have walked all over her had she wanted to do so.

The one time Judith had a certain amount of freedom had been in the summers at The Birches. Then a crowd of girls and college boys would motor out or gather from the vicinity, especially over week-ends. The drive would be filled with cars, some sporty and expensive, others rather like Bill's, and to my childish mind fascinating with the chalked designs and words on them. One of them said *Charleston Charlie*, because those were the days of the Charleston.

Rolled stockings, very short skirts, girdles surreptitiously removed for dances, and the Charleston! I remembered trying to do it with my knock-kneed little-girl legs, and Father catching me up and laughing.

"Stop it, skinny!" he said. "You're still my baby. Let the big girls make fools of themselves. Not you."

But outside of Judith it was the pool that was the center of attraction, and an alfresco lunch was always set out there on Saturdays. There was Prohibition then and no drinks were served, but most of the boys carried flasks, and many a Coke or ginger ale was needled in the shrubbery. I used to watch them, and they would yell at me, "Get out of here, Lois, you little snoop."

I never told on them, of course.

As I have said, it was the day of big expensive summer places, plenty of servants, plenty of everything. Now most of the houses were gone, either torn down for taxes or

183

abandoned, and try as I would I could not remember the names of any of the young crowd I tried so hard to join, and which so completely ignored me.

O'Brien said Judith's story went back a long time, and was not a pretty one. Whatever it was I felt certain it dated back to those week-ends at the pool, and to one of the boys who surrounded her there. Whether she had eloped with him or not he had some sort of hold on her, which her curious egocentrism had built into a deadly menace.

I did not believe he was a menace. I did not believe he had killed Selina Benjamin thinking she was Judith. The note through the window, what he had said when he picked me up and on discovering his mistake dropped me into the pool, were not the acts of a man with murder in his heart. Something else occurred to me, too.

He had not waited to get me out of the water. He seemed to know I could swim. Perhaps, after all, he remembered the little Lois Maynard who had been practically amphibious in those days.

With all that, and my approaching interview with the district attorney the next day, it was early summer dawn when I finally went to sleep, and in no time at all Jennie was pounding on my door.

"You better come down," she called. "The chief's here for you."

It had come, then. I was about to be arrested, and to be arrested, of all things, on an empty stomach! I dressed as carefully as I could, although my morning mood before coffee is distinctly sinister. But the plain fact is that what with apprehension and lack of sleep my hands scarcely obeyed me. I dropped my hairbrush, put on too much make-up and had to wipe it off and start again. And, of course, I pulled a button off the white sports dress I was wearing—as a symbol of innocence—and had to stop to sew it on again.

Chief Fowler was scowling over a cup of coffee when I entered the dining-room. There was no sign of Judith, but Bill

184

was there, looking horrible and explaining that he had chased a strange man in the grounds and fallen, a fact which Fowler obviously did not believe. And, of course, Phil decided to cheer me by being facetious.

"Very nice," he said, inspecting me. "Not that it will save you from the chair, but a good try."

I could not eat. Not with Jennie ogling me with suspicion, and Helga peeping from the pantry door. Not with the story O'Brien had given me to tell, and my own feeling of guilt about it. I did get down a cup of black coffee, however. It steadied me somewhat, as did the announcement that both Phil and Bill intended to go with me to the district attorney's office. Not with me, exactly. I went in the chief's car. But there was a certain amount of comfort in knowing they were behind me.

The cottage was closed as we passed it. But O'Brien's car was standing outside, and I felt a wave of fury which actually shook me. He could sleep, I thought, while I lied myself black in the face with a tale no one was going to believe. And for what? So he could solve the murder years ago of a man I had never heard of and cared nothing about. Why hadn't I come out with the truth? That the ticket had been in the bag, that he had taken it, and that at his behest I had looked up the Benjamin woman.

I still do not know why I had not done it. There had been something in his face when he talked about Flaherty that moved me deeply. He had been like a son speaking of a beloved father. But at least he could have been around, I thought furiously. He could at least say he had suggested I locate Mrs. Benjamin, and that I had given him her bankbooks. Although why they thought I had taken them was beyond me. I certainly could not cash in on them.

Yet my first impression of the district attorney was rather favorable. A smallish man, thin and with gray hair and a pair of keen blue eyes, when I was ushered in to him, he smiled and got up from behind a desk. His name he said as he shook hands was Tarbell.

"I'm afraid this is rather early for you," he said politely.

185

"Sit down, please. That chair isn't bad. Would you like a cigarette?"

He came around the desk to light it, and I found myself relaxing. Somewhere outside were my menfolk, Phil and Bill. And Fowler, who had merely admitted me to the presence, had disappeared. I stiffened, however, when I saw a golf club lying on the desk.

But the district attorney did not mention it. He went back to his seat and surveyed me benignly.

"You know," he said, "you look like a nice girl. A very pretty one, too, if I may say so. I'm wondering just how you got involved in this mess."

"I didn't kill that woman," I said, "if that's what you mean."

"Possibly not, but someone did. And certainly you have done some odd things since, Miss Maynard. Let me tell you what I know. In the first place, you have maintained you did not know her. I accept part of that, for certainly you did not know exactly where she lived. Also your behavior shows it. You described her to certain people in that town of hers, and you located her house.

"You know what happened after that. You broke in and you searched her desk. Your prints are all over it. You took her bankbooks, for some unknown reason, but so far as I know nothing else. Why? She was dead. The bankbooks were of no use to you. I would say she had been blackmailing you, but for one reason."

"I suppose because you can't get blood out of a turnip," I said, attempting to be facetious but inwardly shaking.

He did not smile.

"No," he said. "Because Mrs. Benjamin did not need money. Blackmail is a risky business, so why would she try it? She knew about the money, and it was hers by the will he left. That in itself is curious. Why wouldn't she touch it?"

I didn't know and said so. He went on: "You say you have no money. What about your sister? Ridgely Chandler is a very "wealthy man."

"She has her alimony. That's all. He was smart about that. He made a trust fund for her. The interest is all she gets. On her death it goes to charity. As for my brother and myself, Phil worked his way through college, and I imagine he got Ridgely Chandler to send me."

"I see," he said thoughtfully. "Mr. Chandler has been trying to hush this thing up, Miss Maynard. He has even been in touch with the Governor. But the Governor is a pretty stout fellow. He won't interfere. In fact he can't. Only I don't like that sort of thing."

"Then you don't know the Chandlers!"

He let that pass.

"This is the picture as I see it, Miss Maynard," he went on. "Here's a woman who is well provided for. Her husband had left her some insurance. She had sold the business, and she owned her home. She had adequate means to live as she did, which was very simply. Besides she was a quiet retiring sort of woman, and a churchgoer; not, I think, the blackmailing type.

"Yet she had some reason for being in your grounds the night she was killed. Do you know what that was?"

"I think she was meeting someone there," I told him. "There had been a strange man in the grounds two or three times at night. Once he frightened one of the maids. Another time he threw a rock through my sister's window, and only two nights ago he caught me in the drive, picked me up, and threw me into our swimming pool."

He looked completely incredulous.

"Into the pool? Why? Do you mean he tried to drown you?"

"I don't know what he meant. He didn't stop to explain."

"Still, it seems an extraordinary thing to do. Did you recognize him?"

"No. It was dark, of course. I didn't know his voice."

"Oh, he spoke, did he?"

"He told me I was going to talk, or he'd kill me."

The district attorney was staring at me with what amounted to fascination.

"I don't suppose," he said slowly, "that anyone could invent a story like that. It's too preposterous."

"All right," I said. "If you don't believe it call in my nephew, Bill Harrison, and look at his face."

"I presume it is a nice honest face, but why should I look at it? Especially when I can look at yours."

He was smiling, but I wasn't having any humor at that moment, or any compliments, either.

"Because he chased the same man last night," I told him. "He caught him, too. He's young and he's fast. Only the other man was stronger. I gather he won the round. At least he knocked Bill out and escaped. If you'll call him in—"

He looked a trifle uncertain, which I imagine was unusual. Also he said nothing when I lit a cigarette which, so far as I knew, might be my last one.

"I'll see your Bill later," he said. "Just now I want to talk to you. There are certain other curious angles about this case. For one thing, the Benjamin woman sent the taxi away. Why? Did she expect someone to motor her back to the railroad station? Or—did she mean to stay all night?"

"How could she expect that? None of us even knew her."

"You knew where she lived. The town, anyhow. You went there like a homing pigeon. Don't you think that needs some explanation?"

It was a bad moment. Inwardly I was cursing O'Brien and all his works, but I had to go through with it.

"It wasn't hard to do," I said. "You see, I had this." And reaching into my bag brought out the crumpled water-soaked return ticket. He took it and examined it.

"This was in her purse?" he inquired.

"It must have been. I emptied it, you know. I told them so at the inquest."

"You denied it at first."

"I hated to admit I'd been snooping."

"An inquest is a serious matter," he said, eyeing me. "So is murder. Now why did you keep this ticket? What possible reason could you have?"

"I didn't keep it," I said with complete truth. "It just turned up later. As a matter of fact, the tenant in our cottage found it and gave it to me. If you don't believe me ask him. His name's O'Brien."

He looked at me.

"So O'Brien found it," he said. "The queer thing about this case is the way Terry O'Brien turns up in it. He's a smart cop, but this isn't a New York case, Miss Maynard. Why is a detective lieutenant of the City Homicide Department involved in it?"

"He's retired, isn't he?"

"No," he said grimly. "Apparently he's on a protracted leave of absence, or something of the sort. I wish to God he'd let us attend to our own business in this county, and keep his nose out of it. What kind of game is he playing, anyhow? He's inherited a lot of money, but he doesn't retire. Instead he rents a small cottage from you, pretends to be something he isn't, and for God's sake raises chickens!"

"Maybe he likes them."

He had lost his urbanity by that time. He drew a long exasperated breath.

"All right," he said. "Let's forget O'Brien. I'll keep this ticket, of course. Whether you took it out of the bag or got it some other way, it should have been given to the local police at once. As it is we've wasted a lot of time. What interests me just now is why you broke into the Benjamin house."

"It was the cat," I said, with more assurance. "I couldn't leave it there to die."

"There were neighbors. There was this Mrs. Hunnewell, for instance, the woman who identified her. Why not have called her? Why break a window to get in?"

"I didn't want to be seen there. After all, she had been killed in our pool. But I wanted to know why it had been *our* pool.

189

There must be plenty of others nearer where she lived."

"I suppose your brother and sister did not know of this excursion of yours to the Benjamin house?"

I shook my head. The mention of Judith, however, reminded me of something.

"My sister is convinced someone has been trying to kill her," I told him. "She's psychotic, of course, if that's the word for it. Or is it psychosomatic? But she really means it."

"And she thinks it was this woman?"

"No, of course not. She didn't even know her. I'm sure of that. She thinks whoever did it mistook the Benjamin woman for her. Anyhow she's dead, and Judith's still afraid. More than ever, as a matter of fact."

"Why? Doesn't she say?"

"No. She won't talk about it, but she thinks it's the man who has been haunting our grounds."

"Why for God's sake haven't you notified the police?"

"We did. O'Brien knows all about it."

He looked practically apoplectic, but he managed to control himself.

"What does this fellow look like?" he asked.

"I don't know. Nobody does, unless it's my sister. He's strong. I think he's about medium height. And he has a car, or gets one somehow. I heard him drive off while I was in the pool."

"Your sister refuses to identify him?"

"She says he means to kill her. That's all."

"Have you any idea why? Or why she won't talk?"

I daresay I was pretty well wrought up by that time. I realized, too, that much I had said sounded like complete nonsense without some sort of background. So almost before I knew it I was telling him of Judith's sudden intention to get a divorce, after twenty years of marriage; of our trip to Reno and her fright at the railroad station; of the locks and nailed windows at The Birches; and of Doctor Townsend's conviction that her terror had a real basis. He listened carefully, making no notes, and part of the time with his eyes closed, until I finished.

"Do you think she's afraid of her husband?"

"No," I said positively. "I don't think she ever was in love with him, as I look back, but they got on well enough. Anyhow, he's not that sort of person."

"How can we say what sort of person any individual is? Even children commit murder, and pious women with innocence written all over them. But it wasn't Chandler in the grounds? You are sure of that?"

"Absolutely. Ridge is short. This man is bigger and with a deeper voice. I couldn't be mistaken."

"Do you think she would talk to me?"

"I think she'd faint if she so much as saw you."

He smiled at that. Not much of a smile, but a good try. It was a moment or two before he spoke.

"Had you any reason to associate this Benjamin woman with your sister?" he asked finally. "Or with her divorce? After all, that's a curious story of yours. A woman suddenly decides to leave her husband. She goes to Reno and seems contented there. Then at the railroad station something happens. She faints, and she has been terrified ever since. She won't use taxis, for one thing. That mean anything to you?"

It did not. I said so.

"Any taxi drivers around when this happened? At Reno?"

"One or two, maybe more. I didn't notice."

"Yet a taxi figures in this," he said. "Let's take a purely hypothetical situation. Suppose one night last winter your sister is in a cab with a man and something happens. She's a good-looking woman, I understand. So he makes a pass at her and she—let's say she opens the door and pushes him out. He's killed, and the driver gets out and accuses her of murder. So she's at his mercy. There's blackmail right off, and I've been smelling blackmail in this case right along."

"I don't believe it."

He smiled again.

191

"I'm only guessing," he said. "She has to be afraid of something or somebody, and according to you it happened suddenly. She wasn't prepared for it, so all she could do was cut and run. She chose Reno, and she was followed there."

"What about this Benjamin woman?" I asked. "Where does she come in?"

"I'm supposed to be asking you that. What about her? Why did O'Brien put you on her tail? Because I think he did."

I didn't deny it. How could I?

"I haven't the remotest idea," I said honestly, and rather to my surprise he seemed to agree with me. He said he thought that was about all, and shook hands with me.

"But," he added, "the next time you find a piece of paper the police are breaking their necks to locate, I suggest you give it to them. You'd be surprised how well they know their business."

Phil and Bill were in the anteroom, waiting anxiously, and when he saw Bill's face the district attorney grinned.

"Quite a shiner you've got there, son. Want to come in and tell me about it?"

He kept Bill only five minutes or so. And he was not smiling when he let him go. He looked very sober.

"I'd better have a man or two around your place for a while," he said. "Looks as though this fellow has a gun. No fist ever made a bruise like that." He looked at Phil. "And now, Mr. Maynard, I think it's time you and I had a talk."

I shall never forget Phil's face as he went into that room and the district attorney closed the door behind him.

Chapter 20

It was an hour before he appeared again. He looked as though he had been run through a wringer, and this time the district attorney did not see him out. But he said nothing, merely nodding when Bill insisted that we have lunch in town to celebrate what he called my escape from the chair. Bill's face called for lively interest in the restaurant, but as usual he ate stolidly from soup to nuts, only to stop now and then with what the newspapers would say that night:

"'Socialites Quizzed in Murder Case,'" he offered. Or: "'Woman Novelist Involved in Crime She Writes About.'"

As a result we were still there when the Hunnewell woman came in.

She was accompanied by what I learned later was a local detective, a youngish good-looking man who appeared slightly bored, and I knew what was coming the moment I saw her. I would have to pass her table going out, and I hadn't a hope she would not recognize me.

She did, at the top of her voice.

"That's her!" she yelled. "That's the girl who broke into the house."

I stopped beside her. There was nothing else to do.

"I've just been telling the district attorney about it," I said with a forced smile. The whole restaurant was listening, and one or two people stood up to see me better. "How's the cat? And I hope your husband fixed the window."

Apparently it took most of the wind out of her sails. But not all. She stared at me.

"The cat's all right. I wouldn't say the same for you."

"No?"

"Not with Selina Benjamin gone to her grave, and dead in your pool."

Here the detective handed her a menu and said something in a low voice. She flushed angrily.

"All right," she said. "I'll shut up, but if that girl thinks she's putting something over on me she can think again."

It was three o'clock when we reached our drive, and as Phil turned in I saw that the O'Brien cottage was still closed. A window was open, however, and his car was there. As he had been up most of the night I supposed he was sleeping. But his girls were still in the chicken house, announcing feverishly that they wanted to be let out and fed.

That was when I saw Henrietta.

The little hen was strutting about alone in the front yard, and I knew O'Brien never allowed her there. It was a small thing, of course, but Henrietta where she did not belong, plus the indignation in the hen house, made me uneasy.

As a result I made Phil stop the car and got out, with Bill at my heels. The front door of the cottage was locked, but a window was open, and when no one answered my knocks and calls I made Bill crawl through the window. It was some time before he opened the door. When he did he stood blocking it with his solid young body.

"Get out of the way, Lois," he said. "Phil, come here, will you?"

I didn't get out of the way, of course. I ducked under Bill's arm and got inside, to see O'Brien in his big chair, unconscious and with blood all over the place. He was in pajamas and a dressing-gown, but evidently he had been shot somewhere outside, for there was a trail of blood across the floor from a

194

wound in his right leg. Equally evident was the fact that he had made an attempt to telephone, for the instrument had fallen beside him on the floor.

Not that I noticed any of this at the time. I was screaming for a doctor, Bill says, and that I jerked off his—Bill's—necktie to use as a ligature.

"My best tie, too," he said. "You simply yanked it. It didn't help, either. The leg had stopped bleeding hours before, but there you were, blubbering at the top of your lungs and wrecking a three-dollar tie, all at the same time."

The real wound, of course, was in his chest, but the fact is I do not remember much what followed. I recall the ambulance coming, the care with which they carried O'Brien's big body out to it, and Phil going with it when it left. But I do not remember stripping the chair of its bloody chintz cover and carrying it carefully to the house.

Bill said I was making no sense whatever, that I wailed over it all the way, because I had made it and it had been damned hard to make, and now it was stained and would not wash! And Jennie maintains I handed it to her in the hall and told her to take it out to the incinerator and burn it, which the idiot proceeded to do.

I must have been making quite a fuss, for Judith heard me and came down the stairs.

"What on earth!" she said. "Jennie said Fowler had arrested you."

I glared at her.

"Your friend out in the grounds has killed O'Brien," I said frantically. "Now maybe you'll tell us about him. If you don't I warn you I'll choke it out of you. I mean it."

She did not faint. I was still standing with that bloody cover in my hands, and I knew the sight of blood upset her. All she did, however, was to sit down on the stairs and look blank. She didn't even speak. If ever I saw a human being appear sick and frightened it was Judith that day.

"What do you mean, my friend?" she gasped. "I don't

195

understand, Lois."

"The taxi driver," I said. "That's what he is, isn't it? That's why you won't take taxis. The district attorney knows all about you, the blackmail and everything."

"Blackmail?" she said strangely. "Who on earth is being blackmailed?"

Bill had been standing by, puzzled. He came over and put an arm around me.

"I don't know what all this is about," he said. "But O'Brien isn't dead, Lois. Not yet, anyhow. What's this about Judith's friend in the grounds? The fellow I had the fight with?"

"Ask her," I said. "Maybe she'll talk to you. She knows a lot she's not telling."

Then my knees gave way suddenly, and Bill caught me and eased me into a chair. I suppose it was the sudden understanding of what he had said, that O'Brien was not dead. In any event I shut my eyes. When I opened them Judith had disappeared, and Bill was standing by me with a glass of whisky. Later he helped to get me up to bed, where Helga undressed me, her old face grim.

"Now you go to sleep, child," she said, tucking the covers around me. "That O'Brien will be all right. Phil promised to telephone from the hospital. But he's strong. Don't you worry about him."

"You know him, don't you, Helga?"

"We've had one or two talks," she said evasively. "When he brought me some eggs. That's all."

"What about?"

"Just about the old days. Nothing important. Now you go to sleep and stop worrying. It takes a lot to kill an Irish cop."

So Helga knew who and what he was. I wondered just why he had talked to her, or what he had hoped to learn. But in one way she had reassured me. O'Brien was strong. I remembered the night when he dived into the pool for my bag, and his big muscular body in his trunks. And—because I was trying to forget that scene in the cottage—I thought over what Helga had said. The old days! What about the old days, when Father had killed himself and a police officer named Flaherty had been murdered because he had apparently located a Selina Benjamin, wife of a respected tobacconist! But she might not have been Selina Benjamin twenty years ago. She might have been Kate Henry. Katherine Selina Henry, whose testimony before a grand jury had indicted a boy for murder, and who had disappeared before his trial.

It was nine o'clock that night before we had any word from the hospital. Helga, who would not let Jennie into my room, had brought me a cup of soup and some crackers at seven, but I could not touch them. When the phone rang, I was out of bed in a second. Bill, however, was answering it in the lower hall. He listened for some time. Then: "Good. I'll tell Lois. But listen, Phil, what about Aunt Judith? She's locked in and won't speak to anybody. I'm kind of worried. Think Christy ought to see her?" And after a pause: "No, I suppose not. Well, I'll try it."

He came up to my room. I had put on a dressing-gown over my pajamas by that time, and as my door was open he came in. He still showed the marks of battle. In fact the lurid purple was even deeper, but his mouth looked better.

"They think O'Brien will be all right," he said cheerfully. "Take time, of course. They got one bullet. According to Phil, it was in the apex of a lung, and believe it or not it missed the subclavian artery, whatever that might be. The other wound isn't serious. It went through his leg. But he lost a lot of blood, so they're giving him transfusions. Phil says the hospital is lousy with New York cops. Seems the guy is popular."

I sat down, because my knees had given way with relief.

"Does he know who did it?" I asked.

"Didn't see anybody. Of course, he isn't talking much. Too weak. He was by the pool when he got it. That's all he knows."

I must have looked better, for he lit a cigarette and offered me one.

"What makes with him, anyhow?" he said. "Phil says those

197

city cops look fighting mad; that they all insisted on being tapped for blood, and it was flowing by the quart, so far as he could tell."

"He's one of them," I said weakly. "Homicide."

He whistled.

"Homicide? For God's sake what's he been doing here?"

"I don't know. It's something about an old murder. An officer named Flaherty was killed, and lately something came up that revived it. I don't know what it is, Bill."

"What's it got to do with The Birches?"

"A woman was killed here. Don't forget."

"He was here before that happened," he said, looking mystified. Then he apparently abandoned the puzzle. "I suppose you know there are cops all over the grounds."

All over the cottage, too, I realized. It meant they already had seen the bankbooks and photograph, as well as the clippings. What would they make of the one about Judith? Would they connect her with Selina Benjamin's death? And would they be right? If the golf club on the district attorney's desk was one of Phil's, and they could prove it had been the murder weapon—

Bill's next words penetrated the haze that was my mind at that moment.

"Those guys make it damned inconvenient when a fellow wants to try a job of breaking and entering," he said. "What's the penalty for that, anyhow?"

"Breaking and entering?"

"Look," he said, his bantering tone gone. "I'd better tell you. I'm anxious about Judith. There hasn't been a sound out of her since she learned about the shooting. I've called to her off and on ever since. I've even thrown pebbles at her windows. She won't speak and I can't hear a sound in the place."

I rallied as best I could.

"She's upset, that's all, Bill. And you can't break into her room. That door's too solid. Anyhow it's silly. She has spells like this sometimes. Phil says she did the same thing after

Father died. I wouldn't worry."

"You didn't see her face when she heard about O'Brien," he said grimly. "She looked like death. Either she's scared into a fit or she knows a lot she's not telling. I think she's scared."

"She's been scared for weeks."

"This was different," he insisted. "How about a window? I'm not fooling, Lois. She may be unconscious or even worse."

"Don't be a young idiot," I said. "She's frightened about something, but she likes to dramatize herself, too. You know how she is."

"I know she's as nutty as a fruit cake," he said, with the brutality of youth. "Just the same I think someone needs to look after her. Where can I get hold of a ladder?"

"I thought you said there were police all over the place."

"They're mostly around the cottage and the pool. Anyhow, what can they do? I'm locked out and trying to get into my room. Apologies and all that. Come on. What are we waiting for?"

"Helga may come in, Bill. If she finds me gone—"

"The hell with Helga. Turn out your lights and lock your door. She'll think you're asleep."

If it were not so horrible I could laugh over that excursion of ours. With Phil away, the lower floor was empty and dark. I did not think Helga was asleep, so we avoided the service wing. We groped our way out the rear-hall door, to find it was raining, a hard summer shower which almost sent me back into the house. But Bill took my arm, and we crept around the back of the old conservatory and toward the stables.

"I used to see a ladder there," he said. "Climbed trees with it when I was a kid. Suppose it's still there?"

I was not sure. I seldom visited the stables. Also I was already soaked and considerably irritated.

"Of all the fool things!" I said. "If you think I'm going to climb a ladder and scare Judith to death, you can think again."

"Who asked you to climb? You're the lookout, that's all."

There was a brilliant flash of lightning just then, followed by a clap of thunder. We stuck out like a pair of sore thumbs but, as Bill observed, the glory boys—his name for the state police—didn't like to get their pretty uniforms wet.

"They're all cozy in the cottage," he said, "or back in their barracks. What's the matter with you? You're not easy scared."

We reached the stables at last, and once inside Bill produced a flashlight. He caught a glimpse of me then, and serious as he had been he laughed.

"I wish O'Brien could see you now," he said. "You look as though you'd been dumped in the pool."

"He has seen me exactly like that," I said sourly.

He was not listening. He had located a ladder; not the one he remembered but a heavy pruning one, with an extension to reach the upper branches of trees or to clear the gutters on the roof when falling leaves cluttered them in the autumn. But somehow we got hold of it and started back to the house. It seemed miles to me. I lost a bedroom slipper and could not stop to find it, and once Bill fell and the whole end cracked down on him.

The rain was slackening by that time. I could see a flashlight or two in the shrubbery by the pool, but Bill kept doggedly on, and I had no choice but to follow him. The expedition seemed more and more absurd as we reached the house.

The two windows at the side of Judith's room were almost dark, except for a faint light from somewhere which outlined them, and since one of them was open, it was there we placed the ladder. It made a small scraping sound, but nothing followed. No Judith appeared, no light went on, and Bill suddenly went shy on me.

"You'd better go first," he whispered. "She'd have a fit if she saw a man in her room after what she says about one trying to kill her. Or maybe she sleeps raw. Not afraid, are you?"

I looked up. The ceilings at The Birches are high, and the windows looked fifty feet above me. Nevertheless, the fact that she had not heard the ladder worried me. I tucked up my dressing-gown and having lost my bedroom slipper, put a bare foot on the lowest round.

"Hold it steady," I said, "and don't you dare leave. If she's all right I'll come down in a hurry."

No police had shown any interest in us so far, and the climb was easier than I expected. At the top I stopped and looked into the room. The faint light was coming from the bathroom, the door of which was partly open. There was enough for me to see that Judith was not in her bed, but it was mussed as though she had been, and her dressing-gown was thrown over a chair.

I threw a leg over the sill, and immediately a tin tray, balanced lightly on the upturned legs of a chair, fell with a deadly racket. I realized I had walked into a booby trap of no mean proportions, and I waited for Judith to scream. But nothing happened. There was no sound, not even any movement, and I think that was when I became alarmed. The racket had been enough to wake the dead, but no Judith had appeared at the bathroom door. At first I thought she might be out somewhere, and not until I had seen the bolt shot on her door and the chain on did I realize she must be where I found her.

I found her in the bathtub. She had cut both her wrists, and I was certain she was dead. Not that there was much blood in the tub, but because she felt cold when I bent over and touched her. She was wearing a thin nightdress, and her lips without make-up looked blue and thin.

I was still staring at her, unable to move, when I heard a man's voice behind me. I jumped and turned, to find Fowler in the middle of her room, his eyes hard and a gun in his hand.

"What's all this about?" he demanded. "Why the hell are you breaking into your own house?"

I moved then and he saw Judith. He simply stared, as if he could not believe it.

"It's—your sister, isn't it? Is she dead?"

"I'm afraid so," I stammered. "She feels cold."

He pushed me aside and bent over the tub. Then he strode

out of the bathroom and to the window.

"Get Jenkins up here," he called, "and bring that boy up, too. Then someone get a doctor. Break in the house if you have to, but hurry. Find a telephone."

A uniformed state policeman came up the ladder. He almost fell over Judith's booby trap and looked unhappy as Fowler gave him a nasty look.

"Help me get this woman out of the tub here and put her to bed," he said sharply. "Then wake the servants and tell them to find some hot-water bottles and some bandages. All right. Take her feet."

I was shaking all over, but I managed to speak.

"Is she dead?" I asked.

"I don't know. Pretty close to it, anyhow. Who is your family doctor? Or maybe she'd better go to the hospital."

"She'd rather stay here. I'm sure of that. Of course, it's up to you, but Doctor Christy—"

He nodded and together they carried Judith to her bed and covered her.

"Get Christy," he said to the trooper. "Tell him it's an emergency. Then tell the fellows down the drive to pass him." He looked at me, wet and bedraggled as I was, and he almost smiled.

"If some of these would-be suicides would fill the tub first with warm water they might get away with it. This way the blood coagulates. That's not what's wrong with her. She's taken something."

"What? What do you think she took?"

"Sleeping-pills, at a guess," he said dryly. "Why did you break in? You made a pretty poor job of it, you know. That racket—"

They brought Bill up the ladder just then. He took one look at Judith and collapsed.

"O God!" he said. "So I was right, after all."

Fowler sent us both out of the room. The house downstairs was already crowded with the local police and a couple of state

202

troopers who had been in the grounds and who, until they saw me, were smoking surreptitious cigarettes. The screaming of tires announced Doctor Christy and his nurse, who disappeared up the stairs, and after a time Fowler came down. He found us in the hall. I had pinned back my hair, but Bill still looked completely demoralized. It was Bill that Fowler spoke to.

"You say this was your idea?" he said. "Why? How did you know she was going to try to kill herself?"

"It was just a hunch. She wouldn't open her door, or speak to me. I got scared."

"Why did she have a booby trap under her window? What was *she* afraid of?"

"Wouldn't you be afraid?" I said, putting in my two cents' worth. "She says—she has said all along that someone wanted to kill her. You know we've had a man around the place at night trying to get in touch with her. I told the district attorney about him. She believed he mistook the Benjamin woman for her."

He gave me a not-unfriendly grin.

"So she tries to kill herself!" he said. "That's jumping out of the frying-pan into the fire with a vengeance. I've been in this business a long time, Miss Maynard. I've seen a lot of death and some suicides. But I never heard of killing yourself to avoid being killed."

Chapter 21

Doctor Christy was still in Judith's room when Phil arrived, looking half dead. He found me in the kitchen helping Helga make huge amounts of coffee. I was still in my pajamas and the old dressing-gown, with one foot bare.

"You're a sight," he said. "What in the name of heaven is going on? What are all these police doing here?"

"Swilling coffee," I told him. "And if you can stand another shock—and I mean shock—Judith tried to kill herself tonight."

He looked at me incredulously.

"Kill herself!" he said. "They only told me she was hurt. I don't believe it, Lois. Not Judith."

"I've told you all along there was something wrong with her," I said tiredly. "She tried it all right, Phil, believe it or not. I found her."

I told him my story as best I could, with police wandering in and out for coffee, with Helga listening and Jennie having hysterics in the pantry. He still looked stunned.

"But why?" he said. "She's been taking precious good care that nobody got at her. Then all at once this! I don't get it."

Well, of course nobody did. Not then, anyhow. I got him some whisky, after which he looked better. He reported that O'Brien was badly hurt but not fatally, and as by that time the police had gradually drifted away, we went into the living-room and Phil lit a fire.

He stood in front of it, looking up at Mother's portrait and evidently making up his mind about something. Then he lit a cigarette and turned to face me.

"It's a bad time to come out with this, Lois," he said tiredly. "You've had enough today. More than enough. But you'll have to know sooner or later."

"It's the golf club, isn't it?"

"Yes. It's mine. It hadn't even been cleaned. Only wiped off on the grass and stuck back in the bag. They didn't need a microscope to know it killed the Benjamin woman. Even the scrap of leather fits the grip."

"It didn't kill her, Phil. Remember, she was drowned."

"Why quibble?" he said. "Someone from this house took it and used it. It isn't hard to guess who, unless you think I did it myself."

It was fortunate Doctor Christy appeared just then. He wore the smug expression of a man who has just delivered a nine-pound baby, which was as well under the circumstances.

"Glad to say we've got the stuff licked," he said. "The cuts didn't amount to much. It was the barbiturate that gave the real trouble. She'd had quite a dose of it."

"Enough to kill her?" Phil asked.

"Well, it's hard to say. Enough to give her a good long sleep, anyhow." The chief had come in with him. Now he poured a couple of drinks from the Scotch on a table, and eyed Phil as he gave the doctor one.

"Don't you believe it was a genuine attempt at suicide?" he asked.

I knew what he meant. Someone from the house had taken Phil's golf club and used it on the Benjamin woman, which made our story about the man in the grounds look pretty sick. Phil realized it, too. If Judith had been the one she might have been remorseful enough, or frightened enough, to try suicide or at least to fake it. Phil, however, only looked resentful.

"It wasn't guilt that made her try what she did tonight," he said stubbornly. "It might be fear. Ever since she came here she has been afraid someone was trying to kill her. She's been scared for months. That doesn't spell murder, in my language."

"You've admitted the golf club is yours."

"What else could I do? My initials are stamped on it."

"That rather leaves it up to someone here in the house, doesn't it? And in my language suicide is often a confession of guilt."

But Phil only looked weary and impatient.

"A long time ago," he said, "I gave up trying to understand my sister Judith. She never made sense to me, even as a child. My mother spoiled her, of course. She married a good husband, and he spoiled her, too. She's always had everything she wanted, even a divorce. I'm sorry," he added. "It's no way to talk about a sister, but I've had about all I can take. The point is that she had no reason to kill that woman. None whatever."

"What about tonight?"

"If death was something she wanted—"

"We still have the club, Mr. Maynard. If we leave out the servants, only the three of you are likely to have known where it was kept. You must recognize that."

"Not necessarily," Phil said irritably. "Anyone could have taken it. The house is open except at night. As for me, I am as much in the dark as you are. I haven't played golf for weeks. Any time in the last two months that club could have been taken and never missed."

Fowler threw up his hands.

"If that's your story—" he said, and turning on his heel left us abruptly.

By six o'clock when Helga called us to breakfast the house looked as though a cyclone had struck it, but the police had gone. Even Doctor Christy, after a final look at Judith, had departed, although his nurse remained for a few hours.

"Let her sleep it out," he said. "She's all right now. Those cuts will heal in a hurry. Perhaps you'd better not talk to her about it. Let her explain if she wants to."

I had an idea Judith would do no explaining, but I let that go. Helga was a different matter, however. She stood in the kitchen and surveyed the place: cups all over it, the heel of a loaf of bread, the disconsolate bone of what had been a baked ham, and her clean linoleum covered with muddy footprints. Jennie had retired to her room with a headache, so she was alone when I went in.

"Are you trying to tell me Judith meant to kill herself tonight?" she said aggressively. "Because I won't believe it. Not Judith. Never."

"I'm afraid she did, Helga. It wasn't an act. Her door was locked. So was the one from the bathroom into the hall."

Helga sat down, as though her old legs would no longer hold her.

"It doesn't sound like her," she said slowly. "She was no angel. Heaven knows there were a good many times in the early days when I wanted to smack her good. But what would drive her to a thing like that?"

"I have an idea she thought O'Brien was dead, or dying. It may have been the last straw. I'm sure she felt guilty."

"The real guilt was years ago," Helga said somberly. "There is such a thing as the sins of the fathers catching up with the children."

I must have looked aghast. Certainly she knew she had gone too far, for when I asked her what she meant she clamped her lips shut.

"You must mean something," I persisted. "What did my father do?"

"I didn't say it was your father."

"All right. If you meant Mother, say so," I said impatiently. But Helga was on the defensive now.

"I don't hold anything against her," she said. "But she was a proud woman, Lois, and pride was her downfall."

She would not explain. She went doggedly about cleaning

her kitchen, and at last I left her there. I was sure she knew or suspected a great many things, but I knew, too, she meant to keep them to herself.

It was afternoon when Anne arrived. To my surprise Ridge was with her, as dapper as ever, and Anne looked like a mourner at a funeral.

"Bill telephoned," she said. "I can't believe it, Lois. She'd never do a thing like that. What got into her?"

I had no time to answer. Ridge had brought a huge box of flowers, and after leaving them in the hall he followed us into the living-room. He shook hands with me with his usual formality.

"How is she?" he inquired. "It was an idiotic thing to do. Suppose she hadn't been found in time!"

"What do you mean?" I said sharply. "She didn't intend to be found at all."

He shrugged.

"I hope you don't mind if I question that, Lois. She's threatened it before. You might say it's her way of keeping in the limelight. But she may be disappointed this time. There will be nothing in the gossip columns. I've seen to it."

"So that's the idea!" I said. "She was putting on an act, was she? Well, she didn't stage this, Ridge. It was real, and it was damned near fatal."

Anne was looking bewildered, as well she might, but Ridge was—as usual—the complete gentleman.

"It's possible, of course," he said politely. "I've suspected for a long time she was manic-depressive. Why don't you sit down, Lois? I've had a long drive. Why keep me standing?"

I was, however, too angry to sit.

"I see," I said. "On the upcurve for twenty years and on the down one for the last few months! That's crazy, Ridge."

Anne had said nothing so far. She had dropped into a chair, and lit a cigarette. Now she spoke.

"I don't know what you are talking about," she said querulously. "Why would she try to kill herself? I thought she

208

wanted to go abroad."

"Don't ask me. Ask Ridge. He can explain it!"

"And where's Bill? I told him I was coming out."

"Bill's sleeping," I said shortly. "He was up all night, like the rest of us."

"I'm going to take him home, Lois. This is no place for him: a murder, a shooting, and now this thing about Judith! It's just too much."

"Personally," I said, "I think he's having the time of his life. Anyhow I don't believe the police will let him go—not yet."

"The police! Don't tell me they suspect him!"

I had no time to answer. The nurse appeared in the doorway. She wore a coat over her uniform, and she said Judith was awake and had told her she could go.

Anne bounced out of her chair.

"That's simply idiotic," she said. "I'll go up and talk to her."

"I don't think I would," said the nurse. "She's all right, but she's still very nervous. I couldn't stay, anyhow. Doctor Christy needs me. He took me off another case last night."

I don't think Anne even heard her. She bolted out and up the stairs, leaving the young woman staring after her.

"I hope she doesn't tell Mrs. Chandler about the police," she said. "She doesn't know they were here. It might upset her."

Ridge eyed her thoughtfully.

"Has she said why she did it?" he inquired. "She must have given some reason."

The nurse looked uncertain, as though she had been told not to talk.

"She says she doesn't remember much," she said. "She admits she took too many pills, but only because she needed sleep." She glanced at me. "She'll be all right, you know, Miss Maynard. She's not sick. Only the wrists may bother her for a while. Not for long. The cuts aren't deep."

She left then, saying she had brought her own car, and I was alone with Ridge. He sat down and stretched his legs out.

"Sorry if I annoyed you, Lois," he said. "I thought it was

209

merely another bit of self-dramatization on Judith's part. God knows I've had plenty of them. That's why I brought the flowers, to add my bit to the stage setting."

I nodded. There wasn't much I could say, but I could and did mix him a whisky and soda. He watched me while I did it, as though he was making up his mind to something. It came when I handed him the glass.

"I've been thinking, Lois," he said. "We've known each other a long time. You were only a baby when I used to see you down at the pool. You may not like me, but I think you respect my judgement."

"I suppose I do, Ridge. I never thought about it."

"All right. Let's say you trust me, anyhow. I'll admit I've been in touch with the police ever since that woman was killed at the pool. Has it occurred to you that Judith might have been the one who carried Phil's golf club there?"

"Of course not. Why would she?"

"Suppose she was meeting someone—the Benjamin woman perhaps—and was afraid. After all, it was midnight. She might have carried it for her own defense."

"And killed her with it?"

"Not necessarily. The blow was not fatal. The woman may have been dazed by it, and later fell into the pool."

"The police don't think that."

"They're not saying what they think," he said irascibly. "I'm asking you. Did she know the woman? Had she made an appointment to meet her, by letter or telephone?"

"Not that I know of, Ridge. Anyhow I can't see Judith, terrified as she was, going down to the pool in the middle of the night. You know we've had a man loitering about the place, don't you?"

"So I understand. Have you no idea who it is?"

"No. I think the police believe we invented him."

He made no comment on that. Instead he wandered over to the fireplace, and stood looking at the Laszlo portrait of Mother. It reminded me of something Anne had once said, and of my talk with Helga that morning.

"I've been wanting to ask you a rather personal question, Ridge," I said. "Anne has always believed you financed the Arizona trip after Father's death and the crash. If you did, and Judith resented it—"

"Judith never resented anything to do with money, my dear."

"I am only trying to account for why she left you," I said uncomfortably. "It was kind of you, of course. Mother had no money sense, either."

"On the contrary," he said, his voice low and slightly acid, "she had an excellent money sense. I was younger than I am now, and very much in love. So when she came to me after your father's death and said she was in trouble, I helped her." He hesitated, then he smiled. "I helped her to the tune of fifty thousand dollars in cash."

They left soon after, Anne in a bad humor because Judith would not answer any of her questions, Ridge almost certainly regretting what he had told me. We had had only a moment or so before Anne came in, and I was too stunned to think clearly.

"I can't believe it, Ridge," I managed at last. "What sort of trouble? Surely Mother told you."

He cocked his head on one side, after a habit he had which always annoyed me.

"If I told you I didn't know, you wouldn't believe me, would you?"

"I don't think you'd give her all that money without a pretty good reason."

"They might have been a *quid pro quo*, you know, my dear."

"You mean—Judith?"

"That's rather a crude way of putting it, isn't it?"

"Did she know about it?"

"Not then. She may have learned it later. You might give me credit for sticking to my bargain, too. It hasn't always been easy."

Then Anne came in and soon they were gone. I was still

211

somewhat dazed when I went upstairs. Judith's door was closed and Helga was sitting in the hall, in case she needed anything.

She looked at me sharply.

"You'd better get some sleep, child," she said. "What was Ridge Chandler doing here? It's no place for him."

"He thought Judith was putting on an act."

She sniffed indignantly and I left her there. But I did not go to bed. I wanted to get out of the house and think. Too much had happened in the last few hours. Not only Judith's attempt at suicide and the attack on O'Brien. Both Phil and I were under suspicion of murder, and this time I had no one to help me. Up to then I had never felt entirely alone. I had carried my problems to the cottage, and had come away with renewed courage. Even the last time I had seen O'Brien before he was shot, and when he kissed me—

From the porch I could hear water running upstairs, and knew the men were awake. But I did not want to talk to them, or to anybody.

Instead I went down to the cottage. The police had left the key on the hall table after they had finished with it. I took it and went down the drive. Someone had released the chickens and apparently fed them, for they were clucking contentedly. But I found myself trembling as I unlocked the door and went in.

With the exception of the stained rug, which had been taken away, the place was orderly enough. The telephone was in place, and except for a dusting of powder here and there for fingerprints and the shabby look of the big chair without its cover it looked much as usual. Rather to my surprise the contents of the table drawer were still there, clippings and all, although they had certainly been examined. And, realizing how some of them related to the Benjamin woman, I knew O'Brien would eventually be in for a stiff grilling about them.

I did not touch them, but I picked up the photograph of Walter Benjamin and held it under the lamp. With my hand over the beard the face looked vaguely familiar, especially the

212

eyes. Otherwise I did not recognize it, but I took it with me when I went back to the house.

The men were eating a belated breakfast in the dining-room, or rather Bill was. Phil was having only coffee. He looked half sick, as well he might, but he attempted a smile.

"Don't tell me condemned men eat large meals before they go to the chair," he said. "The very sight of Bill and four eggs makes me shudder."

I took the chair beside him and put the photograph in front of him. He gazed at it without interest.

"Who is the hairy ape?" he inquired. "Friend of yours?"

"Put your hand over the beard and see if you know him, Phil."

He tried it, but he shook his head.

"Reminds me of somebody," he said, "only I don't know who. Don't tell me that's Judith's persistent lover. She doesn't go for whiskers."

It was still on the table when Helga came in with the grocery list. She gave it a long careful look and suddenly dropped the pencil and pad she was holding. I thought she was going to faint.

Chapter 22

The next two or three days passed with maddening slowness. O'Brien was in the hospital in town and gradually improving. I believe Phil saw him at least once, but only for a few minutes. He had apparently no idea who had shot him, or why. According to Fowler, he had been unable to sleep because of the heat and had gone out to the bench by the pool. He had been lighting a cigarette when it happened.

The shots had come from the shrubbery across the pool, he thought, but he had been unconscious for some time. It was daylight when he managed to reach the cottage. He had tried to telephone for help, but the phone fell, and he passed out again. He had had intervals of consciousness after that. During one he had tried to get up and find a ligature of some sort for his leg, but by that time he was too weak to move.

I listened, trying to conceal my surprise. He had not once mentioned the man who had been haunting The Birches. Whatever his reason was I could not imagine, but that he had one I did not doubt. They had recovered one bullet. The other had gone through his leg and was never found. He had been right, however, about the shrubbery. The police found the shell among the rhododendrons where an automatic pistol had ejected it. But Fowler came to the house one morning and asked for me. Phil had gone, and I had just hung up after calling the hospital. He must have heard me from the porch, for there was an odd glint in his eyes.

"You and O'Brien are pretty good friends, aren't you?" he observed.

"We get along," I said cautiously.

"That all? They tell me he's asking to see you."

I felt absurdly cheered, but Fowler hadn't finished.

"I have an idea," he went on, watching me, "you knew who he was when he came here. Knew why, too. I think it's time we had a little talk, Miss Maynard. Don't you?"

"I can't think why," I said. We were both standing and I didn't ask him to sit down. I had no idea what he wanted, but I felt myself stiffening.

"No?" he said. "Well, tell me this. O'Brien goes out sometimes in the night because it's hot and he can't sleep. That's all right. It could be. But why should a man only hunting a breeze carry his gun with him? Because that's what he did. It was under the bench."

"Are you trying to say he shot himself?" I said, startled.

"No. It hadn't been fired. I'm saying he was out there gunning for somebody, only the other fellow got him first."

I made a feeble protest.

"I've told you," I said. "We've had a man lurking about the place for weeks. Only you don't believe me."

"So O'Brien sets out to shoot him! That's pretty drastic, Miss Maynard, even for a New York cop."

He left on that. It was no use telling him O'Brien was merely trying to protect us. He had had the story of our nightly visitor over and over. But I was thoughtful as I went up to Judith.

She did not notice. Ever since we had found her she had simply lain in her bed, with her poor wrists bandaged and her doors locked most of the time. She offered no explanation of what she had done, but she was gentler than I had ever seen her, and grateful for what little I could do for her. She had lost most of her beauty, too. Her face looked pinched and white, and without make-up she was almost plain.

I was trying to induce her to eat some lunch that day when I heard the telephone. I answered it myself, fearful as I had been all along that the press would get the story. It was not a reporter, however. It was O'Brien!

I almost dropped the receiver when I heard his voice, remote but clear.

"Is that you, Lois?"

"Yes. For heaven's sake what are you doing on the phone?"

"Never mind that, and get this quick, while the goddam nurse is out of the room. Got a pad there?"

"Yes. What is it?"

"Take this down. 'A. Morrison. Insist stop further efforts immediately, and contact me.' Sign it 'T.O.' Get it?"

"What am I to do with it?"

"Put it in all the New York papers, under *Public Notices* or the *Personal* column. How soon can you do it?"

"This afternoon, if you're in a hurry. But what's it all about? I don't understand."

His voice was flagging, however. He said to keep it to myself. Then he muttered something about the nurse coming in, and hung up abruptly. I stood there looking at the pad in my hand. Whatever it meant to someone it meant nothing to me. But it was important. There had been urgency in his voice, in the very effort he had made to call me.

With Helga looking after Judith I caught the next train to town and left the notices as he had instructed. None of the people receiving them did more than count the words. I suppose they are accustomed to cryptic messages, but I felt self-conscious as I handed them in.

It was four o'clock when I finished, which left me an hour and a half until Phil's train. I had time to see Doctor Townsend if he was still in his office. I was lucky. He was there, and Miss Robey, his nurse, was even agreeable.

"We have been wondering about Mrs. Chandler," she said. "We haven't heard anything from her for some time."

"She hasn't been very well. Is there a chance I can see

216

the doctor?"

She said I could, although I would have to wait awhile, and eyed me with considerable curiosity.

"I see by the papers you have had a shooting at your place," she said. "Not serious, I hope."

"It was probably accidental," I said mendaciously. "The man was a tenant. He rented a small cottage of ours. But there is always somebody shooting in our part of the country. Of course, it's not deer season, but the natives don't bother about that."

I smiled. So did she. I don't think she believed me, but at least it ended the conversation. She went back to the desk in her small office, and before long a buzzer rang and she disappeared. By the usual system the previous patient had gone out by a different door, so I found the doctor alone. He got up, waved me to a chair, and sat down again.

"I'm glad to see you," he said. "Quite frankly I don't like the way things look. How is your sister?"

"You know about it, then?"

"Your brother called me soon after it happened. He couldn't say much over the telephone, but I got the general idea. Have you any idea what drove her to what she did? Did anything happen to cause any sudden depression?"

"Not to her, at least not that I know of. She's been very nervous, of course, and when Mr. O'Brien was shot we were all pretty much upset. But I think she related the shooting to herself; as though it was part of the plan to murder her. It sounds silly, but I'm sure that's what she believes."

"I don't see the connection."

"It's not easy," I said. "But this O'Brien is a police officer from Homicide here in town. I think he was there to protect her, or partly so, anyhow. Then when she thought he'd been killed—"

"What do you mean by 'partly so'? Was there another reason?"

"I don't know, Doctor. It's a long story, if you have time

217

for it."

He glanced at his watch. "I'll make time, Miss Maynard," he decided. "I've failed in your sister's case, and I don't like failure. Does this story relate to her?"

"Only in part," I said. "It began a long time ago, when a Homicide inspector here in New York was shot and killed. His name was Flaherty, and Lieutenant O'Brien was fond of him. He's never given up the case entirely, and lately I think he felt he was making some progress."

I told him what I knew. It took some time, as I had said, but he listened carefully: from Judith's sudden intention to divorce her husband to her fainting on the train; from the Benjamin woman's death to O'Brien's asking me to locate her home and my breaking into it, including the bankbooks and clippings I had found; and from the strange man who threw me into the pool to Judith's attempt at suicide.

Carefully schooled as he was he looked more and more astonished.

"It's certainly puzzling," he said. "And you've had quite a time yourself. The wonder is that it isn't you who cut your wrists! I gather you think your sister really made a serious attempt at suicide."

"She had locked herself off from any help. I only found her by climbing a ladder and going in through a window."

He smiled for the first time.

"You are rather an amazing young woman," he said. "I don't have many like you here." Then he became professional again. "Was there enough of the barbiturate to have killed her?"

"The doctor thinks so. I suppose the idea was to put herself to sleep while the—the other thing went on."

"To sleep away," he said thoughtfully. "Well, that's not unusual."

"And to do it as comfortably as possible," I observed, and saw him nod in agreement.

"Yes," he said. "Suicides do that sometimes. They go to bed

218

rather than fall on a hard floor, for instance. What about this shooting of Lieutenant O'Brien, Miss Maynard? Have the police any theories about it?"

"None that I know of, unless they suspect me. I think the police believe I pushed the Benjamin woman into the pool. Or that my brother did it. It was his golf club that knocked her out, you know. It doesn't matter to them that we never saw her until she was dead."

He did not smile. He got up instead and went to a window, although I didn't think he saw anything outside. When he turned his face was grave.

"Has it occurred to you that Mrs. Chandler may have done it? The woman came there to see someone. It might have been your sister. That's why you're here, isn't it?"

"I want to know if you think she's capable of a thing like that. Her former husband thinks she is a manic-depressive."

"So?" he said. "Well, in a way aren't we all? We have our ups and downs, but we're not necessarily off balance. One thing strikes me as odd, Miss Maynard. Your sister never told me the circumstances of her leaving Mr. Chandler. Most women do. They go to all lengths to expatiate on such things, to present their reasons, in other words, to defend themselves. She never has."

"She was never in love with him. He knows that himself. I think my mother rather forced the marriage. Judith was very young at the time, you know."

"The sow is not the only creature that kills her young," he said cryptically. "As you know, I've had your sister for some time. I have never thought she was really paranoid. Sensitive and egocentric she was. She had plenty of personal conflicts, but no particular hostility, although I realized she was not fond of her former husband. Nevertheless, as I told you before, she never gave me a real chance. I could go only so far. Then she blocked me. In fact I've been blaming myself for what she did. The last time she was here I told her she was wasting my time, and hers."

I could not think of anything to say. He went back to his desk and sat down, looking unhappy. He opened her file and glanced down at it.

"You see, Miss Maynard," he said, "the picture is somewhat altered. I gather that The Birches was a peaceful place until recently. Then all at once, or close together, we have a death, a shooting, and an attempted suicide. I don't know anything about the Benjamin woman, but I do know about O'Brien. The police have been here, you see. O'Brien was and is a member of the Homicide Squad here in town. He has a fine reputation. But he went into the army, and was invalided out of the South Pacific. Recently he asked for a leave of absence. But he is still a police officer, Miss Maynard, and I think you are right when you say he had a reason for being at The Birches."

I managed to steady my voice. I felt sure what was coming.

"Do you know what that reason was?" I asked.

He shrugged.

"Your local chief of police is a shrewd man," he said. "He has been here. He doesn't think the three events are unrelated. Your brother told him your sister had been consulting me, so he came to see me. What he asked me was if your sister was capable of murder. Or of one murder and the shooting of this man O'Brien."

I had known it was coming, but I felt faint and dizzy. When I did not speak he went on: "I suppose all of us are capable of it, more or less. Greed, envy, jealousy, rage, fear, self-protection, or sheer desperation—who knows what the human animal will do? And, of course, there is always what we call original sin. Whatever it is it may be the matter of a momentary impulse or the result of a long train of unconscious preparation. But we do kill."

"I don't believe Judith would kill anybody," I said stubbornly. "And she's really afraid. She was so afraid that she preferred to kill herself rather than be killed. And there is someone after her. I think he mistook the Benjamin woman for her. He certainly did me when he caught me that night. When he found he'd made a mistake he dropped me into the pool and escaped."

"You're sure you don't know who he is?"

"No. I haven't an idea. If the police have been here you know they've been watching for him."

"They don't entirely believe in him. Nor did I, until you told me all this."

"He exists," I said. "Judith knows who he is, too, but she won't tell. Not anyone. Not me. Not even you, I suppose."

"No," he agreed. "Of course, there is one particular psychosis which seldom accepts treatment. Let's call it guilt."

"Yet she comes here."

"She may want absolution without confession." He glanced through his notes. "You are insistent that she never took a lover?"

"Her husband says so."

"Husbands are usually the last to know," he said dryly. "She may have had affairs, Miss Maynard. Take a woman of her type and the situation between herself and Mr. Chandler, and what can you expect? It might account for a number of things."

Owing probably to my virginal status, he abandoned Judith's sex life, however. I wanted to tell him that I was twenty-eight years old and had lost my belief in the stork at the age of twelve. He gave me no chance.

"Has it occurred to you that her reaction to the sight of this dead woman was rather extreme?" he asked. "She must have seen death before."

"It wasn't a pretty sight, Doctor."

He took a turn or two about the room, looking deeply troubled.

"It's just possible," he said finally, "that it was your sister Mrs. Benjamin came to meet the night she was killed. After all, this woman expected to go home. She must have expected someone with a car to take her back to the station. Mrs. Chandler drives, of course?"

"Yes. But the whole idea is ridiculous, Doctor."

He sat down at last and giving me a cigarette took one himself and lit them both.

"Perhaps. Perhaps not," he said. "I'm out of my field, of course. I'm no detective. But just when did this Homicide man, O'Brien, ask for protracted leave, or whatever they call it? And why did he take your cottage? To watch your sister or to watch over her?"

"I think he was worried about her. He practically told me she was in danger."

"Why? Didn't he say? Your unknown man couldn't have been Walter Benjamin, unless he is still living and had his own reasons for disappearing. You didn't recognize his picture?"

"No. Of course, a beard changes a man."

He looked thoughtful.

"A beard? Would he have a reason for wearing a beard? Unless he had a weak chin or wanted to disguise himself?"

"I don't know why any man wears one," I said. "I think they're horrible."

He laughed at that, and soon after he got up.

"Sorry," he said. "I've given you more time than I should. But I may call you up someday, if that's all right."

"You don't think you should see Judith?"

"At the moment," he said dryly, "I imagine I'm the last person in the world she wants to see." I picked up my bag and prepared to go, but he stopped me. "I hope you don't mind this question," he said. "I think it's necessary. Have you any idea why your sister hated your mother?"

"Hated her? I don't understand!"

He modified it when he saw my face.

"Perhaps the word is too strong. Let's say disliked her," he said. "That has been evident all along. She won't discuss her. She won't even mention her name. I told you once there was a point I could never pass. That is at least a part of it."

"But Mother idolized her," I protested. "The rest of us simply grew up, but Judith was the hothouse plant. Nothing was too good for her."

"Not every hothouse plant flourishes," he said dryly, and prepared to leave.

I had plenty to think of on my way home that day, and it did not help matters to find Anne waiting for me at The Birches. She had come by train and Ed Brown's taxi, and she was still indignant.

"What does Ed mean about my Bill climbing a ladder the night Judith tried to kill herself? And the police arresting him?"

"Your Bill wasn't arrested," I said. "He was helping with what he calls a bit of breaking and entering. As a matter of fact, he was holding the ladder while I climbed it. Only the police grabbed him."

"I suppose that explains everything," she said nastily.

"Sit down," I said. "I'll get you a cup of tea or a high-ball, whichever you wish. And as soon as you're calm I'll tell you the story. Your Bill's all right. He's probably with his Janey this minute. As for the ladder, we needed it to get into Jude's room. I didn't say too much when Ridgely was here, but if it hadn't been for Bill she'd be dead this minute."

Anne chose tea, and I waited until Jennie had brought in the tray, dropped the sugar tongs on the floor, and reluctantly departed before I began. Then I told her, as briefly as I could. She was, like Phil, completely incredulous.

"Then she really meant it after all!" she said. "She's the last person in the world I'd expect to do a thing like that. I thought she was simply playing for sympathy. Or maybe she wanted Ridgely back."

"She doesn't," I said flatly. "But look here, Anne, she really *is* afraid of someone. Not Ridge. This man is a good bit taller than he is, and strong. I only saw him in the dark. But he's been around since. I think he knocked Mrs. Benjamin out and then threw her in the pool, and I believe he shot O'Brien."

She put down her cup.

"It's a pity," she said icily, "that no one ever tells me

223

anything. I send Bill out here to get some good country air while I have to be away, and all at once there's a killer around. I'm taking him back with me, Lois."

I smiled.

"You'd better wait until his face looks better," I said. "He's still not very pretty."

"His face? Did those policemen attack him?"

"No. Bill chased this killer—as we gaily refer to him—a night or two ago and came out second best when he caught up with him. The man got away, but Bill is somewhat battered."

Her face was a mask of horror.

"And you allowed a thing like that!" she said. "My own son, in peril of his life, and you do nothing about it."

"What could I do?" I asked reasonably. "I wasn't there. It was all over when I knew about it. And his lip is healed by this time."

"So they haven't got this—killer?"

"No."

She lay back in her chair and closed her eyes. I knew how she felt. Her quiet domestic life of poor servants, or none at all, of struggling to send her children to good schools, of pot roasts and the price of coffee, of getting Martin off in the morning and seeing him come home tired at night—none of this had prepared her for the drama she was facing.

"I'll be all right after a while," she said. "Let me just rest here a few minutes. I left a note for Martin. He can go out for his supper."

I sat there looking at her. She was older than Judith. She must remember things I had forgotten, or as a child never knew, and I was remembering what Helga had said that morning in the kitchen about the sins of the fathers.

"Do you mind if I ask you something, Anne?" I said.

She opened her eyes.

"What about?"

"About the family. Years ago. Was Father ever in any sort of trouble? I don't mean financial. Anything else?"

224

"Father? Of course not."

"He and Mother, they were happy together, weren't they?"

"They didn't fall all over each other, if that's what you mean. I don't think they quarreled much. But—I've never told this to anybody, Lois; not even Martin—they had a fearful row the day he shot himself."

She hadn't heard anything, just the loud voices and Mother crying hysterically. She had been staying in the house, as I knew, and she heard Father bang out the front door in a fury. It wasn't like him, she said.

"I don't suppose it really meant anything," she went on. "Only it was strange that night at the dinner, Father in full dress and Mother in the black velvet of the Laszlo painting there and all her pearls. I remember wondering at how well they carried on, although I don't think they were even on speaking terms. It was the same night, of course, that he shot himself."

Her voice trailed off, as though she had lost herself in the past.

"Did you know of any trouble Mother was having at that time? She wasn't in any sort of jam, was she?"

"What do you mean by a jam? She was in debt all over town. She refused to recognize the crash, you know."

But she couldn't have owed fifty thousand dollars, I thought. Anne poured herself another cup of tea and set down the pot.

"Of course, she got out as soon as she could after Father's death. She took Judith and went to Arizona. I often wonder if she didn't blame herself. If that was the reason she left. As though she couldn't stand the house any longer. Judith's cough was only an excuse."

I was remembering myself. The hasty exodus, and my standing around childlike to watch the hurried packing of trunks, Mother's face white and strained, and my nurse grabbing me by the arm and shutting me in the day nursery. Curiously enough, I did not remember seeing Judith at all. I daresay she was around, coughing, as Anne said, but I did not remember her.

But, with one of those curious flashbacks of memory that occur sometimes, I was remembering a tall saturnine-looking man, carrying down the bags to the car.

"We had a butler then, didn't we?" I asked.

"I suppose so. We always did have, didn't we?" she said vaguely. "I'd better see Judith, I suppose. She practically threw me out the last time. What on earth will I say?"

"Don't ask her any questions. Just say you're sorry she's not well. Tell her about Martin, or the high cost of living. Talk to her about going abroad. She intends to, as soon as she can get the space. Just any darn thing, but ignore the bandages."

She did pretty well, although I could see she was shocked at Judith's appearance. I think Judith tried, too, although she wasn't successful. They did better over the *Queen Mary*, on which Judith wanted to travel. But she and Anne had never got along, and I was relieved when Anne said she did not want to tire her and got up.

She stayed to dinner that night. Bill, for a wonder, turned up, but he instantly vetoed going back to New York.

"I've got a thing for this Janey girl," he said, "and I'm having the time of my life into the bargain. I'm staying awhile, if Phil and Lois will keep me."

Anne eyed him. His face had improved, but the black shadow around one eye made him a little pathetic. In the end he got his way and, Anne refusing to ride in his jalopy, he drove her to the station in our car. I think she was reassured by the sight of a state trooper on a motorcycle who followed them into town. It annoyed Bill, however, and on returning he stated he had meant to take Janey for a drive that night, but the idea of a policeman making a third did not appeal to him.

Chapter 23

I found Helga with Walter Benjamin's picture that night. She had gone into my room ostensibly to turn down my bed, but she had not done so. Instead she was standing holding the photograph, and her hand was shaking.

"Found this on the floor," she said. "Not very pretty, is he?"

"Do you know who it is?"

"Me?" she said indignantly. "Of course not."

I did not believe her. She was both shocked and frightened, and she scurried out of the room as fast as her legs would take her. I gave her time to get to her room and settle down before I followed her, carrying the picture with me.

She had not gone to bed. Apparently she had been sitting beside the window in the dark, as though she were watching the grounds, and I saw she was careful to draw the shade before she switched on a light. For the first time I wondered if she was afraid, and if so, of what. When I asked her, however, she merely said it was a hot night and she liked the air.

But she eyed the photograph with angry suspicion.

"I told you about that," she said. "It's my bedtime, Lois, and what with company and trays and what not I've earned my sleep."

"Of course you have," I agreed. "This won't take a minute.

Just who is this man? You recognized him, didn't you?"

"With all that hair? It might be the angel Gabriel for all of me."

I gave up. Helga could be stubborn, and the way her jaw was set over her false teeth a Missouri mule had nothing on her. Yet I felt she wanted to tell me something and was afraid to do so. I tried another tack.

"All right," I said. "You didn't know him and he didn't know you. But perhaps you remember what employment agency Mother used, Helga. She must have changed help now and then."

"Not me. I went there as kitchenmaid, and I've stayed ever since."

"But the others. I seem to remember a lot of butlers, for one thing. Where did she get her servants? What agency, I mean."

She threw me a sharp glance.

"She didn't consult me," she said. "My job was my kitchen and I stayed there. Every morning I got my orders. I wrote them down, too, so your mother couldn't say I'd changed anything. And every week I added up my slips, so she knew I wasn't getting a percentage like most cooks. Butlers, too. They get a cut on all the liquor they buy. That Dawson got rich on it."

Dawson! It was the name I had forgotten, and Helga had managed to tell me after all.

"He was there when Father died, wasn't he?" I said casually. "How could he get rich, Helga? We had lost everything."

"Don't ask me," she said. "All I know is he was going to buy a business of his own. That takes money. He was a bad man, Lois. A wicked man. Mind, I don't know anything, but he got that money somewhere that wasn't honest."

"What sort of business, Helga?"

"How would I know?" she said. "And it's no use showing me that picture!" she added. "I haven't got my specs. Left them downstairs. I wouldn't remember, anyhow. Now clear out of here. I want to go to bed."

228

But I held it out to her, and she had to take it. She didn't want to. Her old hands were shaking again, and she gave it the briefest possible glance.

"Never saw him before," she said. "Don't like hairy men. Never did. Who's it supposed to be?"

She knew him all right. But for some reason she wasn't going to tell me who he was, and I knew my whole excursion was a failure. She didn't know anything. She insisted she did not know what agency Mother used to find domestic help, and I left her standing in the center of the room, her mouth stubbornly set. But she said one significant thing as I was closing the door.

"You better let sleeping dogs lie, Lois," she said. "We got trouble enough now. Don't you be stirring up more."

I made Judith comfortable before I went to bed that night. I rubbed her back, realizing that she was thinner than I had ever seen her, and I laid out the two sleeping-pills she was allowed out of the bottle I kept hidden in my room. She hardly spoke at all, but when I had finished she looked up at me.

"Does Doctor Townsend know about me, Lois?" she asked.

"I believe Phil called him up," I said evasively. "Would you like to see him?"

She shook her head.

"I was just tired," she said slowly. "Tired and sort of desperate. I didn't kill that woman, Lois."

"I never thought you did, darling."

"And I didn't shoot O'Brien, either." She gave me a thin smile. "Jennie told me he's in the hospital. I hope he's better. I rather liked him. He's improving, isn't he?"

"Yes," I said. "They say he'll pull through."

"And—have they any idea who shot him?"

"I suppose all cops make enemies. Nobody knows who did it, unless you know something yourself, Judith. If you do you ought to tell it."

But she only gave a slight shudder and closed her eyes.

"What I know wouldn't help," she said flatly. Then she did an unusual thing, for her. She reached up a thin hand and patted my arm.

"I've played hell with your work, haven't I?" she said. "Ever since I came."

I grinned at her.

"My agent says the magazines are going all out for sweetness and love," I said. "That rather lets my Sara Winters out, doesn't it!"

She let me go then, as though she was settled for the night. As soon as I had closed the door, however, I heard her beyond it, locking it and shoving the bolt in place. So, whatever the terror was, it was not over for her.

Phil says that out of the mouths of babes and sucklings what issues is usually a lot of burps. Yet as it happened it was young Bill who solved at least one problem for me. For by that time I was practically convinced that Walter Benjamin had been Arthur Dawson, and that he had been involved in some dirty business in the past which concerned us. It would account for the money in the bank, the change of name, the beard, and most important of all, why his widow had come to The Birches.

It was at breakfast the next morning that I asked Phil if he had any idea from what employment agency Mother had got her household servants. He gave me his usual morning glare— of wanting to read his paper, of to hell with commuting, and of resentment that anybody could expect him to speak until after his second cup of coffee.

"How the devil would I know?" he said sourly. "And why should you care?"

Bill, however, looked up from a four-inch pile of hot cakes soaked with butter and syrup.

"Ludwig's," he said.

"Ludwig's what?"

"Grandmother always went to Ludwig's, according to Mother. So does Mother herself, for all the good it does her."

I went into New York late that morning, but as I sat in the train I became more and more uncertain. I had a lot of

230

unrelated facts and some guesses. What had Ridge Chandler's fifty thousand dollars to do with Dawson, alias Benjamin? Could a man, say of fifty and not too honest, have accumulated the sum he had deposited in the bank so long ago? Or had he been the "jam" Ridge had spoken about? In that case what did he know in order to blackmail Mother?

She hadn't killed Father, of course. There was the note he left, and the dinner party was still going on when it happened. Also Judith was only in her teens in those days, not even allowed to drive a car. Not allowed to do much of anything, for that matter. She had not even made her debut, that winter of 1929-30 and, if she was involved, Dawson had apparently let many years lapse, years when he probably knew she had married well, without bothering her.

It was not Dawson then—or Benjamin, if it was he—who had sent her scurrying to Reno, and I felt rather foolish when I located the Ludwig Employment Agency on a second floor on Madison Avenue. It was a shabby place which showed its age. Old Mrs. Ludwig was dead, the girl at the desk told me, but her daughter was running the business. She was out to lunch, but would be back soon. I sat down to wait in the depressing atmosphere of all such places: the line of women in the adjoining room, the detached young woman at the desk, and the occasional telephone calls.

"I sent her over. Didn't she come?" Or: "Well, I'm sorry. Her references are fine. Maybe if you try her a little longer."

I longed for a cigarette or even a sandwich. I had not stopped to eat. And I could feel the eyes of the women on me, suspicious or hopeful as it might be; hope that I might offer a summer place, cool and with grass. Suspicion because all employers were suspect. They made me feel like an interloper. Things picked up, however, when Miss Ludwig appeared. She was a brisk middle-aged woman, neatly dressed, and as she took off her hat she asked me what she could do for me.

"I'm afraid I'm here under false pretenses," I said. "I don't

231

want to employ anyone. I'm really after information, although after all this time—"

She listened while I explained. I was trying to trace a butler my mother, Mrs. James Maynard, had employed a good many years ago. He was dead now, but his widow had died, too, not long ago and there was some money involved. Rather a large sum, in fact. His name had been Arthur Dawson.

She shook her head. The name meant nothing to her. But she said they still had her mother's old ledgers. She herself used a card index system, but the ledgers were around somewhere.

"If Dawson was on her list, Mother would have it," she said. "She was most particular."

She got the approximate date from me, raised her eyebrows, and then disappeared into a third room which from the glimpse I had of it was used largely for the storage of broken chairs and a chest or two. When she came back some minutes later she had two dusty volumes in her arms and a smudge of dirt across her nose.

"Mother had her own methods," she said, placing them on the desk. "She had one for what she called the ladies, and I'm glad some of them never saw those books! The other is for the applicants. If you'll give me your mother's name again I'll take her first."

She found it, and she looked at me with some respect.

"I see you kept eight servants for a good many years," she said. "And—I hope you don't mind this—your mother is listed as hard to suit but fair. She paid well and expected a good bit."

I didn't mind, so she turned to the other ledger. Dawson was there. At the age of forty he had been in a good many situations apparently, but there was no entry for him after Mother had employed him. Not even the date he had left. She closed the book and glanced at me.

"I'm afraid that's not very useful," she said. "But you have to remember the times. Most people cut down because of the crash, and very few continued to keep butlers, or indeed much

232

help at all. You were too young to remember, I suppose."

I said I was, thanked her, and left. All I had was a sort of negative proof that Dawson had not used the Ludwig agency after he left us. He might have been anywhere, doing anything. The one thing I was sure of was that he was too old to have dumped me into the pool or banged poor Bill into unconsciousness.

Chapter 24

It was rather a shock to find Chief Fowler on the porch when I got home. I had come out with Phil, and Bill met us at the train. Phil groaned when he saw Fowler.

"Well, here it comes," he said. "Two to one I go first, Lois."

Apparently, however, no one was to be arrested. It was a hot day, and the chief had made himself comfortable. His collar and part of his shirt were open, and his Panama hat lay beside him on the chair. Beside him, too, on a table was a pitcher of lemonade and a glass. He got up as we climbed the steps, looking rather embarrassed.

"I took the liberty of asking for something cool," he said. "Hope you don't mind."

"Just so you don't pull out a pair of handcuffs," Phil said.

The chief laughed merrily, or so Phil maintained later.

"Now, now, Mr. Maynard," he said. "You will have your little joke."

"Even in the shadow of the gallows," Phil said. "It is a far, far better thing I do, and so forth."

The chief looked mystified, having never apparently heard of Charles Dickens and Sydney Carton, and Phil turned sour.

"Just what's the idea of the visit?" he said. "Unless you've decided I shot O'Brien."

"O'Brien's a cop," Fowler said comfortably. "A fellow like

that makes enemies, and he knows it. He sends them up the river, and when they get out sometimes they go for him. He's had narrow escapes before this."

So that was O'Brien's story! I almost smiled, but Phil was still irritable.

"Are you here because some gun-happy punk shot O'Brien?" he demanded. "If so, I want a bath and a high-ball. Then I want my dinner. Unless there is something urgent—"

"Well, I don't know whether you would call it urgent or not," Fowler said complacently. "But we haven't forgotten a little matter of murder here, Mr. Maynard. And since the state boys have pulled out—"

"Oh, so they've pulled out, have they?"

"I guess they got word from Albany to quit playing. Or maybe they've decided somebody dreamed up this fellow you all talked about."

Phil snorted.

"You can look at Bill's face here if you want a sign. He'd have a hard time dreaming that up."

Fowler, however, was still in high good humor.

"Funny thing," he said. "These state fellows think they're the cat's whiskers, but now and then they slip up. Take it like this, Mr. Maynard. This Benjamin woman wasn't expecting trouble when she came here that night. Not a bit of it. She was sitting nice and comfortable on that bench down there, waiting for somebody. Smoking a cigarette, too. You didn't know that, did you?"

Phil grinned.

"I don't think it would have interested me," he said. "Not to the point of murder, anyhow."

Fowler's smile faded.

"Well, that's as may be," he said. "At least let's say I have eyes and know how to use them."

He reached into his pocket and pulled out a thin old-fashioned gold chain, with a black-and-white locket as a pendant, and held it out for us to see.

"As I said, those state guys are all right for traffic. Give them a bunch of parking-tickets and they're happy. But they missed this, and how! It's hers, all right. The Hunnewell woman says she knows it well. Now guess where I found it."

I was not guessing, nor was Phil. We did not even touch the thing.

"All right," Phil said impatiently. "You found it and it's hers. So what?"

The chief was slightly deflated, but not much, and he refused to be hurried. He had not been satisfied, he said, with the idea that the blow had stunned the Benjamin woman and she had tumbled into the pool.

"It looked more deliberate to me," he said. "That blow she got didn't knock her out. There was no fracture. Made her head ache maybe, maybe not. But she knew the pool was there. So how did she get into it?"

Nobody said anything, and he went on. He had come back to The Birches that morning and gone over the neighborhood of the pool. He had examined the diving-platform, with no results, and at first, too, the old bench offered nothing. Finally, however, he turned it over and shook it, and the locket dropped out from between the boards.

"You get the idea," he said, returning it carefully to his pocket. "She's sitting there peaceably, and waiting for someone she's expecting. It's a long trip, but she's made it. Maybe she's tired. Maybe she even dozes off. She was a little hard of hearing, too. So she doesn't even know there's someone near her until it's too late. Then *wham*! She gets hit on the head.

"But it doesn't knock her out. She puts up some sort of fight, not much but enough to break the necklace. Maybe she tries to scream. Maybe she does scream. The inside of one of her lips was cut, as though whoever it was tried to gag her with a hand. But she still isn't dead. So she's picked up and thrown into the pool. No woman did all that, Mr. Maynard."

"Look," Phil said. "If you lived in a house full of women, as

236

I do for my sins, you'd know there's very little they can't do. They can move pianos and lift carpets. They break things, too; watch crystals, chains, eggbeaters, toasters, even chairs, by God!"

I glared at him.

"Just in case my brother is suggesting the *wham* came from me," I said, "I had a similar experience myself one night not long ago. A man picked me up and threw me into the pool. If you don't believe me you can ask O'Brien at the hospital. He dried me out."

Fowler looked astonished. Then he smiled.

"Didn't just dive in yourself, did you?" he said. "I gather you're a fine little swimmer."

"If you think I did it to throw you off the track," I said angrily, "you're even more of an idiot than I think you are, and that's plenty. Over and over we have told you about this man, but you still think we've made him up out of whole cloth. Who shot O'Brien? Who threw a rock through my sister's window, or don't you know about that? Who frightened Jennie into hysterics? Who knocked Bill here senseless? And who dumped me into the pool? I say it's the same man who killed Mrs. Benjamin, and if we didn't have a lot of lame-brained police he'd be in jail this minute."

Fowler got up. He even managed to achieve a certain amount of dignity.

"Maybe not," he said. "But lame-brained or not, that golf club came from here. Just remember that, Miss Maynard. You talk a lot. So does your brother. But you don't say very much. And don't think I'm through. Maybe for the shadow of the gallows—whatever that means—you might substitute chair, and not one of those your brother mentioned, either."

He left us then, driving away with a look of determination on his face. Bill grinned.

"Made a nice comeback, the blabbermouth, didn't he?" he said cheerfully. "But the big hunk of cheese doesn't know which end of him is up."

237

"I wouldn't bet on that," Phil said. Then he turned on me. "For God's sake, Lois, what goes on around here?" He stood stiffly, eyeing me with something less than brotherly affection.

"What is O'Brien's game?" he inquired. "And why did you go to him anyway, as you so nicely put it, to dry you out?"

"His place was nearer, Phil. Anyhow it was over. The man was gone, and I didn't see what I could do."

"That's a fine state of mind!" he said bitterly. "We have a maniac about this place. He throws all sorts of capers, and he even probably commits a murder. But I'm not to know. It's supposed to take brains to be a lawyer, but no. A tuppenny policeman named O'Brien calls the shots."

"O'Brien tried to catch him that night, but he got away. He's after Judith, Phil. Not me. That's why O'Brien was here. To protect her."

"That I don't believe," he said, and turning abruptly went into the house.

Dinner that night was a quiet one. Phil was taciturn. He didn't even bother to look with distaste at the dried apricots which were Helga's attempt to economize while Bill was out. And when it was over he carried his coffee into the library, closing the door behind him, which was his signal to keep out.

Nevertheless, I followed him soon after. He was at his desk, but he had not started to work. He had not even touched his coffee. He was holding his head in his hands, and the face he turned to me was without expression.

"I'm sorry to bother you, Phil," I said. "But it's time we had a talk. I've been holding out on you, but with things as they are—"

"Without O'Brien, you mean."

"Partly that. Not all."

"So now I'm to be let into the arcanum! Thanks. Many thanks," he said. "I began to gather that quite a lot's been going on without my knowing it. O'Brien turns out to be a Homicide man. Bill gets his comeuppance. Somebody throws you in that damned pool of yours. Judith tries to kill herself. Just possibly you or I or both of us are about to be arrested for murder, and God knows what else. What do you think I am? A moron?"

"You're always so tired, Phil. Besides, I don't really know anything. I'm as mystified as you are."

He laughed cynically.

"So you accidentally take a ride, see a black cat in a window, discover the Benjamin house, make a liar out of yourself at the inquest, and get dumped—I believe that's your word—into the pool. What else?"

"Do you want me to tell you? Or are you going to think the whole thing's funny? It's damned unfunny, Phil."

He drew a long breath.

"Go ahead," he said. "I'll try to control my sense of humor."

Sitting there, with Phil at the desk and me in a chair, I began with the death of Flaherty, and went on to the train at Reno and O'Brien. I ended with Helga and the picture of Walter Benjamin. Some of it he knew, some of it he did not. He remembered Dawson, but he saw nothing unusual in his disappearance, even if he had changed his name.

"They wander about, these fellows," he said. "Change places often, and if they lack good references they may change their names. Some of them make quite a bit on the side, too, tips from guests, commissions on liquor bills, and so on. If that was his picture you showed me the other night he's changed a lot. Of course, twenty years—"

"And thirty thousand dollars," I reminded him. "Phil, do you think Mother gave it to him?"

He stared at me.

"Mother?" he said. "By the time the estate was settled she didn't have thirty thousand cents. What do you mean? Even if she had it, why give it to Dawson?"

"If he was Walter Benjamin he got it somewhere. She wasn't in trouble of some sort, was she?"

"We were all in trouble," he said shortly. "I was back in college, shoveling snow and washing dishes to finish my last year, and Anne was trying to find a place where she and Harrison could starve to death."

"Yet Mother took Judith and went to Arizona, Phil. I think she was running away from something. Could she have owed a lot of money you didn't know about?"

"She owed plenty," he said, his face grim. "The executors had to stop her credit everywhere. She never had any money sense. It was just something to spend. But real money, no."

I might have told him then about Ridge's fifty thousand dollars. I wish now I had. But he reverted to my story as if he did not care to discuss Mother's lack of financial acumen. He has a clear legal mind, and as he sat back with a cigarette he reviewed briefly what I had told him.

It looked to him, he said, as though I was confusing two different things. One, he said, didn't concern us. That was the murder of Flaherty.

"That's O'Brien's business," he said shortly, "and if you ask me it's a trifle sentimental after all this time. But the other is Judith's, and knowing her capacity for getting herself in a mess it might be anything from mayhem to bigamy."

"I've thought of that, Phil. Could she have run away and married someone before she married Ridge?"

"And the groom has kept his mouth shut ever since? Talk sense, Lois. How about these clippings? You say they're still in the cottage? I might have a look at them."

It was still twilight as we started down the drive. Phil was silent, apparently thinking over our talk and not liking much of it. But when we were fifty feet or so away I heard Henrietta give a loud squawk and flutter her wings wildly.

"That chicken still roost in the cottage, Lois?" Phil asked.

"I think Helga puts her there at night. She sounds frightened."

She *was* frightened. The cottage door was wide open and she was on her way out when we reached it. It took only a glance to see that someone had been there before us. The place had been pretty thoroughly ransacked. The table drawer was open and empty, and the books had been moved about on the shelves. There was no great confusion, however. It had been done in an orderly way, as if someone had hoped it would go unnoticed.

It took only a moment to see all this, and I shot into the kitchen, with that ridiculous chicken practically under my feet. The window there was open, although it had been kept closed and locked since O'Brien had left. I called to Phil.

"He's somewhere outside," I said. "He got out this window when he heard us coming. He can't be far away. Perhaps you can catch him."

I don't think he relished the suggestion. Nevertheless, he took the poker from the fireplace and started for the door. He stopped there to glance at me with a sickly grin.

"God help me if Fowler sees me with this!" he said, and disappeared.

I stood listening. Darkness had fallen suddenly, and I could hear him beating through the shrubbery. Nothing happened, however, no car started up, as I had expected, and Phil found no one. He came back, covered with burs and looking disgusted.

"Why the brainstorm?" he asked. "How do you know whoever it was went out that window?"

"Because it was open. And Henrietta was scared off her perch. You heard her squawk yourself."

He damned all chickens while he picked the burs off his trouser legs. But he was impressed, nevertheless.

"If there was anyone here how did he get in?" he asked. "Who has a key to this place?"

There were only two, I told him, O'Brien's and the one we kept at the house, on the hall table.

"Helga uses it to get the chicken feed from the kitchen," I said, "but she always puts it back. Phil, did you look in the chicken house?"

"No, and I don't intend to," he said grumpily. "I need a vacuum cleaner and a drink. Or reverse it. A drink, then the vacuum."

241

As a result it was I who went out to the chicken house, taking O'Brien's flashlight with me. It was too late, of course. The hens were stirring unhappily, but the shed was empty. The doors were open, however. Someone had been there, listening and waiting for a chance to escape.

It did nothing to soothe my feelings to find the key in its usual place when we went back to the house.

I was still upset when I prepared Judith for bed later on. She was up and about by that time. Her wrists had healed with only small scars, but she continued to stick to her room and her locked doors. The terror, whatever it was, still obsessed her. She had tried to escape it by dying, but when that failed it remained with her.

Yet in a way I thought she was less desperate. Certainly she was easier to get along with. Perhaps when one has deliberately faced eternity as she had one's perspective must be altered, and even death may have lost some of its horror. She was still weak, however. I fixed her bed and got her into it before she noticed chicken feathers in my hair and asked about them.

I could not tell her our invader was back again. It would have destroyed what little equanimity she had recovered. I invented something about a fox after O'Brien's girls, and let it go at that.

She turned over as usual to let me rub her back, not interested in chickens, not interested in much, actually, except to get away from all of us and start a new life elsewhere.

"I've been thinking," she said. "I'll be sure to get a sailing soon, with the rush almost over. And a lot of my clothes are still in the apartment. If Ridge lets you in, would you pack them for me? The trunks are in the storeroom."

"Of course," I told her.

"If you can find Clarice, she might help you. She's a wonderful packer."

Clarice had been her personal maid for several years, but thinking of the raft of servants she always employed for some reason reminded me of Dawson.

"I'll try," I said. "Ridge probably gave her a reference.

Speaking of her, I wonder if you remember a butler we used to have?"

"What butler?" she asked idly. "We had dozens."

"His name was Dawson."

To my surprise I could feel her stiffen under my hands. Every muscle went rigid, and at first she did not speak. Then, "What about him?" she asked. "I think I remember him. It must have been years ago. Why?"

"Only that he was there when Father died," I said. "Phil and I were going over old times tonight. What became of him? Do you know?"

"I haven't the remotest idea," she said.

I was confident she was lying, but I could not be sure. Certainly it was some time before she relaxed. Also certainly she did not revert to him again, and I did not dare to pursue the subject.

But the name had meant something to her, something unpleasant, perhaps even something dreadful, for she was very pale when I went out and she locked and bolted the door behind me.

Clearly whatever her secret was she meant to keep it to herself if it killed her. And as things turned out it almost did.

Chapter 25

I resolutely put Judith's problem behind me when I went to my room that night. I had two reasons for thankfulness. One—an important one—was that sometime during the evening Phil had told me O'Brien was out of bed. The other, of course, was the prospect of Judith's going abroad.

I tried to visualize what it would mean, a return to peace and safety, time to work at my neglected novel, and a move back to Mother's room, warm in winter and with a sunny window for my typewriter. I even played with the idea, if I finished the book, of buying a station wagon instead of our old car. Which shows my state of mind, as well as how little I knew.

But it was dampening to realize that O'Brien would probably leave when Judith did. He liked me. I knew that. He even kissed me in an impulsive moment. Yet I knew instinctively that he was a man's man. He had been a tower of strength to me, and he was as masculine as they come. But he had no illusions about women. It might, I thought, be very difficult for him to love one.

So discouraging was the idea that I crawled out of bed, washed my hair, and after a disconsolate look at my nails, ignored largely since Gertrude's, filed and painted them.

This last was not a good idea. I had to wait for them to dry, which gave me time to think: about the chicken house that night, about Fowler and Selina Benjamin's necklace, even about Doctor Townsend's suggestion that Judith might have carried Phil's golf club to the pool.

Even when my hair and nails were dry I was not sleepy, and I remember that was when I drew the black cat on the pencil pad beside the bed. I always kept the pad there, in the vain hope that some fugitive idea about my work would come in the night.

So far as I know none ever did. All there was on the pad when I looked at it was a list of words with which at some time I had evidently intended to enrich Sara Winters's skimpy vocabulary. I remember "functional" and "integration" were among them, as well as "photogenic," which Walter Benjamin definitely was not.

I drew the cat absently, thinking about the Benjamin-Dawson puzzle, and about the cottage and what had happened there. Not only the theft of the clippings that night. There was the shooting of O'Brien, and before it there was the other time when I wandered in from the pool, soaking wet and furious, and he had used the telephone to order the road block.

Because he knew something I did not. Probably a great deal, for that matter. For I could still see him, able and competent, and annoyed rather than alarmed as I stood dripping before him. He had even known who the man was. It was in his voice when he said, "The poor crazy bastard." And then his poor crazy bastard had come back and tried to kill him. Or had he?

I came, of course and inevitably, to Dawson, and to Judith's reaction that night while I rubbed her back. She was not only shocked. She was instantly on the defensive. Why? If Walter Benjamin was Dawson, he was most certainly dead. I had no doubt O'Brien had verified this. And Helga had recognized the photograph. I knew it, and she knew I knew it.

That was when I remembered Judith in the attic, with the old-fashioned square trunk before her. She had not been looking for her wedding pictures in it, and whatever she was searching for she had not found. Her hands were empty when

245

she left; empty and shaking, as though she had been caught in some nefarious enterprise.

There was no use trying to sleep after that. I got up and putting on a dressing-gown and slippers, I went out into the hall. It was dark, the only light a dim reflection from the bulb left on downstairs for Bill, if and when he came home. But I knew the house too well to need any assistance.

The attic, however, was slightly daunting until I found the cord for the ceiling lamp. Then it sprang into life, a vast repository of the family's history, with its broken furniture, its trunks, some of them with foreign labels, even the old toys Helga refused to throw away. They were on a shelf, and I could see my old doll's house, its contents neatly arranged. It gave me a faintly nostalgic feeling for the old days. For Father, and a small girl standing by a Christmas tree and staring incredulously at what was beneath it.

"Like it, baby?"

"Oh, Daddy, it's wonderful. It's wonderful."

Poor Father. The church had decided he was of unsound mind, so he had received a Christian burial. I had not seen his grave for years, but the last time there had been a potted geranium on it. Helga had not forgotten him.

The trunk of snapshots was where it had been before, under the light. As I raised the lid I was almost appalled. It contained the accumulated snapshots of years, from Phil's boyish efforts to my own with a Brownie later and others probably donated from other sources. But after an hour's hard work I had half a dozen or so clear ones of Judith and her crowd around the pool. In spite of their best efforts I had managed to edge into one or two of them, grinning toothlessly at the camera. Then, when I had almost given up, I found one of a man in a white coat, standing by the picnic table and looking up from slicing a large baked ham.

He was Dawson, right enough, the man I remembered helping Mother and Judith downstairs with their bags on their way to Arizona, and I did not need Phil's cynical writing on the back to identify it. It said: *Dawson catering to the locusts*!

He was clean shaven, of course, a man of forty or thereabouts, and I tried to imagine him at sixty or more and with a beard. Except for the eyes I could not be certain. Nevertheless, I took it, along with half a dozen of the groups around the pool, and putting out the light felt my way down the stairs.

I was in the hall when I saw the man. He was hardly more than a shadow, and he had heard me, for he was flattened against Judith's door as though to escape observation. I must have taken two or three steps forward before I screamed, for the next thing I knew my head struck the newel post, and he leaped over me and made for the stairs.

According to the best fiction I should then have passed out. I did nothing of the sort. I simply lay there and yelled until Phil bent over me and shook me.

"Stop it!" he shouted. "What the hell's wrong with you?"

"The man," I gasped. "He was there, outside Judith's room. He knocked me down."

"Get up and talk sense. What man, and where did he go?"

I got up indignantly. My head hurt and I was sick at my stomach.

"There was a man," I said slowly and distinctly—and furiously. "He was at Judith's door. When he saw me he knocked me down, so I hit that post and may have a concussion. He then ran down the stairs and by this time has escaped. Let go of me, Phil. I'm going to lose my dinner."

He released me in a hurry, and I made my bathroom without a minute to spare. When I wobbled back to the hall Bill had evidently come home, the search below was in full cry, and Judith was standing in her doorway. Or rather she was leaning against the frame, as though she needed support.

"Did you see him?" she asked.

"Only an outline, Jude. I think he was wearing a cap."

She made a queer little gesture of despair, and turning sharply went back into her room. I could hear her sliding the bolt on her door and putting up the chain.

I was in bed when the men came upstairs again. There was a sizable bump on the back of my head, but I got little sympathy for it. They said he had cut a neat hole in the pantry window so he could get at the lock, and the window was still up when they got there.

Phil had already called the police in town. He said a prowl car was on the way out, but the sergeant or whoever took his message thought too much time had elapsed.

"Fellow could lose himself in two minutes among those trees out there," he said.

He proved to be correct. When, an hour or so later, two big boys in blue examined the pantry window and came upstairs to examine me, they found me with a wet compress on my head and slightly gaga from the whisky Bill had poured into me.

"Come in and sit down," I said cheerfully. "How about a drink?"

The idea appealed to them, but they said they were on duty. Maybe another time— And did the fellow who attacked me have a weapon?

"Certainly," I said. "The newel post out there in the hall. Only I hope you don't have to take it away. We really need it."

Phil gave me a nasty look and took them away. It developed that if our man had a car he had not gone toward town. The only car they had seen was a New York taxicab, which had left some people beyond us and was heading back to the city.

The driver, they reported, had seen nobody.

The house settled down at last, Bill having adopted Judith's idea of a booby trap under the broken window and using most of Helga's tinware to do it. I locked myself in my room, however, and having hidden the snapshots behind some books on my shelves, crawled back into bed. I did not expect to sleep, but Bill's whisky must have been operating, for I remember no more of the night.

Of course, there was trouble in the morning, with Jennie as usual threatening to leave and Phil having to raise her wages to induce her to stay. But the effect on Helga was appalling.

She sought me out in the storeroom, where I was making a list of needed supplies, and closed the door behind her.

"Bill says you saw this man," she said. "What did he look like? Was he young or old?"

"I haven't an idea. Not very old, I think, by the way he ran."

"Look, Lois," she said, "can't you get Judith out of here? She's not safe. Nobody's safe either while she's around."

I confronted her, pad in hand.

"Does it occur to you," I said, "that if you told everything you know we might all be safer? What do you know about it, Helga? You must know something."

She drew a long breath.

"I'm not sure of anything," she said slowly. "I only know it has something to do with Judith when she was a slip of a girl. They had to get her out of town, Lois. Your mother was about frantic. Maybe she killed somebody with a car, or maybe she was going to have a baby. And that Dawson—"

"What about Dawson?"

"He knew all about it, whatever it was. He and the madam were shut up in her room for hours one day talking. It wasn't him last night, was it?"

"I think he's dead, Helga," I told her. "Anyhow, he would be pretty old now, wouldn't he?"

"It's got to do with him just the same," she said, her face set obstinately. "You get rid of Miss Judith, Lois. Her middle name's trouble."

But I did not have to get rid of Judith. I found her packing her bags again, and she said she was leaving as soon as I'd packed her trunks in the apartment.

"I'm going to a hotel," she said feverishly. "And I'll sail on anything that floats. I should have gone long ago."

As it turned out, however, she did not go. Only a few days later she was in bed in the hospital in town, being held for murder.

Chapter 26

I never did see O'Brien in the hospital. To my astonishment he came back that afternoon, against the doctor's orders and refusing the ambulance as though it had been a hearse.

He looked much the same, except for the sling that supported his right arm. Perhaps a little thinner and with a slight limp, but his grin was as engaging as ever. When I saw him from the house he was outside in the chicken yard carrying on a one-sided conversation with Henrietta, who gave every evidence of hen hysteria, and when I ran down the drive he looked pleased.

"Somebody's been taking good care of the girls," he said, eyeing me. "Which is more than I can say of you, mavourneen. But O'Brien's back. We'll have no more of these shenanigans. Do you think I could sit on my rump in that hospital and let fellows bang you on the head with a newel post?"

"He didn't, you know," I said. "He was only pushing me out of his way."

"Well, you gave the town police a good story, anyhow. Fowler says how was she injured, and they state 'she was struck by a newel post!' Come inside. I don't stand so good on this leg."

It was what I had learned to call one of his Irish days, which I discovered later only came when he was deeply moved. And once inside I suddenly felt shy. He seemed younger than I remembered, for some reason; and for the first time it occurred to me that he was very good-looking. He was no Adonis. His features were too irregular for that. But any man would have considered him handsome, and a good many women, too.

To my surprise he looked embarrassed. After I sat down he stood on the hearth filling his pipe, and it was some time before he spoke.

"I suppose you wouldn't know why I didn't ask you to come to the hospital," he said at last. "I suppose it's because no man wants his girl to see him laid out and helpless. That's a man's pride, and he has a right to it. But I had another reason, too. I used to lie in that damned bed and figure what I was going to say to you when I got out and we were here together like this. I had it all fixed, words and music," he said. "Only I can't remember any of it."

I'm afraid I blushed, as I had not done for years, but I kept my voice even.

"Personally," I said, "I keep a pad and pencil to jot down fugitive thoughts. You might try it."

"Fugitive!" he exploded. "What's so damn fugitive about it? It's funk, my girl. I'm scared witless, that's all. Only I've changed my mind. I propose to no woman while I have a game leg and an arm in a sling. Besides, I've got a job to do. I may stop another bullet before it's over and not get off so easy. Because this is big-time stuff, my darling."

I managed a smile.

"So I'm to consider the motion passed as read," I said. "Is that the idea?"

He nodded. It was characteristic of him, I thought, to put me aside and get back to his job again without even a break.

"Passed as read," he agreed, and dropped down heavily in his big chair. "Now, what goes on out here? Not last night. I know about that. What have they been doing to you? You look as though you haven't been sleeping for weeks. Has Fowler been bothering you?"

251

"Only now and then. Of course, he is quite sure either Phil or I killed Mrs. Benjamin. He's looking for a motive now. And your clippings and the photograph are gone, just in case you're looking for them."

He was not worried, I saw. Hardly even interested.

"Police take them?" he asked.

"No. Somebody last night. He escaped through the kitchen window while I was bringing Phil to see them."

"Likes windows, doesn't he?" he commented. "Two the same night. Although I can't imagine—" He broke off then, as though he was thinking. "What good are they to anyone? Even the bankbooks. I've got the facts on them."

"Not all of them," I said rather smugly. "I don't suppose you know Ridgely Chandler gave Mother fifty thousand dollars in cash about the time Walter Benjamin made that deposit. Or do you know that, too?"

"I knew it," he said briefly. "At least I knew he'd made a large withdrawal about that time. Did he come out flat-footed and tell you?"

"Not flat-footed. No Chandler is ever flat-footed. He told me, yes."

"Why? Not why did he pay your mother. That's pretty clear. He wanted your sister. But why tell you?"

"I think he was annoyed. Judith had tried to kill herself, and he'd been busy keeping it out of the papers. I think he regretted it later. But maybe a psychiatrist would say it was a part of his build-up; that he had an inferiority complex about his height and this showed him big and generous."

He grinned over his pipe.

"I'll be getting a smart wife someday, God willing," he said. "With a head like that pretty one of yours we could go places. I suppose you know by this time that Dawson was Benjamin."

I gaped at him.

"You knew it all along, didn't you?"

"Well, I had a theory, and I was lucky. I managed to trace him. You see, we're getting along, aren't we?"

"If you mean back to Flaherty—"

"Precisely," he said. "Back to Flaherty is right. It wasn't very long after your father's death that Flaherty was killed. And two weeks later an impecunious butler named Dawson went to a downtown savings bank and made deposits of thirty thousand dollars there."

I got up. All the peace was gone from the cottage, or for that matter all that held us together.

"Are you saying," I asked furiously, "that my own mother had Flaherty murdered?"

"I haven't said anything of the sort," he said patiently. "I think your mother was blackmailed out of fifty thousand dollars. Dawson spent some of it. He bought a tobacco business, remember, and he still had thirty thousand left. That was a sizable sum for those days, my dear. For any days, for that matter."

Slowly it dawned on me what he meant.

"The Preston girl!" I said. "You can't think any of us were involved in that, unless you think my father knew a little cheap East Side prostitute and murdered her."

"Dawson murdered her."

"Dawson!"

"He was in love with her. We never had enough to take to a jury. But Flaherty was sure the Henry woman was lying about young Johnny Shannon. They both disappeared before the trial, and Flaherty was trying to trace them when he was shot."

"You mean," I said incredulously, "someone paid him to kill Flaherty?"

"He was paid for something. Maybe to keep his mouth shut."

"And Mother paid him?"

"I think she did, yes."

"But why?" I said bleakly. "What had she done? She had her faults, but she was never the sort to run around. She had a family, too. We were only kids, except Anne, and she kept a sharp watch on us. Oh, I forgot, our friend the prowler was

253

here again last night."

He looked annoyed rather than surprised.

"How do you know it was Morrison?" he asked sharply.

"Because he was at Judith's door in the upper hall when I saw him. He knocked me down trying to escape."

If I expected him to leap from his chair in any wild expression of sympathy I was certainly disappointed. He only looked tired and angry.

"The damned fool!" he said. "Did you get a good look at him?"

"I wasn't in any position to inspect him," I said. "I was flat on the floor when he leaped over me. And I was good and sick afterward, if that means anything to you."

I was still getting no pity, however.

"You must have some idea about him," he said thoughtfully. "Was he big or little, young or old? And what was he doing at your sister's door?"

"I didn't inquire," I said. "We merely met, so to speak, and parted."

He came over then and put his good arm around me.

"I'm sorry, my poor darling," he said softly. "I'd hoped he wouldn't come back."

"But why?" I said. "What does he want? Why is he trying to kill Judith?"

"I'm not sure he is," he said slowly. "I told you once I might be off on the wrong foot in this case. I still wonder. What does Mrs. Chandler say about all this?"

"He was a burglar after her jewelry. Period."

"Not the tea set in the dining-room?"

"Definitely not the tea set. And don't try to be funny. I have a bump on the back of my head so I couldn't wear a hat, if I ever wore one. You know who this man is. Why don't you turn him in? Or don't you think he killed Selina Benjamin? Maybe you suspect one of us, as Fowler does."

"Don't forget that's still a possibility, my darling," he said. "A woman with a golf club can be pretty formidable, and Judith's attempt at suicide hasn't helped matters any. As a

254

matter of fact, we may find it was Judith Chandler who took the golf club to the pool that night. Whether she used it or not is another question. But Selina was there to meet someone, and I think it was your sister."

I sat back and closed my eyes.

"I don't believe it," I said huskily. "Why would she?"

"Look, my dear," he said gently. "A long time ago someone paid Walter Benjamin—or Dawson, if you like—fifty thousand dollars for some purpose. Maybe to kill Flaherty, maybe not. But Selina Benjamin knows about it. She marries the man, and may have had twenty years of hell with him. Then he dies—he is dead, I've verified that—and she is free. So one of several things may happen. Perhaps her conscience bothers her. Perhaps she sees a chance for more blackmail. Or perhaps, if she wrote the anonymous letter I got, she intends to warn Mrs. Chandler she is in danger."

"So she has to be silenced?"

"She had to be killed."

I got up dizzily.

"I can't bear it," I said. "Judith never killed anybody."

"No," he said, to my surprise. "I don't think she did. Only it's going to be hard to prove."

He let me go then. It was the policeman, not the lover, who showed me out the door of the cottage, and I went home in a bad humor and a mental state of chaos.

I had another sleepless night after that, and at two in the morning I got the pad from my table and tried to make some sort of outline of what I knew. As I kept it, along with the drawing of the cat, I copy it here to show my mental confusion at the time.

The murder of Selina Benjamin.
> *cat*
My visit to her house   *bankbooks*
> *clippings*
The inquest and Phil's golf club.

The story of Flaherty.

The rock through Judith's window. Was there a note?

The man who dumped me in the pool.

Bill's fight with him, or someone, and his breaking into the house.

The shooting of O'Brien.

The theft of the clippings and so on from the cottage.

Helga and Dawson's picture. What does she know?

Judith's attempt at suicide.

They made no sense, of course. There were even none of the clues Sara Winters always sprinkles about, no lost buttons or cuff links, no handy fragments of cloth or fingerprints. Nothing much except Selina's necklace, which only proved she had been at the pool—a fact we certainly knew anyhow—and the golf club, which might have been missing for days without anyone's noticing it.

If I dreamed about O'Brien that night I do not remember it. But I did realize that I was in love with two men; one was big, gentle, and loving; the other was a policeman—and I wondered drearily if the two ever met.

Chapter 27

I packed Judith's trunks in town the next day. She was up and about that morning, and determined to leave The Birches as soon as possible. She even went down to the telephone and tried to make a reservation at the Plaza for the next day. They could not take her until the day after, which infuriated her, and when I left for the city she was calling the various travel agencies. So far as I could hear, the news was still bad. All they could offer was a possible cancellation at the last minute, and she looked rather daunted as she dropped into a hall chair.

"Get my trunks packed, anyhow, will you, Lois?" she said feverishly. "They can be forwarded abroad to me if I get a ship."

She sat there, her color bad, but her mouth set determinedly. She was not able to travel. She was not even fit to be where she was, out of bed and downstairs. But there was a sort of desperation about her that morning which left me without protest.

I lunched at the Waldorf with Ridge that day. He had the keys to the apartment and to the various closets there, and he had located Clarice, who agreed to help me. He himself was not going back.

"I've turned that particular page," he said, his face set. "I don't want to reopen it."

He did not look well. He was nervous, too, although a couple of Martinis relaxed him. He listened to my story of what Judith maintained was a burglar after her jewels, and said she was a fool not to keep them in the bank. But he thought The Birches was no place for her, and said so.

Not until the meal was over and his demitasse was in front of him did he refer to our last meeting and then, I felt, unwillingly.

"About the money I gave your mother," he said; "that was strictly between us, Lois. No need of having it talked about."

"It's nothing I'm very proud of, Ridge. I still can't imagine Mother getting into a jam. Didn't she tell you what it was?"

"I gathered it was serious. That's all I know."

I was tempted to tell him about Dawson, and I have wondered since if things would have been different if I had. But he had paid the check and was ready to go, so I said nothing.

He dropped me at the apartment on Fifth Avenue, but he did not go in. Clarice was waiting in the foyer, and we went up in the elevator together. Her face was alive with curiosity, although she said nothing until we had raised the shades and opened the windows. The huge apartment smelled of moth preventives. It had the moldy odor of places shut up for a long time, and with the furniture and even the paintings covered it was dismal and dark.

Clarice called the houseman to bring up the trunks from the basement, and while we waited for them and I lit a cigarette, she eyed me.

"Mr. Chandler says the madam is going abroad," she said. "Surely she's not going alone?"

"If you mean a maid, she is having enough trouble getting passage for herself."

She sighed.

"I have missed her," she said. "I have a lady now, of course, but she is old and ugly. It was a pleasure to dress Mrs. Chandler. She was always a picture. And such lovely clothes! I

258

do not understand it," she went on when I said nothing. "So gay she was, and then all at once everything is wrong. She does not go out, she has no parties, even some days she stays in bed. In bed all day," she added. "Not even eating! And Mr. Chandler is bewildered, poor man. Why not?"

"She hasn't been well, Clarice. Perhaps that explains it."

She tossed her head.

"She was not sick, Miss Maynard. I have thought—perhaps Mr. Chandler has a pretty lady somewhere and she finds it out. But then I think that is silly. Mr. Chandler is not that sort of man. He is too well-bred."

I might have enlightened her on what Bill would have called the capers of some well-bred people I knew, but the trunks arrived just then and we set to work.

Even I had not realized the breadth and depth of Judith's wardrobe as Clarice lovingly took dress after dress out of their protective bags. She lingered over the ermine evening wrap.

"I always thought that was the reason she had the row the first night she wore it," she said. "It had just come home, and it must have cost a fortune. Not that he said anything when she showed it to him, except that she looked fine in it. I was there, so he couldn't. But after she came home—wow! He must have given her hell."

"I think we won't discuss Mrs. Chandler," I said briefly. "Let's get on with this packing."

She turned sulky after that, but I paid no attention. I was trying to reconcile Ridge's story about that night with what I had just heard. Somehow it made better sense if they had quarreled, Judith's taking out her jewels and more or less appraising them, and her decision to leave him. He must have said some unforgivable thing. Perhaps that she had been bought and paid for with the money he gave Mother and, as he had told me, he felt there had been no value received.

I let Clarice finish the packing and went into the drawing-room and stood looking out at the park. Small boys were sailing yachts on the lake almost under the window and, as I watched, one of them turned over and sank. I could hear the boy's wails from where I stood. It made me think of Judith, whose small craft had so nearly sunk.

Her bags were in the hall when I got home that afternoon, so I gathered she really meant to leave us. I found her in bed, however, looking exhausted.

"Well," I said cheerfully, "your trunks are packed and ready. Ridge let me in and Clarice helped me."

"That snoop!" she said. "Are you sure you got everything? She's quite capable of holding out something she liked."

"She didn't hold out your ermine and sable coat, although she drooled over it. It looks as though it had never been worn."

"I only wore it once," she said. "Do you mind sending me a tray? I'm weaker than I realized."

Obviously the coat was out, as were so many things. If she and Ridge quarreled over it she had no intention of telling me. I saw too that her jewel case was beside the bed, and the safe was open and empty.

"Aren't you afraid of our burglar again?" I said. "What's the idea, Jude? They were all right where they were."

"I'll need them, if I get a late cancellation on the *Queen Mary*. There's a chance I may, at the last minute."

I told Phil at the dinner table that night that she was really leaving, and he drew a long breath.

"It's about time," he said, pushing aside the junket Jennie had served him. "She's my sister, but look at the record! She married a good guy who let her run wild for years. Too much drinking, too late hours, and a lot of parasites around her, picking up the crumbs. Then she leaves him. No reason. Just shucked him like an ear of corn."

"So she tries to kill herself," I said. "That's silly, Phil."

"Well, she's at an uncertain age," he said. "She's been a beauty, too. Now she's fading, and knows it. That's probably the reason."

"Why did she marry Ridge, Phil? She wasn't in love with him. He isn't even attractive."

"Money," he said tersely. "Ten millions of it. I'm not mercenary, but I'd marry a girl with two heads for less than that."

He got up, after giving the junket a look of pure loathing, and lit a cigarette.

"Think I'll go down and see our cop," he said. "The damn fool ought to be in bed. Maybe I can get him there."

Bill was out, so I was alone after he left, and when the phone rang I thought rather hopefully it would be a travel agency with a room for Judith. To my astonishment it was Doctor Townsend.

"I wonder if you will do an errand for me tomorrow?" he said. "It may be a considerable job, but I've been thinking over that last talk of ours. After all, a still youngish beautiful woman doesn't try to kill herself without good reason. And the impulse may still be there."

"She's leaving here the day after tomorrow," I told him.

"For where?"

"The Plaza first, Europe eventually. What do you want me to do, Doctor?"

What he wanted was rather curious. He sounded apologetic as he explained. Briefly, and if I was willing, I was to go the next morning to the public library, where the various newspapers kept their back files, and look over the winter of 1929-30.

"Look for any mention of your family," he said. "Your father's death, if you don't mind, and the society pages, too. It will give you a date or two, anyhow. And see if any of you were involved in any trouble at that time. Outside of the panic, of course. Just see what you can pick up."

I don't think he liked the idea himself. The ethics of it must have bothered him. On the other hand, he was trying to help Judith in the only way he knew, and I understood.

"I'll do anything you think will be useful," I told him. "But I doubt if the society news will be helpful. We were in mourning, you know."

"When did your father die?"

"In January, 1930."

"Why not look before that? In November or December. I think what happened to Mrs. Chandler happened that winter. That's what she blocks off, if you know what I mean."

As a result I went in to the city with Phil the next morning. He was not curious, fortunately. He read the paper all the way, and accepted my statement about needing stockings with no comment whatever.

I had no difficulty at the library, but it was a tough job. The back issues were kept on microfilm, and looking at them through a viewer was troublesome. Also, except for an account of Father's death, which I did not read, and a brief notice that Mother and Judith had gone to Tucson early in February, there was no mention of the family. But purely by chance I happened on the story of the Preston girl's murder.

The story, when I read it, was about the trial. The date was February, 1930. A boy named Shannon, a student at Columbia at the time, had been on friendly terms with a girl of indifferent reputation who worked in one of the five-and-ten-cent stores. She lived in a tenement on the East Side, and one evening in November, 1929, she was heard quarreling with Shannon. Late that night her strangled body was found in her room. Shannon had been arrested, and in February went on trial.

He protested his innocence, but the evidence was all against him. One of the witnesses who identified him before the grand jury was a young woman whose picture was shown.

I sat back and studied it. Given almost twenty-one years and the blankness of a dead face, it was Selina Benjamin. It was her testimony before the grand jury that indicted Shannon, and, although she had disappeared by that time, had helped convict him. Flaherty had believed she was lying, had probably traced her to the town up the Hudson, and been killed before he had seen her.

None of this related to my own family, of course, except for Dawson, whose name was never mentioned. But apparently the jury recognized Shannon's youth, for on its recommendation he was given life instead of the chair.

I found a picture of him after he had been sentenced, but he had turned his face away as if to avoid the camera. All I could see was a well-built youth with heavy hair and broad shoulders. And the young uniformed man beside him and manacled to him, according to the caption underneath, was one Sergeant O'Brien.

I called the doctor, reporting I had found nothing, and later I lunched with Anne. She had a maid again, so we ate, as she said, like Christians. But I did not tell her what I had been doing. Instead I asked her if she had ever heard of a Mollie Preston or a Johnny Shannon. She only looked blank.

"Who are they? I never heard of them."

"I only wondered if they were friends of Judith's years ago. I came across the names somewhere."

"Oh, Judith! If they were a part of the gang around the swimming pool every summer, I wouldn't know them. The amount of riffraff she collected!"

She said Ridgely was selling the apartment and had offered her Judith's huge grand piano.

"As if I had room for it," she said sourly. "Martha wants it, but I told her if she brought it in her father and I would have to move out on the street."

Her real interest, however, was in the fact that Judith was leaving The Birches for the Plaza, and the reason she gave for it.

"A burglar," she said, "and in the house! What on earth did you do?"

"I lost my dinner, for one thing."

I had to explain it, of course, and she looked appalled.

"I suppose he was after that jewelry of hers," she said. "She's acting like a fool about it. Why not put it in the bank? Ridge says it's actually dangerous to carry it about as she does."

I left her soon after, but I did not want to go home. Call it intuition. Call it a hunch if you like, but I was depressed and not a little sad. I could still see O'Brien handcuffed to Johnny Shannon. He had been looking straight at the camera, and there was nothing in his face to show that the boy beside him was going to something worse than death. He looked like a man doing his duty. Nothing more.

Was that what it meant to be a policeman, I thought. To be in Homicide, sending people to the chair or up for life. To build cases against them, stubbornly and doggedly, to grow hard in so doing, and yet to care for some woman, love her, and marry her. Even have children and love them, too.

Because O'Brien could be hard, and I knew it, I did not want to see him that day. Instead I went to a double-feature movie which I hardly saw, ate a hamburger supper, and took a late train home. As both Phil and Bill were out to dinner, nobody met me.

The only taxi at the station was Ed Brown's, and he drove me to The Birches that night. He sat grumpily in the front seat of the rattletrap he called his car, and at the entrance to our drive he stopped.

"Guess you can walk the rest of the way," he said. "I got to get home. Missed my supper already."

"It won't take you two minutes to go on, Ed. I'm tired. Go ahead. Don't be stubborn."

He turned around in the seat and glared at me.

"Too many bullets flying around this place," he said. "Too much sudden death, if you ask me. Either you walk or you stay in the car and I'll take you back to the station. All the same to me."

I was furious, but I knew Ed. I got out grumbling and I did not tip him, which made him clash his gears with indignation. But I need not have worried about seeing O'Brien. The cottage was dark and his car gone.

I was hardly in the house when the telephone rang, and a man's voice asked for Judith. She must have been listening, for she was down the stairs in a hurry. As I stood by I could see she was wildly excited.

"Of course I can make it," she said. "I'll make it if I have to walk. Oh, you're sending a car for me? That's splendid. We have none here. My brother is out to dinner somewhere, and so is my nephew. Another passenger, you say? Where do I pick him up?"

Later on, with police all around, I tried to tell them of her real excitement, her real happiness that night. She was not acting. She was almost the young Judith I had admired and loved years ago. But they did not believe me.

She turned to me from the telephone, her eyes shining.

"What incredible luck!" she said. "A really good cabin on the *Queen Mary*. It's a late cancellation. They're sending a car out to pick up someone or other, so they are having it come for me first, and I'll pick the man up on my way in." She was already halfway up the stairs. "We'll have to hurry," she said. "The ship's sailing at midnight, and I have to get there in time. It's lucky I'm partly packed. You'll have to send my trunks later, Lois. I'll cable you where."

She shot up to her room and I followed her. It was after nine by that time, and the two maids were in bed. I did not wake them. While Judith started to dress I finished her packing, and carried the bags down the stairs. After that there was a considerable wait, with Judith consulting her wrist watch every five minutes. When at last we heard the car grinding up the drive, I was in what might be called a state. It was almost ten by that time, a starless, moonless night, and I remember piling the bags into the big black car without any attempt at order.

Then Judith was kissing me good-by, and with her jewel case on her lap was waving as the car started.

Chapter 28

I waited until the car reached the main road, then with a curious sense of deflation I went back into the house. She was gone, and I realized unexpectedly that I was going to miss her. I went up to her room, which was a chaos of tissue paper, discarded stockings, and all sorts of odds and ends, and for something to do set to work to put it at least partly in order.

There was no need any longer of the bolts on her door or on her bathroom, I thought as I worked. The terror, whatever it had been, was gone. Or was it? The big quiet house seemed full of ghosts: of Mother dying in the walnut bed beside me, of Judith unconscious in it, of the unknown man lurking outside in the hall. I felt somewhat better when, an hour or so later, I saw the lights come on in the cottage and knew O'Brien had come back.

I needed to see him. Not only to tell him Judith had gone, so he no longer felt he had to watch the place at night, but for reasons of my own. I had been badly shaken that day, and my confidence had not yet returned. I needed to see him, not as the man shackled to Johnny Shannon but as the O'Brien I knew, the big kindly man who tolerated Henrietta and even built a roost for her in the kitchen, the man who liked his girls and said he loved me.

The house was still empty when I left it. Neither Phil nor Bill had come back, although it was after one o'clock. And the darkness was appalling. Well as I knew the drive I had more or less to feel my way. Yet darkness meant safety, I thought, in case our intruder was still about. He might not know that Judith was gone, and in fact it was only when I was near the pool that I heard any sound at all.

Someone was in the shrubbery. Whoever it was was moving slowly, as if with a cool deliberation which was worse than any sort of haste. It sent me running madly for the cottage and safety, and fortunately O'Brien heard me coming. He opened the door for me, and it was at that instant a shot rang out. It struck the wall of the cottage beside me as he dragged me inside and shoved me down on the floor as he slammed the door.

"For God's sake!" he said. "What are you doing here?"

He didn't wait for an answer. He left me there and shut off the lights, but not before I had seen his face. He was all policeman at that moment. What's more, he was furious at me.

"Don't move," he said sharply. "He may try again. Where is he?"

"Where he always is," I said hysterically. "Near the pool."

I could hear him getting his gun, and the next moment he was quietly opening the door. It was more than I could bear. Probably I screamed. I know I begged him not to go out, that the intruder was still there.

"He'll kill you!" I yelled. "He's tried once. He'll try again."

"Not now he won't," he said grimly. "That voice of yours was a warning all right. He's gone."

It was some time before I let him go out. I was still crying like a fool, and I knew he was furiously impatient with me when at last he took his gun and a flashlight and went out. I was sitting up drying my eyes when he came back.

"You certainly have a faculty for spilling the beans," he said coldly. "Can't you ever learn to keep your pretty mouth shut?"

Somehow I managed to get on my feet.

"I'm sorry," I said. "I didn't want you shot again. That's all.

267

And I don't like policemen. They're hard. They're not like other people. They have no feelings."

And then I was sobbing on his breast, and his arms were around me, sling and all.

"It isn't cruel to try to get a killer," he said. "It makes the world a better place to live in, mavourneen."

He let me cry it out, my fright and shock, and when I was quieter he offered me a large, very clean white handkerchief. Then he put me into his own chair, and drew up one for himself.

"Let's have this out," he said. "If you ever marry me I'll still be a cop, my darling. It's all I know to be. It's in me, as it was in Flaherty. But I'll be on the side of the law. That ought to mean something."

He was wearing his other face now, the one I knew and loved, and when Henrietta came in, eyeing us in her crooked manner, he put down a hand and stroked her absently.

"Something's happened to you," he said. "You've known all along what my job is. What is it?"

"I saw your picture today," I told him. "It was an old one. You were taking the Shannon boy to prison for life, and you didn't seem to care."

"I cared all right," he said. "What did you expect me to do? Burst into tears?" And when I only shook my head he went on. "Maybe I'd better tell you about Johnny," he said. "Perhaps I should have done it sooner. You see, he was by way of being a friend of mine. I visited him all the time he was shut away and last winter I got him out. He wasn't even on parole. He was free."

"*You* did that?"

"Don't give me too much credit. He'd been a model prisoner, and the case had been purely circumstantial, anyhow. But there he was, free, and with no place to go. You'll have to know his problem, Lois, to understand him. It's not easy to get work for a man like that. He was forty, and his hair had turned white, so he looked even older.

"He lived with me for a while. He was fine. He knew a lot, too. He'd read about everything in the prison library. He was the librarian for a long time but he had one obsession. He hadn't killed the Preston girl, and he wanted his name cleared.

"I think he located the Benjamin woman about that time, although he never told me. Possibly he scared her, too, for she and her husband closed the shop and went away, ostensibly to visit her sister, and Walter Benjamin died there.

"But Selina had to come back eventually. There was the estate to settle, the shop to sell. She must have been afraid at first, but as time went on and Johnny let her alone she gained confidence. There was something else, too. She had joined the church, and her conscience was bothering her badly. I think, too, she began to worry about your sister."

"Judith!" I said, bewildered. "What had she to do with him?"

"I'm coming to her, my dear. She knew Johnny was free. The papers played it up when he was released, and it was she, far more than Selina Benjamin, who had let him go up for life. No wonder she was terrified, or wanted to get out of the country."

"Are you saying Judith killed the Preston girl? That's crazy. It's insane. Judith at eighteen! How could she even know her? Mother watched over her day and night."

"That's as it may be, my dear. Let's say after Reno Shannon meant to see her, and had a reason for it. Perhaps he wasn't normal. The big house does things to men, and he'd been there a long time. I began to worry about him, so I wrote to a friend of mine, the police chief in Reno, and told him the facts. He arranged for Johnny to get a license there to drive a taxicab, under the name of Alec Morrison. He did pretty well out there. Reno is a free-and-easy town. But when I read in the papers that Judith Chandler had gone there to divorce her husband, I didn't like it. I got some leave and went out. Johnny was all right. Apparently he didn't even know she was there, and I didn't tell him.

"He seemed contented, now that he had a job. He even had a girl, although he said he wouldn't marry her until he was cleared of the murder charge. Then, on the day you were leaving, he saw Mrs. Chandler on the train, and she saw him. He hadn't changed much, except for his hair, and his cap hid that. But I didn't like the way he stared at her. There were twenty years of pure hatred in it. She saw it, too, and fainted."

My lips were dry and my whole face felt tight.

"Why did she faint?" I said. "You know, don't you? You knew all the time, didn't you? It was no accident you were on that train."

"No, it was no accident." He reached over and took both my hands. "Look, Lois, this isn't going to be easy. I hate like hell to do it, but just bear with me, that's all. I'm going to begin with your mother. I'm Irish, and the Irish love their children but, as Doctor Townsend would say, we're not cannibals. We don't eat them alive.

"In a way, that is what your mother did with your sister Judith. It's hard to understand why a cat will pick one out of a litter of kittens to prefer, or a hen a chicken. It happens. I've seen it happen. In this case your mother picked on Judith. Why? She had other children, but for one thing Judith was the beauty of the outfit. She had great hopes for her. She was to make a wonderful marriage and restore the family fortunes, and eventually she did make what looked like a good one. To see that happen your mother was willing to go to any lengths outside of murder.

"But Judith herself almost ruined her prospects. Young as she was, Ridgely Chandler was deeply in love with her, but she wasn't in love with him. I don't think she ever had been. In fact, she had a sort of adolescent crush on a good-looking boy who used to come out here to the pool on Saturdays.

"The boy was Johnny Shannon."

I didn't speak. I couldn't.

"I think Dawson knew about it. He probably let her in when she came back. But one night she went to Johnny's room on

270

Morningside Heights and was there until almost morning. That was the night the Preston girl was murdered. He had seen Mollie earlier, to tell her he was through, but when she was killed he was with Judith Maynard, as she was then.

"You see how it was, darling. She was his alibi, and his only one. Apparently no one else had seen him. But he told Flaherty, and Flaherty went to see her. Your mother was there, and Flaherty called in Dawson. They both lied. So did Judith. She sat there in your big city house, Flaherty told me, looking like an angel, and lied her head off. He had left me outside, I was his sergeant, and he came out swearing. 'She was in Shannon's room all right,' he said, 'but she's afraid to admit it. She sat there, knowing that boy may go to the chair, and as much as sent him there.'

"Johnny didn't get the chair. He was young and the evidence was circumstantial. He got twenty years to life. But Judith Maynard knew what she had done. In a way, I suppose that accounts for the life she led after she married Chandler. She was safe, as safe as churches, but there must have been times when she remembered the man up the river, with the best years of his life gone. It killed Johnny's mother, too, but she may not have known that.

"It was some time until the case came up for trial, and before it did, your mother whisked Judith off to Arizona. And Kate Henry disappeared. So did Dawson. But other people had seen Johnny go to the Preston girl's place. I've always thought there was malice in their testimony. He wasn't a part of them. They called him Mollie's dude, just as they protected Dawson, who was raised among them.

"Flaherty got all that, and something more which came from your Helga. She knew Dawson was crazy about Mollie, and she thought he was the one who strangled her. She only thought, which is no good in a murder trial, and before Kate Henry disappeared the police got a deposition from her. It wasn't used at the trial, but it existed and the district attorney's office knew about it.

"Only Flaherty thought she was lying. She was in love with Dawson, it stood out all over her. And somehow he got on her trail. One evening he told me he was sure he had located her, in a small town up the Hudson. He said he was going there the next day, and if he was right Johnny would go free. But he wouldn't tell me what he knew, or even the name of the town, and that night he was shot and killed.

"He was on his way home when it happened. He had driven his car into the garage beside his house when he got it. His wife was waiting for him. She was having a steak for him. People could buy steak in 1930. Steak and onions. When I got there you could smell onions all over the place."

"She didn't last long after his death. Just didn't want to live. But I promised her I'd find his killer if it took me a lifetime, and for twenty years I've carried the bullet that killed him."

He looked at my frozen face.

"I'm sorry, darling, but now you understand what Judith was afraid of. It was Shannon. I don't think he meant to hurt her. He was no killer. But he did want the alibi she could give him. The worst of it was I had lost him after he left Reno. Even his girl didn't know where he was, or if he had changed his name. I suspected he had come to New York and taken a chauffeur's job, or managed to get a license to drive a taxi. It's not easy, but his Reno license would help. But I was sure of one thing. He would try to see your sister. That's why I took this place.

"He did try. You know that. He picked you up, thinking you were Judith Chandler, and remember what he said. You were to talk. That's all he wanted, for Judith to talk and clear him. He threw a note tied to a rock through her window. He even broke into the house and got upstairs."

"He shot you, didn't he?" I said. "And he fired at you or me tonight. If that's not being a killer, what is?"

He shook his head.

"Maybe he's changed," he admitted. "But look at my position. When Selina Benjamin was killed here at your pool I was frantic. She as well as Judith was responsible for those lost twenty years. And I couldn't catch him. He was as slippery as an eel, and I began to think—after I was shot—the hell of a lot more dangerous. That's why I asked you to put those ads in the papers, so he would know I was watching him.

"Then, a day or so ago, I had a glimmer of the sense God gave me. I went over to the Adrian house and broke in. He hadn't been living there all the time. He must have had some sort of job. But there was a cot in the kitchen and some canned food, and behind the garage there was an oil slick, where he had hidden his car."

He released my hands, picked up Henrietta gently, and carried her to her roost. When he came back he bent down and kissed me. I must have been unresponsive, for he straightened.

"I'm a cop, Lois," he said. "And once a cop always a cop. Johnny didn't kill Flaherty. He was locked away by that time. And Dawson is dead and beyond my reach. I verified it. But someone has tried twice to kill me. That shot tonight was for me, not you. I mean to get him, or her, whoever it was."

Yes, I thought drearily, he would never change. He was wearing his policeman's face again, standing there on the hearth, and when I saw it I looked away.

"How can you say he's not a killer?" I protested. "He murdered Selina Benjamin, and threw her into the pool."

"Why?" he said. "Why would he, Lois? He must have been counting on her to help him. Why kill her?"

There was no time for more. Bill's Ark roared and rattled into the drive, and the next minute he was pounding on the door.

"Hiya," he said when O'Brien opened it. "You people know what time it is? What will Judith say?"

"Judith won't say anything, Bill. She's gone."

He grinned.

"What sort of gone? Departed this life or merely The Birches? In any case I shall be brave. I shall bear it like a man."

What with the shot and O'Brien's story, I suddenly realized

I had forgotten to tell O'Brien. He stared at me incredulously.

"You mean she's left The Birches?" he said. "Don't you think you might have told me?"

"There was nothing really to tell. At the last minute one of her travel agencies got a cancellation on the *Queen Mary* and sent a car for her."

"You're sure of that?"

"What else could it be?" I said. "After all, she's been hoping for weeks to get such a break."

Perhaps it is hindsight, but I thought O'Brien looked worried. However, at Bill's suggestion—it appeared that Janey's family was opposed to the demon rum—he mixed highballs for all of us, and it was with glasses in our hands and a general appearance of revelry that Phil found us.

He stood in the doorway in his dinner clothes, unsmiling and indignant.

"What the hell goes on here?" he said. "Do you know what time it is?"

"We're celebrating the fact that our dear Judith is now on her way to England," Bill explained. "She's gone, lock, stock, and barrel, with the emphasis on the lock."

Phil relaxed after I told him what had happened. He sat down, explaining that he had won three dollars at bridge that night, and that something should be done about people who didn't watch their partner's discards. But he did not stay. He said firmly that he was not leaving his sister to any orgy, and insisted on driving me home.

He asked a question or two about Judith's departure, and I sensed considerable relief in him.

"I'm fond of her," he said. "At least I suppose so. But she could certainly raise hell around a house. You can have Mother's room again, too. You'll like that."

I have written this and then reread it. For the plain truth is that I never moved into Mother's room at all. I couldn't face it.

Not until I was in the house did I realize how carefully

O'Brien had avoided telling Phil or Bill about the shot that night. It had been deliberate, I knew. But why? Frank as he had been about Johnny Shannon I knew I had heard only part of the story: that Flaherty's murder was still in it, and Dawson; Judith, too, and perhaps even Mother.

It was hours before I slept. I was back in the drawing-room of the city house, with its Aubusson carpet and its petit-point chairs. It must have been gloomy, that winter day, with Judith crouched in a chair, looking like an angel and lying her head off. And Mother lying, too.

She must have known the truth. She had paid Dawson an enormous sum to keep quiet. But with Flaherty there that day she was seeing all her hopes for Judith gone; Judith on the witness stand, admitting she had spent at least part of the night in Johnny Shannon's room, a soiled angel indeed. And Flaherty watching them all three, for Shannon claimed Dawson had let Judith out and waited for her to come home.

They must have been terrified, all three of them, have known Flaherty did not believe them. I could almost see him there, the law personified.

"I hope you realize what you are doing. You are sending this boy to the chair, or to life in prison. It's the end of everything for him."

And silence. No one speaking, and at last Flaherty grabbing his hat and going out to the young sergeant who was driving his car, swearing.

"She was in Shannon's room all right, O'Brien, but she's afraid to admit it. She sat there, knowing that boy may go to the chair, and as good as sent him there."

Had Father known about it? I wondered. Had Mother gone to him the day of the dinner party and asked for his help, for money to keep Dawson quiet or to get Judith out of town? He must have been in torture that night, honorable man that he was, faced with the dilemma of ruining his daughter's reputation or letting an innocent boy possibly die. Things were

275

bad for him, anyhow. He was bankrupt. He may have played with the idea of suicide before, but this was more than he could take.

So he left that strange note about his conscience for Mother. Perhaps he hoped it would influence her, his last message before his death. But she never saw it, and she was beyond influence by that time.

For the first time that night I wondered about Helga. All along she had known something. Perhaps she had been awake and seen or heard Judith coming home. Perhaps Dawson's sudden affluence had set her to thinking. It was even possible she knew about the tobacco shop and told Flaherty where it was, only to have him shot before he could act on the knowledge.

She must have blamed herself for his death. Certainly it frightened her. I thought bleakly that she had probably been frightened for twenty years.

Chapter 29

It seemed to me I had hardly got asleep when Jennie brought me the news that Helga's arthritis was bad and I would have to help with the breakfast. So it happened that I was resignedly fighting the huge old coal range when the boy came with the milk. He put down the bottles and stood goggle-eyed in the doorway.

"Haven't heard the news, have you?" he inquired.

"What news, Tommy?"

"Man killed last night," he said importantly. "Nobody knows who he is. His car's down in the valley beside the road only a mile or so from your gate. I seen it."

"Killed!" I said. "How dreadful. What happened?"

But before he could answer Phil yelled for his breakfast, and when I came back from the dining-room Tommy was gone. Phil raised his eyebrows when I placed his bacon and eggs in front of him.

"Oh, no! Not eggs again!" he said.

"You'd better thank God for O'Brien and his girls," I said indignantly. "And if it intersts you, the milk boy says a man's been killed down the road."

"There should be a special place in hell for the man who invented wheels," he observed. "And another for the man who added an engine to them. Also for eggs," he added sourly.

"Isn't there such a thing as sausage to be had?"

Which shows neither of us doubted it was the usual car accident. We had one every now and then during the summer. It was hours before we learned the dreadful truth.

Bill slept late that morning, so I fed Phil and took him to the train. O'Brien's car was gone, and at the scene of the accident there was a small crowd in the road. Down below it in the valley both the local police and the state men were busy, but Phil would not let me stay to look. Someone said the body had already been taken away, which was all we knew at the time.

It was still, of course, a matter of purely academic interest to us. Our roads are often tricky, winding around the hills as they do, and when I drove back from the station the police had cleared the place, and down in the valley only the chief, a uniformed man or two, and a half dozen state troopers were there, as well as a photographer from town.

I stopped the car, and Fowler saw me and laboriously climbed the slope.

"Funny thing," he said. "That car down there has half a dozen bags in it. You wouldn't know anything about it, would you?"

I gasped.

"Bags?" I said. "What sort of bags?"

"Good looking. Expensive, I'd say. Your sister's initials are on them. Was she sending them anywhere?"

I looked down at the overturned car. It was on its side, but it was almost certainly the one that had called for Judith the night before. I must have turned pale, for Fowler hastened to reassure me.

"Nobody in it but the driver," he said. "Were you afraid there was someone else?"

"I thought it might be Mrs. Chandler," I told him bleakly. "She took a car like that one to go to New York last night. She was sailing on the *Queen Mary*."

"Maybe someone picked her up after it happened."

"She'd never have left her luggage," I said. "Only, where is

278

she? I don't understand."

"Well, she'd had a pretty bad shock if she was in the car when it left the road. Turned over a couple of times. Might just have wandered off somewhere. Maybe you'd better come down and take a look. It's not bad," he added, seeing my face. "The fellow's gone. Not much blood, either. Head wounds don't bleed much."

I followed him down the hill, my legs shaking and my head dizzy. The men stood aside to let me see the car, but it was not necessary. Judith's bags sat beside it on the grass, and her purse was with them, the big handsome one she always carried.

"It's the car," I said shakily. "It picked her up around half past eleven last night, and I put the bags in it myself."

"Didn't notice the driver, did you?"

"Only vaguely. I know he wore a chauffeur's cap, but we were in a hurry. I don't think he even got out. Only I don't see her jewel case. She had it when she left."

He stood rubbing his chin, which had missed its morning shave, and eyeing the luggage.

"Sure of that, are you?"

"Positive. She had it on her lap."

"Well, you never can tell," he said. "Those boys over there found the car. They were going fishing. One of them might have snitched it."

I had not noticed the boys before. There were four of them sitting on the hillside, and he called them over.

"Now listen, kids," he said sternly. "There's a small bag missing from this lot. Any of you take it?"

They disclaimed it immediately and loudly. They hadn't even touched anything. They had come across it at six o'clock or thereabouts, and they had hailed the first car that passed.

"Anybody else in the car or near it?" Fowler persisted. "A lady, for instance?"

They looked dazed. They hadn't seen anyone but the chauffeur, and he was dead. Fowler let them go, and stood surveying the wreckage.

"This jewel case," he said. "It sort of changes things, doesn't it? Who knew she had it?"

"She always took it with her."

"Might be a case of assault and robbery," he said thoughtfully. "Maybe kidnaping, too. Knock the driver out, grab the case, and take Mrs. Chandler along to gain some time. It wouldn't be hard to send the car over the edge. Road's narrow here."

It had been a stolen car, he said. The owner had missed it when he left the theater the night before, and reported it. As the thief had worn a chauffeur's uniform, no one noticed him.

I must have driven home, although I don't remember doing so. That blessed automatism which I believe comes from the spinal cord at least took me there and into the house. Jennie was taking up Judith's breakfast tray when I got back. I told her not to bother, that Mrs. Chandler had gone to the city, but I did not explain, for O'Brien was limping up the porch steps. He looked exhausted.

"Any extra coffee floating around?" he inquired. "I haven't had time for breakfast."

Still dazed I got Judith's tray and set it before him. He drank only a cup of black coffee, however.

"You saw the bags, I suppose?" he asked.

"Yes. They were hers."

"I'm afraid I have some bad news for you," he said quietly. "For you only," he added. "I've been to the mortuary. The dead man was Johnny Shannon, Lois. And he was murdered, poor guy. Shot."

"Shot!" I said weakly.

"Shot in the back of the head."

In the back of the head! I knew what he was thinking: Judith behind Johnny and learning who he was. Maybe his telling her, and she realizing how all she had built for twenty years was about to be destroyed.

"Hold it!" O'Brien said. "Put your head down."

I tried it, but it was no good. I simply fell forward on the

280

porch floor and passed out.

When I came to I was in my own bed, with Helga beside me. She wouldn't let me talk at first. Finally, however, she broke down. Judith, she said, was still missing, and they were beating the woods for her. Phil had come back from the city, and he and Bill had joined the searching parties. Also Anne was downstairs having hysterics, and—she said this with a certain unction—Jennie had put a bottle of household ammonia under her nose and nearly strangled her.

I had been out, it appeared, for several hours.

Anne was allowed to see me after lunch. She came in like a whirlwind. Judith had been kidnaped and probably killed, she said, and her jewel case was still missing. Also Ridge had called up, suggesting he send out a Homicide detective from New York, and the newspapers had the story. All sorts of reporters had been on the phone, and one of them had asked her if Judith shot the driver. And if so, why?

"A chauffeur?" she wailed. "Why would she kill a man like that? What's happened to this family? It isn't enough that you fall in love with a policeman. Now Judith kills a cab driver!"

I let that pass.

"How could she kill anybody?" I said. "She had no gun. I know. I helped her pack. I think they're all demented."

There was no question, however, that Judith had disappeared. Whatever had happened she had been able to leave the car. Anne was sure she had been kidnaped, and insisted on walking down to the mailbox to see if a ransom letter had arrived. But when Phil came in, late in the afternoon, dirty and utterly weary, he said they were sure she had gone on her own two feet. They found her high-heel marks on the soft shoulder of the road, not far from where the car had gone over.

I was downstairs by that time, to Helga's disgust, and I brought him a drink and some food on the porch. He had had no lunch, and while he ate he said they had got out the Boy Scouts, and were sending for a helicopter.

"She may be dazed and wandering anywhere," he said.

281

"That's pretty wild country. Of course, she may be dead. Whoever shot the driver may have shot her, too. Only he didn't kill her. She got away. But where she got to is anybody's guess."

He had some real information, however. The telephone call had been a phony. The *Queen Mary* had sailed while Judith was still on the road. Moreover, there had been no last-minute cancellations, and none of the travel agencies had called her.

"Most of them close at six o'clock, anyhow," he said.

But the police knew the identity of the dead man. I held my breath, but he went on calmly enough.

"New York driver's license in the name of Alec Morrison," he said. "How on earth did she get him? Was he a phony, too?"

I told him that during the message about the *Queen Mary* whoever it was had offered to send a car for her. It was to stop for another passenger, a man, I thought. The car was to come first to The Birches and then pick him up.

"Very neat," he said. "A holdup, of course. The other passenger was the one who shot Morrison, and took the jewel case. Only where the hell is she? Did he take her with him?"

It seems incredible now that I had not told him about the shot the night before. At breakfast he had been in a hurry, and I had not seen him since. Now I told him, and Anne, having returned from the mailbox, heard me and gave a small shriek.

"Shot!" she said. "Who in the world would want to shoot you?"

"I don't know, Anne. O'Brien thinks it was for him. It was dark, you know."

Phil turned a pair of cold eyes on me.

"Where was all this?" he demanded. "And when?"

"I suppose an hour or more after Judith left," I said guiltily. "I had some things to tell Lieutenant O'Brien, and I saw his light was on. I was at the door of the cottage when it happened."

He was still angry, furiously angry.

"For God's sake, why didn't you tell me you'd been shot at,

when I brought you home from O'Brien's last night? What is he up to, anyhow? It occurs to me that this was a quiet spot until he hit it. Since then we've had two murders and two shootings. And maybe a third death. Your own sister."

I never answered that. The helicopter appeared, flying low and some distance away, and we watched it with fascinated eyes. None of us, I think, noticed the car which had driven up until the man got out of it and climbed the steps.

It was Doctor Townsend.

"I'm sorry to intrude just now," he said, "but I gather from that machine in the air that you haven't located Mrs. Chandler."

"No," I said. "They're trying everything, of course. This is my sister Anne, Mrs. Harrison, Doctor, and you may know my brother Phil. Won't you sit down?"

He did, but he declined Phil's offer of a drink.

"I have a radio in my car," he said. "I gather there is a rumor to the effect that Mrs. Chandler herself shot this driver and then escaped into the woods."

"That's idiotic," I told him. "I saw her off last night. I helped her pack, too. She didn't have a gun. I don't think she ever had one. And she was happy when she left, happier than she had been for months."

"I see." It was a hot day, and he got out a handkerchief and mopped his face. "Of course, I agree with you. She didn't do it. She was quite incapable of such a thing. The reason I came was this: If she could walk at all—and it seems she could—where would she be likely to go? As I drove past the place where the car went over, I realized how wild it was. Knowing her, I don't think she would strike into those hills. She was a sensitive woman and a highly civilized one. It was a dark night, too."

"All right," Phil said, annoyed. "Tell us where she would go. That's your business, isn't it? Knowing what people will or will not do?"

The doctor eyed him calmly.

"Quite definitely," he said. "Wearing the heels she always

did she would stay on the road. Provided, of course, she could get there. She must have been in profound shock."

I suppose Phil was worried half sick, as we all were. Certainly he was exasperated.

"We may discover she took the *Queen Mary* after all!" he said. "Look, Doctor, I'm sorry to be rude, but this is a hell of a situation. Judith hasn't been normal for months. We've put up with her locked doors, her shutting herself away. She tries to kill herself, and Lois here nurses her until she's exhausted. Now we've got this. If the sensational press thinks she killed this Morrison, we can't help it. But if you think we're hiding her here you're mistaken."

Doctor Townsend looked stubborn. He set his jaw.

"I didn't say that, Mr. Maynard. I do suggest a search of the grounds, even possibly of the pool down there. Where else could she go? In trouble most people strike for home. It means shelter, safety. Remember, even if she didn't kill this man she has been through a terrifying experience."

"The pool! Good God," Phil gasped. "Do you think she's there?"

The doctor shook his head.

"I have no idea where she is," he said. "I can only suggest that if she was able to move at all she would try to come here. Where else could she go?"

Chapter 30

Bill returned as Phil went inside for his bathing-trunks. He had no news. He was badly scratched, and one leg of his gabardine slacks was torn from the knee down. Anne looked after him as he followed Phil into the house.

"You would think clothes grew on trees," she said acidly. "Did you ever learn who this Janey is? What's her last name?"

I hadn't an idea, and said so. Anne grunted.

"They never have any," she said fretfully. "They're Nell and Betty and God knows what. I often wonder what Mother would think."

I didn't say anything. Down the drive by the pool I could see a girl in a pair of dirty white shorts who was trying to escape our attention. She had obviously been on the search with Bill and she was tying a handkerchief over what I imagined was a scratch on one of a pair of long and very bare legs. Anne was too short-sighted to see her, but so far as I could tell she was merely any seventeen-year-old, and probably Janey.

The men came out then and headed for the pool. Neither Anne nor I accompanied them. I was too shaken to move, and Anne was weeping into her drink, whether about Judith or Bill's slacks, I did not know. Janey did not move as the procession neared her, but when Bill stopped to explain to her she nodded, turned, and took a quick dive into the water, with a flash of slim legs and in what I imagine was a highly expensive sweater.

Then for fifteen minutes we waited. O'Brien's car drove in and stopped by the pool. When he came up to the house I saw by his face they had found nothing. Anne stopped crying to glare at him when he came up the steps.

"Sorry, old girl," he said. "It's pretty bad. But she's not dead. We'd have found her by now if she were. She's not in the pool, either. I was in it myself around noon, looking for her." He glanced at Anne, or more specifically at her drink. "Hate to cadge your liquor," he said, "but I could do with one of those myself."

He sat down. If Bill had looked exhausted, O'Brien looked even worse. His shirt was torn and his slacks were stained and dirty. Anne gave him a frigid nod when I introduced him, but it didn't bother him. He sat back with his eyes closed until I gave him the whisky. He gulped it down and sat up, as if he had a new idea.

"Ever hear the story about the village idiot and the jackass?" He looked at Anne. "He just thought where he'd go if he was a jackass and—"

"I was raised on it," Anne said, her voice chilly. He ignored it, however.

"It's like this," he said. "I'm a woman, and I've been through something of an experience like—let's say—the driver of my car being shot and the car rolling down a hill. Perhaps I got out before that. Maybe I spilled out. I've got a bump or so or maybe the glass has cut me. But I can still walk. I know there's a killer around somewhere, and I wait awhile. Then it's all quiet. So what? Where do I head for? The woods? They're dark, and I don't know them, anyhow. I do the only thing I can. I head for home."

"We've already heard that from Doctor Townsend," Anne said, still stiffly. "Only she isn't here, Lieutenant."

"How do you know she isn't?" he demanded. "She gets back

286

here, and only God knows what that mile or so cost her. She makes it, but just barely. And the house is dark, locked and dark. So she—" He got up abruptly. "Don't bother about another drink, Lois. It can wait. Has anybody looked in the stable?"

They had not, I thought, and followed him at a dogtrot as he raced down the steps and around the corner of the house. I caught up to him in the birch grove. He had gone rather pale, and he stopped and leaned against one of the trees.

"Excuse it, please," he said, trying to smile. "It's the old wound plus a couple of late ones. I keep forgetting the damned things."

He took a couple of deep breaths and started again. But at first the stable was a disappointment. There was nothing in what we called the carriage house but a rusty old sleigh. O'Brien did not stop there, however. He went through a door at the back and stopped dead in the doorway of the tack room.

Judith was there, on the floor.

She was unconscious, and even when he picked her up and she opened her eyes it was clear they saw nothing. She was a pitiable sight. There was a hideous bruise on her forehead, and one of her hands was badly cut. Her clothes were torn, too, and one of her ankles was swollen, as though she had sprained it.

O'Brien handled her like a baby.

"Get somebody to turn down her bed," he said. "Fill some hot-water bottles, too. And maybe she can swallow a little brandy. It won't hurt to try."

They were all on the porch when our small procession arrived, Phil and Bill still in bathing-trunks, Doctor Townsend immaculate and calm. I shall never forget their shocked faces as we turned the corner of the old conservatory and reached the steps. There were cries of where had we found her, and both Phil and Bill rushed down to help O'Brien. He warded them off, however.

"She's not heavy," he said. "Get out of the way, all of you.

287

She's unconscious."

"Is she hurt?" This was Phil. Anne seemed for once beyond speech.

"She's got a bad knock on the head," O'Brien said. "No fracture, I think. Better notify the police, Mr. Maynard. They'll want to know this. And get a doctor."

"The police?" Phil looked mutinous. "She needs a hospital and medical care."

"She'll get them," O'Brien said grimly. "Only they have to know. At the moment she may be wanted for murder."

There was a shocked silence as we went into the house, and O'Brien did not elaborate. We got her into bed while Phil telephoned Fowler and Doctor Christy, and then followed us upstairs.

"Just what did you mean by that remark, O'Brien?" he demanded angrily. "She's been attacked herself. Look at her!"

"I'm not accusing her," O'Brien said mildly. "The driver of her car was shot in the back of the head. To the chief of police here that means only one thing at the moment. She wasn't attacked herself. She went down the hill in the car, and only God knows why she's alive."

"That in itself ought to prove her innocence to any man with sense."

O'Brien only smiled.

"Not necessarily," he said. "The driver's foot may have been on the gas and started it. It was an old model. Fowler's idea, not mine."

"Then where's the gun?"

"If you'll get out of the way I'll look for it."

"In the stable, I suppose," Phil jeered.

But O'Brien was too late. There had been police in the grounds, and when he got downstairs one of them had already found it. She had dropped it in the grass near the stable door, and one of the local detectives was on the drive with it, wrapped in his handkerchief. Fowler came up on the porch and surveyed the crowd. I was not there, but I was told about it.

"Sorry about all this," he said. "I guess I'll have to talk to Mrs. Chandler."

"She's hurt," someone said. "She needs a hospital."

"Sure," he said. "We're taking her there as soon as the ambulance comes. But I hope you folks understand. That gun Jim has down there has been fired recently. Two or three times if it was fully loaded, and the cab driver was shot, if you don't happen to know it."

"But why?" Anne wailed. "Why would she shoot a man like that?"

The answer, so far as the others were concerned, came late that afternoon. They had taken the dead man's finger-prints, and as I already knew they proved to be those of Johnny Shannon, ex-convict and only a few months ago released from twenty years in prison for manslaughter. I was in the hospital with Judith, so I missed the army of reporters and cameramen that besieged the house.

I stayed in the hospital all night. Judith was still unconscious, and in the morning Phil came in with one of the New York papers and the news that her fingerprints—and only hers—were on the gun. I went out into the hall to talk to him, and to see a policeman sitting there, outside Judith's room.

He handed me the paper.

"Maybe you can make some sense out of this," he said. "I can't. It's tabloid stuff, of course. The news is on another page."

I took it to a window and read it. It had been written by a well-known columnist.

Did Judith Chandler, famous beauty and society woman, kill Johnny Shannon? And if so, why? It was well known, at the time of his trial, twenty years ago, that Inspector Flaherty before his own murder believed him innocent of the Mollie Preston slaying, and that he made at least one visit to the Maynard house, where the then Judith Maynard was queried.

The case was further complicated by the disappearance before the trial of one Kate Henry, one of the chief witnesses for the prosecution. Other witnesses appeared, however, testifying to Shannon's presence in the building at or about the time of the murder, and the noisy quarrel which followed. It was believed that the defense hoped the then Judith Maynard could substantiate Shannon's alibi, but this failed to stand up, and Johnny Shannon was convicted. Not the least curious part of the present case is the participation in it of Flaherty's sergeant at the time, now Inspector Terrence O'Brien.

It was largely due to O'Brien's efforts that Johnny Shannon was released some months ago. It is an odd coincidence that three people concerned in the long-ago murder of an unimportant East Side girl should again be involved in a crime: one of them the victim, another the woman possibly responsible for his life sentence, and the third a police officer who worked with Flaherty on the Mollie Preston case and who had never believed Shannon guilty.

As for Judith Chandler—nee Maynard—herself, it is difficult to believe she would shoot and kill the driver of the car while it was still in motion. Such a course would be purely suicidal. Had Johnny Shannon stopped the car and revealed his identity? In that case she might have killed him in self-defense. But the car was apparently in motion, thus providing the authorities with a highly perplexing problem.

So far there has been no arrest. The police move slowly when any member of a highly respected family is involved. And both the Chandlers and the Maynards have always stood for the best in the city. It is indicative of this that her ex-husband, Ridgely Chandler, is standing by Judith in this trying time.

Phil looked as though he had not slept. He took the tabloid from me and stuck it in his pocket.

"Fowler read it," he said. "That's why the cop's outside her door. She's under arrest whether she knows it or not. Maybe they call it protective custody, but they're holding her for first-degree murder."

That was when I took him into the drab reception room and told him O'Brien's story. He listened stoically.

"So she had to kill him," he said. "She wasn't going to admit she'd sent an innocent man to prison for twenty years. But how did she know the driver was Shannon?"

"I think he told her himself that night, Phil. Only how did he know she was going to need a cab?"

"He must have known she was waiting for a ship. Maybe he did the telephoning himself. O'Brien says all he wanted was vindication, poor devil. What he got was a cold-blooded murder."

It shows how we both felt that day. Neither of us really doubted Judith's guilt. Phil merely wondered how and when she had got the gun. He said she might have recognized Shannon's voice over the telephone and staged the whole thing as a holdup for her jewel case.

"Because the damned thing's still missing," he said. "Anne and I have searched the stable, as well as the whole house, attic and all. If she had it with her, she must have hidden it somewhere along the road."

He was right, of course, but within limits. When the time came it was practically her sole defense.

It was a long time before that happened, however. It was a full week before she began to recover. She would lie in her high hospital bed, not awake and not asleep, in a partial coma which was pitiful to see. It seemed absurd to have a policeman sitting outside her door. Not only because she could not walk—one ankle was badly twisted—but because she made no effort whatever to move.

After a day or two they could rouse her to swallow liquid food and water. That is, she could get them down. Her eyes, however, remained blank, until one day she reached out a bandaged hand and touched me.

"Lois," she said.

It was the first sign of consciousness she had given.

Her skull was not fractured, but she had a bad concussion. Also she had walked on the sprained ankle, and even now I shiver at what that mile or so along the road at night must have meant.

I saw very little of O'Brien that week. He was seldom at the cottage, and I spent my days at the hospital. Once, however, he called me up there.

"Just to keep you from forgetting me, my darling," he said. "And also to let you know I'm still on the case."

"Always the policeman!" I said bitterly. "Are you going to send her to the chair?"

"Not necessarily," he said. "I may be able to surprise you before very long."

"I don't like your surprises. I've had all of them I can take."

He told me not to be like that and then hung up abruptly. Hours and days for his job, I thought dourly, and two minutes for dalliance, as he probably regarded it. I missed him sickeningly.

I am quite sure Judith had no idea she was under arrest at that time. She could not see the policeman from her bed, and under the doctor's orders Fowler and his minions left her strictly alone. I did feel, however, as time went on that her semicomatose condition was partly protective. Once in a while when the nurse was out I would find her watching me, and now and then she spoke. As the missing jewel case was in all our minds, I asked her about it one day.

She seemed to come back from a far distance.

"Jewel case?" she said slowly.

"Yes. The one you had with you when you were hurt, Jude."

"The man took it," she said, and closed her eyes again.

I called Phil in great excitement when I got home. He was cool enough, however.

"Of course she'd say there was a man," he said. "What the hell did you expect?"

By the tenth day, with Fowler growing angrier and more

impatient all the time at the delay, she was able to sit up in bed and even to eat a little. Her memory, too, was slowly coming back. That afternoon for the first time she inquired about the driver of the car.

"Was he dead?" she asked.

"I'm afraid he was, Judith."

"Who was he? Do you know?"

And then all Phil's theories and mine went into the discard.

"He called himself Morrison," I said, "but he was really Johnny Shannon."

"Johnny!" she said. "Oh, not Johnny! I can't bear it."

Then she was crying, loudly, hysterically. The police officer ran in, the nurse came flying, and soon after an intern. I was too shocked to move. They had to push me aside, and later on in the hall I had to answer questions. What had I done? What had I said to her? The intern was particularly insistent.

"Now see here, Miss Maynard," he said. "She didn't go off like that for nothing. She'd been quiet all day. It's on her record, the best day yet. Then all at once she goes off into a fit, and you were alone with her at the time."

I lied. What else could I do?

"I don't know what started her off," I said. "Perhaps she just remembered something."

"I wish to God she could," he said fervently. "You didn't by any chance tell her about the police?"

"Of course not. But she's seeing things now. If she caught sight of that officer—"

"He says the door was closed when she began to yell."

But after that I was limited to two hours a day with her, with the nurse always in the room. Now and then as she improved I think she wanted to talk to me. There was no chance, however.

Ridge Chandler came out to The Birches about that time. He had telephoned frequently, and her hospital room was filled with the flowers he sent and which she did not notice. He looked haggard, as I daresay we all did, and he seemed as bewildered as the rest of us.

293

"Hasn't she talked at all?" he asked. "She must remember something."

"She's beginning to remember, Ridge. She's had a concussion, of course. We do know a few things. She says a man took her jewel case."

"It's hardly news," he said dryly. "We all know it was a holdup."

It was September by that time. It was cool that day, and I had a fire in the living-room. He got up and stood in front of Mother's picture, looking up at it.

"Handsome old girl," he said. "Ever find out what she wanted the money for? The fifty thousand, I mean."

"Maybe to bribe Dawson. You remember him. He was our butler at the time."

"Bribe him? Why?" He stared at me, but I went on recklessly.

"Because Judith was the alibi for a man accused of murder, Ridge. It won't hurt you to know it now. Apparently she lied, for he was convicted. His name was Shannon, Johnny Shannon."

"Good God!" he said. "The man who drove the car! Then she did kill him, after all!"

"That's fantastic, Ridge. She had no gun."

"No? Well, maybe not, although I wonder what became of the one your father used. The police returned it. And it might have been stored away somewhere."

"I never saw it," I said weakly. But I was remembering the night I found Judith in the attic. She had been looking for something, definitely not her wedding pictures. I sat gazing at him, but he merely shrugged.

"Don't look at me like that," he said, his voice irritable. "God knows I don't want to drag my name in the mud. Shannon may have scared her. He had a right to, if she did what you say. I remember the case dimly, but how did you learn about it? You were only a child at the time. I suppose it was this policeman of yours. What's his name? O'Brien, isn't it?"

"Yes," I said dully. "It was O'Brien."

"It could be worse, of course," he said, "even if they prove the gun was your father's. She would probably get a light sentence. She's still a good-looking woman, and if necessary we can show she has not been normal for some time."

"I think she is normal," I said obstinately. "She's been afraid, that's all."

He left me in a wretched state of mind. Judith might have found Father's gun in the attic. It might have been there. Also her handbag was large. She could have carried it with her. But why shoot Shannon and risk her own life when the car went over the edge of the road?

I didn't dare to risk talking to her again. But she was improving rapidly, and one day I realized the armistice was over.

She was better. Her ankle was in a cast, and they were talking of getting her up into a wheel chair. I went home more cheerful than I had been for a long time. When the haze completely lifted she would be able to tell us what had happened, and clear herself. Because by that time I felt sure she was innocent. She had not known the cab driver was Shannon, and why would she shoot an unknown man?

Then Fowler came to see me.

I was alone late that afternoon when he appeared. I had been getting Mother's room ready for Judith when she was strong enough to be brought back to The Birches, so when I heard his voice I went down the stairs to find him in the lower hall with a heavy automatic in his hand.

"Know anything about this gun, Miss Maynard?" he said. "Recognize it, I mean."

"No. What about it?" I asked stupidly.

"It's the gun which killed Shannon," he said. "It also killed your father years ago. I wonder how your sister got hold of it?"

Father's gun! I sat down on one of the hall chairs, feeling faint. But I managed to speak.

"I don't know. I've never seen it before. It wasn't in the house. And she never killed anybody."

"Well, that's as may be," he said. "You have to do a little

guessing in this case. I'll guess, for instance, that the telephone call about the ship was arranged for to impress you. I'll guess she knew this ex-convict Shannon a lot better than you realize. And I'll guess a bit more. She didn't expect to go off the road in that car. She had him stop it before she killed him, but the motor was running, so maybe his foot kicked the gas and she had no time to get out."

"You're making her a monster," I said wildly. "She isn't. She has her faults, but to think she would scheme like that, pack her bags, kiss me good-by, and go out to murder a man—it's crazy."

"Maybe that's the answer," he said laconically. "She'll cop a plea of temporary insanity, or her lawyers will. But it won't do her any good."

He left me in a state of collapse, and when Phil came home that night I gave one look at his tired, haggard face and decided not to tell him about Father's gun. Maybe I was wrong, but he was sure to learn it sooner or later. He was entitled to one peaceful evening, if you could call it that.

When O'Brien called me later he said nothing to cheer me.

"I'm afraid things don't look too good," he said. "Who would think a damn-fool reporter in New York would bring Shannon in? Or that they would check back to your father's gun?"

But the thing was almost over, he said. Judith had not killed Johnny Shannon, and he hoped to prove it.

"I still don't see why anybody wanted to kill him," I said stubbornly. "Why kill *him*? If he'd killed her I could understand it."

"Leave the worrying to me. I can take it. And I'll say this much," he went on. "Several people are responsible for his death. Only one of them killed him, but more than one conscience must have kept its owner awake at night for a good many years."

He did not explain what he meant. He had really called, he said, to tell me that Fowler intended to interrogate Judith the next day, and I was to insist on being present.

"Just go there early and stay," he said. "I'll be there, if I have to break a window. After all, Shannon was in my jurisdiction. He was a New York resident."

Then for a few seconds he ceased being a police officer and became a man. "I'm missing you, darling, but this is my job. Someday soon it will be over, and you'll be my own sweet girl again."

Unfortunately I was not feeling sweet.

"Of course," I said. "In the intervals between cases, you mean. You'll come home to the little woman, put your gun away, and after food, a bath, and a shave you'll look around to see if she's where you left her a week or so before."

"And what could be more wonderful, mavourneen?" He chuckled. "Just promise me you will be there."

"I'm just damn fool enough to promise I will be, with a steak ready for the broiler and your slippers ready for your feet."

The mention of the steak was unfortunate. Flaherty's wife had one ready the night he was killed, and he remembered it. The laughter went out of his voice.

"I'll come home to you, my darling," he said gravely. "That's as near a promise as I can make."

Chapter 31

The nurse had done her best for Judith when I got there the next morning, had brushed her still lovely hair until it shone, and put a little color on her cheeks and lips. They only heightened her alarming pallor, but I did not say anything.

Fowler had said he would be there at eleven o'clock. He came promptly, but he was not alone. He had brought the detective who found the gun, and almost on his heels came the district attorney for the county. Fowler looked displeased when he saw me, and even more so when O'Brien walked in. He did not care either for the presence of Doctor Christy, who sat by Judith's bed. But it was definitely Fowler's show.

He began urbanely enough.

"I don't want to distress you, Mrs. Chandler," he said. "But I think it's time we had a talk."

Judith did not move, but she looked at him.

"What do you want?" she asked, slowly and painfully. "I don't remember very much."

"Well, you remember getting into the car at The Birches, don't you?"

"Yes."

"You were going abroad? On the *Queen Mary*?"

She made an effort.

"Yes," she said. "I got a message they had space for me."

He let that go.

"I see," he said. "So you called a cab. That's right, isn't it?"

She frowned in an attempt to remember.

"No. They said they were sending one for me. Whoever it was said a car was on the way. It was picking up another passenger later."

"Would it interest you to know," he said, still smoothly, "that no such message was ever sent?"

She looked puzzled.

"I don't understand. I got it. My sister Lois knows it. She was there."

The district attorney stirred in his chair.

"I think we'd better get on with it, Chief," he said. "She's not very strong. We know the car picked her up. We know it was a stolen car. Let's take all this for granted."

Fowler scowled.

"I'd like to carry this on," he said. "The car was there, that's the important thing. Now, Mrs. Chandler, you got into the car, and drove on a mile or two. What happened then?"

"It stopped. The driver said he was to pick up the other passenger there and take him to the ship. I said there wasn't much room, with all my bags, but anyhow we waited. Then a man came along the road. He stopped beside the rear door where I sat and jerked it open. I—" she looked about to faint "—I saw he was wearing something black over his face, and I guess I screamed. That was when he shot the driver. He tried to shoot me. Perhaps he thought he had, for I fainted just after that. The last thing I remember is his throwing the gun at me. It struck me on the head."

A wave of shock must have gone through everyone there. Even Fowler looked surprised. Then he smiled.

"I see. So that's how you got the gun?"

"The gun?" She was thinking hard, trying to remember. "But I didn't get it. It was in my hand when I came to."

Nobody believed her. There was sheer incredulity on every face in the room, including my own. Except O'Brien's. He was watching her intently. Fowler smiled.

"That's quite a statement," he said. "You fainted, the car crashed down the hill, after turning over at least a couple of times. And you wake up holding the gun! What happened then?"

"I must have been out a good while," she said. "I could see the car below me. Not the driver. Just the car. I think it was some time before I tried to climb the hill. My foot was very painful, but I couldn't stay there with that man around. That's really all I remember."

"Not quite," Fowler said. "You knew where you were, didn't you? You didn't go toward the town. You turned toward The Birches. No woman in a stupor did that, Mrs. Chandler. And you carried the gun with you."

"Are you saying I walked back home? With an ankle like this?"

"You did, unless someone took you there. Perhaps you'll claim this highwayman of yours did it! That's where you were found, anyhow. In the old stable at The Birches. The gun was there, too, the gun that killed Johnny Shannon."

I watched her, but the name did not startle her as it had before, although she went very pale.

"I never shot anybody," she said swiftly. "Not in all my life."

"But you knew Shannon?"

"A long time ago I knew a Johnny Shannon. He was a student at Columbia. He came a few times to the swimming pool at The Birches."

"Did you know he was driving the car that night?"

"No. Not until—" She stopped. She had made a misstep, and she knew it.

"Now we're getting places," Fowler said with considerable satisfaction. "Suppose you tell us why he stopped the car where he did. There were no houses near. Shannon wasn't picking up a passenger. This masked man wasn't a thief after your jewel case, either. Matter of fact, isn't it possible there was no such man?"

I think she gave up then. She lay back on her pillows with her eyes closed, and the nurse held some aromatic ammonia under her nose. Doctor Christy spoke for the first time.

"I'm warning you, Fowler. This is no time or place for accusations. I said she could tell her story. That's all."

"If her story's a bundle of lies, I didn't promise to accept it."

Then O'Brien spoke.

"Suppose you let me tell it for her," he said. "I knew Johnny Shannon. I knew him off and on for twenty years. I knew he'd been trying ever since he left the pen to get a statement from Mrs. Chandler which would clear him of the murder which sent him up the river."

Fowler eyed him with acute dislike.

"I don't see where you come in on this," he said. "I'm supposed to be doing the questioning."

"Right, but I'm not asking questions. I'm telling you what Mrs. Chandler will have to tell, sooner or later. She knew Johnny Shannon never killed the Preston girl, and she knew it because she was in his room the night it happened. She was with him, in his room on Morningside Heights, from eleven o'clock to four in the morning. The Preston girl was killed at or about midnight."

There was a dead silence. No one in the room moved.

"She was pretty young at the time. Even then I think she might have come forward and cleared him, but her mother terrified her into keeping quiet. I'm only going to ask her one or two questions, Fowler. The rest is up to you." He glanced at Judith. "You heard me, Mrs. Chandler. That's the fact, isn't it? And when Johnny Shannon got you in the car it was in the hope you could be induced to clear him?"

She nodded weakly.

"I thought he would be acquitted at the trial," she said. "But Mother took me to Arizona, and when I learned he had gone up for life I was in bed for weeks, sick."

"You didn't invent this masked man, did you?"

301

"No. He was there. We were to wait for him. He was to be a notary, or something like that. He was to take down what I said, and I was to sign it. Johnny told me after he stopped the car. I didn't know who he was until then."

"There was no real message about the ship. You know that now, don't you?"

"I think Johnny learned somehow that I hoped to sail. I realize now it must have been his voice over the telephone."

"And the rest is as you've told it?"

"About the man? Yes."

O'Brien grinned and looked at Fowler.

"Your witness, Chief," he said.

Fowler was sulky. It was a moment or two before he leaned forward in his chair and spoke to Judith.

"Isn't it a fact, Mrs. Chandler," he said, "that as soon as you learned Shannon was released you went around in terror of your life? You lived behind locked doors for fear he would kill you?" *Corny*, I thought bitterly. But Fowler went on. "And isn't it a fact that when you learned his identity in the car that night you shot him before, as you thought, he would shoot you?"

O'Brien got up.

"This isn't a trial before a jury, Fowler," he said. "Mrs. Chandler will not answer that question while I'm here, or until she has a lawyer to defend her."

Fowler looked ugly.

"All right," he said. "She'll get a lawyer. She'll probably get a dozen of them. She married a Chandler, didn't she? But maybe you forget we've had two murders." He looked at Judith. "Did you know the woman who was knocked out and then drowned in your swimming pool not long ago?"

Judith closed her eyes, and the spots of rouge on her face stood out sickeningly. But her voice was clear.

"No. She was a complete stranger to me."

"Yet someone at The Birches took a golf club down there that night. You know that, don't you?"

"That doesn't necessarily follow," O'Brien said. "A good many people had access to those clubs. You did yourself, probably. So did I."

Fowler was seething with fury by that time. He got up and jammed on his hat.

"I had a vague idea that I was in charge of this case. If New York Homicide is taking over, I'd like to know. Now I'm getting the hell out of here. Maybe O'Brien can produce this masked phantom, if there ever was one. This whole business looks to me like a conspiracy to protect Mrs. Chandler. But don't think I'm through. I'm only beginning."

He stalked out of the room, not without a certain dignity, and a moment later I heard his car starting. The detective he had brought heard it, too. He shrugged.

"So he leaves me here," he said. "Looks like I'll have to bum a ride into town. But don't discount Fowler. He's got plenty on the ball."

That he had something was evident when he came to The Birches that night.

O'Brien had disappeared when the others did. He left an envelope for me with the clerk in the office at the hospital, but there was no letter inside. There was merely a prescription blank, on which he had written just three words. They were enough, however, to make me happy, and the early part of the evening was very pleasant.

After all, there was no real case against Judith, as Phil agreed with his lawyer's mind when I told him about it.

"Unless they can prove she had a gun," he said. "And that I doubt. It's up to the gun and the jewel case. Prove one and locate the other. Then maybe you've got a case. Or maybe you haven't."

We had another reason for feeling somewhat cheerful that evening. A real-estate agent in New York had called Phil up, and said he had a faint nibble for The Birches.

"Not too strong," he said, "but they can pay plenty if they take it. Scared of the atom bomb, I gather, and have a raft of children. Only," he added, "don't have any more murders out there. You'd be surprised how a whacking good one affects the real-estate market."

It shook me, rather. So much of my life was tied up in the place. In the spring the magnolias, pink dogwoods, and cherry and other fruit blossoms made it look almost bridal. And the silver birches were there the year round, lovely in the snow, tall and dignified always. Father's garden, the pet cemetery, the stall in the stable where Fairy, my little pony, was kept—

"Oh, no," I said when Phil told me. "How can we?"

"How can't we?" he retorted. "I have an idea you won't be here long anyhow, and I'm not staying on alone."

As it happened, Bill had brought his Janey to dinner, and Helga had extended herself—and the grocery bill—to give her what she called a bang-up dinner. Janey was a nice slim little thing. Bill must have known dozens exactly like her, with their girlish voices and rather shy good manners. And she did have a last name, after all. Not too surprisingly it was Jones. Just why Bill found her unusual I couldn't see, and Phil's only comment was that she ate enough for a laboring man, that when she stood up you would have thought a hard-boiled egg would show, and she didn't even bulge.

He watched them as they wandered out to the porch.

"Funny kids these days," he said. "Those two are as romantic as a pair of china doorknobs. Ever occur to you that we've knocked romance for a loop by taking the clothes off the youngsters and bringing sex out into the open?"

But I was in no mood to argue, so he let it drop. I was tired, and I had not liked the way Judith looked when Fowler spoke about the woman in the pool. I did my best, turned on the radio, so Bill and Janey could dance in the hall, and was about to go up to bed when I heard a car stop in the drive.

It was Fowler, and he had brought Ridge Chandler with him. Both men looked sober, and Fowler asked to see us both alone. I knew then there was trouble, bad trouble. And there was.

304

Chapter 32

We took them into the library, and against Bill's despairing glance firmly closed the door.

"What's all this about?" Phil asked gruffly. "Judith's told you all she knows, hasn't she?"

Ridge gave his usual glance at Mother's portrait before he sat down. Fowler remained standing.

"I've been checking back a bit, Mr. Maynard," he said. "I don't like to bring up anything unpleasant, but after this length of time— You remember your father's death, of course."

"I do. Did you expect me to say I'd forgotten it?"

"You went to his office that night, I believe? After it happened?"

"I did. Is that any business of yours?"

"I think it is. You saw the gun he used."

"It was there, yes."

"Do you know what happened to it later? I mean, what became of it?"

"Good God, no," Phil said violently. "I never wanted to see the thing again." He pulled himself together. "Sorry, Fowler," he said, more quietly. "It was all an unholy mess. I had to help go over his papers. We were wiped out, of course, and my mother was in poor shape. We had to get rid of the town house, too. There was a lot of confusion."

"That's why I brought Mr. Chandler," the chief said smoothly. "He was attentive to your sister Judith at that time, so he was there a good bit. All right, Chandler, let's have it."

Ridge looked uncomfortable.

"I don't like being dragged into this, Phil," he said, "especially since Judith is involved. But the fact is the police returned the gun to your mother. I was there when it came."

"What's all this about?" Phil demanded. "What has Father's gun to do with any of us? You're talking about twenty years ago, man."

"I'm talking about the past few days," Fowler said importantly. "As your sister here already knows, the gun which killed Shannon, Mr. Maynard, was your father's gun. I have the serial numbers. It was registered in the city in his name. He bought it when we had some burglaries out here in this district years ago."

Phil looked dumbfounded.

"Father's? You're sure of that?"

"I've seen his gun purchase permit, Mr. Maynard. Here's the description of the gun." He took a paper from his wallet. "Thirty-eight Police Positive Colt, blue finish, four-inch barrel, weight twenty-two ounces. It's the same gun your sister dropped at the stable. No doubt about it."

"Are you telling me," Phil said hoarsely, "that my sister had my father's gun, and killed Shannon with it? Why, for God's sweet sake?"

"I think you'll find she had a reason," Fowler said smoothly. "Anyhow it's the gun which killed him. That's one thing O'Brien couldn't stop. I sent it and the bullet to Ballistics in the city. They match all right. Got the report tonight."

Ridge had been quiet. It was obvious he disliked being there, disliked Fowler, disliked Phil and myself, probably disliked even the kids in the hall. Now he spoke.

"I suppose Lois has told you about today," he said, "but I don't think it will ever come to trial. She can be certified if necessary as of unsound mind."

"She's as sane as I am."

Ridge shrugged his elegantly padded shoulders.

"I am willing to testify to the contrary," he said stiffly. "Judith has not been herself for a long time. The attempt at suicide shows it clearly. She had everything to live for—health, adequate means, and a considerable remnant of her former beauty. When she wanted a divorce—for no reason whatever—I saw she got it."

He glanced again at Mother's painting over the mantel and smiled faintly.

"I not only gave her everything she wanted after our marriage, I helped her out of trouble before it. Lois knows it. I told her some time ago. But after hearing Mr. Fowler's account of today at the hospital, I feel I should make my own position clear."

He looked at Phil, but he was lighting a cigarette.

"What *is* your position, Ridge?" Phil asked. "You're not married to Judith now. You're not even a member of this family. Just why are you here?"

Ridge flushed,

"I might say I came to ask for the fifty thousand dollars I gave your mother twenty years ago after your father's death. It might just possibly interest you. I don't know."

Phil looked stupefied.

"Mother?" he said. "Why did she need it? It never showed on any of the bank statements."

"I paid it in cash. She wanted it that way, in small bills if possible. Even in those days of Prohibition it wasn't easy. I rather think my bank thought I was bootlegging."

If it was meant as a pleasantry it got nowhere.

"Just why did she want it?" Phil asked grimly. "She wasn't being blackmailed, was she?"

"I'm quite sure she was. At the time I thought I was paying to keep my future wife's name out of the newspapers. She had been out driving with some lad or other, and the car had hit a woman. It hadn't killed her, but she was badly hurt, and this was to remunerate her. That was the story I was told.

"It wasn't true, of course. I know it now. But I was very much in love, and so—"

He shrugged again.

"What I was actually doing was to bribe the butler you had at the time—a man named Dawson—to keep his mouth shut about the fact that Judith had been—let's say indiscreet—with a boy named Shannon. She had spent most of a night in his room, and she was his only alibi for a murder he was supposed to have committed while she was with him.

"I suppose Dawson had let her out of the house, and let her in again. He may have followed her, too. I don't know. But as a result this boy, Johnny Shannon, was convicted and served twenty years to life in the pen. I don't need to tell you it was this same Shannon she shot and killed two weeks ago with your father's gun."

Nobody spoke for a moment. Phil looked profoundly shocked. Out in the hall Bill and Janey were shooting craps. We could hear the dice rattling on the bare floor. Then Phil moved.

"Why would she do such a thing?" he said. "If Shannon had shot her, I could understand it. But you say she killed him. Why?"

"You'll have to ask her," Ridge said. "I suppose she was afraid of him, for one thing. But if all this comes out, as it may, she can claim he threatened her. She shot in self-defense."

Fowler got up.

"I think I'd better say what I came to say," he said, "and then get out. As you know, I've been holding Mrs. Chandler as a material witness, but this matter of the gun changes things. As a matter of fact, I have a warrant for her arrest in my pocket. She can't be moved yet, of course, and if she can prove self-defense it won't go hard with her. Or put it another way. Say she's been erratic at times. Has a psychiatrist, hasn't she? And the maid here, Jennie, says she's kept herself locked in ever since she came. There's a defense, too—mental case."

He said something about not liking scandal when it touched

the old and prominent families who had summer homes there. Secretly, however, I thought he was enormously pleased with himself as he went out. Bill and Janey were still noisily shooting craps. Both sprawled on the floor, as though there was no warrant in Fowler's pocket; as though Judith had not taken Father's automatic from the trunk in the attic which held his fishing-rods and old hunting-gear; and as though Ridgely Chandler had not tonight paid her back for the years she had not loved him.

Phil and Fowler were already on the porch when Ridge tried to put an arm around me as he said good night. I freed myself quickly. "I hope you're happy," I said. "That story was unnecessary and uncalled for, Ridge. The gun was enough. The rest was pure spite, because she hated you. You couldn't forgive that, could you?"

He gave me a cold smile.

"No," he said. "You learn fast, don't you?"

Then he was gone, and Phil and I were left to our own unhappy thoughts. Some time later, after making cocoa for the kids, I found him in the library carefully inspecting the Laszlo portrait. He turned when he heard me.

"She must have had some dreadful times," he said slowly. "Times when she couldn't sleep for seeing an innocent boy shut away for the rest of his life. All of it so Judith could marry Chandler, the pipsqueak of a man who was here tonight." And then he said something I shall always remember.

"Maybe we are better now than we were then," he said. "There's not so much pride of the wrong sort, of money or place, or social position. Mother was of her world, but her world has gone kaput. I'm glad you're marrying O'Brien, Lois. He's a cop, but he's also a gent."

It was the next day that Judith told me about the woman in the pool.

She was looking better. The nurse had brushed her hair, and piled it high on her head. But I felt her real beauty was gone for good. There comes a time in every woman's life, I suppose, when she has to say farewell to the best things nature has done for her; the flawless skin goes, the lovely eyes fade, and she knows she is over the hill and, as the Indians say, going to the sun.

Evidently she had not yet been arrested. Fowler had not served his warrant. But now there were two men in the hall outside her door, one in uniform and one in plain clothes. They greeted me civilly enough, but there was a subtle change in both of them, a watchfulness, an alertness I had not noticed before.

Judith was alone when I went in. She seemed glad to see me. She had never been a reader, and the long hours must have hung heavy on her hands. But the look she gave me was a wary one.

"What was all that about yesterday?" she asked. "Didn't they believe me?"

"I think they hoped you would remember more, Jude."

"I don't. I can't." She passed a hand wearily over her tired face. "But I must talk to somebody or I'll go mad. Lois, what do you remember about Mother? Before she moved out to The Birches? You were pretty small, weren't you?"

"I was seven, almost eight, when Father died."

She was watching me carefully.

"Was there anything queer about Father's death?" she asked.

I was startled.

"Not so far as I know. There has never been any doubt he killed himself."

"I suppose he did," she said, and was thoughtful for a minute. Then: "I didn't shoot that man, Lois. Believe me, what I told was true. But I think I did something else equally dreadful. I think I killed the Benjamin woman." I must have looked horrified, for she went on gravely. "I tried to save her, as God is my witness, but I never was a good swimmer and she kept going down." She shuddered. "I had to tell you," she said. "I can't take any more. Is that policeman still out there?"

"He can't hear you. What do you mean, you tried to save her?"

310

"She was in the pool when I got there. Somebody meant to kill her. You see how it is. I'm under suspicion for what I did not do, and in a way I am guilty of something they don't even suspect! I suppose that's life for you, or maybe death."

It was a longish story she told me that day, her poor face raddled and her hands shaking. It began, she said, after she came back to The Birches from Reno. She didn't get much mail, but one day Jennie brought her a letter from the mailbox. It warned her she was in danger as Shannon was free. But that was all, and she knew about Shannon already. Nevertheless, the letter scared her, she said, but she did nothing about it until another one came. But by that time she was pretty desperate. The new one was rather ominous. It was signed Kate Henry, and it said Shannon was trying to get his case reopened.

"I'm through with it," it went on. "Dawson's dead. He killed Mollie Preston, and if I go on the stand I'll tell them so. But Johnny's counting on you to alibi him. I think we'd better talk this over."

She ended by saying she would be at the pool on a certain night, and Judith was to meet her there. Judith was terrified. She was afraid Johnny would be there, too. She went, however. In the hall she picked up one of Phil's golf clubs, for defense if necessary. It was all she had. She never owned a gun. I knew that, didn't I?

"You were looking for something in the attic one night, Jude. They think you found the gun there."

She shook her head.

"No. I had hidden a letter from Johnny in your old doll house, Lois. It was under one of the floor mats. But it was gone. Perhaps Mother found it, or Helga."

It was, she said, one he had sent her after his arrest, begging her to tell the truth and save him. It had almost killed her. She was in love with him, and perhaps someday she could produce it. But by that time it was too late. Dawson had been bought off, Flaherty was dead, and Mother took her to Arizona.

"What do you mean by someday, Jude?"

"I thought he would be acquitted. If he wasn't—"

But Mother had all those months in Arizona to work on her. Mother and Ridge. She was pretty young, she said, so when Ridge proposed to her—knowing the truth, as he did—she shifted the burden to him.

"Only he never did anything," she said bitterly. "He didn't even try to get Johnny out. At first I thought he was afraid of his mother. She was a terrible woman, Lois. But she died and still he refused to help Johnny. I gave up then."

She went back to the pool. She said the bench was empty when she got there, so she waited, the golf club beside her.

"It was dark, but there was some starlight," she said. "I sat down and waited, but the woman didn't come." Then she heard someone in the shrubbery. Whoever it was didn't appear, and suddenly she was terrified.

"I forgot all about the golf club," she said. "I simply beat it. I ran back to the house and sat on the porch, and before long I heard Ed Brown's taxi. It stopped to let someone out and went away, and after a while I screwed up my courage and went down to the pool again.

"She was there, Lois, but she wasn't on the bench. She was in the pool, floundering around in the deep end. I tried to reach her. I got down on my knees and tried to catch that awful hair of hers, but I couldn't hold her. I suppose I should have gone in after her, but I'm a rotten swimmer. Anyhow it was too late. She sank right before my eyes, and she never came up again."

She said she waited for a while. Quite literally she could not walk. The woman's hat came up and floated, then it sank, too, and after a bit she picked up the golf club and went back to the house. It never occurred to her the golf club had been the murder weapon. She simply put it back in the bag and forgot about it. But she had been almost frantic, anyhow. For one thing, she had got pretty wet, and she had spent most of the night drying and pressing her clothes.

"I had my traveling-iron, of course," she said, as though it mattered.

The curious thing was that until much later she did not even

312

know the woman's identity. I realized she still did not know who she really was.

"Her name was Kate Henry, but she married Dawson. He'd changed his name to Benjamin, so she called herself Selina Benjamin. I imagine he told her the whole story, including the murder of a Homicide man named Flaherty. Inspector Flaherty."

That was when I realized I had lost her. The new frankness, even the friendliness, was gone. It was as though a hand had been drawn over her face, wiping out all expression.

"If he told her Mother was mixed up in the death of Flaherty he was lying," she said sharply. "He probably had plenty of enemies. I guess I've talked too much, Lois, but I wanted you to know. I had nothing to do with the Benjamin woman's death. Do you mind ringing for the nurse?"

It was the first time Flaherty's name had entered the case, and I told O'Brien about it that night.

"She's right, of course, except it's odd the way she reacted. Someday she'll come clean all the way, and she'll feel better when she does. It's the gun that bothers me now. Who had it all this time? Sure it wasn't in the attic?"

"I'm not sure about anything."

I went out to the porch with him, but he did not go back to the cottage. He kissed me lightly—he was definitely a man who did his own courting—and said he wanted a few words with Helga.

"She's probably in bed," I protested, but he only grinned.

"It won't be the first time I've disturbed her virgin slumbers," he said. "And 'tis a sorry spectacle she'll be, mavourneen."

I always suspected him when he lapsed into his Irish vernacular. It meant he was getting away with something I was not to know about. But he gave me no chance to question him.

He kissed me again and disappeared toward the service wing. I never doubted he had a key to it. And he had.

Chapter 33

I never have known whether Fowler served his warrant or not.
I did not see Judith the next day, for the offer for the property
became definite that September morning, and the prospective
owners arrived en masse to inspect it.

The children loved it. There was a little girl of seven or so
with a front tooth out who reminded me of myself at the same
age. But, of course, one of the boys promptly fell into the pool,
and I had to dive in after him while the mother screamed her
head off. I think the husband liked the pool, nevertheless. He
gave me rather a tired smile as I got my orders.

"I'm afraid it will have to go, my dear," he said as I stood
dripping beside him. "At once, if you can manage it. I want the
kids out of town as soon as possible."

I changed my clothes after they departed, and went out into
the grounds again. A man had already arrived at the pool. He
was struggling to open the sluice gate, and I stood there
watching him. Just so I must have stood years ago, with Father
holding my hand as it began to fill. Looking worried, too.

"You'll have to learn to swim, baby," he said. "We can't
have you falling into the thing unless you know how to get
out."

I went over to his garden. It looked dreary at the end of the
summer, but the birches still stood, tall and proud, over the
little cemetery. They seemed to be whispering to each other.

and I sat down under them and wept. My eyes were still red when Anne arrived later in the afternoon. She looked hot and tired, but exultant about her share of the money involved as she sat fanning herself on the porch.

"Of course, the price includes the furniture, such as it is," I told her.

"But not Mother's portrait!" she protested. "You wouldn't sell that, Lois."

"No. You can have it if you like. Phil doesn't want it. Nor do I."

My voice probably sounded bleak, for she stared at me.

"I rather thought you'd want it."

"I'll probably have no place for it, Anne."

"Then you *are* going to marry that policeman."

"I'm not sure. He hasn't really asked me yet."

She had a glass of iced tea in her hand, but she did not drink it. She was flushed with indignation.

"I think Mother would turn in her grave if she thought you were serious about him," she said. "A policeman, and an Irish one at that! Good Lord, Lois, have you lost your mind?"

I wanted to say Mother was probably whirling if she knew all about us. I did not, of course.

"I didn't know there was anything wrong with being Irish."

"Maybe not, but a policeman! A cop! What do they call them? A flatfoot!"

"He's hardly that, Anne. He's a lieutenant in the Homicide Department. Also he's a college man. He can even read and write. And before I forget it, Janey has another name. It's Jones."

I don't think she even heard me.

"Even Judith made a good marriage," she said scornfully. "You'll go far before you find a finer man than Ridge Chandler, even if she did divorce him. And my Martin may not be a millionaire, but he's a gentleman. That policeman, with his chickens! You're not really serious about this, Lois, are you?"

"I'm as serious as all hell," I said. "He's a man, and a real

315

one. I'm terribly in love with him. And I'll tell you something else you don't know. Ridge Chandler may be a gentleman, but he bought Judith just the same. The exact price was fifty thousand dollars. Or so he says."

She dropped her fan and did not bother to pick it up.

"I don't believe it," she said flatly. "Why would he do a thing like that?"

"To save her reputation, and incidentally to send a man to prison for murder."

Sitting there, with Anne clutching a glass of iced tea she never drank, I told her the story of Judith's early days, as I had it from both Ridge and Judith herself. Her rather long face grew longer as I went on, her nice eyes bigger. I rather think her greatest shock was Ridge's part in it, for it was the only comment she made.

"He must have been crazy," she said. "After all, a Chandler—"

"He meant to marry her. He paid the fifty thousand dollars to save his family name. Not ours."

She did not even know of Judith's arrest! It surprises me now to think how little she really had known all along. But when I came to Father's gun she was stunned.

"What became of it, Anne?" I asked. "You know, after he died. Did the police send it back to us?"

"I don't know," she said. "I don't remember seeing it. Of course, with all the confusion at the time— Does it matter?"

"Matter? It may send Judith to the chair, or to life imprisonment. It was Father's gun that killed the cab driver, Anne. He had a license for it, and the police have traced it. Ridge says it *was* returned. To Mother. He was there when she got it."

She was too stunned even to put her glass down properly. She put it on the edge of the table, where it toppled to the floor and smashed. It belonged to a set Mother had brought from Venice on her wedding trip, but she ignored it.

"Why?" she said. "Why would she kill such a person? She wouldn't even know him. How could she?"

316

"Because he was the man she sent to prison, the Johnny Shannon I told you about."

Thinking now of that talk I realize I had the whole case before me. The clues, as Sara Winters would say, were all there. But it was like not seeing the forest for the trees. I was too close, too tired, perhaps too stupid.

Sitting there on the porch, the house quiet behind us, I told her as much as I knew, beginning with Father's suicide and the note he left, and ending with the warrant for Judith's arrest. I told her about Flaherty and Mollie Preston. I told her about Dawson and the bribe, and about Selina his wife, who had sworn away Johnny Shannon's liberty and then married Dawson under the name of Benjamin. I even told her of my excursion to their town, and the tobacco shop there. And finally I repeated Judith's story about Phil's golf club and how near we had come, Phil and I, to arrest because of it.

She tried to smile. After all, if Ridge was a Chandler she was a Maynard and the Maynards have their own standards of behavior.

"Bill says I'm a lame-brain," she said, "but I've got at least part of it. Only I thought Judith was claiming it was a holdup."

"She does, only they don't believe her. How would a thug like that get Father's gun? It was his gun. The slugs matched."

None of us except Bill ate much dinner that night, although Helga was celebrating the sale of the house with fried chicken and an angel-food cake, undoubtedly the largess from O'Brien's girls. All Phil had to say was the warrant had been served and Judith was under arrest.

He pushed away his dessert, which was the ice cream he usually liked, and excusing himself went out into the grounds. Even Bill seemed subdued. He and Janey had had a fight, he said, but there were plenty of other fish in his particular ocean.

"The more I think of it the more I understand Joseph Smith," he said.

"Joseph Smith?" Anne said, looking puzzled. "Who on earth was he?"

She took Bill with her while she went over the house, so I

was alone on the porch when Doctor Townsend drove up. He had been dining somewhere in the neighborhood, but as the others were about to play canasta, which he detested, he had made an excuse and left.

"I understand Mrs. Chandler is getting better," he said. "Terrific shock she'd had. It would have killed a lot of women."

"She's a worse one today," I said. "She's been arrested for murder, Doctor."

I think he already knew it, but he drew a long breath.

"I suppose it was inevitable, but still—"

"You don't think she did it, do you?"

"Almost anyone will kill, if sufficiently desperate," he said. "In fact"—he smiled faintly—"there is a school of thought which says we are all killers, only restrained by the laws we ourselves have made. The point is, why? Why would Mrs. Chandler kill this man? She doesn't even claim he attacked her. It's easier to believe in her highwayman."

The district attorney, he said, had been at the dinner party that night and admitted the case was puzzling. For instance, if she had used the gun, why carry it back here with her? She was in shock, of course. He asked me if I knew Ballistics showed it was the murder weapon, and I nodded.

"Even semiconscious as she was," he said, "wouldn't she have thrown it away somewhere? Down a bank. Into a creek. Even into your own swimming pool? She was not completely in shock. That came later. She knew her way here. She even knew where the stable was."

He left soon after, leaving me somewhat cheered but still bewildered.

It was almost nine o'clock when O'Brien arrived. We must have looked like a normal family party, with Anne serving coffee from Mother's big silver service on the table before her in the living-room and Phil passing benedictine in one of Father's handsome decanters. There was a small fire going, too, and I tried to forget how soon we were leaving it. Or, for

318

that matter, what was to come.

Because I knew O'Brien had something to say. His voice over the telephone was his policeman's voice.

"That you, Lois?"

"Yes. Is anything wrong?"

"No more than usual," he said. "I'll be at The Birches as soon as I can make it. Don't let Helga go to bed. I'll want her."

He hung up, without so much as a good-by, and I went upstairs in a fury and put on my blue silk dress, which had withstood the water in the pool after all, and remade my face.

When he did come he had evidently stopped at the cottage, for he was freshly shaved and he wore a fine pair of gabardine slacks and a tweed sport jacket. He had had a haircut, too, and not since the case began had I seen him so resplendent or with such an air of tired dignity.

He took the highball Phil gave him, but he did not sit down. He stood by the mantel, glass in hand, and surveyed the three of us.

"I'll try to make this short," he said. "Some of it's damned unpleasant, and much of it Lois knows, but it has to be told. First of all, try to imagine Judith Chandler's state of mind last winter when she read in the papers that Johnny Shannon was free. She never doubted he would try to kill her. She has never doubted it since. But I didn't believe it. I met him when he came out, and eventually I gave him enough money to go west. What he really wanted was to be exonerated, and I told him I would try to do it. There was no revenge in him. He had had a long time to get over that, but it's hard for an ex-con to get anywhere, and he had studied law in prison. Once cleared, he could practice somewhere.

"He wrote me from Reno that he was driving a taxi and even saving some money. He hadn't changed a great deal. He had been a good-looking boy, and except that his hair was white he was still much the same.

"I had a leave coming, and so I went out to Reno to see him. He was doing all right. He had a small room there. He even had

319

a sweetheart. But he had an obsession, an *idée fixe*. He wouldn't marry her until his name was cleared.

"Then he saw Judith at the train in Reno. He was driving a taxi, and she was beautiful and smiling and—well, reeking of prosperity. She wore a mass of orchids, I remember. It made him pretty bitter, I imagine. All I know is what his girl wrote me. He'd left Reno after that and come east, and I began to worry. In Reno he'd changed his name to Alec Morrison. I knew that. But if he'd changed it again, or dyed his hair— There are twelve million people in and around New York. There are several thousand taxi drivers, too. His Reno license would help him there.

"I spent days going over the list of cab drivers in the city. Also I put other men on it. I even advertised for him. But the plain fact is I had lost him. He knew where to find me, but he never showed up. And the first time I saw him after Reno was after he had been killed.

"All this is merely to tell you why I took the cottage here. I began to realize he might not be entirely normal, and I stayed up a good many nights when he began to haunt the grounds. As you all know, I never caught him."

He stopped then, and I thought he was listening for something. All he did, however, was to ask me if Helga was still up, and to bring her in if she was. She looked startled when I told her. She waited, too, to put on a clean apron, and I saw her old hands were shaking.

"What does he want?" she asked. "If it's about the eggs, why let them go rotten? I've fed his chickens enough to pay for them."

It was not about the eggs, of course. He stepped forward when she followed me into the room and gave her a chair. True to her training she sat only on the edge of it, but his voice was pleasant as he spoke to her.

"I want you to tell me something," he said. "It won't do any harm now. It may even help. I think you have known all along more than you have ever told."

"This is my family," she said bleakly. "It's all I have."

"That's understandable," he agreed. "But go back twenty years, Helga. You knew Miss Judith was out the night the Preston girl was murdered, didn't you?"

She swallowed hard.

"Yes, I knew it," she said defiantly. "Those children were like my own, Lieutenant. And there was trouble enough, with the money all gone and Mr. Maynard shooting himself. Anyhow, who would believe me, with both Judith and her mother against me? I didn't even see Dawson let her in that night. I only heard it."

"What time was that?"

"It was after four in the morning. My legs were bad and I'd gone down to the kitchen for some aspirin. When I think of that murdering devil blackmailing the madam, after what he'd done himself that night!"

"What had he done, Helga?"

"What? He'd strangled the Preston girl. That's what. Crazy about her, he was, and at his age! Jealous, too. I heard him often, over the pantry phone, begging to get her to see him. He was out that night, too. I heard him go and come back. He had big ugly hands. They were strong, too. That's what he did it with."

I think all of us were shocked. I know I was. But O'Brien was not interested in Dawson or his possible guilt.

"So you let this Shannon boy take the rap for something he didn't do," he said. "You knew Miss Judith was his alibi for that night. Why did you do it, Helga?"

"I didn't know him," she said defensively. "And I couldn't prove anything, could I? That's what Mrs. Maynard said, too."

"Oh, so you told her?"

"Sure I told her."

Phil got up. He was very pale.

"Are you saying my mother knew all this and did nothing about it?"

"She knew, Mr. Phil, but I swore on the Bible I wouldn't

321

talk. And I didn't. Until now, if it will help Judith any. That's why I took the things from the desk in the cottage, and you nearly caught me. I hid in the chicken house that night. The photograph was Dawson all right, no matter what he called himself."

She looked at O'Brien.

"You said you were only going to ask me about the gun," she said.

But Phil had not finished. He went across the room and stood over her.

"How much of this did my father know?" he demanded, his face frozen.

"Don't you go blaming your father, Phil," she said. "He was the best man I ever knew. I think he knew Judith had been out that night, and why Dawson was blackmailing your mother. But he didn't know she'd been with the Shannon boy. If he had he'd have gone right before a jury and told them. That's what he was like."

Phil turned. He gave a despairing glance at the Laszlo over the fireplace. Then he sat down and put his head in his hands. Anne had not moved. She was staring straight ahead of her, but seeing nothing. As for me, I felt dizzy and sick. Mother, carrying that guilt all those years, dying with an innocent boy spending the best years of his life behind stone walls, and still not talking. Father's suicide, too, that gentle kindly man driven to desperation and unable to raise the money to save Judith's reputation.

I think O'Brien had not meant to let things go so far, although he certainly knew them.

"Now about the gun," he said. "You know it was returned after his death, don't you?"

"I gave it to Mrs. Maynard with my own hands," she said.

"Have you ever seen it since?"

"No. It's never been around. I know every inch of this house. It's never been in it."

322

Chapter 34

Nobody spoke for a minute or two. Then O'Brien drew a matchbox out of his pocket. He opened it and looked at it.

"For twenty years," he said quietly, "I have been on the trail of Inspector Flaherty's murderer. I've carried the slug which killed him in this box, and yesterday when the chief of police here in town sent to Ballistics in New York the gun Mrs. Chandler brought back with her, I was present when they tried it out.

"It was the same gun. Think about that for a minute. It had killed your father, but by his own hand. It had wounded me, although that's not important. It had murdered Johnny Shannon. I dug a slug from it out of the cottage wall. It comes close to convicting Judith Chandler of murder. And it killed Inspector Flaherty twenty years ago. That's quite a record.

"I want you all to think about Flaherty for a moment. He was a good cop. He had to take the risks of his job, as we all do. But he was no man's fool. He did not believe Johnny Shannon was guilty. He told me your sister Judith was lying, and—I'm sorry—your mother, too. Then one day he told me he had located Dawson and meant to get the truth out of him.

"But he made one mistake. He told both Judith and your mother, and that night he was murdered."

He shoved the matchbox back into his pocket and going over to the hearth looked up at Mother's portrait.

"A mother will do many things for a dearly loved daughter," he said slowly. "Or to save her own place in the world, her social position, or the good name of her family. But I do not believe murder is one of them. And quite definitely she did not shoot me, or Johnny Shannon. Nor did it seem likely Johnny had shot me, not with that gun.

"You see, the whole case turned on the gun. It still does. And I haven't been working alone. When Shannon came east I went to the commissioner and told him the story, that he had come east and Mrs. Chandler might need protection. He knew who she was. Who didn't? And he didn't want her killed. So I got an extended leave and took the cottage by the main road. The papers said she was here at The Birches, and from the start I felt sure Shannon was about the place at night. I even knew he was in the cottage the first day I saw it. He'd taken a drink of water and his prints were on the glass.

"I never caught him, however, and then a woman whose name was Selina Benjamin was drowned in your pool. I knew from the railroad ticket in her bag where she had come from, and when the Hunnewell woman who lived next door identified her, I was positive she was the Kate Henry whose testimony had largely convicted Johnny. She had seen him in Mollie Preston's room and heard them quarreling, and she'd identified him in the line-up before she disappeared.

"It looked as though he had killed her. He had a motive, right enough. But the golf club was not his sort of weapon. I don't imagine he had ever used one in his life. I know now that Mrs. Chandler took it to the pool and left it there. At least so she told me today. There is no proof, of course. Nor was there any proof of her story about a holdup." He smiled. "I've heard even more imaginative stories many times, and the local men are positive she invented it. But today it had become a matter of fast work or she would go to jail. As I told Lois—"

We had never heard Ed Brown's taxi drive up, which shows the state we were in. But we heard his voice.

"Now mind you," he said, "twenty minutes and no more.

It's my bedtime."

"Oh, shut up, sourpuss," a woman said. "I'm not paying you until I get back to the station. Take it or lump it."

She came briskly up the porch steps, and O'Brien went out into the hall.

"Come in," he said. "I'm glad you got here."

"So am I! I thought the old bastard out there was going to dump me in the ditch."

It was Clarice, Judith's personal maid, and now shed of her fine manners. She gave a sharp look around the room as O'Brien brought her in.

"And maybe I ain't scared," she said. "You didn't say this place was spooky. What's the idea of a man stopping that rattletrap and shining a flashlight in my face? The driver nearly jumped out of his skin."

I thought O'Brien looked annoyed. He did not bother to introduce her. He put her in a chair near the door and stood by her.

"You telephoned, as I told you?" he asked.

She merely nodded. She was surveying all of us, especially Helga. She grinned at her.

"In kind of high-class company, aren't you?" she said. "What goes, anyhow?"

Helga looked disgusted.

"It's none of your business," she said. "Keep your mouth shut until you're spoken to."

O'Brien ignored them both. He looked down at Clarice. "Did you bring the list I asked for?" he inquired.

"All I could remember," she said.

She fished in her handbag, bringing out the usual lipstick and compact, a fine embroidered handkerchief which probably belonged to Judith, and finally a sheet of paper. O'Brien glanced at it and shoved it in his pocket.

"Did you see the gun?"

"I saw *a* gun. At the police station here in town. It looked the same. I can't be sure."

325

"When did it disappear?"

"It wasn't there when I went back with Miss Maynard to pack Mrs. Chandler's clothes. That's all I know."

Phil glared at her.

"Are you saying my sister took this gun, and had it with her when she left for Reno? I don't believe you."

O'Brien, however, did not let her answer. He motioned to Helga, who got up, and hauled some change out of his pocket.

"Pay off Ed Brown, will you?" he said. "And take Clarice here back to your sitting-room. I'll see she gets back safely. Give her a cup of tea or something. She's had a trying evening."

If anyone ever looked less like giving Clarice a cup of tea than Helga at that moment, I can't imagine who. But Clarice took a hand.

"You might make it something stronger," she said. "I've still got the shakes."

As a result she left carrying a tall glass of whisky and soda, and looking definitely more cheerful.

Phil stirred.

"Why all the mumbo jumbo?" he demanded. "If you have a case against Judith, let's have it."

O'Brien was still standing. One of his pockets sagged, and I knew he had a gun in it, but no one else apparently noticed. It frightened me, that gun. It seemed so unnecessary somehow. No one was going to attack him, although Phil looked rebellious enough for anything.

"I'm sorry," O'Brien said. "I didn't locate Clarice until tonight. I'd like to go back to the night Johnny Shannon was killed and Mrs. Chandler was hurt. You see, it was carefully arranged as a holdup. A masked man with a gun, the driver shot, and the jewel case taken. But even the best plans slip. This one did, for the simple fact that the engine of the car was still running, and some movement of the dying man pressed on the accelerator.

"I'll go a little further. Johnny Shannon expected to meet a man there, the one he told your sister was to take a deposition from her to clear his name. But he had not expected a mask. Something was wrong and he knew it. He may have put the car in gear then.

"However it happened, the masked man shot him and thought he had shot your sister. There is a bullet hole near where she sat. But she had only fainted, as it happened. He took the jewel case and was backing out of the car when it started.

"Mrs. Chandler says he threw the gun at her. I think she is wrong. It was jerked out of his hand. It may have struck her. I don't know. What we do know is that she did not go all the way with the car. She fell out as it turned over, and after she came to she had the gun in her hand. She's vague about all this. It's still possible she grabbed at it as he pointed it at her.

"She wasn't out very long. She was in shock and in pain, but she started back to The Birches. Remember, she thought the masked man was still around; so she carried the gun with her. For the same reason she did not use the drive. She took to the shrubbery. Her memory has improved now. I talked to her today, and she says she remembers that. She also remembers that near the pool she stumbled and fell, and the gun went off."

He glanced at me.

"That cleared up something which bothered me for some time, a shot both Lois and I heard that night. It was a couple of hours after the so-called holdup. The killer should have been gone a long time, establishing an alibi, or at least getting the hell out of there. At any time someone might see the car and investigate, and he needed— Keep down, Phil," he said quickly. "Don't move. Don't try anything."

He jerked the gun out of his pocket and I was suddenly faint. Phil, who had been out so late the night of the murder! Phil, who had little or no love for Judith. And Phil, who might have had Father's gun for years.

O'Brien, however, was not looking at him. He was watching one of the open windows. It was near the old conservatory, and in the sudden silence we all heard what O'Brien's quick ears had caught before we did, the crushing of glass under a careful foot. It was followed almost immediately by a hand pushing back the curtains there, a gloved hand holding a gun.

The two shots were almost simultaneous. O'Brien's, however, was first. It knocked the gun into the room. The hand disappeared, and young Bill outside was yelling at the top of his lungs.

"Quick! I've got him."

Almost immediately men were shouting all over the place outside, and O'Brien, wearing his grim policeman's face, was dropping his own gun back into his pocket and swearing under his breath.

Anne was staring incredulously at the window, and Phil was grinning crookedly at O'Brien.

"By God," he said. "I thought you meant to shoot me!"

O'Brien did not answer. Fowler came in, looking flushed and apologetic.

"He took the back road," he said. "Came on foot down the hill by the stable. That's how we missed him. Narrow squeak, wasn't it? That nephew of theirs is some boy!"

"Too narrow," O'Brien said. "Did I kill him?"

"Got him in the arm. That's all. The boys are taking care of him all right. That his gun?" He went over and carefully picked it up. "Bought it yesterday in Bridgeport," he said. "We had the other one."

Anne was still looking dazed.

"Who was it?" she said, her lips white. "The man at the window. Who was it, Lois?"

"Ask Lieutenant O'Brien," I said shortly. "He hasn't bothered to tell me."

O'Brien smiled, for the first time that evening.

"It was—and is—a gentleman named Ridgely Chandler," he said, and put his arms around my shaking body.

Chapter 35

I suppose I should have known. As I said earlier, I had all the clues. Except for Dawson, dead for months, who outside of Mother or Judith had a motive for killing Inspector Flaherty? And who was desperately determined not to have Shannon's case reopened, as Selina Benjamin had agreed to do?

Ridge, I thought, had been a superb actor, or perhaps it is hard for women to think of small dapper men as killers. He would not be looking like a killer even now, sitting with dignity in the station house while a police surgeon dressed his wound.

"There is, of course, some absurd mistake, Doctor. If you will look in my wallet you will see my name on a number of things."

His name! His proud family name, for which three people had died.

How far he meant to go that night I do not know, but, as O'Brien said later while we sat around the fire and the men had drinks and Anne and I cigarettes, he had felt all along there was a smart scheming mind behind a good bit of what happened.

"He killed Flaherty years ago," he said. "As you've said more than once, Lois, he was a Chandler, and the Chandlers don't marry young women who have had to acknowledge being on more than friendly terms with a lad like Shannon. His old she-dragon of a mother was living at that time, too. So when

Flaherty got on the trail of Dawson he knew what it meant.

"Don't make any mistake about him. He knew Judith was lying, but he had lost his head entirely over her. In a way he was hardly responsible for what he did. I'd like to say this, too. I don't think your mother gave him your father's gun to shoot anyone. Most likely she simply didn't want it in the house.

"It's a queer thing that he kept it for twenty years. Clarice knew it was there. She did his mending, and she often saw it. Then the day she and Lois packed Judith's clothes she looked for it and it was gone. She didn't think much about it. He wasn't living in the apartment, although some of his clothes were still there. But she noticed it. When I located her she told me.

"He must have gone through hell when Johnny Shannon was released. I imagine Johnny called him up or saw him. He was determined to be cleared and he wanted his case reopened. Chandler had felt safe for a long time, but he knew I'd never given up the search for whoever killed Flaherty. And Johnny knew a lot. When he left the pen he located Selina Benjamin, who had testified against him before the grand jury, and scared her and Dawson so they left town.

"He even came out here and saw Helga, but he found her hard to deal with. She was willing to help him, but not if it hurt Judith. Also she had no real facts, as you all know now.

"So a lot of people were scared, if scared isn't too mild a word: the Benjamins, both the Chandlers, and even Helga. But the worst of the lot was our friend Ridgely. He wasn't in love with his wife by that time, but in an odd way he was proud of her, her looks, even her publicity. It was a long time since any Chandler had figured in anything but churches and hospitals.

"Then he had a respite of sorts. Johnny got discouraged and left town. Judith was getting a divorce and preparing to live abroad. It wasn't until she came back here and he learned I had taken the cottage that he began really to worry. I was bad news and he knew it.

"The story had to be stopped at all costs. I think Johnny told him where the Benjamins were. The husband was dead by that time, and Selina had come back to clear his estate. Don't forget, Selina was a real danger for him. She had lied and largely convicted Johnny, but only so Dawson could get your mother's bribe of fifty thousand dollars. You can't hide that amount of money, especially if you get it in cash, as Chandler did.

"I believe Chandler went to see Selina, and she realized she had a knee lock on him if Johnny's case was reopened. Her bank says she deposited five hundred dollars, again in cash, about that time, and it wasn't from Judith Chandler. She was in Reno.

"But Selina had changed. She took his money, but her conscience was bothering her. She had seen Johnny, with his hair snow-white at forty. It gave her some idea of what the years had done to him. And when he came back from Reno she began to worry.

"She notified Chandler of his return, and it's evident he knew who was haunting the grounds here, the unknown who was trying so desperately to see Judith. Very probably he came here himself in the hope of killing Johnny. I knew he was in the grounds the night he shot me. That was later, of course. After Selina's body was found in the pool.

"But about Selina and her death. I know she called Chandler over long-distance at his office in New York—I have the record of the call—to say she was going to see Judith that night at the pool. You can hear how it would go.

"'Why?' he would say. 'What good will it do you?'

"'It might do Johnny Shannon a lot of good. He's back. He came to see me yesterday.'

"'Don't be a fool. If the case is reopened, you'll have to go to the pen for perjury.'

"'Let's say I have a conscience, or have got religion. They might go easy on me.'

"It was something like that. His secretary heard his part of it and remembered it.

"Judith's story fits it exactly. The woman was late and she herself was afraid. She forgot the golf club and left it there, so when Selina waited on the bench it was beside her. Probably Chandler meant to shoot her, but a shot is noisy and I was near by in the cottage. The club was better. He knocked her out with it and dragged her into the pool.

"He was, you see, getting rid of his troubles one by one. Selina was the first, after Flaherty. I came close to being the second, and Johnny himself was to be the third. Don't forget Judith, either, if the case was reopened. She was frightened, but she wasn't the shivering obedient girl she had been before. She was a woman now. Perhaps she knew Chandler had bought and paid for her, and hated him for it. Or she might have developed the same conscience as Selina Benjamin.

"Then one day Johnny himself went to see him. The secretary knows it. She let him into Chandler's office and he was there a long time. When he came out he looked pleased.

"'Something nice happen to you?' she said.

"'About the best there is,' he told her. 'Wish me luck tonight, will you?'

"'Of course. Is it a girl?'

"'No girl is as important as this is.'

"That's when the scheme was hatched," O'Brien said. "He was to get Judith and then pick up Chandler on the road. Chandler was to have a paper ready for her to sign, admitting her presence in Shannon's room the night of the Preston girl's murder, and confirming his alibi. Just what pressure they meant to use I don't know. Or what Shannon meant. Chandler had other plans.

"I know it sounds cracked, but Shannon wasn't entirely normal. It was obsession at its worst. And remember, from Chandler's point of view, how nearly it came off! Only the unexpected happened. Judith wasn't killed, and she carried off his gun. I have to guess a bit here. She says she came to with it in her hand. He may have followed her down the hill and thinking the fall or his shot at her had killed her, put it in her

332

hand himself. Or she may have caught at it when he pointed it at her. I think this last is more likely. I doubt if he stayed around there very long. He had his car hidden near by, and he beat it back to the city.

"It still stood as a holdup, of course. Only he had grabbed her jewel case, and no matter how wealthy a man is, it takes a lot of guts"—he grinned at Anne—"to throw a quarter of a million dollars' worth of baubles into a river, or one of the reservoirs.

"Chandler didn't have that sort. The damn fool has been carrying them locked in the trunk of his car ever since. He had a special lock on it, but, we opened it today. They were there.

"I don't think he knew we had them. The case is still in the car. But I knew he was after me. I knew too much. I believed Judith's story when no one else did. And I had his gun. Only he and I knew it had killed Flaherty. When I asked him to meet me here tonight I was confident he meant to kill me.

"So I laid a trap for him, and got him."

It was the end of the story. Months later, after all sorts of appeals, Ridgely Chandler was convicted of Johnny Shannon's murder. But I will always believe he actually went to the chair for the shooting of one Inspector Flaherty, dead for twenty years. As O'Brien says, the police have long memories when it comes to a cop-killer.

As always happens, many things were not brought out at his trial, although Homicide had them. A search of the Benjamin house, for example, disclosed a singular document fastened with Scotch tape to the back of the high old-fashioned tank of the toilet in the bathroom. It was signed by Benjamin himself, and notorized.

I, Walter Benjamin—born Arthur Dawson—do hereby swear that I had nothing to do with the murder of Inspector John

Flaherty. Flaherty was shot and killed by one Ridgely Chandler. I followed him that night and saw him do it.

This is to state that the money I received, fifty thousand dollars, was for the purpose of confirming Judith Maynard's alibi in the death of Mollie Preston, and for no other purpose whatever.

Which was curious, to say the least, since Helga still believes he killed Mollie himself.

Of course, you get used to things like that when you marry a policeman. During the long months since I began this story of my sister Judith I have done much of the work at night. The long endless nights when the telephone rings and O'Brien picks it up, says "yeah" a couple of times, and then throws on his clothes and looks around for his gun.

He is a captain now. I don't think he has to carry it, but it's a matter of habit. He feels undressed without it. Sometimes it's in his shoulder holster or stuck in his leather belt. Or again he merely drops it into a pocket. It is automatic. He doesn't always know he does it. His mind is out somewhere in this huge city where we live. I get a hasty absentminded kiss and he is gone.

I go back to the kitchenette and get the coffee ready for his return. Not percolated. Just ready to turn the current on. But I never go to sleep again. I sit and wait or I sit and write. But even as I write I am waiting, for the sound of his key in the lock of the apartment, for his strong arms around me and the tenderness of his voice. For if he is both a police officer and a man, at least the man is mine.